I'll Find You Where the Timeline Ends

I'll Find You Where the Timeline Ends

KYLIE LEE BAKER

HODDER CHILDREN'S BOOKS

First published in Great Britain in 2025 by Hodder & Stoughton Limited
First published in the United States in 2025 by Feiwel and Friends, an imprint of Macmillan Publishing Group, LLC

5 7 9 10 8 6 4

Text copyright © Kylie Lee Baker, 2025
Illustrations copyright © Karmen Loh, 2025
Book design by Aurora Parlagreco and Abby Granata
All emojis designed by OpenMoji, the open-source emoji and icon project.
License: CC BY-SA 4.0

The moral right of the author has been asserted.

*All characters and events in this publication, other than those clearly
in the public domain, are fictitious and any resemblance to
real persons, living or dead, is purely coincidental.*

All rights reserved.
No part of this publication may be reproduced, stored in
a retrieval system, or transmitted, in any form or by any means, without
the prior permission in writing of the publisher, nor be otherwise circulated
in any form of binding or cover other than that in which it is published
and without a similar condition including this condition being
imposed on the subsequent purchaser.

A CIP catalogue record for this book
is available from the British Library.

ISBN 978 1 444 98534 4

Printed and bound in Great Britain by
Clays Ltd, Elcograf S.p.A.

The paper and board used in this book
are made from wood from responsible sources.

Hodder Children's Books
An imprint of
Hachette Children's Group
Part of Hodder & Stoughton Limited
Carmelite House
50 Victoria Embankment
London EC4Y 0DZ

The authorised representative in the EEA is Hachette Ireland, 8 Castlecourt Centre,
Dublin 15, D15 XTP3, Ireland (email: info@hbgi.ie)

An Hachette UK Company
www.hachette.co.uk

www.hachettechildrens.co.uk

"미라선생님, 수현선생님, 승진선생님, 지원선생님, 솜이선생님, 민아선생님, 지은선생님하고 지민선생님에게,"

제가 책 천권을 쓴다 해도 선생님들이 저한테 얼마나 큰 자리를 차지하는지 표현을 다 할 수 없을 겁니다. 저를 돌봐주셔서 감사드리고 이 책은 선생님들께 바칩니다.

To Suhyeon, Jiwon, Seungjin, Mira,
Somi, Mina, Jieun, and Jimin:

Even if I wrote one thousand books, I would never have enough words to tell you how much you mean to me. Thank you for taking care of me. This book is for you.

Chapter One

SEOUL, EUNPYEONG
Present Day

As far as new lives went, this one was my favorite.

This time, I was in Seoul on the last Tuesday in September. As I crossed the stepping stones over the Bulgwang stream, Kim Jihoon held my backpack in one hand and followed me unquestioningly across the water, looking at me like I actually mattered, like I was someone he would remember ten years from now, even though I knew he never would. I had already looked up how he died, and I wouldn't be anywhere near him when it happened.

It was the end of my first month as Mina Yang, eighteen-year-old American exchange student, the only child of an American consultant and a flight attendant for Japan Airlines. I got to attend a public school this time, which unfortunately made my presence a bit more conspicuous since there weren't a lot of foreigners. But it was better than private international schools, where everyone was some sort of alpaca farm heiress or had a parent who invented and trademarked the color Teal. My family probably had more money than all their families combined, but the problem was that we weren't allowed to use most of it. We weren't important enough to access our ancestors' fortune, but we were important enough to die for them.

Jihoon hopped to the next step and suddenly we were sharing a stepping stone, his hand on my arm to steady me. I hugged my bag of honey butter chips to my chest, the plastic creaking in protest and threatening to pop, which would be both embarrassing and a tragic waste of snacks. I looked away, a nervous smile on my lips—not because someone like Jihoon could ever faze me, but because boys tended to feel more comfortable around nervous schoolgirls than ruthless undercover agents. I took a step back to the next stone, hoping I looked somewhat cute and playful rather than like a startled pigeon fleeing in a panic and pooping everywhere.

Jihoon was both the tallest guy in my homeroom and currently leading Mr. Oh's exam score board. He had an inoffensive smile and smelled like soap and walked his little sisters to school. When we first met, he'd complimented my shoes, then promptly spilled orange juice on my shirt and ripped off his own shirt to offer to me in a panic.

I'd only been in class with him for a month, so it was a little soon to start planning a wedding. But every morning, he wordlessly passed me a tiny bottle of mostly-frozen Yakult, which I felt fairly certain was an indication of love. All in all, it seemed like a nice beginning of something more.

I was an expert in beginnings because I'd had a lot of them—I moved every three to six months, ping-ponging between different parts of Korea, Japan, and the States. That was how I knew there were worse ways to start over than with Jihoon.

Plus, kissing him would earn me one hundred infiltration points.

In other lives, I'd had to prove how good of a chameleon I was in much more humiliating ways, like convincing my elderly neighbor to ride a tandem bike with me, or pretending to be a delivery driver and carrying thirty packs of Buldak fire ramen out of the corner store without paying. All things considered, having Jihoon as a mission was a pretty lucky draw. It would be a lie to say I would have paid him much attention if he weren't my assignment, but it would be a double lie to say I hated his dimples when he smiled or the way our classroom brightened when he laughed.

Jihoon teetered on the edge of the stepping stone, then righted himself with an undignified flapping of his arms, his face red.

"Are you not strong enough to carry my bag?" I said, smiling and crossing my arms. I was walking the tightrope between Shy New Girl Who Needs a Boy to Save Her and Mysterious Foreigner Who Can Get Away with Being a Little Sassy. Most boys liked some combination of the two. The last month had been a delicate dance of pretending to be perpetually lost in school so he'd walk me around, playfully asserting the superiority of sushi over kimbap while eating lunch together, and flubbing a few Korean quizzes so I could ask him to explain my mistakes.

When I'd first planned out this mission, I'd aimed to wrap it up in three weeks. That was when the azaleas bloomed on school grounds, and I'd been dropping hints for days about how much I loved them. Sure enough, when Jihoon walked me home from school, he presented me with a bouquet of purple azaleas. I hugged him and hesitated before letting go, and that was when he was supposed to kiss me.

But instead, he'd only tucked an azalea behind my ear with a soft smile and said he'd see me at school tomorrow. Now I was behind schedule, all because Jihoon was the one boy in year three who was stingy with his lips.

"Maybe I should take it back," I said, reaching for my backpack with a playful smirk.

"No, absolutely not," he said, holding my bag high above me.

When I reached for it anyway, he strapped it to his front like some strange double-sided turtle and put his hands proudly on his hips. "Pretty girls shouldn't carry their own bags."

"Pretty?" I echoed, looking up as if the word surprised me.

Jihoon blushed as if he hadn't meant to say it out loud. He stopped on the middle stone, halfway across the stream, and put his hand in his pocket.

Before I could think to stop myself, I copied the gesture. My hand slipped into my skirt pocket, closing around the small box inside. Jihoon was hiding something, and in my line of work, this was almost always a bad thing.

But before I could crack open my box and crush him with thousands of years' worth of hand-me-down Japanese magic, he pulled out a tiny blue silk bag and offered it to me with both hands.

"For you," he said quietly.

Slowly, I released my grip on the box in my pocket and accepted the bag. I pulled on one of the drawstrings and emptied the contents into my palm.

A bracelet.

A strand of tiny polished white-and-green-jade beads held together by a silver clasp. Each bead looked like its own dream, a miniature planet of bright clouds and green mist.

"My noona told me that the Hanja for your name means 'beautiful jade,'" he said, staring at his scuffed shoes.

He was sweet, but wrong. The characters for my name could mean "peaceful beauty" or "beautiful beauty" or "that beautiful one over there," none of which made a ton of sense, but there was definitely no jade. But of course, he was thinking of Mina as a Korean name. It was one of the few names that sounded "normal" in Korean, Japanese, and English, which of course was 100 percent intentional for someone like me, who had to lie a lot.

I turned the bracelet over in my hands, considering my next

words. We were balanced on the edge of something more. One wrong word could destroy everything—that was how it always was in the beginning. Saplings were so easy to kill.

"Why are you giving me this?" I said, as if I didn't already know the answer.

Jihoon took a steadying breath, then finally tore his gaze away from his shoes and looked at me, the bright edge of the waning summer sun glowing in his round glasses. "Because, Mina," he said, "I like you."

The smile that broke across my face wasn't a lie, even if the reason behind it was.

One hundred points, I thought as I dropped my gaze to Jihoon's lips. I was 124 points away from a promotion. Crossing the threshold would put me in the running for an associate agent position after graduation. Associate agents didn't have to pack up and move countries at a moments' notice like my parents, who were only floating agents. Real agents could have homes, build lives, use their real names.

I opened my mouth, about to say something nice and normal like *I like you too*, but the words died in my mouth when I saw what—who—was behind him.

"No," I whispered.

"No?" Jihoon said, going pale.

I shook my head quickly. "No, I didn't mean . . . I just meant . . ."

I was being too obvious, staring over his shoulder with panic written plain across my face. He started to turn around, which was the absolute worst thing he could have done. If he saw who I was looking at, I'd have to convince him to follow me to the office, where he'd get waterboarded with condensed magic until he lost his memory of the last day, and then he'd definitely fail his calculus test tomorrow.

"No, don't look!" I said, reaching for his arm.

But instead of stepping to the next stone, my foot slipped off the edge. My stomach lurched, and I slipped headfirst into the shallow water.

Jihoon reached for me, his fingers brushing my arm as I fell. Of course, he had absolutely no balance because of the double-sided-turtle-backpack situation, so rather than catching me, he crashed down on top of me with the combined weight of both of our bags.

My face bit down into the gravelly river bottom. I reeled back and frantically shoved him off me, for a moment genuinely afraid I would drown in the most embarrassing way possible. Distantly, I registered the bag of honey butter chips popping under my stomach, spilling into the water. I stumbled to my feet, my face numb from the impact, my teeth sore. The small amount of eyeliner I'd decided to risk wearing that morning was now running down my face, and my wet shirt was almost definitely see-through.

I clapped a hand to my pocket, where my small box was thankfully still sealed shut. I pulled out my phone, which had already gone full brick mode, the screen not responding at all to my touch. And my backpack . . .

"My backpack!" I said, tugging at the straps. It was still latched firmly to Jihoon, who flopped back and forth as I pulled, his glasses splotched with water droplets.

"What?" he mumbled.

"You're getting my bag wet!" I said, pulling harder. "My calculus notes—"

He bent his arm so I could slide the bag off his front, then rose unsteadily to his feet. I turned my back to him, slamming the bag down on one of the stepping stones. Water had soaked through the bottom, so I yanked out my notebook and tried to shake it dry.

"Mina, are you okay?" Jihoon said behind me.

I shook my head, not trusting myself to speak. I was already pitifully behind on calculus compared to my classmates, thanks to a few unfortunately timed years of American education. Korean and

Japanese students did this kind of math in their sleep. My parents had pulled enough strings to get me into this school, and if I flunked out or had to repeat a year, I could kiss all my pending infiltration missions goodbye. Descendants were supposed to be exquisitely unmemorable, blending seamlessly into whatever situation they fell into. Getting booted for being the oldest and least intelligent girl in year three would definitely not impress my superiors.

I needed to excel wherever the descendants put me, or else I'd never have access to the files that would tell me the truth.

"Mina?"

The ink from my ruined notes ran down my wrist, staining the sleeve of my school shirt. Slowly, I looked up and locked my gaze with the person standing in the alley, shooting as much anger as I possibly could into my glare. Even as she stared impassively back at me, the anger flickered out quickly. She was only doing her job. *Our* job.

A glimmer of white beneath the water caught my eye. Jihoon's bracelet sat among the gravel and dirty water, but I didn't move to pick it up. It was a bad idea to trust someone like me with beautiful things.

"I have to go," I said, turning back to Jihoon. "I need to run home and change before my after-school class."

"I can walk you there!" he said, squinting at where he guessed I was standing, since his glasses were still in his hand.

"*No!*" I said—too loudly, making him flinch. "I mean . . . no, please, I already feel so embarrassed." This part wasn't exactly untrue, but there were bigger problems than embarrassment right now. I reached out and touched his hand. "Can we finish this conversation later?" I said, smiling in a way I hoped looked sweet even when I felt like a drowned puppy.

"Okay," he said, nodding eagerly. "Whatever you want, Mina."

But I didn't want this—hurting Jihoon, fleeing from every good thing, either because I ruined it myself or because I had to move again.

If I wanted to, I could quit my job when I turned twenty, and it would only cost me a hundred pages of paperwork and a thorough mind scrub. I could be a normal girl, holding hands with Jihoon right now instead of pushing him away.

But I would never do that.

The descendants were liars and guardians of secrets. The only way I would know the truth was if they trusted me, if I was one of them.

I turned around and clambered back onto the stepping stones before Jihoon could offer to help me up, then stormed down the street. I glanced over my shoulder to make sure Jihoon had walked away, then turned to the alley. My socks squished in my shoes with every wet step until I reached the person waiting for me.

There I was—another version of me—standing next to the CU store with my arms crossed.

This Mina was wearing a black hoodie, the collar of her school uniform peeking out underneath. Her hair was tied up in a way I knew meant I hadn't had a shower in a while because I was swamped with homework. I almost felt bad for her. I might have, if I couldn't still taste mud between my teeth.

I'd been on the other end of this interaction many times, so I knew how this worked. There was no room for politeness or considering anyone's feelings. Things like that weren't important to descendants of Ryūjin, the Japanese dragon god.

Long ago, Ryūjin's second daughter—Otohime—fell in love with a human and gifted him a box of time magic. The human mishandled it and unfortunately ended up as a pile of lint. But even though he got what he deserved, the damage had been done—once you brought magic to Earth, it was pretty hard to take it back.

Otohime's descendants went down to claim her magic, but

found that they weren't the only dragons who'd spilled a bottle of time magic on Earth and were frantically trying to mop it up. The Korean descendants were already downstairs, thanks to the last wishes of one of their dragon clans.

None of them realized, at first, what kind of price they would have to pay for playing with time.

In the beginning, it must have been fun—to bend time to your will so you never had to suffer any consequences, or regrets, or nostalgia. But the descendants realized slowly, and then all at once, that the timeline was very easy to break and very difficult to put back together. It was actually quite challenging to change the past without creating a paradox, undoing your own birth, or accidentally ending the world. After about a century (or no time at all, depending on where you were standing) the whole timeline turned into a pretzel twisted around on itself.

I obviously had no memory of that timeline, but I'd heard rumors of pterodactyls snatching humans off the sidewalk, sweet potato trees so tall that falling potatoes split skulls open, the extinction of all domesticated dogs, etcetera.

These days, the descendants were a bit more organized.

It was too late to fully contain time travelers—that cat got out of the bag centuries ago—but the majority of the descendants didn't need much convincing to see the importance of having the world in one piece. Both Korean and Japanese dragon descendants worked together to correct the timeline back to its original state—to before reckless rogue travelers had their fun with it—in exchange for our living expenses and a respectable stipend. But there were plenty of rogue travelers still running free, so it was a constant battle of making adjustments, fighting the selfish chaos that would tear a hole in the universe.

I was raised to be a trilingual superweapon of a descendant, able to work wherever I was needed, worth my weight in dragon gold . . . assuming that I could pass calculus.

I stopped in front of my Echo and crossed my arms, mirroring her stance.

"*What?*" I said. There were more colorful things I could have said, but I knew my mentor was probably watching somewhere, trying to stay out of the way but making sure I didn't mess up the timeline too badly.

The other Mina turned and picked up a bottle of banana milk from the outdoor table, then dumped it all over my—not her—shoes.

"Sorry," she said, not sounding particularly sorry. But of course I was never sorry either.

I grimaced, looking down at the shoes that I definitely would not be able to wear to school tomorrow because they would never dry in time. "Is that all?" I said. "Any more infiltration missions you want to ruin for me while you're here?"

She shook her head, reached into a pocket of her bag, and tossed a handful of confetti over me.

I sputtered as one of the tiny pieces got in my eye, waving my hand to disperse the rest of it. "*Are you serious?*" I said.

But even through the haze of paper, I saw her turning away. When the confetti settled, she was gone.

I hope that was worth it, I thought.

But of course it was—that was the whole point of time traveling. Every single action we took, even something as insignificant as tying a shoe or taking a sip of coffee—had a ripple effect across the entire universe.

Maybe there would be a mudslide tomorrow, and my school sneakers would have gotten sucked into the silt and caused my death. Or maybe it was imperative to the integrity of the universe that I ran the washing machine tonight because that tiny amount of water would be stolen from the mouth of an ancient fish that was destined to go extinct. Or maybe I would wash my shoes and find the laces unsalvageable, then be forced to go out and buy new shoelaces, and the receipt printer would jam and the cashier would have to go to the back room to replace it, where she would meet the man she was meant to marry.

I had trouble justifying the confetti, though. Sometimes I was just a jerk.

I jammed a pinky into my ear, trying to fish out another piece of confetti before it wormed its way into my brain. Death by confetti was a hilarious way to go, but I had a lot to do before my death day.

In my pocket, I clutched the tiny tortoiseshell box full of time. It constantly radiated heat that spread through my bones. I held it tight and started to trudge to headquarters, aka the "after-school classes" that Jihoon had been walking me to. In the distance, the ten-story tower cut through the smog overhead, the one-way glass of the top levels gleaming like a lighthouse beacon.

Somewhere up there, someone knew the truth about my family.

I would make them trust me, maybe even love me. And only then, with their throats exposed and backs turned, would I take what I wanted.

While I no longer had a dragon's scales or claws or fire, no one could take away my teeth.

Chapter Two

Once I finished my job, there was nothing to do but take a bite of my cheese corn dog and wait for the bloodshed to begin.

It was Friday, August 12, 2011, 7:47 P.M., one minute before a disaster that would change the course of history. But even a decade of distance from that afternoon's swim with Jihoon wasn't enough to stop me from cringing in between bites of corn dog. Once I'd arrived at headquarters, I'd barely had time to change out of my soaking wet school uniform before my mentor had dragged me on another mission.

It might have been a good distraction, if I weren't the kind of person who relived my most embarrassing moments in a cold sweat at three in the morning. I took an angry bite of my corn dog and tried to focus. This mission was too important to mess up because of a boy.

I was standing in Yongma Land—a sad excuse for a family theme park in a tiny overgrown section of forest, and the best park in Seoul before Lotte World became popular. In the present day, it was rusty and deserted. But right now, it was a visual assault of flashing lights in colors that human eyes probably weren't meant to perceive, the air thick with grease from the fried dough and corn dogs, with a faint undertone of vomit. For only 10,000 won, children could climb into buckets held up by giant octopus tentacles and swing in nauseous circles, or run around the scattered plastic gnomes with their leering facial expressions, or crawl through the fairy houses braided with overgrown flowers just starting to die as summer wound down.

I'd stood in this exact place in 2025, fourteen years after the park shut down.

By then, it was just a deserted ghost playground that you could visit for 3,000 won and use as a pretty backdrop for Instagram photos. There was only a slight risk of tetanus from all the rusted metal, and a slightly higher risk of being haunted by carnival ghosts, which probably made it worth way more than 3,000 won.

Two thousand eleven was the last year the park was supposed to be open. At least, until a rogue descendant had interfered.

I supposed there were more insidious actions than keeping a family-owned amusement park open another decade, but that was hardly the point—descendants couldn't go around picking and choosing what parts of the original timeline we liked best. If enough people did that . . . well, it was the fastest way to end up with ten-foot-tall spiders roaming the streets. Again.

My mentor—Jang Hyebin—inhaled her corn dog as she stood beside me, then glanced unsubtly at mine. I handed it to her without comment. I had only taken a few bites and was starting to feel sick thinking about what would happen because of me.

At twenty-five, Hyebin was the youngest descendant in Korea to ever hold the position of senior agent. Legend said she could work 24/7 because she took micro-naps every time she blinked, and that she'd lived the equivalent of ten lifetimes with all the time traveling she'd done. Others said that her brain worked at two times the potential of the average human's because she'd simply burned all her memories of her life before she started her job. Some even said she had more Red Bull than blood in her body, and I suspected that rumor was actually true.

As lucky as I was to be shadowing someone like Hyebin, standing next to her always made me feel conspicuously uncool. She was even taller than me, but her height somehow made her look like a fashion model, while mine made me look more like Godzilla. She had an unusually sharp face with purple shadows under her eyes and bangs that hid her burning expression, the rest of her hair a jagged wolf cut stopping at her shoulders. Part of me wondered if she was also mixed race like me, because she looked so unlike anyone I'd ever seen. But of course, you couldn't just ask Jang Hyebin questions.

She might have looked too memorable for this line of work, but she had an uncanny ability to slip like a shadow into any time period and go totally unnoticed, like the sheer force of her anger repelled other people's gazes.

It was a bit harder for someone like me to blend in.

I did my best by dyeing my hair a few shades darker and ironing it perfectly straight, but there was only so much I could do about being mixed. If I wore glasses that were in fashion from whatever time period I was visiting, older people wouldn't stare at me from a distance the way they would foreigners with blond hair or dark skin. But the second anyone made eye contact with me, their expressions changed. No one had ever looked me in the eye and thought I belonged here. But they were right—I didn't belong here, or anywhere.

"Look," Hyebin said, pointing at the Viking ship ride with her—my—corn dog.

As the ship swung high to the right—far higher than it was supposed to—the passengers lifted in their seats with a delighted yell.

Rides were supposed to be scary, after all. No one ever thought something would go wrong until the moment it did.

On the next upswing, all the safety bars released.

The passengers flew forward, tumbling headfirst into the other half of the boat with screams that were no longer delighted. Some of the passengers hit the cement platform below and didn't get up, bright bursts of their blood splashing across my face. As I tasted salt, I was suddenly glad I'd given Hyebin my corn dog. She'd assured me that no one would actually die, but then again, Hyebin wasn't exactly above lying.

In the original timeline, a mechanical failure on the Viking ride combined with an inexperienced operator resulted in eleven injured and two lawsuits that the park owners couldn't afford. Yongma Land closed down within six months. A lot of factors led to the accident, but the last chain in the sequence was that the man who operated the Viking ship ride had gotten a flat tire and ended up stranded on the side of the road right before his shift. His substitute was an eighteen-year-old who didn't know how to stop the ride.

At least, that was how it was supposed to happen.

Until this morning, when a rogue descendant heroically gave the Viking ride operator a lift to work. No accident, no lawsuit, and Yongma Land lived on in perpetuity.

The change had set off alarms all over headquarters—the descendants kept a close eye on Yongma Land because a lot of rogues saw it as an initiation, trying their hand at cause-and-effect, getting their first taste of unsupervised, unsanctioned power.

It was my job, as a "loyal" descendant, to take that power away.

That was why I'd handed the Viking ride operator a bag of chili fries.

I already bought these, but I feel sick from the rides and don't want to waste them, I'd said with big, innocent eyes, standing under the green neon light of the octopus ride so I looked slightly ill. I might have been behind schedule with Operation: Kiss Kim Jihoon, but that didn't mean I had no clue how to infiltrate a scene.

The operator gratefully accepted my fries and went to the bathroom a few minutes later, where he was currently locked in a stall with the door jammed shut, and absolutely no one was operating the ride. The timeline would correct itself, and it had only cost me 4,000 won at the snack bar.

No matter what country I worked in, the higher-ups preferred this indirect approach to adjusting the timeline. They called it the butterfly principle, based on the theory that a butterfly flapping its wings could indirectly cause a typhoon on the other side of the world. For descendants, the principle basically boiled down to this: Never solve a problem at its source. Making a small change from a distance creates fewer unwanted ripple effects and makes it harder for rogues to undo your work.

For instance, rather than crashing a car, we'd drop a persimmon out a window. A seagull would eat the persimmon, which would give it violent indigestion, and it would poop all over the windshield of a passing car, which would run a stop sign and plow into the car we'd wanted to crash in the first place.

The timeline architects said it was more resource efficient this way, but I doubted that was the real reason. It was probably so that we could pretend that the end result wasn't our fault.

I took a step back as another person crashed into the pavement, their forearm crunching beneath them. A crowd was gathering around the fence now, screaming and pointing. The octopus ride spun in my peripheral vision, its flashing lights making me nauseous.

"All right," Hyebin said, tossing the two corn dog skewers in the trash. "Let's see if you pulled this one off." She pushed back against the crowd, heading toward the exit and waving for me to follow. "Wipe your face!" she called over her shoulder.

I swallowed, the few bites of corn dog sitting heavy in my

stomach. I'd done what I was told, but that didn't necessarily mean I'd succeeded—a lot of things could go wrong on a mission without revealing themselves right away. Maybe I'd bought the last corn dog and ruined the day of a future war general who would flatten the earth in retaliation. Or maybe a famous artist had seen my face and would showcase a portrait exhibit titled *Nervous Foreigner Eats Corn Dog*, which would have all sorts of butterfly effects. That was why Hyebin and I never spent more than a few minutes on any assignment.

My time with Hyebin was my first field experience. In Japan and the States, I'd spent hours every day after school in a classroom with other descendants. We'd studied time travel principles and infiltration techniques and case files of other descendants who'd nearly destroyed the world with their carelessness. I'd finished all my classroom hours just before moving from Tokyo to Seoul, where I had the great fortune of attempting to master time travel in my third language.

Over the last month, Hyebin had taught me many things that a classroom never could: how to move unnoticed through a crowd, how to get through most interactions as quickly as possible, how to walk through the past like it was made of glass and I was a wild elephant who could shatter everything if I turned around too quickly. Until I was cleared for independent travel, we did our missions together.

After all, the descendants didn't let just anyone travel through time. No matter how much they needed more descendants, a descendant you couldn't trust was worse than none at all—it was too easy to make mistakes that would end the world. Hyebin graded me on every mission, and her score combined with my infiltration mission points would determine whether I could move up the ranks and be trusted with important tasks, or if I was better off being fired and brain scrubbed.

That was the worst-case scenario, because I had no backup plan for the rest of my life. I had never thought about college, didn't have the extracurriculars to get into an American university because all my time after school was spent working for the descendants, and didn't have the grades to get into a Korean or Japanese university. I wasn't even studying for the Korean college entrance exams—I'd told everyone that I was applying to international schools. There was no option but to keep plowing forward with the choice I'd made.

I dragged my sleeve across my mouth, wiping off the blood, and hurried after Hyebin. "Are you sure that no one died?" I said as we left the fairground. I could still taste blood, which somehow couldn't overpower the taste of corn dog.

"Would it matter if they did?" Hyebin said, her gaze flat. "Would you have gone against orders?"

"No," I said, before I could even think about whether or not I meant it. I knew that insubordination was the fastest way to guarantee I never got top-level security clearance.

"People die," Hyebin said. "Our job is not to stop death, it's to make sure everything is the way it's supposed to be. There's no way to save everyone in the world from dying."

"Yes, Sunbaenim," I said quietly.

Hyebin was making that face that I knew meant I'd annoyed her. Blue and red lights gleamed off her dark eyes as police cars drew closer.

She held her hand out stiffly. "Come on."

I took her hand, grimacing at the feeling of corn dog grease between our palms. I was sure Hyebin hated touching me, but it was a necessary step when using our powers.

Hyebin was not a descendant of Ryūjin like me, but of one of the Korean dragon families. Instead of boxes of time, the Korean descendants all had yeouiju—orbs of concentrated magical power. Korean legend said that fledgling dragons claimed their final and all-powerful form when they caught a yeouiju in their mouths. Though the mythical dragons were gone, some of their descendants—like Hyebin—still carried yeouiju full of immense power.

For now, since I wasn't cleared for independent travel, Hyebin's powers carried us both across the timeline. She held tight to my hand and pulled out the glowing yeouiju from her pocket.

"Are we clear?" she said.

In other words, *Are we about to accidentally traumatize anyone by vanishing into thin air?*

First, I scanned the empty street for humans. When I didn't see any, I closed my eyes and listened for footsteps or car engines but could only hear cicadas and the low buzz of streetlights. Lastly, I raised my gaze to the sky.

"No," I said.

"No?" Hyebin pressed.

I nodded to a telephone pole, where a security camera was mounted high up, angled toward us. Descendants had to avoid showing up in photos or videos while on missions.

"Where should we stand to avoid it?" Hyebin said, even though she knew the answer.

"Directly under it," I recited. "Unless there's another camera on the next pole, in which case we should move into the forest."

Hyebin nodded in approval—the closest she ever got to praise—and walked toward the pole. Once I confirmed that there weren't any other cameras nearby, her greasy grip tightened painfully around my hand. She closed her eyes and took a deep breath, and as she exhaled, her bones bloomed with light.

She opened her eyes, which were now piercing blue, her normally shadowed face glimmering. The light rushed across her skin and spread to my hand that was locked tight around hers, her palm as hot as a shooting star. The warmth surged into my bones and the edges of the world began to blur.

Time flowed like silk around us, the years whispering across my face, glinting beneath my fingertips, tightening around my throat. Most people thought of time as an unyielding constant, a sworn promise of sunrises and sunsets and shifting seasons. But only the descendants knew that time was nothing more than the whim of a forgotten god—it promised nothing, often lied, and had sharp, glistening teeth.

When I opened my eyes, we were standing on the same street as before, but the sky was an ominous gray, the light gone. The air tasted wet with an impending storm, clouds gathering overhead. The arrangement of parked cars had changed, the sidewalks were cracked with weeds bursting through them—a scene I remembered from the present, which meant we were back in 2025. I looked over my shoulder at Yongma Land . . .

Where the carnival lights were still as bright as ever.

The delighted screams of children carried across the hill, the mechanical whir of rides and scent of fried foods along with them.

I failed, I thought, going as still as a rabbit under Hyebin's glare. Maybe if I didn't move, she would forget I was there and go home without skinning me for a stew.

Foreign transfers like me didn't typically get to do this much fieldwork—the only thing saving me from toiling away in the classroom was my high scores on the infiltration simulations in Japan. If I started failing these missions, there were a dozen domestic descendants who would be happy to train with Hyebin in my place.

"Don't throw your pity party just yet," Hyebin said, arms crossed. Of course she could tell what I was thinking by reading my face. "What time is it?"

Tentatively, I pulled out my phone. "Three?" I said, wincing at Hyebin's glare that told me that was the wrong answer.

"Descendants don't round up, Yang," she said.

I looked back to my phone, which said 2:59 P.M. At once, I understood.

Maybe one minute didn't make much of a difference to a regular human, but to a descendant, it meant everything.

I tucked my phone in my pocket and turned toward Yongma Land once more.

The wind picked up, its high-pitched shriek swallowing the sound of children's screams and wheels scraping over metal tracks. A flurry of dead leaves blew across my vision, and I held up a hand to shield my face as they spiraled up and up toward the white sky, dimmed behind a veil of smog.

When I lowered my hand, Yongma Land was deserted.

The sign, once brightly lit, was now yellowed and cracked. The octopus ride spun lazily in the wind, but all the colors were pale, all the rides empty, the grass yellow and dead.

"Here it is," Hyebin said, flashing me her phone, where she'd pulled up a Wikipedia article on Yongma Land.

> **Yongma Land** is an abandoned amusement park in Seoul in operation from 1980 to 2011.

It worked, I thought. I bit back a smile, only because I knew Hyebin didn't like it when I was smug.

The timeline refreshed every hour, on the hour. None of the changes a descendant made would go into effect before then. Afterward, only descendants would remember the secret world of what used to be, the world we had irrevocably changed.

Any Echoes not on their origin timeline during the refresh were dragged back home by the timeline itself, a process which Hyebin had likened to "being forced through a cheese grater one hundred times," which usually left people maimed if not dead. It was like the timeline's immune system—a safety precaution to prevent paradoxes. Some descendants had a gene that made them immune to the pull, but the only way to test it was to try to weather a refresh, and the cost for being wrong was ending up as a puddle of time jelly.

"Great," Hyebin said, already turning away. "That should earn you a few experience points. Now come on, I'm starving."

I wasn't sure exactly how the descendants had built a BBQ restaurant that existed outside of any timeline, but with meat this good, I wouldn't question it.

The restaurant sat in a limbo where time didn't pass, which was helpful for descendants who desperately needed a dinner break but didn't have time for one. It was a traditional Korean restaurant, the kind of place that made you leave your shoes at the door and sit on the floor and never let you leave hungry. There was no menu, because apparently they could cook whatever you wanted.

A white expanse of nothingness blared through the windows of the restaurant, the flat plane of a world without time. Hyebin had warned me not to stick my fingers out the window in case the timeline bit them off, and I still wasn't sure if she was joking. The only way in or out of the restaurant was through a hidden door in a bathroom stall marked OUT OF ORDER in Saejeol station.

Within thirty seconds of us sitting down, waiters crammed our table full of kimchi, bean sprouts, spinach, and a huge bowl of gamja-tang in the center—the staff had an uncanny skill for knowing just what Hyebin wanted to eat. She ladled a big chunk of pork and potato into my bowl before filling her own and digging in as if I wasn't even there.

This was the only place I'd ever seen Hyebin sit down to eat. Most of the time, she ate like a cat, gorging herself on prey when it was available in preparation for long stretches of going without.

This was what my life would be like if I ever became a senior agent like her. Ironically, the people trusted to wield time had so little of their own. But at least Hyebin didn't have to move around like my parents, who had never been promoted past floating agents, and at this point were too good at their jobs to justify changing them.

But my fate hadn't been sealed yet. I could still be like Hyebin if I worked hard enough. I could still have access to the kinds of files that the boss handed her without question. I'd seen them once in her scrying pool—the record of an ex-descendant, marked LEVEL 1 SECURITY CLEARANCE. But she'd closed the file before I could get a better look.

"Sunbaenim," I said, stirring my soup. I didn't feel particularly hungry after the corn dog. And the blood. "How many points will I get for this mission?"

Hyebin plopped a piece of dried seaweed on top of her rice and folded it up with her chopsticks. "I don't know, six or seven?" she said. "Successful infiltration less than twenty years in the past, about ten seconds of direct interaction with a human—which you could cut down next time, by the way . . . I'll put it down for six, unless the analysts find any ripple effects we missed. You in a hurry or something? You're still in school anyway."

Only six points? I thought, staring down at my food to hide my expression. Missions close to the present weren't worth much because the stakes were lower, but I was still on my twenty-year leash until I got promoted. I needed to clear five hundred points before I could even be considered for a full-time agent position, and I was currently sitting at 376.

"I just want to see something more interesting," I said, praying the excuse made enough sense to Hyebin that she would believe it. "I can travel through time, but I haven't actually seen anything that unfamiliar, you know?"

Hyebin shook her head, cracking open a bottle of soju and flicking the cap. "You turn nineteen this year, right?" she said.

"Um, yeah. In December."

Hyebin nodded and poured a shot, then slid it toward me across the table.

"Trust me, you don't want to work too far in the past," she said. "They have weird diseases. If you want to move up faster, you're better off earning infiltration points in the present. They're meant to be practice runs."

That was easy for Hyebin to say, since she wasn't the one who'd belly-flopped into a stream in front of Jihoon and had to face him at school the next day. My other choices for infiltration missions were even more humiliating.

For ten points, I could pretend to be pregnant and sit on the pregnancy seat on the train from Bupyeong Station to Sindorim Station. For fifteen points, I could convince my calculus teacher to give me his favorite pen (the one he loved more than his children). Or, for twenty points, I could convince Choi Seoyun—the most popular girl in my year—to switch socks with me.

There was a smattering of two- or three-point missions that were slightly easier, but they all required time that I didn't have. For now, the best way to get access to level one files was to keep my head down while I trained with Hyebin, focus on Jihoon, and try not to flunk out of school.

Hyebin was watching me expectantly, so I picked up the shot glass and tapped it against hers. I turned away as I drank it—I was younger, so it was the polite thing to do—but I could sense her gaze burning the side of my face, and I knew that there was no lying to Jang Hyebin.

At dusk, when I felt slightly warm from soju but not quite drunk enough to forget the sound of children smashing into pavement, I walked home alone. Hyebin had stayed with me as far as my train stop, which was only a few minutes from my apartment. *If I can trust you to fix the timeline, I can trust you to walk home alone*, she'd said.

I pulled my jacket tighter around me as I emerged from the subway, crossing the car bridge above the shallow stream that Jihoon and I had fallen into earlier that day.

My parents had chosen to live in Eungam because it was a perfectly inconspicuous place—still in Seoul, with access to all of its trains, but the sort of place no one bothered going unless ends lived there because there were absolutely no tourist attractions. This late at night, the people selling handbags and bracelets along the bridge had packed up, and the brightest light was the Emart sign at the end of the road, like a North Star but for groceries and flip-flops instead of Jesus's birth.

I came to a stop at the top of the bridge, looking out across the river that ran off into the horizon, caged in by trees on both sides that were just starting to turn orange. I liked this part of Eungam most at night, when there wasn't a constant stream of people pushing you forward, when you could stop against the railing and breathe the smell of cinnamon hotteok and see the vast, uncountable stars behind the fine dust veil. I took a deep breath and imaged for a moment that this was my home, that I could be this version of Mina forever. I held my breath, tightened my grip on the railing, and clung to that feeling for a few beautiful, selfish seconds.

I exhaled, my grip going limp.

I could never go home again. Home was not a beautiful place, or a clear night, or a country, or a language. Home was a person, and that person was gone.

Tears burned at my eyes, so I turned away and headed for my apartment. I still had to study calculus, after all. I took out my key fob and turned the corner, and that was when I saw him.

In the narrow alley just to the left of the street vendors, a young man in gray dress pants and an untucked white shirt—half a high school uniform—was picking something up off the ground. He had a black face mask and pale blond hair, which meant he was either a foreigner or a K-pop wannabe. But the blond hair was far less distracting than what he had in his hand.

A yeouiju, glowing blue in his palm.

Using one this close to the main road was reckless—even I knew that. He hadn't even noticed me gaping at him, and he wasn't wearing a watch, so he was breaking at least two important rules at once. The only people so careless were ones who didn't have to worry about getting demerits, and those were . . .

Rogue descendants.

I took a step forward and my foot crunched down on a leaf. The boy turned around.

His dark eyes captured the light from the streetlamp above him, his gaze flaring like a passing comet before it locked onto me. He squinted, fist clenched around the dark object he'd picked up, then paused. His eyes widened and he took a startled step back.

"Mina?" he whispered.

I frowned. "Do I know you?"

He drew his yeouiju close to his chest, then turned and looked at something on the other side of the building. With an apologetic smile, he pivoted and ran around the corner.

I hurried after him, but when I rounded the corner, there was nothing but a dark, empty parking lot.

I sighed and took my phone out of my pocket, pulling up Hyebin's number—I was supposed to call Hyebin to report him. Every second I kept this to myself was technically violating protocol.

But my finger hovered over the call button, and after a few seconds, the screen went black. I looked up to the window of my apartment, still dark because neither of my parents had made it home yet. They were out working, like always, for their bosses who would never promote them, even after stealing from them.

If I reported this, there was no way I'd get to sleep tonight. Hyebin would tell me to go back to headquarters to write a detailed make sure no rogues tried to insert themselves into the royal family again. Rogues seemed to think it was hilarious to try to get their own faces on the 10,000 won note instead of King Sejong, even if they could only enjoy it for a few moments before other descendants swooped in to correct the timeline.

"Are you hungry?" my mom said, pulling up a stool and peering into the high cabinets.

I was, but for actual food. To my mom, "cooking" meant "assembling a snack plate." She was a highly skilled agent, fluent in three languages, yet had managed to break five rice cookers before making the executive decision that we were a takeout family. That was after she'd already ruined our kimchi fridge because she thought it was a freezer and packed it to the brim with ice cream. We were still scraping chocolate chunks off the ridges.

She dropped a few boxes of snacks on the counter and hopped off the stool. Her boss often sent her home with processed food from across the timeline, like some sort of bonus to distract her from the fact that she hadn't been promoted in twenty years, and I hated that it actually worked. Last week, she brought home a box of dalgona candy from the sixties, which she claimed were definitely different from the kind you could buy in Emart today. There was also hamburger gummy candies from the '90s, Apollo sugar sticks from the '80s, and occasionally a fried pork cutlet vaguely shaped like Pikachu, which was apparently a thing in the early 2000s.

I grabbed a box of chocolate cereal before my mom could empty out all our cabinets onto the counter. She smiled and snatched a few of my cheese balls, then passed me a carton of milk.

I tried to pour myself some cereal, but a red rectangle came flying out of the box and fell into my bowl. It took me all of two seconds to realize it was my mom's passport.

"Shit!" my mom said, snatching it. "I mean, *Oh no!* You didn't hear me swear."

"I'm eighteen," I said.

My mom sighed and shook the crumbs off her passport. "I forgot that was in there," she said, before looking around for a safer place to hide it.

My parents and I had three passports, three names, three identities.

In Korea, I was Yang Mina. In Japan, I was Yamamoto Mina. And in America, I was Mina Young. When I was a kid, I'd asked my parents which name was my real name, and they hadn't known how to answer because they didn't want to give me an identity crisis (and they'd also lost my actual birth certificate and weren't sure themselves).

My mom had somehow gotten it into her head that we had to hide our unused passports in different places, in case the Korean police investigated us for identity fraud and found all our passports in her nightstand. I felt fairly certain the descendants would intervene rather than let valuable employees rot in jail, but try telling that to a worried mother.

The door unlatched again and my dad appeared in the doorway.

"Meet any princes today?" he said to my mom, bending down to untie his boots. He was dressed in a military uniform because there were only so many roles a white man could realistically play in Korea's past. He spent most of his days interfering in switchboard operations during the Korean War, undoing the mistakes of rogue vigilante travelers. The war was a hotbed for unauthorized rogue interference, so there were always plenty of timeline inconsistencies for my father to clean up in order to prevent a paradox from devouring us all.

My parents had met when my father was studying abroad at the University of Tokyo. Only my mom was an original descendant of Otohime, the Japanese princess who'd bestowed boxes of time on the world. But the Japanese descendant branch was notoriously short-staffed and shrinking along with the declining Japanese population, so they'd been willing to train my dad as long as he'd help my mom make lots of descendants. But the joke was on them, because my parents had only had me.

At least, as far as they could remember.

Honestly, it didn't make much sense. The bosses had made their expectations explicitly clear to my parents as a condition of their marriage—two children, minimum. My mom had never mentioned any trouble having another kid, and the descendants had no shortage of money to throw at that sort of problem, which was a tier-one priority. Yet, somehow, there was only one of me.

When I was growing up, my clothes and shoes had always been hand-me-downs, supposedly from a cousin I'd never met, who my mother couldn't tell me much about. Until I was ten, all my bedrooms had a bunk bed. I slept on the bottom bunk and stared up at the springs of the upper bunk with a strange fixation, somehow knowing innately that the upper mattress wasn't mine. We didn't have a single family photo from before I was ten, and the pictures from that year looked oddly asymmetrical—my mom's hands on my shoulders where I stood in front of her, my dad's hands awkwardly tugging at his pockets, like he didn't know what to do with them.

There was only one photo that made sense. It was a picture of me when I was seven, swinging on a playground set in Michigan, a girl with long brown hair on the swing beside me. Both of us faced away from the camera, looking toward the sun over the fence, the light illuminating our silhouettes in gold. My mom had written *Mina + ?* on the back and said she couldn't remember who the other girl was—she must have been a neighbor's kid. But I knew better.

If I ever had another girl, I would have named her Hana, my mom once said. *It's just like your name—it works in Japan, Korea, and America. I'd have two little chameleons.*

And then, a month ago, when we'd first moved into this tiny

excuse for an apartment in Seoul, I'd found a note waiting for me on my pillow:

When you're ready, come find me. I will keep you safe.
—Hana

Manipulating the timeline was an art, not a science. It was difficult to completely extract a single event—or person—without creating a thousand other undesired ripples, so sometimes you had to let the loose ends be and hope for the best. For all their snobbery, the descendants didn't always clean up after themselves that well.

That was why, when they tried to erase someone, they often left pieces behind.

Somewhere on the timeline, I had a sister.

I couldn't remember her face or her voice, because those things had been stolen from me. But I felt her absence in the empty chair at the kitchen table, in the loose threads of her worn hand-me-down sweaters that felt like her arms around me, in the cavernous silence in my room at night, the certainty that once, somewhere, in some timeline, there had been another heartbeat in my room, so close to mine.

My dad took out a bag of chips and laughed when my mom's American passport fell into his bowl. My mom smiled and handed him a Coke, and something about their joy made my milk taste sour. They did not miss Hana, not even a little bit. You couldn't miss someone you didn't remember.

If I ever got caught, the other descendants would erase me too. Would my parents still smile and laugh and happily eat junk food and feel perfectly fine about their lives without me? Or would they know, like I knew, that they harbored a secret love in their heart for someone who was no longer here, and now that love had nowhere to go?

"I made a bunch of people fall off a carnival ride today," I said, because I wanted my parents to stop smiling.

"Yikes," my father said, turning toward me. "Yongma Land again?"

"Someone really wants that park open," my mom said, shaking her head. "I don't see why. I like it the way it is now. And so many K-pop idols have done photo shoots there! The haunted carnival aesthetic is so beautiful."

"Yes, it's the *aesthetic* that you appreciate in those photos," my dad deadpanned.

"They're all too young for me!" my mom said, her face red.

"Don't you think it's wrong?" I said.

My parents stilled. They both tried to speak at the same time, closed their mouths, and looked at each other.

"Don't we think *what's* wrong?" my dad said carefully.

Unquestioningly taking orders from higher-ups, even if it ends up with children bleeding on the pavement? I thought. *Or maybe your own child disappearing?* "Putting someone out of business," I said instead. "Shouldn't we feel bad about that?"

"Mina, we're not designing the timeline ourselves," my mom said, setting a gentle hand on top of my own. "I don't trust myself to make those kinds of decisions, do you?"

"*I* certainly don't," my father said. "I can't even decide what to eat for dinner, much less the fate of the entire world."

My dad laughed at his own joke while my mom rolled her eyes good-naturedly. "The descendants have saved the world many times," she said. "They have a plan, even if we can't see it right now. All you have to do is trust."

The next day, I hurried into calculus class two minutes before the bell, hoping that it wasn't enough time for Jihoon to start a serious conversation. Our seats were next to each other, and suddenly changing now would draw more attention to us than it was worth.

"Morning," I said to him, sliding into my seat. He turned around and brightened like he'd just noticed me, even though I knew he'd carefully tracked my steps across the room while trying to look unflustered.

"Morning, Mina!" he said, reaching into his bag and pulling out a bottle of Yakult. Apparently he'd forgiven me for my weirdness by the river, and I was more than fine with pretending it had never happened.

"Thanks! Sorry for running off yesterday," I said, laughing awkwardly as I accepted the bottle. I would play it off like it wasn't a big deal, smooth over the memory in his mind, do absolutely anything but act like he'd nearly caught me time traveling.

"Don't worry," he said, holding a hand out when he saw me "struggling" to peel the foil lid back. I passed him the bottle and he peeled it easily and handed it back to me, our hands brushing for just a moment longer than necessary. "What are you doing after school today?" he said.

"More classes," I said, shrugging and sinking down in my seat, cradling the Yakult. "It's too bad, though. They're so far away and it's boring walking there all by myself . . ." The end of my sentence trailed off in an unspoken invitation. I stared resolutely at the Yakult, resisting the urge to peek at Jihoon's face.

"I have English tutoring right after school," Jihoon said mournfully, like he was telling me about a funeral. "I would walk you, but—"

"No no, don't miss your class," I said quickly, only because it would be rude to say otherwise. It was all part of the delicate choreography—don't be too needy, make him think about you during class instead. Still, I would have loved to wrap up this mission before reporting in.

I was about to innocently suggest that we meet up after his class, but the words died in my throat when I caught a glimpse of dark eyes in the doorway. The shadow retreated behind the fogged glass of the half windows between our classroom and the hallway. Hyebin.

I didn't have time to consider what Hyebin was doing at my school because Mr. Oh swept into the classroom and greeted us before loudly shutting the door. I stared resolutely ahead as he announced that he'd finished grading our exams and was going to pass them back.

I could hardly even remember taking that test last week—that was when Hyebin and I had been tasked with catching one very specific duck from the Han River in 2005, which our bosses thankfully understood would take us more than one attempt. Nearly every day after school, I'd been knee-deep in the water, swinging a net at feral ducks while Hyebin tried not to shoot me with a tranquilizer gun.

Mr. Oh set my test face down on my desk before moving to the row behind me. I lifted the corner of the paper and dared to peek, then held my breath and turned it over.

67%

I slammed the paper back down, praying no one else had seen.

This was my only class with Jihoon, and I couldn't afford to flunk out of it. Maybe he would still see me outside of class, but he'd probably second-guess his interest in me once he realized I wasn't smart like him. Besides, having to tell the descendants I needed a new slate of infiltration missions because I'd gotten held back a year was definitely not going to get me promoted any faster. Maybe they'd refuse to assign me anything new, and I'd be stuck collecting points six at a time with Hyebin. If I were better at math, I could have calculated how long that would take me to reach five hundred, but I was too afraid of the answer to try.

I sat in a daze through the rest of class, trying to listen to Mr. Oh so I wouldn't fall even further behind, but I felt like *67%* was branded across my vision. Dragons were supposed to be highly intelligent, but apparently my dad's human genes had overridden that particular trait.

When the bell music finally played, I grabbed my bag and shouldered my way out of the classroom before anyone else, terrified that Jihoon would ask how I did on the test.

"Mina?" I heard Jihoon call, but I pretended not to hear him and hurried into the hallway, where Hyebin grabbed my arm and yanked me into the nearest bathroom.

"My phone is on!" I said. "You could have texted me!"

Hyebin slammed a gloved hand over my mouth, shoving me back into a stall. The leather smelled of fire, the scent stinging my eyes.

"Shut up," she said, her eyes dark.

Something was wrong with Hyebin.

Her face looked gray and thin under the weak bathroom light, her eyes tinged red. Instead of the joggers and pullover sweatshirts that she normally wore until she had to change into a costume for a mission, she wore black leather that didn't look like it belonged to any time period in particular, tight to her skin, meant to make her disappear into the shadows. She dropped her hand from my face, and as she reached for her pocket, her jacket swung back, revealing a gun against her belt.

"*You brought a gun into my school?*" I whispered.

"I said *shut up*," Hyebin said. "Give me your hand."

I held out my hand without thinking, and Hyebin dropped something cold into it. When she pulled back, I held four bullets in my palm, glowing from the overhead light.

"Hide these somewhere, and don't bring this up when you see me," she said. "I was never here."

"Don't bring this up?" I said, my blood suddenly cold. There was only one reason Hyebin would ask me this. "You're an Echo, aren't you?"

Hyebin didn't dignify my question with an answer. Instead, she drew her face mask up over the bottom half of her face and stormed out of the stall, yanking open the bathroom door. The stall door swung shut, and I looked down at the shells in my hand that suddenly felt impossibly heavy.

Two weeks ago, I'd seen Hyebin loading a gun with quick precision before heading out for a mission deemed too dangerous for me to join. We kept our guns with the police and our ammo at headquarters—unlike the American branch, we only brought out guns here if they were absolutely necessary.

I closed my fist around the shells, their coldness spreading through my bones.

If Hyebin had given me bullets, one thing was certain: Someday, I would need to use them.

With fingers I could hardly feel, I opened up the smallest pocket at the front of my backpack and dropped the bullets inside. *All you have to do is trust*, my mom had said last night. I hoped, more than anything, that she was right.

· 🦋 ·

When the final bell rang and all my classmates went to their hagwons to study until their brains bled, I went straight to the café a few blocks from my apartment to do exactly the same thing, but for free. Jihoon had class, and Hyebin had meetings, so for once, I was on my own.

I claimed the window table with an outlet and slammed my calculus book down, determined to steamroll my worries under the weight of differential equations. It would be humiliating if the reason I never became a full agent wasn't to do with my being Japanese, or American, or any sort of skill related to wielding time, but rather that I was just really bad at math.

I knocked back a tall cinnamon latte and kept a piece of cheesecake at the corner of my table as a reward, because it had been a royally shitty week and if I couldn't date Jihoon or pass calculus or get a promotion, I deserved to drown my misery in sugar and cheese.

After ninety minutes of toiling through my homework and sneaking bites of cheesecake, I pulled up some explainer videos in English on YouTube, hoping switching to another language would reboot my brain. With my headphones on, peering intently at some math nerd trying to explain my homework to me on my smudged screen, I almost missed when someone dropped into the seat in front of me.

I looked up, unable to hear the words out of the stranger's moving lips because the calculus video was still playing through my headphones.

The first thing I noticed was bright blond hair. *Foreigner or K-pop wannabe*, I thought instantly, but of course I had already had that thought. I had seen this person before.

He was, undoubtedly, the rogue traveler I'd seen running away the other night. Today, he was wearing an oversized white T-shirt and black sweatpants, his blond hair slightly damp. He pulled off his black cloth mask, and I nearly choked on my next breath. He could fight Jihoon for the title of Cutest Guy in Year Three. He had the kind of bright, disarming face that you saw on subway posters where impossibly beautiful actors advertised bottled tea or snail cream or Samsung phones by holding them close to their airbrushed faces.

I took off my headphones. There were many things I could have said, things that a more experienced and assertive descendant might have said. Hyebin probably would have cuffed him to the table before he could blink. But somehow, spectacularly, all that came out of my mouth was "You're going to knock my cheesecake off the table."

He blinked, then his gaze dropped to my cheesecake, which was teetering precariously on the edge of the table. He quickly shoved it back to the center. "Is it strawberry?" he said. And there was that same warm voice, which had no business being that smooth and low coming from a guy who couldn't be more than nineteen. Jihoon's voice still cracked, which always made him flustered and made me less nervous about my infiltration mission. But talking to this guy in my third language made me feel like my mouth was full of pine cones.

When all I did was stare back at him, he let out an awkward laugh. "Sorry, let me start over. You're Yamamoto Mina?"

I shook my head—how did he know my Japanese name? Something about his undivided attention and his big brown eyes made me want to melt into the floor. So I did the only thing I could think of—I pulled out my phone.

"*Wait wait wait!*" he said, holding out a hand, eyes bright with alarm. "What are you doing?"

"Calling my mentor," I said.

"Why?" he said. "What have I done?"

I frowned. "I saw you last night."

"What?" he said, drawing back. "I wasn't here last night."

"No, I saw you outside *my apartment* last night," I said, my grip tight around my phone.

He shook his head. "That's not possible. Look, can you just give me a moment to explain before you call Hyebin?"

My finger froze an inch away from my phone screen. "You know my mentor's name?" I said. I probably should have been worried at that point, but I was too confused to think about any worst-case scenarios yet. This wasn't the weirdest thing that had ever happened to me, but usually awkward and confusing scenarios were the result of my own Echoes, not random cute guys in cafés.

He grimaced. "I don't really have time to explain that part," he said. "Please, can you just listen to me for a minute?"

I drew back against the booth, clutching my phone to my chest in case he tried to grab it from me. I still didn't want to spend the next week filing a rogue report, but it seemed this problem wasn't going to go away on its own. Maybe if I turned him in, I would at least be rewarded with some more points and get one step closer to a promotion.

He leaned back slightly, like he could see my thoughts rapidly sliding out of his favor. "If you call Hyebin now, I'll run," he said, hands braced against the table as if to push himself off and get a running start. "They'll probably never find me, but here's one thing I know for certain: I'll never see you again. And if I never see you again, then in fifty years, the world will end."

The café seemed to quiet at his words, the whirring of the coffee bean grinder and clinking of mugs such oddly mundane sounds compared to the bomb this guy had just dropped. Who the hell discussed the apocalypse in a Caffebene over a plate of cheesecake? I wondered if I'd had too much sugar and was starting to hallucinate.

"The world doesn't end in fifty years," I said at last. This I knew for certain. I had seen the entire timeline laid out in scrying pools at headquarters.

"No," he said, shrugging, "because you haven't called Hyebin yet, have you?"

I frowned. "I'm pretty sure that's a logical fallacy."

"Look," he said with a sigh. "How about this: Listen to me talk for five minutes. I'll . . . I don't know, buy you another piece of cheesecake for your time, okay? Then after five minutes, you can decide if you want me to get lost, or if you want me to keep talking. Worst-case scenario, you wasted five minutes of your life and got a free piece of cheesecake."

I glanced down at my half-eaten cheesecake. I hated to think I could be bought so easily, but . . .

"Fine," I said. I set a timer for five minutes on my phone and placed it on the table between us. If nothing else, this would make him go away so I could get back to studying. He glanced uneasily at the countdown, then sighed and straightened up.

"My name is Kim Yejun," he said, switching to Japanese—a skill common for descendants but less so for anyone else. He glanced around in case anyone else was listening, but we were in a quiet corner of the café. "I'm a descendant, just like you. But I don't work for the organization anymore, because I've been on the run ever since I found out the truth."

"The truth?" I said, raising an eyebrow.

Kim Yejun nodded. "I know you're new there. I know they don't tell you much, but you know why they have you make adjustments to the timeline, don't you?"

I frowned. Had Hyebin sent him just to give me a pop quiz? "To correct it back to how it was before rogues started interfering," I said. "The original timeline."

"Yes," Yejun said, "except it's not the original timeline at all."

"Of course it is," I said, starting to regret giving him the chance to talk. Clearly he was some conspiracy theorist who had tumbled down one too many internet wormholes.

"But you wouldn't know that, would you?" he said, leaning closer. Suddenly illuminated by the overhead light, his eyes looked black with starry flecks of brown, like constellations in a summer sky. "You live on this timeline just like everyone else," he went on. "The moment it refreshes, you believe that this is the way it's always been."

I shook my head. "Why would anyone try to change the timeline?"

Yejun let out a sharp laugh. "Money, of course. The descendants have no honor anymore. They can be bought by whatever company will pay them enough to build a future where their company succeeds. The descendants are driving us headfirst into a brick wall of climate change, and they don't even care."

I pressed my lips together tightly, eyeing Yejun up and down for some sign he was joking. "The Japanese descendants follow the same timeline," I said.

"Yes," Yejun said, nodding vigorously, "because Korea and Japan are in on it together."

I sighed and shut my laptop. The idea that Korea and Japan would conspire together about anything was even more unbelievable than a secret second timeline. The descendants only cooperated across countries because they didn't have a choice—you couldn't exactly fix the timeline in two different ways at once. "Why would you tell me this?" I said. "Is this some sort of test? You think I'll just believe anything some stranger tells me?"

His expression crumpled at my words, a sudden sadness pulling at the corners of his annoyingly beautiful brown eyes. "I'm asking because I need your help," he said, lowering his gaze. "I know you're new, so in a lot of ways, telling you isn't ideal, but I need *your* help, specifically."

"*Why?*" I said. Surely there were much more qualified descendants he could have chosen from. Ones with way more experience and points to their name.

"You're not Korean, so you have a different source of time magic than me," he said, shrugging. "If we combined our powers, we'd both be able to use half as much, and the respective amounts would be so low that neither of our agencies would be able to track us. We could move freely around the timeline, totally unseen."

I blinked slowly as his words sank in. "You decided to come to me with this proposal that could get both of us erased . . . *because I'm a foreigner?*"

He winced. "Well, it sounds bad when you put it that way."

The timer on my phone went off. I silenced it, then stood up and started packing up my books.

"Are you going to call Hyebin?" Yejun said, eyeing the door like he was ready to run.

I should have. But Hyebin wouldn't get here in time, and I wasn't about to tackle this guy in the middle of a coffee shop, so it would mean a lot of paperwork for me and he would escape regardless. "I'm going to finish packing up my bag, and then if there's still a rogue sitting in front of me, I'm going to call Hyebin," I said. "But maybe, if I'm alone by the time I finish packing, then I'll have no choice but to accept that this was all a caffeine-induced hallucination which will *never happen again*, and I can move on with my life."

Yejun sighed, his expression wilting. I turned away as I put my laptop back in its case, zipped it up, and slipped it into my bag. By the time I bent down to get my charger, Kim Yejun was gone.

A 5,000 won note was sitting on the table, held down by my plate. On the napkin was a note in messy handwriting:

Cheesecake money

I crumpled up the napkin and used it to wipe the table clean, then shoved the 5,000 won in my wallet—hey, money was money. I stormed home, where hopefully no more handsome boys would pop up when I wasn't looking. He'd lost his mind if he thought I'd help a stranger with an idea like that. It would only end one way: with me scrubbed from existence. I pictured my parents alone in their tiny apartment telling jokes late at night, happily eating their stale cereal, and not missing me at all.

If the descendants didn't destroy me, calculus class would.

Last night, I'd been so busy trying to make sense of my class notes that I'd completely forgotten we had a workbook chapter due today. I'd downed my daily bottle of Yakult like a shot of soju and otherwise pretended Jihoon didn't exist while I tried to do calculus at hyperspeed before Mr. Oh arrived. I glanced up at the clock and grimaced. *I'm a time traveler; how am I always running out of time?* I thought.

The uninvited guest at my study hour certainly hadn't helped my concentration last night. In between equations, I found myself playing back his words in my mind.

If I never see you again, then in fifty years, the world will end.

I shook my head, wishing I could beg Hyebin for a partial brain wipe to erase the memory. The words had somehow gummed to the inside of my brain, as well as the memory of Kim Yejun's dark eyes as he leaned across the table. The more I thought about his proposal, the more ridiculous it seemed. The idea that the fate of the world could depend on someone like me—currently scrambling to make up my calculus homework, wearing mismatched socks because I woke up late—was the most hilarious thing I'd ever heard.

The bell music played, but Mr. Oh still hadn't arrived, so I plowed ahead with my homework. If I hadn't been so preoccupied with calculus, it might have occurred to me that Mr. Oh never showed up late, that there must have been some reason for it.

I finished a passable attempt at my homework and dropped my pencil, slumping back against my chair with a sigh of relief just as the door at the front of the classroom slid open. Mr. Oh walked inside, and a student following closely behind him turned around and slid the door shut.

"Attention class," Mr. Oh said, standing at the front of the classroom and gesturing to the student. As he turned around, my blood ran cold.

"We have a new student today. Everyone please welcome Kim Yejun."

Chapter Four

There were very few times in my life that I'd considered cracking open my box of time magic for an unsanctioned redo. The moment that Kim Yejun walked into my classroom and winked at me was one of them.

I decided that after school, I would petition HQ for a do-over so I could call in sick that day, or better yet, throw myself from the third-story window. I reeled back in my seat at Yejun's eye contact, sure I looked like Mr. Oh had just dragged roadkill in behind him. My fist clenched around my pencil, which snapped in two and clattered loudly to the floor.

"Does he know *her*?" one of the girls in the back whispered unsubtly. Beside me, Jihoon had gone full statue mode, everything frozen except for his eyes, his gaze darting between me and Yejun.

What did Yejun think he was doing here?

Did he really think he was handsome enough to stop me from calling Hyebin to have him dragged off in handcuffs? The girls whispering in the back probably would have argued *yes*, but they wouldn't be ripped from the timeline if they made a mistake.

"We're one desk short," Mr. Oh said, frowning, "but for now, Im Daeun is absent, so you can take her seat beside—"

Yang Mina, I thought mournfully as Mr. Oh finished his sentence. Of course Daeun had to have food poisoning today of all days. Maybe I could go back in time and eat her spoiled kimbap for her so I could be trapped on a toilet instead of between Jihoon and Yejun.

Yejun slid into the seat beside me and pulled out a notebook. I could feel Jihoon's questioning gaze searing the other side of my face, so I looked straight ahead, pretending to be totally oblivious. I needed to tell Hyebin about this, but I was in the front row and couldn't exactly whip out my phone and start texting—Mr. Oh didn't need an excuse to fail me. So instead, I sat perfectly still and did my best to become a piece of furniture. Mr. Oh might as well have been speaking Russian, because I wasn't retaining a single word out of his mouth. I heard one of the girls in the back whisper my name and slouched down in my seat, as if I stood any chance at hiding under the sterile classroom lighting.

I'd spent the past month carefully designing this new life, one where I was completely unseen. A person first and a foreigner second, the chameleon the descendants needed me to be. I cut my hair into annoying wispy bangs like the popular girls, even though they poked me in the eyes. I made a point of never standing up straight so that I would seem shorter. I talked as little as possible so no one could make fun of my accent. And in a single moment, Yejun had made sure everyone knew my name.

I decided in that moment that I hated Kim Yejun.

It was easy for someone like him. Sure, maybe he was having fun attracting stares with his bleached-blond hair now, but when he got sick of it, he could dye it back and be a normal person again, while I never could.

My grip tightened around my second pencil, which creaked threateningly.

"Yang Mina?"

I tensed. Mr. Oh was looking at me, tapping the blackboard. "The derivative of the function," he said in a tone that told me it wasn't the first time he'd asked.

I quickly scanned the equation, but with all my classmates staring at me—and two boys on either side of me—I could barely remember my own name much less how to do calculus. My brain felt like an old laptop overheating, fans whirring loudly in my ears. No one thought I belonged in this class anyway. They were all waiting in anticipation for my wrong answer. Normally I could brush it off, but something about failing in front of both Yejun and Jihoon made me want to cry. Yejun would realize I was too stupid to help him with anything, and Jihoon would be glad he wasn't dating the dumbest girl in class.

I could have been smart, I wanted to scream.

Maybe I had been, in a life where I hadn't had to transfer schools every few months. Where I'd had the time to become good at something, to actually take an interest in what I learned instead of always trying to catch up, spending nights watching Crash Course videos because I didn't have any friends to ask for help.

Yejun raised his hand. "Seonsaengnim?" he said. "Could we do another example? This is different from how we did it in my old school and I want to make sure I understand."

Any other teacher might have resented the interruption, but Mr. Oh was used to talking to a class of half-dead third years who would sooner eat dirt than speak to him before nine in the morning, so he gleefully started to break down the problem on the board. I slumped back in my chair now that I'd escaped the jaws of calculus unscathed and no one was staring at me anymore.

Once I was fairly certain Mr. Oh had forgotten about me, I

turned and shot a glare at Yejun. I hadn't asked for his help, and he'd lost his mind if he thought it meant I owed him anything, but he only winked like we had some secret, and my second pencil snapped in my hand.

For the rest of the class, Yejun did his best to become Mr. Oh's favorite student. It seemed that he not only knew all about calculus but *enjoyed* it. Mr. Oh was probably going to send him a fruit basket in gratitude after class. On my other side, Jihoon was staring unsubtly at both me and Yejun.

The music started playing over the intercom to signal the end of class, but before I could stand up, a shadow fell over my desk.

"Let me carry your bag," Kim Yejun said, snatching it from the back of my chair before I could. In my peripheral vision, Jihoon stared open-mouthed while the girls behind me whispered.

"Mina, you know him?" Jihoon said.

"No," I said, before Yejun could answer. "And I can carry my own bag." *And the phone inside it*, I thought.

Yejun smiled like I was telling a joke, tugging my bag higher on his shoulder. "But I want to talk to you," he said, smiling sweetly. "Come on, I have English next."

So do I, I thought. Of course it wouldn't be enough for Yejun to crash only one of my classes. He'd probably copied my entire schedule. Maybe he even gave Daeun food poisoning—skilled descendants were good at manipulating the world to work in their favor.

"Come on, *Yang* Mina," he said, smirking conspiratorially. As if emphasizing my fake name in front of my classmates would win me over. But he was already leaving with all my things, so I had no choice but to follow. I cast Jihoon an apologetic glance and hurried after Yejun.

"What do you think you're doing?" I whispered as soon as we made it into the hallway. "What part of 'leave me alone' don't you understand?"

"And what part of 'the world will literally end' do you not understand?" he said, smiling through clenched teeth. "Forgive me for being persistent, but the stakes are rather high."

"And you think stalking me will convince me to help you?"

"Is it a crime to want an education?" Yejun said, nearly rounding the wrong corner before I yanked his sleeve, pulling him toward the English classroom. It was the one class I was decent at, so I couldn't afford to be late.

I stormed through the door and pointed to my desk, which, thankfully, had no empty seats next to it. Yejun sighed and dropped my books on the desk, then plopped my bag on my seat. For one glorious moment, I thought I'd bested him.

But then Yejun reached into his pocket, took out an envelope, and placed it on top of my notebook.

"What's this?" I said, glaring like he'd dropped a dead rat on my desk.

"A love confession," he deadpanned, then moved to the back of the room to take the empty seat in the corner.

I should have thrown it in the trash just to see the look on his face. My life would have been a lot simpler if I had.

But the envelope wasn't fully closed, too overstuffed to seal, and I could see the frayed edges of a stack of photographs. *Who even prints photos anymore?* I thought, before my curiosity got the better of me and I dumped the stack on my desk.

The first picture was a shot of the Bulgwang stream—I could tell by the giant *M* painted on the officetel in the background, the one right next to my apartment. It looked like Yejun had photoshopped it too much, because the sky was a blazing blue, the shrubs bursting with flowers. He'd even photoshopped solar panels onto nearby buildings, their reflections bursts of white light that the camera couldn't capture clearly.

I flipped the photograph over.

April 7, 2025, Timeline Alpha was scrawled across the back.

I scoffed. Whatever "Timeline Alpha" Yejun had invented didn't seem that different from this timeline, at least not enough to justify risking my life for. Was that really his best argument? *"Betray the descendants so we can live in a world with five more solar panels!"*

I cast the photo aside and examined the next one. This one was a wide shot of Gyeongbokgung Palace—I recognized the three arches of the main gate with the two tiers of roofs on top. But the interior looked different than I remembered—the Gyeongbokgung of today had vast courtyards of pale dirt between sparse buildings, but the palace in this photo had far more buildings, and instead of white dirt there were blooming gardens and curved ponds. All the temporary fencing for construction was gone, which meant it must have been sometime in the future. I flipped the photograph over.

October 1, 2017, Timeline Alpha

Yejun really was audacious.

Imperial Japanese soldiers had demolished Gyeongbokgung Palace in the early 1900s, and Seoul had planned a fifty-year reconstruction plan for it that still had twenty years to go. Was Yejun really trying to convince me that the palace was still standing in 2017? That the Japanese had never occupied Korea? He was out of his mind.

The next photograph was a board game café in Hongdae—I'd gone there on Christmas last year with my parents, so I recognized the shelves packed with board games, the fairy lights, the exposed brick walls, the window overlooking the street, and the ramen restaurant on the other side. And there at the table . . .

. . . was me.

My hair was cut to my shoulders and I wore a fuzzy gray sweater that I'd never seen before, but that was undoubtedly me, smiling over a game of Don't Break the Ice. I held a can of Sprite in one hand, the silver watch my parents had given me reflecting sunlight off its face. I knew it was me, yet somehow this looked like a complete stranger.

I was the opposite of Hyebin—while she could blend in anywhere, somehow I looked hilariously out of place in every year, like I was an orphan of the timeline, never at home no matter where I went. In the few photographs my parents had taken since I started high school, I always looked like my skin was an itchy costume I wanted to peel off, my eyes haunted, my smile like I'd been forced to grin at gunpoint.

But the Mina in this photo looked completely relaxed. Her hair was my natural shade, not dyed darker to match the other girls', and this Mina had also forgone the trendy eye-poking bangs.

How did Yejun get a picture of me?

My gaze slid to my right, and what I saw next was even worse.

In the photograph, a girl sat across the table from me, a wave of long, coppery brown hair—the same shade as mine—blocking her face. Her sleeve was rolled back, revealing a silver watch. A watch that my father had brought back for me from America for Christmas. It was from a specialty store—a Swiss watchmaker in Grand Rapids made his own watches from the discarded parts of vintage luxury watches. It was a gift no one else in Korea should have had . . . unless my dad hadn't bought one just for me, but for *us*.

Hana?

The bell music played and Ms. Choi stood up from her desk to begin class. I quickly crammed the photographs in the envelope and stuffed them into my bag. I cast a nervous glance back at Yejun, whose infuriatingly pretty eyes looked so full of hope. I turned around quickly, sinking into my chair.

It's just a badly photoshopped picture, I thought again and again, trying to sear the sentence into my brain.

But somehow, my stomach still clenched like I was falling from a great height, the last photograph burned across my vision. I couldn't let go of it in the same way I couldn't ignore Hana's absence. It was the way the stars felt just slightly off-kilter, the way that empty chairs somehow took up more space than full ones, how the trees leaned a bit too far to the left. Hana's disappearance had cast the whole world off-balance.

I sat rigid in my seat as Ms. Choi started passing back papers. I couldn't even remember the topic, but I knew I'd turned mine in three days late—Hyebin and I had been on a mission in Gangneung and I'd lost track of the days with all the driving back and forth. I always saved my English homework for last because I could type up something while half asleep and it would be good enough to impress my teachers.

Not this time. I peeked at the corner of my paper and saw *70%* in bold. A ten-point penalty for each day late.

I jammed the paper into my folder and slammed it shut before anyone could see.

Dragon descendants were supposed to be fast learners, good at retaining large amounts of information, excellent students. I was descended from a literal god. And yet, here I was, about to lose my chance at finding Hana because I was too incompetent to handle basic high school classes.

As soon as the bell music played, I grabbed my books and rushed into the hallway before Yejun could catch up. I heard him call my name, but I hurried to my locker and stuffed my books in my bag.

"Mina?" he called. "The photographs—"

"Just how stupid do you think I am?" I said, slamming my locker shut and glaring at him. I needed to stick to the plan. The way to find Hana was by infiltrating headquarters, not by trusting a random guy who bought me cheesecake.

"I don't think you're stupid," he said, frowning. "These are relics from the other timeline. I thought if I showed you proof—"

"It doesn't prove anything," I said, tugging my bag over my

shoulder. "Look, I know I'm not as smart as our"—I glanced around in case anyone was listening—"classmates," I said at last. "I know I'm a foreigner and no one trusts me. But if you want me kicked out of the descendants, you're gonna have to try harder than that."

He reeled back as if I'd slapped him. "I don't want you to get kicked out," he said, his voice so gentle and hurt that if I were anyone else, maybe I would have fallen for it.

Descendants are good liars, I reminded myself, turning around before he could say anything else to try to persuade me. I sensed him following me, but I stormed into the girls' bathroom—the one place he couldn't follow—then locked myself in a stall and took out my phone.

I found a rogue, I texted Hyebin, a cold jolt of satisfaction washing through me. She didn't respond right away, but that was normal—she never let anything break her focus.

What wasn't normal was that five minutes later, while I waited for the sound of Yejun walking away, she still hadn't responded.

Hyebin never spent more than three minutes on any single mission. Even if she'd just started when I texted her, she should have been done by now.

I gnawed my lip. The thought of going through the rest of the school day with Yejun trailing after me sounded about as fun as walking barefoot over needles.

I tugged a long pink sweatshirt out of my bag and pulled it over my head, covering up most of my school uniform, then shoved open the sliding window and climbed outside, crushing decorative plants as I landed. I walked confidently down the front stairs of the school—that was what Hyebin taught me—no one questioned where you were going or what you were doing if you looked confident—and made it out to the street. If Hyebin wouldn't answer her phone, I would tell her myself.

Maybe skipping school wasn't the smartest idea for someone in danger of failing, but all I could think about was that photo of maybe-Hana, and how happy Yejun was to taunt me with the only thing that I cared about. Punching him in the face and getting kicked out of school was arguably worse than disappearing for a few periods.

I stormed toward headquarters, bending my knees so I wouldn't roll down the incline again. My school sat at the top of a hill, all of western Eungam spread out beneath me.

Before I'd come to Seoul, I'd imagined polished glass skyscrapers that echoed the whole city back at you, flashing neon signs, and a sky lit by fluorescent office lights instead of stars. But that was just the rich parts of Seoul.

Here, on the western side, the tallest buildings were a mix of faded gray concrete and weathered brick, each with perfect rows of square windows like a thousand gaping mouths on haunted faces. Far in the distance, a row of identical concrete skyscrapers stood like sentinels, the barrier between Seoul and the mountains of Gyeonggi. With the haze of fine dust blown over from China, the tops of the distant buildings blurred away, like everything beyond the border of Seoul was no more than a dream.

As I descended the hill, the street rose higher and blocked my view to the west. I reached street level and waited at the intersection, wordlessly accepting a handful of commercial fliers that some old lady handed me. A bicycle sliced diagonally through the crosswalk and nearly ran over my toes, but I made it to the other side of the street unscathed and could finally breathe easier with my school far behind me.

After a few minutes, I reached the tallest building in Eunpyeong. On paper, it was a grocery store, but in reality it was something far more important to humanity.

Emart was the Korean equivalent of Walmart if you could only build up instead of out; a towering Eye of Sauron in the western part of Seoul, except instead of black slate and evil incarnate, it was full of seven-dollar peanut butter and old ladies trying to run me over with their shopping carts. It was ten stories of everything you could possibly want to buy, plus an eleventh floor that was mysteriously always "under construction."

I grabbed a two-pack of banana milk on the first floor, because after dealing with Kim Yejun all morning, it was the least I deserved. I hesitated for a second at the smell of the bakery, my hand lingering over the knotted sausage-and-cheese bread, but thought better of it because Hyebin would surely not appreciate it if I had greasy hands. I picked up a prepackaged vegetable kimbap and hurried upstairs, swearing under my breath when a family with a grocery cart blocked the entire escalator. I managed to rush around them and cut ahead before they could turn the corner for the next escalator, then I was fast-walking as subtly as humanly possible up to the clothing level.

A headache started brewing behind my eyes. I groaned, closing my eyes against the bright fluorescent lighting. *Just what I needed.*

I knew this kind of pain well—the kind of headache that cast star flashes across my vision and threatened to pop my eyes out. It was a symptom of timesickness, which you only felt if you were part of an incomplete time loop. I hadn't yet gone back in time to pour banana milk on my own shoes, so that was probably why I was feeling sick. I would have to check my new missions to see the exact time and date I needed to close the loop.

As the escalator carried me up, the flip-flops and BB Cream on the lower level disappeared into the depths of the basement, followed by the pots and pans and shower curtains. The escalator dumped me out on the electronics floor, but there was still one more level to go.

I skirted around the edge of the floor, to the elevator marked OUT OF SERVICE, and hit the lightless call button four times while stuffing a piece of kimbap in my mouth. Headquarters paid ridiculously high rent to this building, so it was somewhat of an unspoken rule that descendants could help ourselves to whatever we wanted, as long as we didn't cause a scene.

The elevator doors opened and I stepped inside, finally cracking open my long-awaited banana milk. But the moment it touched my lips, I remembered the curdled scent of it that had soaked into my sneakers after my Echo poured it over me. Even after I'd run my shoes through the washer twice, they'd smelled faintly of rotten milk and feet. I grimaced, lowering the bottle as the elevator dinged and reached the eleventh floor.

I entered the sterile lobby, where Seulgi was sitting on her desk, kicking her feet and texting. She looked up as the doors opened and waved with one hand while continuing to text with the other.

Min Seulgi was the world's most unlikely security guard. She had a higher concentration of dragon blood than most descendants, so she looked about eighteen even though she was closer to thirty-five. She wore tulle dresses and circle lenses and looked like her thin arms would snap if she tried to carry her groceries home, but she also had claws that could slice cement like cream. It was her job to make sure no humans wandered into headquarters, and to cut down anyone who tried to get through anyway.

"Hi Seulgi-nim," I said. "Want some banana milk?"

She looked up, a sharp flash of gold blazing through her eyes.

I tensed, taking a step back. Had I said something wrong? Was banana milk offensive to dragons in some way?

"How did you know it was my favorite?" Seulgi whispered.

I relaxed my shoulders and handed her the bottle. "Lucky guess," I said.

The nail on her index finger sharpened into a claw as she stabbed through the foil, then downed the bottle in half a second as the claw retracted into her hand. "Thanks, Mina," she said, wiping her lips on her sleeve and stepping aside to let me into headquarters.

The glass doors slid open automatically as I passed through, sensing the tiny amount of dragon blood running through my veins. I stepped into an office space with sad beige walls and framed paintings of dragons. Each door had an ominous dragon's head knocker with gemstone eyes that gleamed as you walked by. I thought it was a weird decorating choice, considering that humans didn't use human heads as door knockers.

I tossed my opened banana milk in the trash as I strode past the rooms for costuming, yeouiju maintenance, claw and fang repair, the mail, and headed straight for the scrying area.

The southern side of the lair was an open floor plan, lit only from the sunlight through the anti-glare windows—one-way glass so that we could see out but no one could see in. Overhead lights caused too much glare for our purposes.

The other descendants knelt in rows on the floor before shallow-reflecting pools, their fingertips tracing delicate arcs into the water before them. No one looked up as I walked in, too engrossed in their own work. This was perhaps the only place on earth I could blend in, because everyone here was too busy to think about anyone but themselves.

I grabbed a floor cushion from a stack in the corner and sat in front of an unoccupied pool with a white marble rim. My reflection glared back at me, her hair sticking up from how I'd haphazardly yanked the sweatshirt over my braid. I rinsed my hands with a small bowl and cup beside the pool, toweled them off, and dipped a fingertip into the water.

Words floated to the surface of the pool, prompting me to enter a password. We all had signatures that could unlock different information in the scrying pools depending on what kind of clearance we had. My signature was a mixture of my names written in English, Japanese, and Korean—something a stranger wouldn't be able to forge.

All the descendants used bodies of water to communicate—dragons were water creatures, after all—and these reflecting pools offered the highest resolution and greatest amount of privacy. Perhaps the later generations of descendants would have preferred to work over email rather than water scrying, but good luck convincing the Dragon King to use a keyboard. There was also the extra layer of security—anyone who wasn't a descendant could never hack our systems and find our secrets. They would find nothing but chlorinated water.

As soon as I finished my signature, the screen glowed with moving images playing back my last few missions with Hyebin—the domestic violence rally in 2005, the bakery incident in 2007, the typhoon in 2009. All of them had a blue ring around them because Hyebin had marked them as complete.

I opened the tab for new assignments, expecting to find the mission to go back and pour banana milk on my own shoes, but there was nothing there.

That's strange, I thought, as the headache flared behind my eyes. Normally, if I had a timesickness headache, I'd find the reason for it right here, with a bright red ring around it for INCOMPLETE MISSION.

The timeline architects reviewed all our missions and checked for unintended ripple effects. If we deviated too much from the plan and caused problems down the line, they would tell us to send back Echoes to make minor corrections, and those missions were supposed to populate here. Whenever I saw another Mina, it was theoretically because I'd made a mistake on a mission and been sent back to fix it, dragging along a disgruntled Hyebin to supervise.

The banana milk–wielding Mina's mission should have been here.

I splashed the pool, the ripples distorting the screen, and waited until the water settled again to see if it changed anything—you couldn't really turn a scrying pool off and on again, but it was worth a shot. Still, my NEW MISSIONS page was empty.

Maybe my headache was really just a headache. I'd thought I

was good at telling the difference, but if today had proven anything, it was that I wasn't as clever as I thought.

Footsteps echoed behind me, and suddenly Hyebin's reflection appeared in my scrying pool. I turned around.

Hyebin was wearing black leggings and a gray hoodie thrown over the top. She panted like she'd just run up a flight of stairs, her face flushed red. "Oh good, you're already here," she said.

"I texted you," I said. "At my school, there's—"

"We can deal with that later," Hyebin said. "There's an emergency we have to handle first."

"*We?*" I said. Usually, I wasn't allowed to go with Hyebin on any mission of real importance.

"Yep, you're shadowing," Hyebin said, waving for me to follow her. "Look but don't touch."

"What's the emergency?" I said as she all but shoved me toward the clothing designers, who urged me to sign their scrying pool so they could access my size.

"We're going on a neutralization mission," Hyebin said.

I froze, my whole body suddenly stiff as the costumers tried to wrench my sweatshirt off. "Neutralization?" I echoed, even though I already knew what that meant.

Maybe Hyebin thought I hadn't heard of it—I probably should have acted like I didn't, but she was too preoccupied to notice. "Yes," she said, nodding gravely. "We've found a traitor, and we're going to erase them."

Chapter Five

"Do not, under any circumstances, use this," Hyebin said, holding out a pistol.

I stuffed my hands deeper into my jacket pockets and made no move to accept it.

Costuming had outfitted me and Hyebin in a slick black material that looked like leather but was designed to match the exact hue of night shadows. The descendants had poured a lot of money into finding the color scientifically proven to be the least noticeable under Seoul's streetlights. It was reflective in photographs, blurring anything around it.

"I'm not firearm trained," I said.

"That's why it's not loaded," Hyebin said, pulling back the slide and showing me what I assumed an unloaded gun was supposed to look like—not that I would know. "But pretend it is, and don't point it at anyone or I'll kill you."

"Why do I need an unloaded gun?" I said, crossing my arms.

"Protocol," Hyebin said. "We log five people out on a

neutralization mission, we check out five pistols. It's not optional, Yang."

Hesitantly, I took the gun from Hyebin. My palms were already too sweaty and I nearly dropped it, which made Hyebin grit her teeth and let out a pained sound. The costumer had already clipped a holster into the front of my pants, which I'd naively hoped was decorative. I looked to Hyebin hopefully, but she only rolled her eyes. "I'm not stuffing a gun in your pants."

I tucked it in gingerly until it slotted into place, and Hyebin nodded in approval.

"Why do we need these?" I asked.

"Because," Hyebin said, waving for me to follow her down the hallway. "You only get one chance to neutralize someone. If they get away, they know they can't trust us anymore and they go rogue. We never see them again."

"So you *shoot* them?" I said. The descendants hated coming face-to-face with bloodshed, so this seemed like a bizarre choice.

"Rarely," Hyebin said. "But we keep our options open. The stakes are too high to not have a backup plan for your backup plan."

I supposed that made sense. Rogues were almost impossible to capture because they weren't afraid to play with time. The descendants, on the other hand, were as conservative with their adjustments as possible. That was why potential rogues didn't simply get kicked out onto the street after a thorough mind scrub—anyone smart enough to actually succeed in betraying the descendants was too dangerous to set free.

Including Hana.

Hyebin pressed the elevator button and held the door open with one hand, waving me in.

"These missions can be a bit . . . intense," Hyebin said, looking pointedly away from me. That was rare for Hyebin, who had no fear of prolonged eye contact. Half our conversations felt like a staring contest because she glared unblinkingly at me until I looked away in submission.

"In what way?" I said, shifting from side to side, the holster scraping against my stomach.

Hyebin stared at her own reflection in the mirrored walls, lips pressed tight together. "We have close to a hundred percent success rate because we always have the element of surprise. We make the decision and execute it in the same hour, before the timeline refreshes, so the traitor never has the chance to know."

"Okay," I said slowly, sure there was more she wasn't saying—none of that was surprising enough to make Jang Hyebin look nervous.

"We have to go before they've actually committed any crime," Hyebin said, quieter. "That way they won't be expecting us."

There it is, I thought, the metal elevator walls suddenly cold against my spine. "So they won't know why they're being taken?" I said.

Hyebin said nothing, because Jang Hyebin didn't answer stupid questions.

"Why not just convince them to change their plans instead?" I asked.

"That's not possible," Hyebin said. She finally turned to face me, but her eyes were strangely dim. "Once a traitor, always a traitor."

Is that what everyone said about Hana? I thought. *That she didn't deserve a second chance?* I looked away from Hyebin, this time not because I was wilting under her gaze, but because I couldn't bear to look her in the eye knowing that she'd erased innocent people. *Once a traitor, always a traitor.* What a joke. The descendants were capable of wiping out entire species, saving continents, changing the moon cycles, and ending wars. Of course they could change a single person's loyalty if they cared enough to try.

Hyebin's gaze snapped forward at the sound of footsteps.

"Sajangnim!" she said, bowing.

Sajangnim? I thought, bowing and shuffling behind Hyebin to make room before I could get a good look at who was approaching. *Sajangnim* meant "boss," and there was only one person I'd heard Hyebin refer to with that title.

The shadow announced his arrival first, a cold bath of night eclipsing the doorway and then the whole elevator. I held my breath as he entered—I'd heard legends that looking directly at a dragon could kill a human. Each one of their scales told the story of a single human life, and all of that combined suffering would cause your heart to burst. Surely the boss of this branch was the closest to a real dragon I would ever get.

A young man in a black suit entered the elevator, ducking under the doorway. All dragon descendants were tall because of our serpentine ancestors, but he was the tallest I'd ever seen. He looked about Hyebin's age—too young to be anyone's boss—and had hair that glimmered silver under the elevator light like a polished pearl.

He caught my gaze as I rose from my bow, his eyes flashing gold.

Hong Gildong.

It was a fake name, of course—the Korean equivalent of John Doe—because the descendants most closely related to dragons had names that couldn't be spoken in any human language.

"Sajangnim, this is my shadow, Yang Mina," Hyebin said, gesturing to me.

I bowed again for good measure, even as his smooth, silvery voice said: "I know who you are."

How? I couldn't help thinking, but knew better than to say out loud. I didn't like the idea of a powerful descendant like him knowing anything about me. He could squish me like a grape if he was having a bad day.

"All neutralizations require his explicit approval," Hyebin explained.

That means that he approved Hana's neutralization, I realized, going very still. Hong Gildong glanced over his shoulder at me suddenly, as if he could sense my racing pulse. I was standing in an elevator with someone who had known my sister and destroyed her.

Hong Gildong's piercing gaze was the only thing forcing me to stay still, to take steadying breaths, to try to calm my racing heartbeat. The elevator felt impossibly warm, my vision sparkling gold at the edges from the sudden surge of adrenaline. I glared at my reflection in the mirrored wall, unsure how I still looked like a normal high school girl when inside I felt like a burning city.

Hong Gildong turned back to the elevator doors, and I let out a breath. He nodded at two high-level agents who ran to catch up. I'd seen both of them in the scrying room before but couldn't remember their names. They bowed and slid into place on either side of Hong Gildong.

"It's time," Hong Gildong said.

Wordlessly, Hyebin pulled her arm back, and the elevator doors slid closed. She grabbed my hand and reached for the hand of the agent in front of her. They all held hands, except for Hong Gildong—the agent nearest him laid a gentle hand on his forearm.

Hyebin had told me that taking someone's arm instead of their hand when sharing time magic was a sign of respect, and that I should never offer someone my arm unless my hands had literally been chopped off (and even then I should apologize profusely). But of course someone like Hong Gildong commanded that kind of respect. I couldn't really imagine him holding hands with a subordinate. Hong Gildong pulled out his yeouiju, and the elevator began to glow.

Light speared through my body.

I had only ever felt Hyebin's time magic before, so I'd never realized that anyone else's would feel different. But while Hyebin's magic felt like stepping into a sauna, Hong Gildong's felt like being flayed by the sun.

Centuries rushed through me in a single breath—I tasted glimpses of the dawn of Korea, golden palaces, dragons circling the moon in fluid arcs, starlight on my tongue, fire at my fingertips. Then I was crushed into the dirt of a world at war, blood and silt breathing me in. I was the skeleton of a city climbing with glass hands into the sky, black ribbons of road unfurling across dirt, nauseous voyages to sea, wordless secrets and broken bones and bright, blazing gold beneath it all.

The magic flashed in front of me like a passing train and then disappeared, leaving me breathless and squeezing the life out of Hyebin's hand.

I barely registered the sound of the elevator doors opening.

Hyebin nudged me, and my legs moved automatically to follow the other descendants, but I couldn't even feel my feet. I stumbled after them into a mall, squinting under the fluorescent light. I could hardly remember what year we were in, what year we'd come from, what we were doing here, as if I'd lived a thousand lifetimes in the single breath that Hong Gildong's magic had run through me.

The other descendants moved in silence toward the exit. They glinted between customers like minnows, smoothly evading humans so no one would be forced to move to avoid us, which would impact the timeline. I focused all my energy on blending in with the other descendants, minding each footstep as if dancing an intricate ballet, just as Hyebin had taught me. I couldn't imagine the shame if I tripped into a human in front of Hong Gildong, who would surely never promote me if I couldn't do something as simple as *walk*.

The automatic doors slid open, and we stepped into the night.

The crowd on the sidewalk flowed faster than the elderly Emart shoppers inside, so I had to focus more intently on avoiding humans while staying as close to Hyebin as possible. I followed her around a few sharp corners until we drew to a stop in front of a café with flower garlands in the window. Several customers sat at the outdoor tables, where strands of fairy lights illuminated their ceramic plates of pastries and steaming cups of coffee.

I knew right away which person was our target.

There was only one woman sitting alone. Surely the descendants wouldn't grab someone off the street in front of their spouse or friends, so it had to be her. She was wearing a green summer dress, her auburn hair tied in a ponytail. Her back was turned to us, but I could see her reflection in the window of the café as she carefully tore off a piece of croissant, then adjusted the shopping bags at her feet.

I imagined Hana sitting down to eat a croissant and ending up dead before she could finish it. My headache returned, and my throat tightened with nausea.

All three descendants turned to Hong Gildong, who checked his watch, then nodded.

The two high-level descendants shot forward.

Before I could blink, each of them grabbed one of the woman's arms. One of them clapped a hand over the woman's mouth, sweeping her into the alley. They'd moved like a passing shadow, so fast that no one on the street so much as turned to look. Hyebin swooped in and cleared the table, snatched the bags, and shoved the chair back in place. In the blink of an eye, it was as if the woman hadn't been there at all.

I tensed when I realized even Hong Gildong was gone, and I was standing alone in front of the café. I hurried into the alley, barely catching Hyebin's glare as she waved for me to hurry up. The descendants dragged the writhing woman into a building, and I slipped inside behind them.

"Lock the door," Hyebin said over her shoulder.

I bolted the door, sealing us in an office space filled with drab furniture and pale carpets. The other two descendants kicked rolling tables and chairs out of the way and pressed the woman to the floor, finally releasing the gloved hand from her mouth. The woman had wide honey-brown eyes and pink lipstick smeared on her cheek, her auburn hair falling loose from a silk hair tie. She gripped a descendant's wrist with a thin hand, a loose engagement ring sliding up and down her finger.

Hong Gildong took a step forward, crossing his arms.

"Sajangnim?" the woman said as his shadow fell over her. "What's going on?"

"Oh Jia," Hong Gildong said, no longer using the cool and indifferent tone he'd had in the elevator. Now his words echoed as if spoken into a deep cavern, so low that they hummed through the floor and vibrated in my bones. Hyebin had told me that long ago, dragons could cause earthquakes with their harsh words.

"You have betrayed our ancestors and knowingly defied orders, damaging the timeline that the rest of us work tirelessly to protect," Hong Gildong said. I couldn't help taking a step closer to Hyebin at the sound of his disapproval, like some instinctive part of me knew to fear him. I could taste Oh Jia's terror in the air, for she had gone very pale, her hands trembling and eyes wide.

She shook her head, slowly at first, then frantically, her struggling renewed. It was useless, for the other two descendants still had her pinned to the carpet. "I didn't!" she said, looking between me and Hyebin, as if either of us could save her. I looked away like a coward, but I could still hear her desperate words choked with tears, her panicked breaths, her cries as she struggled to get up.

I couldn't have helped Oh Jia even if I'd wanted to. My feet felt rooted in place, my blood so cold that my teeth were chattering. Maybe it was the effect of standing so close to an angry, powerful descendant like Hong Gildong. Or maybe it was because I knew exactly what it meant to erase someone.

"On October 11, 2033," Hong Gildong went on, "you took an unauthorized trip back to 1951 and deliberately interfered with the war."

Oh Jia let out a choked sound of disbelief. *"That hasn't happened yet!*" she said, thrashing against the hands. "I won't do it, I swear! I wouldn't betray you."

Hong Gildong sighed and stepped back. "You already have," he said, nodding at Hyebin.

Hyebin strode forward, and I suddenly felt exposed without her between me and Hong Gildong. Hyebin straddled the woman, digging through Oh Jia's pockets until she pulled out a glowing blue yeouiju. Its light pulsed weakly, illuminating every bone in Hyebin's hand and casting a ghostly glow over the room. Hyebin passed the yeouiju to Hong Gildong with both hands, then helped hold the woman down.

"Oh Jia," Hong Gildong said, "I hereby sentence you to complete erasure from all timelines."

I froze, the words repeating in my head as if echoing across an endless cavern.

All timelines.

Meaning, there was more than one.

But there wasn't time to think about it, because Hyebin pried the woman's jaw open with a *crack*. Hong Gildong knelt down and forced the yeouiju between Jia's teeth with the heel of his palm. Oh Jia coughed, trying to force it back out, but the yeouiju slid down her throat, its light fading as it disappeared inside her.

Oh Jia gasped for breath, the only sound in the sudden darkness. The other descendants stood up and took a step back.

That's it? I thought. Somehow, I'd always imagined that erasing someone meant killing them and tossing their corpse into some void for the timeline to devour. But Oh Jia was still breathing, even as she lay flat on the carpet, tears spilling unstopped from her eyes.

On Oh Jia's next ragged breath, she opened her mouth as if struggling for air that wouldn't come. Then her jaw yawned wider and wider, lips peeled back to reveal her teeth, and I didn't realize until her jaw hit the carpeted floor that it wasn't *opening*, it was *dissolving*.

Her face crumbled inward like wet sand, sparks of gray ashes flying from her fingertips as the invisible fires of time seared through her flesh. In half a breath, she'd changed from a person to a pile of ashes that the carpet breathed in, and then she was gone forever.

This is what they did to Hana, I thought, my ears ringing. I pictured them holding her down this way, ignoring her as she screamed and cried. Was she a child when it happened? Would they even care? In the reverent darkness, the unofficial moment of silence, I turned my gaze to Hong Gildong.

He gave the order. He remembered my sister, and yet he had dragged me on this mission to watch another descendant's undoing. I closed my eyes and tried to imagine anything except Hana turning into dust, but the thought seared through me, hotter and brighter than Hong Gildong's time magic, than the sun itself. I felt like I'd swallowed an entire star, that it had burst into a supernova in my stomach, ready to devour the world as soon as I opened my mouth. I was standing next to the person who *erased my sister*.

"Let's go," Hyebin said, shoving my shoulder.

I opened my eyes, unclenching my fists one finger at a time. I couldn't react now, because I wasn't supposed to know about Hana. If I ever wanted her back, I had to wait.

When I looked to where the woman had been, even her muddy footprints had vanished, her handbag missing from the corner where Hyebin had tossed it.

I tried to conjure the memory of her face in her last moments but could no longer visualize her at all. I couldn't recall what color her coat had been, or the sound of her voice, or the bright fear that I knew had been in her eyes. I had a hazy recollection of her existence, but it was like her memory had been ripped out from the root, leaving only a hole behind.

Feet stopped in front of me, but I tensed when I realized it wasn't Hyebin as I'd expected.

"Yang Mina," Hong Gildong said. Up close, the gold in his eyes gleamed even brighter, like staring into a gilded kaleidoscope.

"Yes, Sajangnim?" I said stiffly, withering under his gaze.

"This is your first neutralization?" he said, even though he surely knew the answer.

I nodded. "Yes, Sajangnim."

"I realize it's rather . . . disturbing," he said. "Walk with me for a moment?"

"Sajangnim?" Hyebin said behind him, looking between us in confusion.

"Hyebin, you finish up," Hong Gildong said, passing her the gun in his belt, probably to return to the police station. "I'll bring Mina back when we're finished."

Hyebin's stern gaze drifted to me, as if warning me not to say something I'd regret, then she bowed and hurried away.

I stood alone with Hong Gildong, my stomach clenched like I was staring down the edge of an abyss. If I could make him respect me, then he would trust me the way he trusted Hyebin, and one day I would have my truth.

Hong Gildong waved for me to follow him into the night. Unlike Hyebin, he didn't seem concerned about lingering too long in any one particular time period. No one even seemed to notice him, despite his hair the color of starlight. The crowd parted easily around him as he walked unhurriedly down the street. Even the smoke from passing food sellers seemed to blow away from him, the whole world a sea parting to let him pass.

He drew to a stop on a bridge overlooking the Bulgwang stream, the same place I'd paused to look at the sky, thinking about Hana.

"I don't like to do these sorts of missions," he said at last, resting his hands on the railing. He wore an array of rings in various shades of silver and gold, his fingers glistening like claws under the moonlight. Descendants with stronger dragon blood couldn't resist the temptation to hoard riches. "It seems unfair in some ways, doesn't it?" he said. "Everyone makes mistakes."

Surely this was a trick question. I bowed my head slightly while thinking over my answer. "No," I said quietly. "I trust your decisions, Sajangnim."

He threw his head back and laughed, the sound star-bright as it echoed across the water. "It wasn't a test, Mina. I was only making conversation. It's a flawed process, I know that."

He turned toward me, the gold in his eyes flaring bright. "To err is human, and in many ways, descendants are closer to humans now than the dragons we came from. But what many of us have forgotten is that we're not, and will never be, human."

I swallowed and nodded. Hong Gildong certainly didn't seem human, but I didn't see how *I* could be anything else.

"Humans are allowed to make mistakes," he went on. "It's necessary for their growth. But descendants cannot make mistakes."

He looked to me as if expecting a response, so I nodded in agreement. "Mistakes are dangerous in this line of work," I said, something Hyebin had said to me many times.

"Exactly," Hong Gildong said. "This is what it means to be a descendant. We were not put on this earth to be heroes. If we do our job correctly, no one will ever thank us, and some will even hate us. But we are stronger than humans, so we bear the shame in our hearts so that they don't have to. Does that make sense?"

"Yes, Sajangnim," I said automatically, even though none of it did. All I could think about was Hana on the ground, her tortoiseshell box forced between her teeth. He was right about one thing—we were no heroes. Even in this moment, we were existing unnecessarily outside of our origin timeline. Surely Hong Gildong planned to smooth over any ripple effects later on. He could adjust the timeline as he wanted to, yet he claimed the timeline was his god, that he was helpless to do anything but what others had already determined.

But I'd given the right answer, so he nodded in approval and turned back to the sky. "Do you know why I wanted to come here?" he said.

I shook my head.

"It's a clear night," he said, pointing overhead, "a good view of Horologium."

"I'm . . . sorry?" I said, squinting into the darkness.

He gestured for me to step to the left, then pointed once more. "It's my favorite constellation," he said. "It looks like a clock and a pendulum. Do you see it?"

I followed the direction of his finger, frowning at where he pointed. I could just barely make out the crooked shape of a swinging pendulum, etched into the sky by six dim stars.

"As long as they're stationary, pendulum clocks are the most precise timekeepers in the world," he said. "Descendants cannot afford to overlook a single moment. That is what this constellation reminds me."

"That's . . . poetic," I said politely. But I must not have sounded very enthused, because Hong Gildong laughed.

"By the way, Mina, I've begun planning next year's roster. We are, as you know, a bit short-staffed. I would love to have you continue to work with Hyebin, but I feel compelled to remind you that you have a quota to hit."

My face burned. "Yes, Sajangnim," I said stiffly. "I won't disappoint you."

"I should hope not," he said, smiling knowingly before turning back toward headquarters. His grin lasted only a moment, but I swore that his teeth caught the glare of moonlight, illuminating the sharp points of his fangs.

Chapter Six

"I hate weddings," Hyebin said, as if that wasn't patently obvious from the way she was storming across the reception hall and tugging up her green velvet dress, which she wore with the enthusiasm of a snake clinging to its own dead skin. Unfortunately, her normal sweatpants wouldn't cut it for a wedding of this caliber.

Apparently, one of the wedding guests was a future K-drama actor, but I wasn't allowed to know his name. Celebrity-adjacent missions were highly classified ever since a descendant had tried to twist the timeline so that she could marry Min Yoongi from BTS. All I knew was that thanks to a butterfly effect from a rogue agent, the actor was going to get food poisoning here and miss an audition, ruining his acting career. He was supposed to be the first Korean actor to win an Emmy, so it was paramount that we corrected the mistake.

Hyebin stormed up the stairs rather than wait for the elevator, jammed two envelopes of gift money at the bride's attendants in exchange for banquet tickets, then all but ran down to the banquet hall while I tried not to trip in my heels.

"Who wants to spend this much money just to be a slave to their in-laws?" Hyebin said under her breath.

"People in love, maybe?" I said.

Hyebin's eye twitched, but she didn't turn to glare at me like usual, hurrying down the stairs.

She hadn't looked me in the eye since yesterday's neutralization mission.

I couldn't tell if she was just busier than usual, or if she felt strange about me seeing her help turn another descendant to dust. She didn't seem the type to care what other people thought, but then again, I knew very little about her other than her work.

If it meant keeping my cover until I could find Hana, would I have held someone down while Hong Gildong jammed a yeouiju down their throat?

I didn't know the answer, which was why I couldn't judge Hyebin for it.

Still, all night I'd dreamed of Hong Gildong holding down a faceless girl in a striped sweater with a silver watch on her wrist, coppery hair splayed out around her on the gray carpet.

Mina! she'd cried, reaching out for me just before Hong Gildong jammed a box of time magic between her teeth.

I'd woken up before Hana turned to ashes, then emptied my backpack on the floor in a panic and clutched Hana's note to my chest.

Hong Gildong had tried to scorch all of Hana Yang from the timeline, but somehow, against all odds, some small part of her had survived and was trying to protect me. Her note was proof that she wasn't completely gone.

Hyebin yanked me by the wrist right before I could collide with a wedding guest. *Minus one point for unauthorized physical interference with a scene*, I thought grimly.

"Are you awake?" Hyebin said under her breath, her grip painfully tight around my wrist. "You're usually better than this."

"Yes, sorry," I said quickly, focusing on the way my high heels pinched my toes and my strapless bra dug into my rib cage—anything to ground me in the moment.

"Don't be sorry," Hyebin said, releasing my wrist. "Be better."

We hurried to the crowded banquet hall, a vast redbrick basement decorated with fake ivy and fairy lights. Some guests swarmed around buffet tables under a glittery arch on the left, and others sat at round tables with fake floral centerpieces. Guests from three different weddings ate together while the brides and grooms in hanbok walked around to greet them.

Senior agents had run a few scenarios to determine the strategy with the fewest ripple effects, and had ultimately decided that I needed to set off the fire alarm and evacuate the hall. But the pull-down alarms were all on security cameras, and descendants weren't supposed to appear in photos or videos while on missions, so I needed to set one off the old-fashioned way.

"If we have to be here, I'm at least getting some cake out of it," Hyebin said, eyeing the dessert table. "You got this, Yang?"

"Got it," I said, already mentally calculating my score after finishing this mission. Hyebin's gaze lingered on me for a moment as if she didn't believe me, but apparently the siren call of cake was too loud to ignore, because she turned and disappeared into the crowd.

I wove my way to the back of the hall, scanning the ceiling until I spotted the smoke detector overhead. Just as the case file described, I found a neat stack of gold paper napkins beside the silverware. The napkins would go up in a quick burst of flames directly under the fire alarm, forcing everyone outside with minimal fire damage.

I readied the lighter in my pocket, eyeing the emergency exit just a few feet behind the table, where I was supposed to take my leave as soon as I finished. I flicked the wheel of the lighter and a flame bloomed in my hand.

"Mina!"

I froze. Even in the crowded room, the word sounded bright and clear. It wasn't Hyebin's voice, and she was the only person who would have called for me here.

Mina! the girl in my dream had said, struggling against Hong Gildong. I didn't know what Hana's voice sounded like, but that only meant she could be anyone at all.

"Mina!" a voice said again. But this time it wasn't the faceless girl in my dreams—the sound was coming from behind me. I turned, squinting through the sunbeams cast down from the skylight. Someone was approaching, her face blurred by the light. It was just like in Yejun's photograph of me in the board game café— the other girl in the photo was looking over her shoulder, turning to face the camera, the sun from the high windows blaring across her face, and as she turned all the way around I could finally see—

"Mina, you can't run in here!" said a woman, bursting through the crowd and scooping a young girl off the floor. "Stay with Eomma!"

Clouds rolled across the skylight, extinguishing the glaring sun. The woman walked away, her own Mina in her arms. I tried to imagine Hana again, but now I could only see a pile of ash.

Someone bumped into me.

I stumbled into the table and fell over the napkin pile, the lighter still clutched in my hand. With a sudden *whoosh* of light and heat, the tablecloth caught fire.

The decorative ivy must have been highly flammable, because the flames raced across the table in bright sparks, like a dragon's tail flashing through the decorative arrangement of seeded bread rolls. A woman in hanbok was trying to serve herself some cake, but the long dangling goreum of her top draped over the flowers and caught fire, devouring the front of her jeogori. She screamed, dropping the plate and reeling back into a guest, who dropped a bowl of kimchi jjigae to the floor.

It occurred to me then, as I watched a bride go up in flames and fall over shattered dishes, that Hyebin was going to kill me.

I spun around, looking for some sort of liquid to douse the bride with, but someone else got there first.

Hyebin shoved her way through the crowd and overturned a punch bowl on top of the bride. As the woman sputtered and the flames fizzled out, Hyebin cast the bowl to the side with a clatter, then turned to me, her eyes blazing gold, the tablecloth still alight behind her.

Oh no.

Hyebin seized my wrist and yanked me out the emergency exit, into the street. Time magic surged through my arm as we walked, window displays in each shop shifting, the street signs morphing, the crowd patterns speeding up as people flickered in and out of existence.

She carried us back to the present in broad daylight? I thought. The only reason Hyebin would do that was if the whole mission was a wash, if she knew it would all have to be redone anyway.

She stormed into a side street and finally released me, standing at the mouth of the alley with her hands on her hips. She hadn't pushed me, but the sudden loss of tension sent me off-balance, and I fell hands-first into a puddle. I tried to get up, but Hyebin's furious gaze pinned me down.

"*What the hell was that?*" she said. Her eyes had turned blistering gold, forcing me to lower my gaze in submission. Blood trickled from between her fingers, and I realized her claws had descended, cutting into her palms.

"I'm sorry, Sunbaenim," I said, folding into a bow.

"*Sorry?*" Hyebin said, letting out an incredulous laugh. "You think that fixes anything? I have to wipe this mission from the timeline and do it all over again. Do you have any idea how busy I am?"

"I'm sorry," I said again, wishing I could drown myself in the murky puddle. "I'll fix it," I said. "Just let me—"

"No."

I looked up slowly at Hyebin. "No?"

"You're done for today," she said. "This is pointless if you're not focused. The stakes are too high for you to mess up."

"I tried my—"

"*Don't say that*," Hyebin said, raising a hand to silence me. Four puncture wounds on her palm glistened with blood where her claws had sliced into her skin. "Whatever you do, do not tell me *that* was you trying your best. Because if it was, I need to tell HQ that you're wasting my time."

I curled in on myself, feeling impossibly small at her feet.

"This wasn't even a difficult mission," Hyebin went on. "How could I send you farther into the past if you can't even do this? You're unfocused. Clumsy. You don't listen. You're so . . ."

"Human?" I finished quietly.

Hyebin closed her mouth, but the look in her eyes told me I was right.

Humans are allowed to make mistakes, Hong Gildong had said. But descendants weren't.

Even a single drop of dragon blood was supposed to make you skilled, graceful, beautiful, brilliant beyond measure. But somehow, I was none of those things.

I could blame it on how often I'd moved countries, or my teachers, or my human father, or Hyebin, or Yejun, or even Jihoon . . . but I was the common denominator in every equation. I thought of the bracelet Jihoon had given me, now lost in the mud at the bottom of a stream. People trusted me with beautiful things, and I destroyed them.

"I want to try again," I said quietly. When Hyebin didn't respond, I looked up. "*I want to try again*," I repeated, my eyes damp. "Let me start over. I'll be better, I—"

"Go home, Mina," Hyebin said. Her eyes were no longer angry, but somehow that was even worse. As if she'd finally realized I wasn't worth her time.

I hung my head so I wouldn't have to see her walk away. When the sound of her footsteps had faded, I folded forward into the puddle and let my tears fall.

I could almost feel Hana then—her hand on my back, stroking my hair, wiping my tears with her sweater sleeve. It was too faint to be a memory, more like the soft hands of a dream, as real yet intangible as moonlight on my cheek. *Mina*, she whispered. And maybe it was nothing more than a wish, or maybe it was one of the torn shreds of another timeline fluttering past me in the wind. Of this I was certain: Hana had loved me in a way that Hong Gildong could never erase.

When you're ready, come find me, she'd written. *I will keep you safe.*

I thought of her silhouette in Yejun's photograph from Timeline Alpha, and how the version of me that sat across from her had looked so calm and bright. Maybe, in that life, with Hana by my side, I'd been someone better. Smart, skilled, strong.

I rose to my feet, and the ghostly hands fell away. I was shivering and damp and alone.

"I'm ready," I whispered.

About a block from headquarters, I realized that someone was following me.

I'd just dropped off my clothes and grabbed my school bag, then hurried outside so I wouldn't risk running into Hyebin again. I'd planned to go home and study calculus until I crushed the shame of failing Hyebin under indefinite integrals, but it seemed that the universe had other plans for me.

Hyebin said descendants had predator senses, and while I doubted I could so much as scare a pigeon if my life depended on it, I still had an innate ability to sense when someone was watching or following me. Of course, one of the only dragon senses I'd inherited was paranoia.

I took a sudden left turn, and sure enough, the figure followed me. I could hear their fluttering heartbeat as I took off faster, speed-walking into the Eungam subway station. I rushed down the stairs and fumbled for my T-money card as I hurried through the turnstiles, just barely sliding through the train doors before they closed.

I watched the station flash away in the windows as the train glided smoothly into the dark tunnel. At last, there was silence.

Still, I couldn't bring myself to move, clinging with sweaty hands to the metal pole. I thought of the neutralization mission, how maybe today was the day that sealed my fate as a failed descendant and now Hyebin and Hong Gildong were after me. I felt dizzy, so I pressed my forehead to the cool metal pole to ground myself.

When the doors opened up at Hapjeong Station, I hurried across the platform before I could get stuck behind any ajummas and vaulted up the stairs two at a time. I slipped through the closing doors of another train and dropped into the closest seat. If anyone was following me, I'd definitely lost them now. My heartbeat hammered in my chest as I imagined the feeling of my tortoiseshell box crunching between my teeth, scratching down my throat, my whole body turning to dust.

Then, as the train took off again, I heard it.

A heartbeat.

At the other end of the train, the shadow had found me.

I straightened up, suddenly wide awake with adrenaline. When the doors opened at Hongik University, I raced out of the car, past the subway bakery, past the vendors selling shoes, past the racks of discounted clothing that I nearly toppled as I tried to escape.

Mina, a voice whispered.

I froze, tripping the people behind me in the crowd.

If the descendants wanted me dead, they wouldn't have given me time to run. I thought of the photograph in my backpack, the girl just about to turn around in the sunlight.

Maybe I wouldn't have to find Hana. Maybe she would find me first.

A hand closed around my wrist.

I screamed, right in someone's ear, and a man screamed back in mine. We fell against the tiled walls as I wrenched my arm away, reaching for my tortoiseshell box.

The stranger straightened up, his blond hair glowing white under the station lights.

"*Kim Yejun?*" I said, shoving my box back in my pocket. "You were following me?"

"Sorry, what? I think you just blew out my eardrums," he said, jamming a pinky in his ear.

I let out a sharp laugh, shaking my head. Though I'd wanted to personally feed him to Hyebin piece by piece yesterday, I'd take an annoying guy like him over a team of descendants trying to kill me any day.

I sighed and glanced at the exit. "I'm hungry," I said, turning without another word and heading up the stairs

"Was that an invitation?" Yejun called after me, following even though I didn't answer.

I squinted in the sunlight as I emerged from the station, turning away from the main road. Unlike the wide streets of Eunpyeong, Hongdae was an area for tourists, so all the stores and restaurants were crammed close together and stacked on top of each other. Colorful signs jutted out from every floor, advertising bakeries, BBQ restaurants, noraebangs, and themed cafés. Clothes racks spilled onto the streets under thin tents, right next to vendors selling hotteok and spiral potatoes on sticks. Hardly anyone drove through such a dense area, so the streets were filled with people instead of cars. Big cities often felt soulless, but here, under the kaleidoscope of neon lights and the scent of crispy chicken and pork belly, Hongdae had a beating heart.

I strode toward the center, winding my way through the crowd until I stopped in front of a restaurant with star-shaped paper lanterns in the windows.

"Are you coming?" I said, glancing over my shoulder.

Yejun took a hesitant step closer. "Is that okay?" he said.

It wasn't, not really. But something about sitting in my cramped apartment all by myself when I was supposed to be working felt immensely pathetic.

"You're paying," I said, shoving the door open.

A waiter led me and Yejun around a narrow corner to a small room with cool, pulsing lights. There was no room for anything but booth seats on either side of the table, a window overlooking the street, and a button to summon the waiter. Seoul had lots of restaurants like these, which were ideal for discussing things you didn't want just anyone to overhear.

Yejun slid into the booth across from me and set his bag down. "Mina," he said, "I—"

"I want yangnyeom chicken," I said, pointing to the menu. "And cheese tteokbokki."

He nodded quickly and scanned the menu before calling the waiter back. I sat in silence, staring at the table while he ordered. Yejun must have read my mood, because he wisely allowed me to stew without saying a word. I didn't talk until the soju came, then poured us both a shot and shoved his glass at him.

"Jjan," I said as I raised my glass, staring him dead in the eye. He winced at the eye contact.

"I'm nineteen, you know," he said after taking his shot.

"Congratulations."

"I'm older than you," he pressed.

"That's why you're paying."

"You're not supposed to look at me when you drink."

"I'm not supposed to be talking to you at all," I said.

He smirked. "Fair enough. So what changed your mind?"

My eye twitched at the memory of the bride going up in flames. "*I'm* asking the questions right now."

"Okay," he said with a shrug. His eyes were so big and earnest. I glared down at the menu again rather than look at him.

"Where did you get that picture of me in the board game café?" I said, tugging at my sleeves.

"The restaurant," he said as the waiter returned with tteokbokki. He smiled politely and served me before serving himself.

"What restaurant?" I said after the waiter shut the door.

"*The* restaurant," he said, picking up a piece of tteokbokki and admiring the long pull of mozzarella before plopping it on his plate. "The one that sits outside of time. Anything inside it isn't impacted by timeline changes. Any pictures on your phone would be deleted once it reconnected outside the restaurant, but paper photographs stay the same. All those pictures were in the shoe rack."

I grimaced, pouring myself another shot. That meant I'd been unknowingly carrying around paradox paraphernalia, which was definitely a crime.

"But why was there a picture of *me*?" I said.

Yejun frowned. "I don't know," he said, twirling the cheese around one of his chopsticks. "I know that's a bad answer—"

"It's not an answer at all."

"—but I don't have a better one for you. The timeline wipes my memory just like everyone else's."

How convenient, I thought, putting more tteokbokki on my plate so Yejun couldn't take the part with all the cheese. Did he honestly think I would agree to his plan when he wouldn't explain a thing? I didn't know what I'd expected him to say, but it looked like all I was going to get out of this night was some free food.

Yejun set his chopsticks down and rolled up his sleeves, so I seized the chance to grab the best-looking pieces of chicken and plop them on my plate. As he pulled back his left sleeve, three lines of text appeared on the inside of his forearm in dark ink—a tattoo.

I frowned and tried to read it upside down, but he caught my gaze and turned his arm to face me.

> My dearest Yejun,
> I love you always
> In every timeline

I set down my chopsticks, drawing back against the booth. *In every timeline.* "What does that mean?" I said.

"It was written on a napkin that I found in my shoe at the restaurant," Yejun said, picking up another bite of food. "I was afraid I'd lose it or forget it, so I wanted to make it permanent."

"But why?" I said. "Who is it from?"

Yejun hesitated before taking another bite. His gaze dropped, the tteokbokki sagging in his chopsticks. "I think it's from my mom."

"What do you mean you *think*?" I said, stabbing a piece of tteokbokki. Every time we spoke, Yejun only left me with more questions.

He pressed his lips together, gaze darting around the various dishes at the table like he couldn't decide where to look. After a moment, he crossed his arms, hiding the tattoo. "The thing is," he said quietly, "I have no memory of ever having a mom."

My hand froze, tteokbokki falling from my chopsticks to my plate with a wet splash. "What?" I whispered.

"I know it sounds crazy," he said. "Everyone has a mom, right? Sometimes they die, or leave you, but they never just . . . don't exist. And yet it was always just me and my dad, and I don't understand why I never asked, why he never told me anything about her before he died."

I felt a strange ringing in my ears, a crystal vibration that hummed through my whole body, like I was suddenly hollow. Surely Yejun wasn't saying—

"There's just this hole in my life," he said, staring at the steaming food on his plate. "Even when there's no reason to feel upset, it's like I just know something is wrong. Something is missing. It's like I had all this love for someone and—"

"And now there's nowhere for it to go," I said, setting my chopsticks down, no longer hungry.

The steam from the food spiraled between us, the room vibrating with music, a pulsing heartbeat through the floor below.

Yejun cleared his throat. "Do you—"

"My sister," I said quietly. "I think she's . . . like your mom."

Yejun's gaze softened. "I'm sorry, Mina."

I stared at my slowly cooling plate of food rather than acknowledge his words. I didn't want him looking at me like I was some wounded animal. I didn't want him looking at me at all. Unless . . .

"Do you think," I said, "hypothetically, that my sister still exists on Timeline Alpha?"

Yejun stared at me without blinking for a long moment, as if searching for something in my eyes. "Hypothetically, yes," he said. "Bringing back Timeline Alpha requires eliminating the person who split the timelines in the first place, the person responsible for erasing other descendants."

"Hong Gildong," we said at the same time. I laughed at how earnestly we'd both said such an obviously fake name.

"He has to die for this to work?" I said.

Yejun nodded slowly, edging away like he was afraid of my response.

I thought of the way Hong Gildong had stood over the woman we'd neutralized—I'd wanted to at least hold on to her name, to keep her alive in that small way, but that memory was gone.

But even if I couldn't remember her face, I could remember *his*. The bright flash of gold in his eyes as he'd looked down on her. The twinkling amusement in the corners of his mouth when I spoke, like I was someone to laugh at, someone who could never hurt him. He knew exactly who I was, exactly what he'd taken from me.

"I need help learning calculus," I said at last. "If I fail, then I'll lose all my infiltration missions and get kicked out for not meeting my quotas."

Yejun smirked. "You want my hypothetical help?"

I placed my hands in my lap, looking him dead in the eye. "No."

The smile fell off his face. "No?" he said tentatively.

"Not hypothetically," I said, my voice wavering.

The words I was about to say could spell out my death. No, worse than death—my erasure from all timelines.

But I would do it for Hana. For the person I could have been in another world. For the truth.

"Help me pass calculus, and I'll help you fix the timeline," I said. "I want to put things back the way they're supposed to be."

Yejun stared at me blankly for a moment, then a grin spread across his face. He lifted his Sprite—too eagerly, spilling half of it on the table. "Here's to the way things are supposed to be."

I raised my soju glass against his can, and this time I turned away as I drank.

From the window, I looked down on the busy street below and imagined all the people transforming into their real selves, the signs on all the shops changing colors, the sky clearing up, the flowers blooming. The world would shed this dead skin, and below it, I would have my answer.

Chapter Seven

On the first day of my life as a traitor, I leaned over the railing of a bridge and stretched my honey-coated fingers toward the sun. The Han River rushed below, a fleet of orange kayaks bobbing by while bikes flashed past on either side of the water.

Almost there, I thought.

A single ladybug darted around me, scarlet against the white sky. I leaned even farther over the railing. What good was being tall if I couldn't even do this much? I stood up on my toes, my weight tipping forward.

The ladybug hovered around my palm for a moment, then landed on my ring finger.

I tipped forward, my stomach dropping as the balance shifted, and suddenly my feet were off the ground and the river was opening its jaws.

Hyebin yanked me back by the belt and jammed a plastic bag over my hand, tugging it tight with a drawstring.

"Got you, asshole," Hyebin said. "The ladybug, not you."

"I know," I said, though I never really knew with Hyebin.

It had been one day since the flaming bride incident, and I'd shown up early for work with extra Choco Pies and chips to placate Hyebin. I'd had two extra coffees that morning so my focus would be laser sharp, but my blood was buzzing from the caffeine and I desperately had to pee. Worst of all, my bones screamed that Hyebin must have known about my deal with Yejun, that she was just waiting for the right moment to kill me in the most satisfying way.

At least she hadn't said a word about the wedding incident. Maybe she was truly too busy to hold grudges, or maybe my extra bags of honey butter chips had really earned my forgiveness. Still, though she didn't seem outwardly upset, she'd pointedly avoided eye contact all morning.

She grabbed my wrist and examined the ladybug through the plastic, then pinched it to death inside the bag.

"Let's go," she said, turning around as if she hadn't left me with a sack of sticky bug guts on my hand.

The briefing for this mission had been particularly short on details—it was a cleanup for an error another descendant had made, a quick three years into the past. I'd only done one cleanup before, where a descendant had blown his nose on a mission and tried to throw the tissue away but missed the trash can. A seagull ate the tissue and choked to death in the middle of the bike path, then a human moved its corpse to the side and got *E. coli*, causing a massive outbreak. But I didn't know the crimes of this particular ladybug.

Hyebin and I hid in a public bathroom stall, where her time magic carried us back to the present. I'd tried to wash up, but she said we would miss the bus, so I ended up crammed into a crowded bus with a honey hand that was quickly hardening inside the bag.

"Are bugs really worth your time?" I said, grimacing at the bug guts under my fingernail. "Isn't this below your pay grade?"

"You'd be amazed how integral most bugs are to the ecosystem," Hyebin said, the city flashing past as the bus rattled down the road. All the seats were taken, so we were clinging to the same metal pole by the back door. "This particular species was supposed to go extinct six years ago, but one hitched a ride on an agent's ear. We've been chasing it down for years."

"Was it really that hard to find?" I said. The descendants regularly tracked down *people* without issue. How could an insect be that stealthy?

"Normally, no," Hyebin said, "but this one disappeared during daylight savings."

I blinked. "But there's no daylight savings in South Korea?" I said, suddenly unsure.

"Yes, not *anymore*," Hyebin said. "It was tested in 1988 for the Olympics. So there's no 2:00 A.M. through 2:59 A.M. in the spring, and there's duplicate times for 1:00 A.M. through 1:59 A.M. in the fall that year. It complicates things."

I frowned, suddenly grateful I wasn't training to become a timeline architect—my brain hurt just imagining how to fix that kind of problem. "And the timeline refresh didn't just . . . squash it?"

"Well, no, because it wasn't on the timeline," Hyebin said, like it should have been obvious. "It went from not being on the timeline at all to landing at three A.M. on May 8. It was kind of like being born on that day—1988 became its new origin timeline."

"So, it survived the refresh because it was hiding in a time that didn't exist?" I said.

"Yep," Hyebin said. "Then it got deprioritized until it ate one too many spiders and caused a tsunami. We kind of had to deal with it then."

"Well now I feel like I should be checking more carefully for bugs after missions," I said, running a hand through my hair and imagining half a dozen insects falling out.

"As long as you don't have head lice, you should be fine," Hyebin said, grimacing like it wasn't actually a joke.

The bus turned a sharp corner and I stumbled into Hyebin, who grumbled and went rigid like my touch was radioactive. "Watch it," she mumbled, looking out the bus window rather than at me.

Normally, Hyebin looked at ease in every situation, which was why she made such a good descendant. She was so confident that she could probably barge into any stranger's house and raid their fridge without anyone questioning it.

But now, with her tight grip on the pole as the bus rattled her side to side, she seemed out of place. The way she gazed out the front window felt too calculated, too obvious. Maybe it was an extension of my dragon senses of knowing when I was being followed—maybe I also knew when I was being watched . . . or deliberately *not* watched.

One thing was certain: This wasn't about Yejun.

If she knew about him, she would look angry, not nervous. In fact, she would already have my head on a pike.

"Mina," Hyebin said, her voice low, her gaze fixed on my reflection in the scratched bus window. "I was wondering . . ."

I held my breath as I waited for her next words. Call it a dragon sense, or a hunch, or just overactive anxiety, but I sensed that her next words were of great importance.

She opened her mouth as if to speak, then closed it and looked away.

"This is our stop," she said.

As we stepped off the bus and walked back to headquarters, I realized that I had learned something valuable that day.

I couldn't lie to Jang Hyebin, but Jang Hyebin couldn't lie to me either.

The city unfolded beneath me as I rode the bus up to Namsan Seoul Tower that afternoon. It was a tourist trap, one of the Top Ten Places to See in Seoul. Maybe Yejun hoped the crush of foreign tourists would make a good distraction when we started destroying the timeline in broad daylight.

It was a bad-air day, so the panoramic view from the top of the hill hid behind a silk veil, and I doubted the view from the observation deck was much better. People came here to take scenic pictures of the whole city from behind fingerprinted glass, but they were going to be disappointed if they came today.

I stepped off the bus and lingered outside the main entrance, staying far away from the neon love staircase and the locks that annoying couples clipped to all the railings to promise their eternal devotion—I was pretty sure that maintenance had to come around with clippers every month and prune the gate just so no one got tetanus from all the rust.

Yejun hadn't told me how to find him once I arrived, and I felt too awkward waiting by the door, so I ducked into the OLED tunnel by the main entrance. There were panels like this all over the tower—screens so crisp that they looked more like windows to another universe. This one played a video of outer space rushing over my head, like I was in a rocket spiraling upward into oblivion.

The sharp brightness of the digital stars made my eyes hurt, yet another headache stabbing into my skull. I'd had a headache all morning and Advil hadn't even touched it, supporting my theory that it was timesickness. But I didn't know how to fix it when I couldn't figure out where I'd left a loop open.

In the panels overhead, the spinning stars grew dim. The camera panned to the fiery red surface of the sun, scarlet flames lashing their tongues at the darkness, gold simmering beneath the surface. Something about its brightness ignited a warmth inside my rib cage, relaxing my muscles, forcing my jaw to unclench.

Dragons were creatures of water, not fire, but we were also drawn to gold. It was a symbol of power in both Korea and Japan. Every year, there was a golden dragon dance in Tokyo that was meant to celebrate the return of golden dragons to heaven.

Descendants were only echoes of dragons. But sometimes—like now—I could sense the sizzling embers of who I used to be, the fire waiting for oxygen to breathe it back to life. I looked at my hands, imagining my nails sharpening into claws.

A shadow spilled across my feet as someone blocked the light behind me. I turned around.

Yejun stood at the mouth of the tunnel, a Paris Baguette bag in one hand and a backpack slung over his shoulder. With stars flashing by in the OLED panels all around him, he looked like a falling star tearing through the night sky.

"Yes, I got your cheesecake," he said, grinning and waving for me to follow him.

"I didn't say you had to get me cheesecake every time we met," I said as I emerged from the tunnel, snatching the bag from him anyway and peering inside at the slice of cheesecake with a little plastic lid over the top—strawberry, just like I'd had at the café. I hated that he'd remembered. He probably felt so smug about it, probably expected me to be impressed.

Yejun shrugged and turned left, away from the lobby entrance. "It seemed like an investment in my safety. I don't know how you eat something so heavy, though. Have you ever tried banana milk mixed with melon milk and a ginseng candy chaser? That's the best dessert."

"That sounds disgusting," I said.

"Excuse you, I don't insult your precious cheesecake," Yejun said. He came to a stop in front of the panda garden—a staircase decorated with round plastic pandas for tourists to take pictures with—and sat down next to a particularly chubby panda, waving for me to sit. I sat a careful distance from him as he unzipped his backpack, pulled out a small plastic tray, and set it on the bench between us.

"Is this a picnic?" I said.

Yejun shook his head, rooting around in his backpack. "I'm showing you the plan," he said. Then he pulled out a bottle of strawberry milk, peeled back the foil, and poured it across the tray.

I flinched as some of it splashed onto my skirt. "Why does your plan involve wasting milk?"

"Milk is less reflective than water, so it's better for scrying," Yejun said, already tracing his signature into the shallow pool. "You don't want to leave a paper trail, do you?"

"I . . . guess not," I said, frowning at the aggressive fake-strawberry scent. I leaned closer as Yejun opened a file and text appeared in the pale pink surface.

1. Popularize candy corn in Korea
2. Rescue the dung beetles
3. Save the MV *Sewol* ferry
4. Final shift 😊

I looked up at Yejun for some indication that he was joking, but he was grinning like he expected a compliment.

"What the hell is this?" I said.

"It's how we're going to save the world!" Yejun said, leaning closer.

"With *candy corn*?" I glanced over my shoulder as the next shuttle bus pulled in, seriously considering just taking the cheesecake and going home.

"The candy corn isn't the point," Yejun said, shoulders drooping as it seemed to dawn on him that I didn't share his excitement. "These are our goals. We're going to strategically undo some events that are key to this timeline's stability. Think of it like . . . this timeline is a big ship with a bunch of anchors cast into the sea. We're going to pull up the heaviest ones."

"And how do you even know what these 'anchors' are?"

He shrugged. "It's how they made Timeline Beta, but in reverse. I might have looked at some . . . sensitive paperwork before I went rogue . . . Which might have been the reason I got chased out in the first place."

"So you're not very sneaky, is what you're telling me?" I said, raising an eyebrow.

"Hey, I'm still alive, aren't I?" he said.

I briefly contemplated throwing myself off the tower. What had I gotten myself into? Surely the way to get my sister back couldn't depend on dung beetles.

But then again, this was pretty consistent with the butterfly principle—never solve a problem at its source. If a ladybug could cause a tsunami, maybe a dung beetle could save my sister.

"And what is 'final shift' supposed to mean?" I said.

The grin slid off Yejun's face. "Once we pull up all the anchors," he said, "we make one last change, and Timeline Alpha just sort of . . . clicks into place."

"And that change would be . . ."

"Hong Gildong started the entire timeline separation process," Yejun said, lowering his voice. "He was the first domino in creating Timeline Beta, which means, for us—"

"He's the last?"

"Best for last!" Yejun said, nodding.

I imagined Hong Gildong on the ground, the look of fear in his eyes as I pried open his mouth and shoved his yeouiju down his throat . . .

I supposed that I could put up with Yejun for a while if that was the payoff.

"Okay," I said. "How do we get candy corn into Korea?"

Yejun patted his bulky backpack. "I came prepared," he said. "But for that, we need to go inside."

He picked up the tray and dumped the strawberry milk into the grass, then shook the tray out and crammed it back into his bag.

I followed him to the main entrance, where he tried to hold the door for me, but I shoved him through first.

"You can buy me cheesecake, but don't hold doors for me," I said. I didn't want us looking like a couple. Maybe people could think I was his disgruntled foreign cousin.

"Seems a bit arbitrary, but okay," he said. "Any other rules I should know about?"

"I'll let you know when you break them."

But he only smiled at this too, like he thought I was joking. I was glad at least one of us found this whole situation amusing, rather than the scariest and possibly worst decision I'd ever made. I contemplated making a run for it with my cheesecake—I hadn't technically broken protocol yet.

We approached the main desk, where he loudly asked the woman for two tickets to the top of the tower. I didn't want him to pay for me, but the only thing I hated more than him in that moment was the idea of causing a scene by arguing with him. He wasn't doing it to be generous—he knew it would annoy me.

I swore that once I found Hana, I would never talk to Yejun again. I despised how he played the world like a concert pianist, how nothing seemed hard for him at all, how none of it really mattered. Dragons were always supposed to look at ease while undercover—something that Yejun had clearly mastered, while Hyebin said I always looked like an ostrich ready to jam its head into the sand.

Yejun returned with two tickets and an infuriatingly smug grin. "It's a good cover," he whispered in my ear. "The elevator, I mean."

"Thanks, I've taken Time Travel 101," I said under my breath, hiding it with a plastic smile as we approached the staff member who took our tickets and gestured for us to pass through.

"What did you have to do to make sure we got the elevator to ourselves?" I said as we waited for it to arrive. "Slash the tires on the shuttle bus?"

Yejun shook his head. "It's an advanced time travel strategy," he said. "I call it . . . 'checking the weather.'" He nodded toward the foggy skyline beyond the windows. "No one wants to pay for a scenic view when the city is covered in smog."

I let out a sharp laugh. "The staff must think we're strange."

"People have thought more offensive things about me," he said, shrugging and bowing slightly to another staff member as the elevator doors opened.

As soon as the doors closed behind us, Yejun pulled his yeouiju out of his pocket and held out his other hand to me.

"The year 2007, March 5, 15:45:11," he said.

I stared at his hand as the elevator went dark, the OLED screen on the ceiling lighting up with an image of outer space. What, exactly, did he want me to do?

When I didn't move, he sighed. "I do wash my hands, you know," he said, rolling up his sleeve, "but you can take my arm if I repulse you that much." But now I could see the tattoo with his mother's note, and that was even worse.

"It's not that," I said, dropping my gaze to the dark floor. Above us, the screens played a video from the perspective of a bird—or a dragon—sailing through clouds, dodging airplanes, flashing through the atmosphere. "I've never . . ."

"Oh," Yejun said, blinking. "You've never used your time magic before?"

I glared at the floor, wishing the darkness of outer space would swallow me whole. He made it sound like he'd thoroughly researched me, so I thought he knew this. But once again, I was less than what everyone expected.

"That's fine," he said, shrugging.

I looked up. He was smiling again like it truly didn't matter.

"My magic will reach out to yours," he said, holding out his hand again. "Do you remember the date?"

"The year 2007, March 5, 15:45:11."

Yejun smiled and nodded, moving his hand closer. "Remember that. You'll know how to do the rest."

The elevator rose higher into the sky, gears whirring, my ears aching from the change in pressure.

Slowly, I set my hand in his.

Time magic rushed through me, nearly knocking me off my feet. It was as if the sun had breathed me into its core, enveloping me in liquid gold. Its warmth washed away the tension in my muscles, soothed away my timesickness headache, sparkled across my skin. Other people's time magic felt like an unmaking, but Yejun's was a symphony of light.

His eyes gleamed blue, and I sensed the bright spark of his smile even before it crossed his face.

Do it now, he said. Or at least, I thought he spoke the words out loud. His mouth didn't move, but the words rang through my blood. *The doors will open soon.*

I had no idea what I was doing, but Yejun seemed so certain I would figure it out. This was supposed to be a natural reflex for all dragon descendants—it should have been easy to access the vast library of time that my ancestors had saved for me.

But as Yejun's magic hummed through me, my own magic stayed trapped in the tortoiseshell box. I was filled up with his light, but my own body was a cage of darkness.

The year 2007, March 5, 15:45:11, I thought, hoping that repeating the time would prompt my magic to come out.

Look, I would love to help you out here, but if I use any more magic, the agency will detect it and come running, Yejun said, an edge of panic beneath his words. The light in his eyes flickered, his grip on my hand growing colder. What would happen to him if all the time magic he released didn't go anywhere? Would he be stuck in between dimensions like at the restaurant? Or would he go halfway to his destination and be unable to come back without using more magic and alerting the agency?

I closed my eyes and gripped his hand tighter, my other hand clutching the tortoiseshell box as if I could wring the time magic out of it. But all I felt was Yejun's bright magic singing through my skin, and none of my own.

I don't know how, I thought, my eyes closed so I wouldn't have to see the look on Yejun's face, the disappointment I knew would be there. He thought I could help him find his mother and save the world, but he'd picked the wrong girl. *I'm sorry, I don't know how.*

My grip loosened around his palm, his magic growing quieter as only my fingertips brushed against his skin.

But then, another voice cut through the dying embers of magic.

Yes, you do.

My eyes snapped open.

I felt it then, as real as Yejun's hand in mine—I had done this before.

Maybe in another timeline, maybe in a moment that no longer existed. But nothing could be erased completely, and everything I had ever done—everyone I had ever been—was still inside me.

I relaxed my shoulders, imagining Hana in front of me, her hand instead of Yejun's closed tight around mine.

You know how to do this, she would say. *You've always known.*

I let out a breath, a white cloud of condensation fogging the air between me and Yejun, washing the world away.

I fell into a frigid ocean, sand scraping my palms, sparks of salt water stinging my eyes. The dark waters rose over my head and filled my mouth, my lungs, my soul.

I was on the back of a turtle racing against the current, years flashing past me in glinting silver scales. I reached my hand out and centuries bled through my fingers. Time was mine, as infinite as the ocean and its cold, devouring expanse.

I was floating in a lightless sea, weightless in a palace of pearls and seashells.

I was a princess of time at the bottom of the ocean.

I was a man on the shore dissolving into dust.

I was the sharp teeth of a dragon god.

I opened my eyes and caught my reflection in the elevator, my irises gleaming violet.

I am a descendant, I thought, as my magic reached out and seized Yejun's. The colors tangled together into royal blue, darkening Yejun's eyes and brightening mine. His heartbeat pulsed through me, bright and fast with excitement.

"The year 2007, March 5, 15:45:11," he said, just as the elevator clicked into place at the top of the tower.

The elevator doors opened, and we stepped out into a wall of light.

Chapter Eight

The gray clouds of the present day had lifted. Sunshine blared through the 360-degree windows at the top of the tower, where schoolchildren and tourists pressed close to the glass and took pictures. Above their heads, white paint traced the silhouette of the mountain range that was usually hidden by fog, but today was carved in gray and green across the horizon.

As I stepped off the elevator into this new world, I was sure the tiles would disappear beneath my feet and drop me into the pale blue sky. Visiting the past with Hyebin had always felt like riding shotgun while she reluctantly chauffeured me around the timeline, but arriving with my own magic was like writing my own story—*I* had conjured the blue sky and glass skyscrapers and shadowed mountains disappearing into the horizon. This world was my creation.

Well . . . mine and Yejun's.

I realized belatedly that I was still holding his hand and took a deliberate step away from him, stuffing both hands in my pockets.

"Not bad," he said, "though you cut it a bit close there. I thought the timeline was gonna chop me in half for a sec."

"Can that actually happen?" I said, imagining the elevator doors opening to a pile of severed limbs.

"Let's not find out," Yejun said, waving for me to start walking.

I followed him outside, half a level down, where people were allowed to gawk at the panoramic views from behind carefully installed fences to make sure no one plummeted all the way down. There were more love locks hitched to the fences on this level, which Yejun walked annoyingly close to before shrugging off his backpack and pulling out a shoebox that looked like it had been stabbed to death with a blunt pair of scissors.

"Would you like to do the honors?" he said, holding the box out to me.

I edged away, crossing my arms. "What's inside?"

"Don't you trust me?" Yejun said with a pout.

"Not at all."

Something rustled inside the box, and I took another step back. "Is there something *alive* in there?"

"I sure hope so," Yejun said, turning away and holding the box over the railing. "Otherwise, this was a waste of time."

Before I could ask what he meant, he took off the lid.

A flurry of butterflies surged from the box and spun into the air, fluttering red and yellow and orange into the blue sky. They swirled around us, their delicate wings tickling across my face. I blinked quickly rather than swat them away—squishing a butterfly to death on my own eye was probably bad luck, not to mention gross.

A yellow butterfly landed on Yejun's nose. He laughed and looked at it cross-eyed for a moment before gently blowing out a puff of air. It fluttered between us before joining the others in the sky. Yejun smiled as he watched them disappear.

He turned to me, then laughed. "Someone likes you," he said.

I froze. "What?"

He reached forward, gently tucking a strand of hair behind my ear. I had half a mind to twist his wrist backward—and probably would have if not for the people around us—but when he pulled back, he had an orange butterfly on his finger.

"This one didn't want to let you go," he said.

"Oh," I said, wanting to smack myself for not saying something halfway intelligent. Yejun always knew what to say, and here I was, fumbling through a simple conversation.

"Maybe your hair smells like nectar," he said, turning to the railing and holding his hand out until the butterfly took off, chasing after the others. He waved as they dispersed. "Thanks for your hard work!" he said. Then he turned to me. "See? That wasn't so scary, was it?"

I tucked my hair back, oddly conscious of how it smelled. "How will this change the timeline?" I said, rather than answer.

He squinted in the sunlight, stepping closer to me to avoid its rays. "What fun would it be if I told you that?" he said.

"*Fun?*" I said. "Is this supposed to be fun?" Betraying the descendants and plotting the downfall of Hong Gildong wasn't exactly my favorite pastime.

He shrugged. "As descendants, there are so few surprises left for us," he said. "Isn't it nice to leave a little bit of mystery? Something to wonder about?"

I let out a sharp laugh, then realized he was serious. "I can wonder about what's for lunch today, not whether or not the world is going to end."

"How boring," he said, picking up his Swiss-cheesed shoebox under one arm. "If you really must know, these thirty-four butterflies will pollinate a slightly higher number of golden asters on Jeju Island, where a Swedish billionaire will vacation in five months. His daughter will pick one of the flowers and tell her dad that yellow is her new favorite color, so he'll start to buy her everything yellow that he can find. He'll buy more shares in a candy company and get his daughter a private tour of the factory where they make butterscotch, and his investment will allow the company to distribute in Korea—at his suggestion—with a social media campaign that emphasizes the honey in candy corn, with lots of pictures of bees and flowers and, of course, golden asters."

"Wow," I said, blinking at the last of the butterflies on the horizon. "That's . . ."

"Impressive, I know," Yejun said, smirking. "I was training to be a timeline architect, so I'm good at scripting scenarios."

It *was* impressive, but I wasn't about to tell that to Kim Yejun. "Did you get caught because you bragged too much about breaking the rules?"

Yejun scowled. "I got caught because I left a paper trail. Hence the milk."

"I think milk can only do so much to protect us," I said. "Now, are you going to help me with calculus, or are we gonna stand here until the timeline wipes us?"

"Right," Yejun said, rolling his eyes. "Heaven forbid you help save the world out of the goodness of your heart. How could I forget the importance of calculus?"

Heat rushed up to my face, but Yejun had already turned away, waving for me to follow him like I was a dog. I stormed ahead, elbowing him out of my way just so he would have to walk behind me instead. When we took the elevator back down, if he noticed that my grip on his hand was tight enough to crush bones, he didn't say a word.

Back on the lower level of Namsan Seoul Tower in the present day, Yejun slurped his bubble tea while shaking his head at my poor attempt at calculus. "That's wrong," he said through a sticky mouthful of boba.

My grip tightened on my pencil. I consciously relaxed every muscle in my hand—I was snapping too many pencils these days. "Why?" I said as patiently as I could manage.

"Because that answer defies the laws of physics," Yejun said.

It had been forty-five minutes, and we'd only gotten halfway through the first page of my homework. I was starting to think that all this had been a mistake. I'd betrayed the descendants in exchange for an hour-long torture session.

Yejun sighed and set his bubble tea down, then plucked my pencil from my hand and scooted his chair closer to mine. I instinctively pulled my chair away, but he raised an eyebrow and shot me an unimpressed look. "You can read the worksheet from all the way over there?"

"Dragons have excellent vision."

He rolled his eyes, then hooked his ankle around the leg of my chair and yanked me closer. "Get over it, I don't smell that bad," he said. He crossed out my indecipherable attempt and started to underline parts of the question. "'If a ball is thrown into the air, when will it reach its highest point?'" he read. "Okay, so to figure this out, you need to know the velocity at the highest point. Do you know what that is?"

I glared at the worksheet, wishing the answer would suddenly come to me or I'd get struck by a bolt of lightning, either one was fine. I could tell by the way he asked that I was supposed to know the answer.

This was a terrible idea, I thought. *I've just given Kim Yejun an excuse to laugh at me.*

I stayed perfectly still, hoping Yejun would just tell me the answer. But instead, he pushed his chair back and started to untie his shoelaces.

"What are you doing?" I said, leaning away.

"Demonstrating," he said, kicking off his shoe and removing one of his socks.

"What does your foot have to do with anything?"

He balled up his sock, then tossed it experimentally from hand to hand. "I didn't bring a ball, so this will have to work." Then he threw his sock straight up in the air, nearly hitting one of the overhead lights.

"Stop that!" I said, grabbing his arm. "No one wants to get hit in the face with your sweaty sock!"

"What's the velocity at the highest point?" he said, ignoring me. "You said dragons have excellent vision, so watch."

He tossed the sock up again. The lady working at the bubble tea counter was staring at us, whispering nervously to her coworker, and I wanted to melt into the floor.

"I don't have robot eyes that measure velocity," I said, tugging at his sleeve.

"You don't need them," he said, pulling away. "Just *watch*, Mina." Then he threw the sock into the air again.

This time, my gaze focused on the sock as it arced higher and higher. The bubble tea shop, the beams in the ceiling, the crowds moving past us—everything disappeared except for Yejun's sock. It moved up and up and up, then slowed down until it was suspended for one single moment, motionless in the air.

Then the sock fell back down. Yejun caught it with one hand, and the sounds of the food court filtered back in.

"It's zero," I said quietly, looking at my feet.

"Great," Yejun said, putting his sock on. "So substitute that back into the equation."

I picked up my pencil, but my fingers felt numb. "That was stupid," I mumbled under my breath.

"Rude," Yejun said, yanking his shoelaces tighter. "I was trying to help you."

"No, not you," I said. "Of course it's zero. I was overthinking it."

"Oh," Yejun said, sitting back. It was the first time since I'd met him that he didn't seem to have his next response spring-loaded. He took a long, noisy slurp of bubble tea.

"Calculus isn't that important anyway," he said. "In fact, it's really boring." He inhaled the last of his boba from his cup and set the cup down. "I need to refuel."

I pushed my sealed bubble tea toward him. "Take mine."

"Do you not like bubble tea, or are you just mad that I bought it?" he said, pulling the cup toward himself anyway.

"I'm already eating cheesecake," I said, nodding to the half-eaten slice. "Too much dairy." I'd inherited a few useful Asian genes from my mother, like the not-sweating-very-much gene and the mostly-straight-hair gene, but also a few unfortunate ones like the violent-diarrhea-when-consuming-too-much-dairy gene. I'd taken Lactaid this morning, but I wasn't about to push my luck in front of Kim Yejun, of all people.

"Oh," he said, drinking my tea. "Do you want a dairy-free one?"

I shook my head. "I want to finish this worksheet." *And I don't want you to keep buying me things*, I thought.

"Are you sure?" Yejun said.

"I'm sure."

"Do you want anything else to drink?"

"No."

"To eat?"

"No."

"Is dating Kim Jihoon your infiltration mission?"

I dropped my pencil, blinking up at Yejun. My face suddenly burned. "Did you think bombarding me with questions would trick me into answering that?" I managed.

"Are you trying the same tactic now?" he said, smirking.

I snatched my pencil off the floor. "No more questions. Only calculus."

"It's just that you pay a lot of attention to him, but you seem different when you do," Yejun said. "Sort of like you're lying."

I clenched my teeth, embarrassed that he'd figured it out so easily. But I didn't think of it as lying—Jihoon was sweet, and talking to him made me forget the catastrophes in every other area of my life. It wasn't like I pretended to enjoy his company. "You don't know me," I said. "How would you know how I act?"

"I think I'm getting to know you," Yejun said, shrugging and slurping boba up his straw. "We already have a secret together. Strangers don't share secrets. I bet you don't have any secrets with Jihoon."

"And where did you get that idea?" I said. "On another napkin in a shoe rack?" He was right, but he didn't need to know that.

Yejun grimaced. "That's a very reliable form of communication," he said, crossing his arms.

"Anyone can stuff some garbage in a shoe rack," I said. "It's hardly proof of anything."

Instead of answering, Yejun set down his drink and stared at it as if deeply contemplating the boba. My gaze fell to the tattoo on his arm, and I realized too late that he was probably thinking about his mother and her note. I hadn't been talking about her, but he probably thought I had been.

"Yejun—"

"It's not just a napkin," he said at last. "I have a shoe."

I blinked. "A shoe?"

He nodded earnestly. "A green velvet shoe with a short heel and a bow on the front," he said. "I found it in my dad's closet. And before you ask—it's not his size."

"I wasn't going to ask that," I said.

"The shoe tells me a lot," Yejun said, looking out at the view of Seoul from the cafeteria—it wasn't quite as impressive as from the top level, but from here it looked like we were floating in a gray cloud.

"Someone with a shoe that color was probably artsy. Maybe she painted in her spare time. She also must have walked around a lot, since the heel is so small. Either that or she was close to my father's height and didn't want to look too tall. I looked up the brand, and it's not very expensive, so she was probably practical and liked to save money for things that really mattered. I bet she was the kind of person who liked to mend clothes and re-sole shoes and make old things bright and pretty again."

He smiled softly to himself, then shook his head and turned back to me with a sigh. "Anyway," he said. "That's what I like to think. When you don't have all the facts, sometimes you just have to make your own story, since it's all you're ever going to get."

I looked down at my worksheet, wishing we could talk about calculus again. If Yejun's mother had really been erased like he thought, then she must have betrayed the descendants and tried to warn Yejun with the napkin. She'd found a fate worse than death because she believed in the truth.

My parents would never do something like that. If their boss told them to roll over and die, they would do it without question.

"I should go home soon," I said.

Yejun frowned. "But you haven't finished your cheesecake."

I sighed and shoveled the last few bites into my mouth, then bundled up the trash. Yejun wisely stayed quiet as we packed our bags and headed outside to catch the shuttle bus. I'd learned *some* calculus today, at least. Probably not enough to make me a straight-A student, but I just needed to pass, not perform a miracle.

We'd hardly taken three steps out the door when I saw him.

"Oh no," I said, drawing to a stop.

"What?" Yejun said, whirling around as if the danger would pop out of the bushes.

The bushes.

"Shut up for a minute," I said, before shoving Yejun into the nearest bush just as Jihoon rounded the corner with his little sisters.

Jihoon froze at the sight of me, then a smile broke across his face and he started walking faster, tugging his sisters along. I glanced at the slightly misshapen bush, which thankfully stayed silent.

"Mina!" Jihoon said, jogging up to me. His little sisters stumbled after him, all but dragged up the hill, then peered at me with wide eyes. "Are you leaving?" he said.

I screamed internally—I could have said no and stayed here with him, but Yejun would probably find a way to join us, and that was the last thing I wanted.

"Yeah, sorry," I said.

"No no, it's fine!" Jihoon said quickly. "If you're busy now, how about we hang out later? Like this Friday?"

I was scheduled for a 3:00 to 5:00 shift with Hyebin on Friday, plus studying for calculus, but I could probably fit in a date with Jihoon. It was technically work, after all, so maybe Hyebin would even let me go early.

"Sure," I said, forcing a smile onto my face. "We could get dinner?"

The bush rustled beside me. I pretended I hadn't noticed, but Jihoon and both his sisters turned toward it.

"Must be a raccoon!" I said quickly. "You should keep your distance. It might bite."

Jihoon's sisters ducked behind his legs. "Oppa, I want to go inside," the older one said.

"We will, Jiwoo," Jihoon said, patting her hair before turning back to me. "Yes, let's get dinner! I love dinner!" he said. "I'll text you?"

"Sure," I said again. Yejun's annoying observation kept playing in my head, making me hyperaware of my body language.

It's just that you pay a lot of attention to him, but you seem different when you do. Sort of like you're lying.

But I wasn't really lying, was I? I actually wanted to get dinner with Jihoon. It was better than squishing bugs with Hyebin.

"Is she your girlfriend?" Jihoon's younger sister asked.

"Okay let's talk later!" Jihoon said, his face bright red. "Bye, Mina!" he called over his shoulder, dragging his sisters toward the main entrance.

I waved, making sure to keep the smile on my face until the door closed behind him.

Yejun popped his head out of the bushes, his hair tangled with leaves. "You're lucky that my curiosity is stronger than my desire for chaos," he said. "I could have made that very awkward."

"And I could have punched you in the face, but it's a good thing we're both feeling merciful today," I said.

"Ooh, did I hit a nerve?" Yejun said, standing up and brushing himself off. "Nervous about your pretend date?"

"It's not pretend," I said, heading for the shuttle as Yejun shook leaves off his backpack.

"What, I can't even joke after you crammed me into a bush?" he said. Something in his tone had shifted—his words had a sharper edge to them now.

I paused, looking over my shoulder. "I'm sorry about the bush, but I didn't see many other options," I said.

He scoffed. "The option to be seen with me was too intolerable?"

For the purposes of my infiltration mission, yes, I thought, but of course I didn't want to tell Yejun that, because then I would have to admit he was right about my mission. If I hadn't hidden Yejun, it would have looked like we were on a date, and I couldn't exactly tell Jihoon we were just trying to destroy the timeline platonically.

"I'll keep that in mind," Yejun said when I didn't answer. He wouldn't meet my gaze as the shuttle pulled up, and we rode in silence back down the hill.

Chapter Nine

My mom might have been content with being a takeout family, but I was starting to feel like my veins were full of oil. I couldn't stand any more takeout pizza, so I did my best to chop up some kimchi and make some semblance of a meal with the frozen rice, vegetable bags, and freezer-burned garlic cloves. A runny egg and some scallions on top would fix just about anything, anyway.

I made extra, hoping my parents would be home to eat it but knowing they probably wouldn't be. I hadn't seen them at home in days, so they were either coming and going while I was at school or they hadn't returned at all. It wasn't unusual for floating agents, so I wasn't worried yet.

As I scraped some rice onto a plate, a sharp pain stabbed behind my eye and my hand twitched, dumping so much rice out that it spilled over the counter. I'd been getting headaches more frequently lately, but every time I checked, the banana milk mission still hadn't populated in my assignment list. I would have to talk to Hyebin about it the next time I saw her.

My eyes throbbed again and I set down the pan, sliding back against the cabinets. I fished an ice pack from the freezer and slapped it over my eyes as I lay down on the floor. When the pain faded, I realized I was lying across my mom's shoes, which were spilling out of the overstuffed shoe rack in the hyeon gwan and slowly migrating into the kitchen. I tossed the ice pack in the sink and gathered up the shoes so no one tripped and fell to their death when returning home at three in the morning.

As I matched up all the boots and sandals, I thought about Yejun's mother and her green shoe. What if my mom dissolved like Yejun's mom and left nothing behind but a mismatched shoe? If I got caught, maybe Hong Gildong would erase my parents too just for good measure—raising two traitor daughters probably wouldn't look good on their records, even if none of it was their fault. I tucked my mom's boots into the rack as gently as possible. No matter what happened to me, I had to make sure my parents were safe.

I grabbed my backpack and fished out my wallet, then pulled out Hana's note and read it with one side of my face pressed against the cool laminate of the front door, letting her words and the cold temperature slow my heart rate.

When you're ready, come find me. I will keep you safe.

I tried to imagine, as Yejun had, what kind of person Hana was. I pictured her hunched over a desk, writing the note with a fine-tip pen, blowing on it to dry the ink. I already knew what clothes she would have worn, because I had her hand-me-downs. I pictured her in my striped pink-and-orange sweater, gray sweatpants, and maybe fuzzy purple socks. Yes, that felt like something Hana would wear. But still, I couldn't imagine her face at all. I could only see her shoulders, her spine, her coppery hair draped down her back. Maybe my imagination just wasn't as good as

Yejun's, or maybe I just didn't want to be wrong, to love someone who wasn't real.

Hana will keep me safe, I thought, hugging the note close to my chest. *She promised. She wouldn't promise that unless she was still here, somehow.*

The door pulled away and I fell into the hallway, where my dad took a startled step back.

"Oh, sorry!" he said, frowning as I scrambled to my feet. "Were you . . . sleeping on the floor?"

"I was rearranging the shoes in the shoe rack," I said quickly, folding up the note and stuffing it in my pocket so he wouldn't see. "Sorry, I didn't expect you home so soon."

I all but ran back inside, too conscious of the wary look on my dad's face as he sat down to untie his boots.

"I made kimchi fried rice," I said quickly, trying to disperse the awkwardness from the air. "Or something close to it. Want me to add another egg for you?"

My dad took his time putting his shoes away before answering. "Are you all right, Mina Bean?" he said. "You seem . . . on edge."

I swallowed, feeling like I was on another infiltration mission. *Of course I'm on edge*, I thought. *I'm a traitor waiting for the guillotine blade to fall.* But I couldn't say that to my dad, and denying it would only make him more suspicious.

"Just a lot of work at school," I said, looking away. "Calculus is hard."

My dad nodded sympathetically, the tension leaving his shoulders. "Make sure you're getting enough sleep," he said. "You're not a calculator—your brain won't work if you don't recharge it."

"I'll go to bed after I eat," I said, cracking an egg over the pan of rice. I could feel my dad's eyes on me as I cooked, so I ate as fast as I could before saying good night and hurrying to my room. Once I locked my door, I let out a breath. I pulled down the shades and put Hana's note back in its designated place in my wallet, safe and secret.

· 🦋 ·

"That's twenty-five," Hyebin said as I dropped another eunhaeng into her bag.

"It's twenty-six," I said, frowning and swaying precariously on my tree branch as it wobbled in the breeze.

"I know how to count, Yang," Hyebin said.

I sighed and resigned myself to plucking another two eunhaeng just to placate Hyebin.

After school on Monday, Hyebin and I traveled to May of 2013 for a mission of paramount importance: plucking twenty-seven pieces of stinky fruit off one specific tree in Olympic Park. Eunhaeng looked like yellow cherries and smelled like garbage when they fell to the ground and burst under people's shoes. Removing twenty-seven of them from this tree was supposed to prevent a truck rollover on the highway in three days, though I hadn't bothered to look up exactly how that worked. I'd stayed up half the night finishing my calculus homework, so at this point, if Hyebin had asked me to lick eunhaeng off the sidewalk, I probably would have done it just to finish the mission quickly.

I stretched higher, trying to reach the closest eunhaeng, but my fingertips barely brushed it. I wasn't keen on taking a heroic dive and plummeting to the ground.

"Reach for it, Yang," Hyebin said. "You move like my grandmother."

I hesitated before making another grab, looking over my shoulder at Hyebin. "You have a grandmother?" I said before I could help it. I'd always thought of Hyebin as totally unattached, floating around across the timelines without a tether.

Her expression went blank. "Everyone has a grandmother," she said—a calculated non-answer.

"Is she a descendant?" I said, stretching my wrist. I imagined an older version of Hyebin and cowered at the thought. The only thing scarier than Jang Hyebin was Jang Hyebin with the authority of a halmeoni.

Hyebin took so long to respond that at first, I thought she hadn't heard me. When I looked over my shoulder, she was staring into her fruit bag. "I'm the only descendant left in my family," she said at last.

I frowned, peering down between the branches. "What? How is that possible?"

"They all opted for the brain wipe," Hyebin said, shrugging as if it didn't matter.

When descendants turned twenty, we could opt to turn in our magic and have our memories scrubbed rather than serve the timeline. As tempting as it was at times, my mom told me that it wasn't as simple as it seemed. The descendants didn't put new memories in place of the years you'd spent training. Instead, they ripped out everything even remotely related to time travel. If Hyebin's parents had had their memories erased, there were probably huge chunks of Hyebin's childhood they couldn't remember at all.

No wonder Hyebin seemed like such a lone wolf. She really had no one.

"I'm sorry," I said.

Hyebin's expression twisted like she'd eaten something sour. "I'm not," she said. "They're not the ones pulling stinky fruit from a tree right now. Speaking of . . ." She gestured impatiently toward the tree.

I sighed and turned back to the tree, tugging myself up high enough to pluck the last two eunhaeng. I let out a breath as I dropped them into Hyebin's basket. That was one more mission I'd managed not to mess up. Ever since the wedding incident, I was hyperaware that the next mission I failed would probably be my last.

I was just about to climb back down when a low rumble shook the earth.

I grabbed the nearest branch for support as the leaves and

eunhaeng trembled. Hyebin steadied herself on the ladder and looked around.

"Earthquake?" I said, digging my hands into the bark as the ground shook even harder.

Hyebin ignored me, narrowing her eyes and peering around as if she could smell a change in the air. The world lurched again and I smacked my head against the side of the tree.

"We have to go," Hyebin said suddenly.

"Uh, okay," I said. "What should I do with the eunhaeng?"

"Yang, *now!*" Hyebin said, her eyes wide.

I reached out for her hand, but another vibration shook the ground, and Hyebin's ladder tilted to the side, her fingers sliding away from me. Hyebin hopped off the ladder and landed easily on her feet as it clattered to the ground, then hurried to pick it up and settle it against the shivering tree again. I clung to the trunk, praying that the whole tree didn't topple over with me on it.

On the horizon, a wave of white began to roll in.

At first, I thought it was a tsunami, but those were far more common in Japan than Korea. Something that resembled ocean foam rolled closer and closer, until I realized it wasn't water at all, but . . . nothing.

It was as if a wave of bleach was flooding the horizon, stripping the colors from the storefronts and sidewalks, leaving the world a vacant white with nothing but ghostly outlines of what remained. The wave devoured the skyline and all the buildings on the horizon, slowly ripping a hole in the sky. People on the streets sprinted away, tripping over each other and running out into traffic.

My fingers on the upper branch stung with a sharp coldness. I looked at the branches overhead, now white as a birch tree, the eunhaeng gray like rocks. The wave of white had begun to wash over my hand, which was quickly going numb.

I scrambled to a different branch as the whiteness crept farther down the tree, breathing frigid air over me. I was positive I had never learned about anything like this in my descendant classes.

Hyebin gave up on trying to steady the ladder, tossing it aside with a frustrated cry when the ground shook even harder beneath her. She cast a nervous glance over her shoulder at the white approaching from all sides, then held a hand out to me, one palm glowing blue. "Just jump!" she said.

It was too far to jump. I was going to crush her into the ground. "I don't think—"

"Yes, *don't think*!" Hyebin said, her eyes wide and desperate. "Just jump!"

As always, I listened to Hyebin.

I dropped from the tree right as the whiteness devoured my branch. My left hand closed around Hyebin's, and the world exploded into color.

We tumbled to the sidewalk, crushing a display of grapes spread out on blankets in front of a market. An old woman started yelling at us, but Hyebin had already rolled to her feet and yanked me upright, gripping me by the shoulders.

"Are you okay?" she said.

I looked to my hand, which had returned to its natural color. "I think so," I said, though I lurched unsteadily to one side because the ground felt a bit more like gelatin than cement.

Hyebin frowned and tugged at a lock of my hair near my face. Before I could ask her what was wrong, the lock fell in front of my eyes, and I realized it was stark white. Frantically, I tugged at the rest of my hair, relieved that most of it was still brown. "What was that?" I said.

Hyebin passed the grape vendor a 50,000 won note and mumbled an apology before tugging me away from the scene of the crime, then uttered the most terrifying words I'd ever heard Jang Hyebin say.

"I don't know."

Chapter Ten

Hyebin forced me to see the medics, who examined each of my toes with exquisite care and poked around the inside of my mouth until they determined that the mysterious wave of nothingness hadn't rearranged my organs. Somehow, I'd escaped with only a lock of white hair.

By the time the medics were finished with me, Hyebin had done enough research to determine that the bleach tsunami was most likely a timeline fluctuation. She marked it in her report as an Unexplained Illogical Behavior While on an Alternate Plane of Time, the catch-all phrase for Something Very Bad That We Don't Know How to Fix.

"I've read through some past incident reports," Hyebin said, fingers dancing across the scrying pool. "Similar events have been reported due to unresolved paradoxes, which started the process of timeline decay."

"Decay?" I echoed, hugging my backpack to my chest.

"Think of the timeline like a piece of wood, and paradoxes

are like hungry termites," Hyebin said, now using both hands to pull up different files at once. "We can never eliminate paradoxes completely—time traveling is inherently paradoxical—but we try to keep the amount of paradoxes below a certain percent. Otherwise, the holes get too big and strange things start happening."

My lock of white hair fell in front of my eyes, and I hurriedly tucked it behind my ear. "On a scale of one to ten, how panicked should I be?" I said.

"The paradox seems to be isolated for now," Hyebin said, rather than answer my question, "but I have to do some more digging to find the cause."

"What could cause this?" I said.

Hyebin shrugged. "People messing up their assignments, open time loops, unauthorized traveling . . . there's too many possibilities."

Unauthorized traveling? I thought back to Yejun releasing the butterflies into the sky at Namsan Seoul Tower. My hands broke out in a nervous sweat, so I jammed my fists into my pockets. Had Yejun and I caused this? Did bringing back Timeline Alpha mean destroying the current timeline while we were standing on it? On any other day, Hyebin probably could have read the terror in my eyes, but she was too preoccupied with the scrying pool to even meet my gaze.

"In case it wasn't obvious, I'm too busy to train you today," Hyebin said. "Go home. Text me if you spot any paradoxes."

"Right," I said, jumping to my feet. I'd take any excuse to leave before I sweated through my shirt and blurted out all my sins to Hyebin.

I tried to bow, but as I lowered my head, pain blared behind my eyes, my vision flashing white. It was that same timesickness headache, but so sudden and sharp that it felt like someone had taken a pickaxe behind my eyes. For a moment, I actually thought my eyeballs were going to pop out and roll across the floor of Hyebin's office.

I reached out for balance but only managed to grab a handful of potted plant before I felt hands on my shoulders.

My vision cleared just as Hyebin pushed me back into my chair.

"What's wrong?" she said, gripping my face, her dark eyes scrutinizing me. When I couldn't find the words to answer right away, she scowled and shook her head. "Those medics are useless."

I swallowed, my throat suddenly dry. The pain had faded a bit, now back to a dull ache. "It feels like a timesickness headache," I managed, though my tongue felt heavy in my mouth. "But according to my scrying pool, I don't have any open loops."

Hyebin pressed her lips together, then turned back to her desk. She grabbed an item too small for me to see, then slammed the drawer shut and knelt in front of me. With one hand, she took my wrist, then with the other she tore open an alcohol wipe between her teeth and swiped it across my arm. Before I could ask what she was doing, she pulled out a thin needle and poked it into my wrist.

I flinched, but Hyebin held my arm steady so I couldn't pull away. As soon as the surprise faded, I realized my headache was just . . . gone. I blinked, glancing experimentally up at the light, which no longer seared my eyes. My gaze dropped to the thin needle sticking out of my arm.

"What did you do?" I said.

"Acupuncture," she said, tossing the alcohol wipe in the trash.

I shook my head. "I've tried that before," I said. "It's never worked for me."

"Because you're not human," Hyebin said. "Human acupuncturists can't help you because your nervous system is different from theirs."

I feel pretty human, I thought, wincing as Hyebin plucked out the needle. "You've had this kind of headache before?" she said, sitting in front of her scrying pool.

"It didn't start today, if that's what you're asking," I said. "I don't think the paradox scrambled my brain or anything like that."

She made a wordless sound of acknowledgment, her fingers dancing across the pool and her frown deepening.

"You're right, you don't have any open loops," she said, glaring at her reflection in the water.

"The architects must have missed something," I said. "I saw one of my Echoes a few days ago."

Hyebin's gaze snapped up. "You did?" she said, her expression grave. "Are you sure?"

"I'm sure," I said, even though the intensity of Hyebin's gaze could have scared me into forgetting my own name. "But that just means the architects made a mistake, right?"

Hyebin's lips pressed together. She nodded stiffly, averting her gaze. "Probably," she said, as if the word had been choked out of her throat. "I'll ask them about it." Then she turned back to me, her expression softer. "I want to check you again, just in case. I don't trust those medics."

It was no use arguing with Hyebin, so I kept my mouth shut while she poked me and tested all my joints. She took a step back, which I took as a signal that she was finished, but she was still looking at me like I was a wilted salad or something equally displeasing.

"Text me in three hours with an update, then again before you go to bed," she said, crossing her arms.

"You have work to do," I said, shaking my head. "Really, I'm fine."

"I wasn't asking," Hyebin said. "Do it or I'll show up at your apartment and kick the door down."

I swallowed and nodded quickly. Hyebin didn't make idle threats.

I bowed—this time without falling on my face—and headed for the door, but Hyebin didn't simply wave goodbye like usual. Instead, she followed me into the hall and trailed behind me all the way to the elevator. She pressed the elevator button, then waited in silence with me until the doors opened. I bowed and stepped into the elevator, but she held the door open with one arm.

"Be careful, Mina," she said. Her words were so quiet, the only thing she'd ever said to me that didn't sound like an order.

"I will," I said. "I'm just going to grab a coffee and go home. The only danger at Caffebene is too much processed sugar."

I laughed awkwardly at my own joke, but Hyebin's expression stayed cold because Jang Hyebin never smiled. Wordlessly, she pulled her arm back and turned away, letting the elevator doors slide closed.

I let out a breath, sinking back against the wall. The minute the elevator doors opened on the bottom floor, I took off running.

I had to talk to Yejun.

· 🦋 ·

I drummed my fingers on the table, checking the time on my phone. Yejun was late. He'd agreed to meet me in fifteen minutes, but that was twenty minutes ago.

I was waiting at the same café where I'd first met him, the same type of cheesecake on the corner of the table—after nearly being obliterated from existence, I deserved it.

If the timeline decaying really was our fault, we needed to change our plan. Fast.

I couldn't find Hana if I got sucked into a vacuum. And of course, I didn't want other descendants or humans to get hurt in another paradox. I also wasn't particularly keen on destroying the entire universe by accident. Whatever calculations Yejun had done for his plan to recover Timeline Alpha, he needed to run them again.

After another ten minutes, I texted Yejun to hurry the hell up, but the text went unread. He was probably taking his sweet time just to annoy me.

But then I thought back to the sudden wave of nothingness that had surged across the horizon that morning. Hyebin said it was an isolated incident, but a decaying timeline didn't care about prior appointments. What if Yejun had gotten sucked into a paradox on his way here?

I took a quick bite of cheesecake—I'd read that eating activated your parasympathetic nervous system and told your body that everything was fine, but everything certainly did not feel fine right now. Yejun was annoying, but that didn't mean I wanted him wiped from existence. He was supposed to help me pass calculus and find Hana.

In my mind, I could picture him being unmade by the timeline, his shiny blond hair and absurdly pretty eyes dissolving into stark whiteness. I stuffed a bigger bite of cheesecake in my mouth, tapping my phone screen again just to make sure I hadn't missed a text. I finished my cheesecake, which sat like a rock in my stomach, and tried to tell myself that I didn't care at all what happened to Yejun.

Then, through the windows, someone with blond hair and a blue raincoat hurried down the sidewalk. The tightness in my stomach untangled and I sank down in my seat, quietly humiliated that I was actually glad to see Kim Yejun.

Except . . . he walked straight past the café.

He stormed down the sidewalk, his expression stern as he passed the front door, drawing to a stop in front of . . . another Yejun.

The second Yejun was clutching a takeout bag in one hand and his school bag in the other. He jolted back at the sight of the first Yejun, holding the takeout bag protectively against his chest.

One of them is an Echo, I realized. Hopefully the one without the takeout, since I was hoping that was for me.

From where I was sitting, I could only see the face of the second Yejun, his expression slowly darkening as the Yejun in the blue raincoat spoke. His mouth moved as he said something I couldn't discern. Then the blue raincoat Yejun reached out, tugged on the other Yejun's hoodie strings to throw him off-balance, yanked his school bag off his shoulder, and took off running down the street with it.

I jumped to my feet, but the Yejun with a takeout bag had already righted himself and stomped into the café, looking annoyed but otherwise fine.

"Your bag!" I said, rushing to meet him at the door. There was still time to catch him if—

"It's fine," Yejun said, brushing past me and slumping down in a chair. "Let him go."

"But"—I shifted from foot to foot, my limbs burning with adrenaline—"you just got mugged."

"Yeah, by myself," Yejun said with a forced smile. "So I must have had a good reason for it. And at least I know I'll get my bag back eventually. I wish he'd done it tomorrow, though. My laptop was in there, with my only copy of my English essay."

I sat down slowly. "Are you . . ." My question faded at the end when I realized it sounded precariously close to concern. I swallowed it down and backpedaled. "How can rogues have Echoes anyway?" I said, crossing my arms.

Yejun raised an eyebrow. "Any descendant can have Echoes," he said.

I shook my head. "But you're not getting correction missions from the timeline architects."

"Yeah, so it must be an organic Echo," Yejun said, shrugging. "Sometime in the future, I'll go back and do that of my own volition. God knows why."

Organic Echo? I thought. I'd never heard of that, probably because I wasn't allowed to just pop back in time on my own yet. Could the Echo that had poured banana milk on my shoes have been organic too? But I couldn't think of a single reason why I would go back in time to do something like that to myself.

"It doesn't matter," Yejun said, sitting up straight. "My wallet was in my back pocket, so I just lost my laptop and a couple chewed pencils. More importantly . . ." He pushed the takeout bag toward me and grinned expectantly.

I uncrossed my arms, tentatively opening the box. Strawberry cheesecake. Of course.

"Exactly how much cheesecake do you think I eat?" I said, my face warm.

Yejun shrugged. "Is there something you'd prefer over cheesecake?"

"Passing calculus."

"They don't sell that at CU," he said. "But they do have *this*." He reached into his jacket pocket, then plopped an open bag of candy corn on the table. "We did it," he said. "We brought this monstrosity to Korea."

I stared at the bag, a strange lightness filling my chest. It was weird to see such an American candy with Korean words on the package, but there it was, in all its neon glory.

Somehow, I'd thought I would feel the timeline shift when we pulled the first anchor. I'd hoped that memories of Hana would start to come back to me slowly as the timeline carried us closer together, like rivers converging as they neared the sea. But it was a day just like any other day, except today there was candy corn.

"Monstrosity?" I said, as I processed his words.

"Oh yeah, it's awful," Yejun said. "Have you tried this? We've unleashed chaos on the world."

"I lived in America, of course I've tried it," I said, snatching the bag off the table. "And if you don't appreciate it, I'll eat it."

"Be my guest," Yejun said. Then he paused and frowned at me. I didn't understand why he was looking at me so intently, until he spoke. "Did you dye your hair?"

I tucked the white lock of hair behind my ear. "There was an incident with the timeline," I said under my breath, checking to make sure the barista wasn't standing too close.

Yejun sat up straight. "Are you okay?"

"I almost got bleached out of existence, but I seem to be fine," I said, shrugging. "I'm more worried about the timeline collapsing."

"Why would the timeline collapse?" Yejun said, reeling back.

I explained to him what Hyebin had told me in her office, and his expression sank into a frown.

"Do you think it's because of us?" I whispered.

"I don't see how it could be," Yejun said, glaring at my cheesecake like it was singularly responsible for the paradox. "Every change we're making is the exact opposite of something that's already been done. That could only undo prior adjustments, not tear a hole in the timeline. Besides, I ran every scenario multiple times. We're not doing anything even remotely dangerous to the integrity of the timeline. The worst we could possibly do is accidentally cause firebellied toads to have nineteen toes instead of eighteen."

"Fire-bellied . . ." I shook my head. That didn't matter right now. "So if it's not because of us, then why is the timeline decaying?"

"I don't know," Yejun said, slumping back in his chair. "Maybe the timeline is resisting major change? Or maybe someone dropped their cell phone in the wrong time period and it has nothing to do with us at all."

Sunlight flashed off the window of a passing car, and I flinched at the memory of the horizon peeling itself open to bright white. The present had always felt solid beneath my feet, but now I imagined the earth falling open like a trapdoor beneath me.

"Did Hyebin seem worried?" Yejun said.

About me? Yes, I thought. But that wasn't what Yejun was asking. "I mean, she let me go home, so she probably doesn't think the world is going to end *tonight*, but who knows about tomorrow."

"Then I'm not worried either," Yejun said. "She wouldn't send you home if she thought the earth was going to eat itself, right?"

"Right," I echoed.

"In that case," Yejun said, "let's talk about something much scarier, like calculus."

I blinked. "The timeline is falling apart and you want to talk about *calculus*?"

"That's why I'm here, isn't it?" he said, grinning. "Or do you just like making small talk with me?"

I rolled my eyes and pulled my calculus assignment from my folder, slapping it down on the table.

"Eighty-five!" Yejun said, beaming. "Have you celebrated?"

"Eighty-five isn't that good," I said, my face warm as I sank back in my seat. "You don't have to pretend it is."

Yejun's expression softened. "Who's pretending?" he said. "It's a big improvement, Mina."

I shook my head. "Dragons should be able to do this kind of math in their sleep."

"Why?" Yejun said, scowling. "What the hell do you think dragons used calculus for? For people like us, high school is just a game to pass the time, and right now, you're winning."

"Winning?" I said. "That's generous."

"Not dying," Yejun amended. "Now take a celebratory bite of cheesecake."

"I already had a piece before you got here," I said.

Yejun ignored me, unboxing the slice he'd brought and scooping up a piece on my fork. "*Celebrate*," he commanded, holding the piece in front of my face.

I rolled my eyes. "You don't have to—"

"*Acknowledge your success*," Yejun said, jamming the piece of cheesecake toward me. He came dangerously close to forking my eye or smearing cheesecake across my nose. I sighed and bit the piece off his fork.

Yejun sat back and set the fork down, then reached into his pocket and tossed a handful of confetti over me.

"*Where did you even get that?*" I said through a mouthful of cheesecake, shaking it out of my hair. "Don't throw confetti in a restaurant! Someone will have to clean it up!"

"How about we study somewhere else today, as a reward?" he said.

I made him wait for my response until I'd finished carefully wiping the confetti off the table and dumping it in the front pocket of my bag, which had inhaled half the confetti anyway. "Isn't the cheesecake the reward?"

"I'm training you like a bear," Yejun said. "Building positive associations in your mind with calculus."

"Who trains a *bear*?"

But Yejun had already risen to his feet and was busy putting the second slice of cheesecake back in his bag, slinging the takeout bag over his shoulder. "I have the perfect place for us to go," he said.

"Where is it?" I said, edging away.

"There are amazing pastries there," Yejun said, rather than answer directly. He held out his hand expectantly. I looked up at him, positive my face was bright red. He couldn't just *offer to hold my hand* so casually!

"What are you doing?" I managed to say.

Then his fingertips pulsed blue and he winked conspiratorially. I realized, with a flush of heat to my face, that he wasn't offering to hold my hand just because he wanted to—he wanted to time travel.

"Not here!" I said, looking around.

"The café's empty and the barista is restocking in the back!" he said, pouting. "It's the perfect time!"

"Security cameras!" I said, feeling like I'd turned into Hyebin.

"The one facing us isn't recording!" Yejun said, looking over his shoulder at the one pointed at us. "See, there's no blinking red light like on the other one. This isn't my first time around the block, Yang."

He took another step forward, extending his hand. "The year 2016, April 1, 7:59:59," he said.

It was a bad idea. I waited for Hana to reach out through the timeline and yank my hair for being reckless, or for Hyebin's Echo to burst in and pull me away for a mission, or at least for my heart to clench in fear. But there was no one here but me and Yejun, his outstretched hand glittering with blue light as he waited for my answer.

"Hurry up, before the barista comes back," he said.

Before I could answer, his magic spiraled around his hand, blue light in tattered ribbons whispering toward me. It wasn't until something purple flashed by my vision that I realized my own magic was awakening in my palm as well, purple tendrils stretching out toward Yejun.

I lifted my hand experimentally, and thin threads of both of our magic reached out to each other, twisting together into an indigo braid. Even though I wasn't touching Yejun yet, his heartbeat echoed through me, his thoughts tangled like ivy around my own, his dreams lay out before me as bright as summer constellations in a clear sky. His magic reeled me in, and before I could stop myself, I clasped my hand around his and the world fell quiet.

It was as if I'd slipped beneath the cool surface of a pond—his magic swallowed every sound, the real world suddenly a thousand miles away. The walls of the café dissolved, the tiled floor crumpled beneath my feet, and an endless expanse of violet light suspended us in its warm infinity. There was nothing in this quiet world except for me, and Yejun, and the light singing through us.

For the first time in my life, it felt easy to exist. It was as if the timeline had finally stopped rejecting me and I'd returned to my origin point after a long voyage. The moment felt inevitable, like every timeline had converged in this brief, delicate second. No matter what changes the descendants made to the timeline, it would always bend and twist to bring me back here.

This had never happened when traveling with Hyebin. I probably should have been worried, or at least questioned it. But as Yejun smiled and tightened his grip around my hand, I didn't want to dissect the moment with theories or questions. I just wanted to be here, the way flowers and trees and mountains simply existed without needing to justify it.

Blue light wrapped in ribbons around us, time whispering through the air in all directions. I held tight to Yejun's hand as the timeline breathed us in.

· 🦋 ·

We arrived in front of a café with BLUE BUNNY in teal bubble letters above the door. The sun had come out, the smog had cleared away, and the little bell above the door jingled as an employee unlocked the door. The smell of bread wafted over me in a warm haze.

As the last of our time magic fizzled out, I became sharply aware of my hand still gripping Yejun's, our fingers tangled together, the sweat between our palms.

"Mina," Yejun said, "I—"

But I was terrified by whatever he was going to say next, so I tore my hand away and stuffed it into my pocket.

I knew—because for a brief moment I had known all of his heart—that Yejun had felt the same strange connection that I had.

But he was still Kim Yejun, the annoyingly smug rogue traveler who had forced his way into my life and was ruining my infiltration missions. Our magic had reacted strangely together, but that didn't mean anything. No one really understood the intricacies of time magic.

"What did you want to show me?" I said, examining the display case of fake croissants and macarons instead of looking at Yejun.

I pretended not to notice how his reflection stared at me in the display window for a moment too long. Then he shook his head and opened the door. "Come on," he said, greeting the staff and holding the door open for me—two things he wasn't supposed to do while time traveling—but the café smelled good enough that I didn't want to waste our few minutes here arguing about it.

"Pick whatever you want," Yejun said as the door swung shut behind him, "but I recommend the croffle."

"Croffle?" I said, frowning at the cream-and-fruit-covered waffles in the display case.

"Croissant waffle," Yejun said. "This shop specialized in them." He leaned closer, switching to Japanese and whispering in my ear. "They went out of business in 2017. I haven't been able to find a croffle as good as theirs since then. It's like my Moby Dick."

"A croissant bit off your leg?" I said.

"Croffle," Yejun corrected. "You want one or not? They sell out fast."

What I wanted more than anything was to obliterate the last three minutes from my memory, but since I couldn't have that, free pastries would have to suffice.

"Two croffles, please," I said to the cashier, then stepped aside so Yejun could pay.

As much as I wanted to buy one of everything in the pastry case, my sweet tooth wasn't a good enough reason to cause ripple effects. Just being here was already risking . . .

A spike of dread lanced through me. I gripped Yejun's arm, squeezing a pained sound out of him. "Won't this mess up the timeline?" I whispered.

He handed the cashier a 10,000 won note and shook his head. "I already ran this scenario. Effects should be minimal."

"When did you run this scenario?" I said, releasing his arm as the cashier plated two croffles and set them on the counter. Yejun thanked her and picked them both up, then walked toward the tables before answering.

"This morning," he said, shrugging and pushing one of the croffles toward me. It had berries and whipped cream on top and a little jar of syrup next to it. "I finished my ramen and figured I might as well, rather than waste the broth."

"You used broth as a scrying pool?" I said, trying with all my might to focus on Yejun and not the steaming pastry in front of me. *Come on, Mina, the fate of the timeline is more important than dessert.*

"You could scry in a toilet bowl if you wanted to," he said, slicing into his croffle. "At least, for the kind of basic scenarios that I run. If you have high-security clearance, your files are all locked to your personal scrying pool, but no one ever trusted me that much. Are you gonna try your croffle or what?"

I still wanted to know what had possessed Yejun to run this particular scenario before meeting me today, but I supposed that could wait until I had a bite of croffle. I cut off a piece, dipped it in the whipped cream, and ate it.

"Oh my god," I said. "I'm gonna kill you."

"Why?" Yejun said, dropping his fork.

"Because this is incredible, and I can't just pop back in time whenever I want it."

Yejun beamed. "I told you!" he said. "Congrats on passing your calculus test, Yang. Remember this moment the next time you want to give up on studying."

I stuffed another piece of croffle in my mouth so I wouldn't have to respond, pretending I didn't notice the way Yejun was smiling at me instead of eating his own dessert.

If he'd run this scenario, that meant he'd planned to take me here even before he'd arrived at the café. He'd thought about me beyond the scope of our mission, had carefully planned a safe trip for me that wouldn't destroy the timeline. We were at a café by ourselves for a reason other than work or school and had literally just held hands on the way here—did that make this a date? The more I thought about it, the more my brain felt like scrambled eggs burning in a nonstick pan. I took another huge bite of croffle so Yejun couldn't ask me a question and imagined that *he* was the one giving me a bracelet as we crossed the stream instead of Jihoon. I imagined Yejun steadying my waist so I wouldn't fall off the stepping stone, Yejun's hands tucking azaleas behind my ear, Yejun whispering *I like you, Mina*.

Yejun checked his watch again, then turned his attention to his napkin and began to fold it. After a few moments, he had a tiny napkin crane in his hand, which he set on the table next to us.

I stopped chewing, slowly setting my fork down.

That's why we're here, I realized, swallowing the rest of the croffle, which felt like cement going down.

"You're making an adjustment, aren't you?" I said, my voice flat. He hadn't come here for me at all. This wasn't a date—it was work. Suddenly no longer hungry, I dropped my gaze to the shredded remains of my croffle.

"What, you mean the crane?" Yejun said. "No."

But I was good at reading between the lines, and I knew his words were too careful. He meant: *No, the crane isn't the adjustment. Something else is.*

I debated abandoning my croffle in protest but decided that stuffing the rest of it in my mouth in one bite would have the same effect. I finished chewing, wiped my mouth, then sat back and crossed my arms. "I'm ready to go back," I said.

"Did you . . . not like the croffle as much as you thought?" Yejun asked.

"I liked it, and I'm ready to go back," I said. "Or did you have something else to do here?"

"I . . . well, yeah there was one more thing," Yejun said, edging away from me as if he sensed this was the wrong answer.

"Then do it quickly and let's go."

Yejun seemed to wilt at my cold tone, and I almost felt bad for him but kept my irritation simmering by glaring at the paper crane. This was just a job to him, and to me. I didn't need to be kind.

Yejun clapped his hands together, suddenly smiling again. "Okay, how about this?" he said. "I'll do a bunch of things, and you try to guess which one is the adjustment."

"Is this a game?" I said.

"Yes!"

"Then no."

"Too late, it's already happening," Yejun said. He stood up, stuffed the rest of his croffle into his mouth, then cleared our plates. While still chewing, he took out his wallet and placed a 5,000 won note in the tip jar, then waved for me to follow him outside.

"Where are we going?" I said. He was walking faster now, and I had to jog to keep up with him. "Shouldn't we go back?"

"I'm on a mission!" he said, mouth still full of croffle.

He ducked into a Daiso and dodged an old woman in the checkout line, then snatched a stuffed bear off the shelf.

Please don't let that be for me, I thought as the cashier bagged the bear. Yejun checked his watch, foot tapping impatiently. As soon as the cashier handed him the receipt, he rushed outside, barely dodging a biker on the sidewalk. At least he'd finished the croffle at that point or he probably would have spit it everywhere.

The pedestrian light switched on and he jogged across the street.

"Slow down!" I said, barely evading a flock of schoolchildren. "Are you trying to get me flattened by a car?"

"I'm trying to make it hard for you!" he said over his shoulder. He reached a small footbridge over the Bulgwang stream, checked his watch, then placed the bear on the edge and patted it on the head before turning around and rushing in the other direction.

Over the next few minutes, he folded a receipt from his pocket into a paper boat, which he set sailing down the stream, then walked across said stream and soaked his pants up to his ankles, and finally, removed one single dandelion from the grass and tucked it behind my ear. I flinched at the touch of his fingers on my cheek. *He's just working*, I reminded myself.

"There!" he said, sitting down on a bench and panting. "Now tell me, Yang Mina, what was the adjustment?"

I sat down on the opposite side of the bench, my left eye twitching as the wind blew dandelion parachutes into it. "Are you not worried about ripple effects?" I said stiffly. "Don't tell me you ran all those scenarios too."

"I like running scenarios!" he said, edging away as if this actually embarrassed him. "It's like solving a Rubik's Cube."

I sighed and sat back. "If I guess right, can we go home?"

He nodded quickly. "Pinky promise," he said, holding out his pinky, which I pointedly ignored.

I crossed my arms and played back the last five minutes in my mind. Yejun had checked his watch before every strange thing he'd just done, and all his actions seemed weird enough to be actual adjustments. That was . . . except for one thing.

"You asked for a bag for the stuffed bear," I said. "It was the last one the cashier had."

Yejun raised an eyebrow. "*That* was the weirdest thing I did?"

"You knew you were going to put the bear on the bridge, so you didn't need a bag," I said. "Besides, you keep trying to tell me the descendants are causing climate change, yet you would go out of your way to get unnecessary plastic?"

Yejun smiled, leaning back. "The cashier is going to have to grab more bags in the back, causing the line to build up," he said. "One customer is late for work and will put his candy bar back rather than wait."

"And then what happens to him?" I asked.

"He won't choke to death while driving and run through a crosswalk," Yejun said, shrugging.

"Are you serious?"

"Yup," Yejun said, grinning. "That guy is an entomologist, and he's going to save the dung beetles. It's nice to save lives for once instead of ending them, isn't it?"

It was true—more often than not, it felt like my descendant work involved making things worse, just because that was how things were "supposed" to be.

My anger toward Yejun slowly faded—it was hard to keep glaring at a guy who had just prevented a traffic accident. I slowly uncrossed my arms. "So the croffle place being near this adjustment was just a coincidence?"

"No such thing as a coincidence," Yejun said. "There are a lot of ways to save the dung beetles—thirty-six, in fact—but only one of them involved croffles, so, naturally, that was the one I picked."

In a way, he still did this for me, I thought. *Just . . . for me and also the dung beetles. Does that make it better or worse?*

"Well, okay, *two* of them involved croffles," Yejun said, "but the second one also involved arson, so I scrapped that idea."

I laughed, startling one of the ducks toddling down the path in front of us. "Good call," I said. "I suppose this isn't the worst place you could have brought me as a reward."

"I'll take that as a compliment," Yejun said, bowing melodramatically. "But if you could pick next time, where would you go?" He spread his arms out across the back of the bench as he spoke. When had he scooted closer? I leaned slightly forward, careful not to lean back against his forearm.

"I don't know," I said, staring at my lap.

"Come on," he said. "If you could travel anywhere in the timeline and the descendants couldn't stop you, where would you go?"

To Hana, I thought at once. But of course, I had no idea when that was, or if any moment from that timeline still existed. I tried to conjure my happiest moment in my mind, a day I'd love to go back to, but I could only seem to recall a blur of airports and moving boxes.

"October 1, 2015," I said at last. "Before lunch."

"Why then?" Yejun asked.

I looked down at my shoes. "My parents took me out for lunch and told me I was a descendant," I said.

At the time, it had been exciting. What kid wouldn't be thrilled at the idea of time travel being real? But that was also the day that any dream of what I could have done with my life had died. I must have had dreams before that day, but I couldn't remember them. Maybe if I'd run away, things could have been different. Maybe if Hana had left when she found out, she'd be hiding in Tokyo instead of wiped from existence.

"I get it," Yejun said quietly. I believed him, because I'd tasted the sadness in his soul in the moment our magic touched. Being a descendant felt like a great adventure on some days, but it was also lonely, especially for a rogue like him.

"What about you?" I said when the silence had stretched out too long.

Yejun crossed his arms, leaning back in thought. He looked up at the sky as a flock of birds arced overhead. The clouds shifted and the sun fell at a sharp angle over the stream, which glinted like it was full of crystals.

"Here," he said at last.

I frowned. "The Bulgwang stream?"

He shook his head. "This moment. Right here, right now."

I recoiled, gripping the edges of my skirt with hands that were suddenly sweaty. "Why?" I said.

"Because right now, I feel hopeful," he said, still looking at the sky, a calm smile on his face. "It's not every day that I get to feel this way."

Hopeful? I thought. It was a strange word for a descendant to use. Hope was a shield against uncertainty, and there was so little uncertainty in the life of time travelers. Descendants didn't have hope, we had timeline adjustments.

But in that moment, as I watched the flock of birds grow smaller on the blue horizon, the sun warming my face, I felt it too—that warm ember of forbidden hope deep inside me, a secret that existed only in this moment.

Chapter Eleven

Sprinting to school in the morning wasn't my favorite activity, but that was the consequence of staying up thinking about paradoxes and forgetting to set your alarm. The irony of a time traveler running late wasn't lost on me.

As if that weren't a bad enough omen, the air quality was also in the red zone, the sky a sickly shade of gray. I'd grabbed one of my dad's large dust masks by accident and it was slipping off my face as I dodged old ladies pushing their carts on the sidewalk, desperate to cross while I still had the walk light. I was pulling my weight in calculus class recently, thanks to Yejun's tutoring, but that didn't mean I could afford to lose any participation points by showing up late.

I ran past the bench by the stream where Yejun and I had sat only a few days ago. I found myself slowing down, my gaze lingering on the empty seat. I shook my head and forced myself to keep walking, not to recall in vivid detail how the sunlight reflected in Yejun's eyes and made them look golden brown, or how long his eyelashes were, or how delicately he'd touched my face, or . . .

I let out a frustrated sound and stormed past the bench.

It wasn't my fault I was acting like this—Yejun looked like an actor from a face soap commercial. Who *wouldn't* feel nervous if he wanted to hold their hand all the time? Plus, he was tutoring me, and people fell for their tutors all the time—something about emotional transference or admiration for kindness and intelligence or some other knee-jerk reaction to being helped. Falling for Yejun was like getting sucked into white water rapids—there was nothing I could do about it.

About two blocks from school, I gave up on trying to hold my sweaty mask tight to my face and accepted that I was just going to breathe in toxic smog today. It wouldn't be the most dangerous thing I'd done by a long shot. I was coughing within half a block, but it would wear off once I got inside. At least, I hoped so.

As if the universe was intent on sabotaging me that morning, a minitruck turned a corner too sharply in front of me, dumping its load of watermelons into the street.

By some miracle, I managed not to crush my toes under any melons or get hit by a car in the chaos. Traffic came to a standstill; drivers peered out their windows wondering whose job it was to push the watermelons out of the road, or if they should just barrel through them.

That was when I saw Yejun.

I didn't normally run into him before class because he always strolled in right before the bell. But that morning, I spotted his blond hair from the other side of the crosswalk. *Am I actually later than Kim Yejun?* I thought, grimacing. *How far I've fallen.*

But as the crowd dispersed on the other side of the street, Yejun placed his hand on the waist of a girl next to him.

I drew to a stop in the middle of the sidewalk, my breath caught in my throat. Yejun knew other girls? When had he even had time to get that close to someone? I squinted but couldn't figure out who the girl was—everyone wore the same school uniform, and almost every girl had dark hair. She and Yejun turned the corner and disappeared.

I felt the inexplicable urge to turn around and run back home, go back to bed and try again tomorrow. My face felt hot, my skin prickling, throat tight with something dangerously close to tears.

Of course I wasn't the only girl Yejun was trying to charm. Maybe he needed me to fix the timeline, but he needed another girl to make him dinner, another to drive him around, another to help him bleach his frustratingly perfect hair. He was handsome enough that all he'd have to do was ask nicely and let them hold his hand for a bit and they'd do whatever he asked, just like me.

I thought back to earlier this week, how I'd wondered if he'd taken me on a date, and my face burned with embarrassment for having been so foolish, for thinking Yejun would ever want me that way. We were only working together because I was a foreigner—he'd said so himself. The other girl was probably smart and sweet and fluent in Korean, probably didn't have huge feet and hair that frizzed in the rain and was probably an acceptable height for a high school girl instead of a crooked string bean like me.

I stomped up the stairs to the school's main entrance and stopped in the bathroom even though I was running late, just to make sure I didn't look like I'd been crying before I walked into class. I carefully molded my face into an expression of indifference and strolled unhurriedly into homeroom, dropping into my seat between Yejun and Jihoon.

"Mina," Yejun said at once, brightening as he saw me.

"Morning," I said stiffly, turning my back to him and facing Jihoon with a smile. Jihoon went still like a prey animal, gaze shifting between me and Yejun before tentatively holding out a bottle of Yakult.

"I thought you weren't coming," he said quietly.

"And miss this?" I said, peeling back the foil on the yogurt bottle. "This is my favorite part of the morning."

Jihoon smiled. "Really?"

I flinched as something sharp poked me between the shoulder blades. I glanced over my shoulder at Yejun, who had jabbed me with a pencil. "Mina," he said, smirking like watching me and Jihoon was amusing to him. I swallowed down the urge to splash the Yakult in his face. "We need to talk after school."

"I'm busy," I said, turning back to Jihoon.

But of course, Yejun didn't take the hint.

"With what?" Yejun said over my shoulder. "It's important."

"I have plans," I said. "Right, Jihoon?"

Jihoon went still. "I . . . uh . . . yes!" he said, finally catching on to the dangerous edge of my smile. "Whatever you want, Mina."

"Unbelievable," Yejun said. "Anything for a few points, huh?"

"Points?" Jihoon echoed.

I will murder you the moment we're in private, I vowed silently, whirling around and glaring at Yejun.

"Caffebene loyalty points!" I said, smiling at Jihoon and praying I didn't look too murderous. "If I get two more, I can get a free coffee. You like coffee, right?"

"Uh, yeah," Jihoon said, shoulders relaxing. "We can go there."

Mr. Oh hurried into the classroom and mercifully ended the conversation. I spent the rest of the period desperately trying to think of nothing but calculus, only so I wouldn't plot out elaborate ways to push Yejun out the window without getting caught.

As soon as the bell music played, I looped my arm around Jihoon's and swept him out of the classroom before Yejun could try to talk to me. I should have felt bad for using Jihoon as my human shield, but he didn't seem to mind.

I spent the rest of the school day avoiding Yejun like it was an Olympic sport, taking sick satisfaction from the fact that he seemed genuinely annoyed. It served him right. He always looked so unbothered—it would be good for him to actually feel something for once.

I all but dragged Jihoon out the front door once school was finally over.

"I think I forgot my calculus book," he said, glancing back at the school building.

"Leave it," I said, lacing my fingers through his. He jolted like I'd electrocuted him, then his muscles relaxed and he pressed closer to me, letting me lead him quickly down the hill. The last thing I wanted was to run into—

"Mina!"

I sighed, walking faster, but Yejun hurried down the stairs after us. "I don't know what your deal is, but there is actually important stuff that we need to talk about," he said.

If anything was that urgent, you wouldn't have time to go chasing after girls, I thought. I let go of Jihoon's hand and crossed my arms. "What, a calculus emergency?" I said.

"Calculus?" Yejun said.

"Yes, because that's all we talk about outside of school," I said, positioning myself between Jihoon and Yejun. "You tutor me in calculus. That's the only reason I talk to you."

Yejun scoffed. "Obviously," he said. "I would never spend time with someone like you for any other reason but charity."

My eye twitched, and I looked away so he wouldn't see how much his words stung. Of course he would have preferred to work with literally any other girl in class.

"Uh, that's kind of harsh," Jihoon said quietly.

"It's fine," I said, even as Yejun's expression softened.

"Mina," Yejun said, "I just meant—"

"We're going," I said, grabbing Jihoon's arm and turning him around. I fully intended to keep walking and ignoring Yejun until he gave up, but I drew to a stop as I saw who was standing at the bottom of the hill.

"Mina Bean!"

No way, I thought, blinking quickly. Had yellow dust gotten into my eyes? *No way is he here.*

But sure enough, there was my dad, standing at the bottom of the hill, waving with both hands. At least he was wearing jeans and a T-shirt instead of the military uniform he wore more often than not these days, which would have been hard to explain. He jogged up to the three of us, smiling.

"I got a dinner break for once!" he said. "Isn't it great? I thought I'd surprise you and we could go out to eat together. Unless you were busy . . ." He looked unsubtly at Yejun. "Are you Mina's boyfriend?"

"*Dad!*" I said. What was it about Yejun that looked inherently more boyfriend-like than Jihoon? Poor Jihoon looked like he'd just been slapped in the face.

But Yejun only grinned. "Just her calculus tutor at the moment," he said in English—since when could he speak perfect English? "But why rush into things? I'm Yejun Kim."

He held his hand out to my father and gave him a strong handshake. I wondered if I could push him down the stairs and make it look like an accident.

"This is Jihoon," I said, tugging Jihoon forward by the arm. "Jihoon, this is my dad," I said in Korean.

Jihoon bowed and sputtered out a greeting, which my father took in stride.

"Wow, you sure are popular, huh, Mina?" he said. "No wonder you're stressed. Fighting off guys left and right."

"She's very popular," Yejun said in English, while Jihoon looked desperately between us, unsure what was happening. "Everyone loves her."

"They don't," I said. I turned to my dad. "Thank you for coming, but I'm not hungry."

My dad's expression fell. "But you texted me that you wanted BBQ," he said, pulling his phone out of his pocket. He struggled for an embarrassingly long amount of time to navigate his own phone, then showed me his most recent text, a single ominous word.

From: Mina Bean 🖤
BBQ

I frowned. As much as I loved Korean BBQ, I definitely hadn't texted him that. I'd been too preoccupied with Yejun and Jihoon to even think about dinner yet.

Yet...

I thought back to Yejun's organic Echo in the café. Maybe I wasn't thinking about dinner *right now*, but I definitely would be in the future. The message had clearly come from my phone, so it must have been from some version of me. Another Mina had sent it.

And if she had, there was definitely a reason for it.

"Oh yeah, I forgot about that," I said quickly. "Just so busy with school, you know." I turned to Jihoon. "I'm so sorry, can we catch up later?"

I squeezed his hand, which was maybe too forward in front of my dad, but it made Jihoon blush and nod quickly. He probably would have agreed to climb into a one-way rocket to the moon if I'd asked him in that moment.

"Yeah, of course," Jihoon said. "You should spend time with your dad."

I flashed Yejun a smug grin. He couldn't fight for my time when Jihoon had so graciously handed me over to my dad.

"No worries, Mina," Yejun said smoothly, as if he were the one I'd apologized to. "Jihoon and I can hang out while you're gone."

My stomach dropped. Yejun wouldn't try to ruin my infiltration mission just to annoy me, would he? It wasn't like he could just tell Jihoon I was using him to get points with the other time travelers.

"You want to hang out with me?" Jihoon said, blinking at Yejun.

"Perfect!" my dad said, clapping his hands together. "I bet you boys could use some guy time anyway."

"Oh, absolutely!" Yejun said, slinging an arm around Jihoon's shoulders and yanking him close a little too harshly, his smile sharp. "We'll have lots of fun."

"That settles it," my dad said. "Come on, Mina, I made a reservation at your favorite barbecue place."

"Okay," I said weakly, casting a wary glance at Yejun and Jihoon as I followed my dad down the hill.

"I got it," my dad said, snatching the tongs from my hands and laying sheets of pork belly across the grill on the table before I could do it first. My dad liked to call the person who manned the grill "Meat Daddy" even though I'd repeatedly told him he wasn't allowed to say that in public.

He'd brought me to a BBQ restaurant in Hapjeong, which wasn't that busy on a weekday. I'd stuffed my backpack and school jacket into a plastic bag so they wouldn't absorb the smell of meat, then gone to town on the kimchi while we waited for the pork to cook.

I couldn't remember the last time I'd sat down for a meal with either of my parents. As my dad hummed the tune that our rice cooker played when it finished and crammed the grill full of way too much meat, I realized he had more gray hair than I'd remembered, that the smile lines around his eyes had carved deeper into his skin. Was the stress of his job wearing him down, or was he just getting older? Even though we lived together, I felt a bit like a boarding school student who only saw her parents on holidays. I put some extra kimchi on his plate and helped him rearrange the meat on the grill so everything would cook evenly.

"What do you think about Hokkaido?" my dad said as he dropped some slightly scorched meat on my plate.

Hokkaido was on the northernmost island in Japan. We'd taken a sleeper train there a few years ago for Christmas. I remembered little of it except the hot springs and fishing out moss balls called marimo from the lake and pretending they were little green pets.

"I guess it's nice," I said between bites of meat.

"Great!" my dad said, waving a piece of pork in the air. "Because we're moving there!"

My chopsticks clattered to the table, precious meat lost to the floor.

"*What?*" I said.

"We've been transferred," my dad said, adding more meat to my plate, as if that would distract me.

I shook my head, my appetite gone. "When?" I said.

"Well, your mother and I are leaving on the fifteenth," my dad said, expression sobering as he seemed to catch on that this wasn't good news to me. "But your supervisor says you have some work to finish up, so you can come the week after you're done."

I shook my head, gripping the edge of the table. The fifteenth was only six days away. How was I supposed to pull up all the anchors of Timeline Beta if I wasn't even in the same country as Yejun? More importantly, would I be able to find Hana in Japan? She'd left the note for me in Seoul, so some part of her was still alive here.

"Are you sad because of your new boyfriend?" my dad said. I grimaced, still not sure if he was talking about Jihoon or Yejun. When I didn't respond, my dad sighed and set down his chopsticks. "I'm sorry, honey," he said. "You know I'd let you stay if it was up to me."

I shook my head. Of course it wasn't up to him—nothing ever was. My parents were only floating agents, so they had no say in their lives and never would.

But I didn't have to live like them.

I was less than ninety points away from getting promoted to a full agent, and Jihoon was the key.

If I could convince him to kiss me, I'd pass the point threshold and could submit my application. Then, if Hyebin was willing to put in a good word, I might actually stand a chance at staying in Seoul and finding Hana.

I let out a breath. *It's not over yet*, I reminded myself. *Hana isn't gone yet*. I drank the rest of my water like a shot of soju, then slammed the cup down.

My dad watched me warily. "Are you gonna be okay, Mina?" he said.

I nodded, my mind already far away as I mapped out my next series of texts to Jihoon. We had a date tomorrow, after all. I would finish the mission then.

"I'm great," I said, stuffing a burnt piece of beef in my mouth and tearing through it with my sharp teeth.

Chapter Twelve

During the two-hour mandatory workshop on scrying pool maintenance that night, I'd missed three calls and twenty-one texts from my dad. I nearly dropped my phone as I scrolled through the notifications, sure that absolutely everyone must have died.

As soon as I unlocked my phone, a picture of a fat panda sitting in a basketball hoop filled the screen.

I blinked, then scrolled down through my dad's texts, which were all pictures of pandas behaving like large furry toddlers. At the very end he'd asked if I wanted fried chicken for dinner tomorrow, complete with six chicken emojis.

Clearly I hadn't done a very good job concealing how much I didn't want to move, and now he was worried. Annoyingly, he also seemed to think food solved all my problems. And pandas, though I was fine with that part.

I'd typed out half a response when a hand seized my backpack strap.

I let out an undignified squawk as I was yanked back, catching the attention of a couple waiting in line at the pharmacy ten feet from me. *Am I really being jumped between a ramen shop and an Emart?* I thought.

I whirled around, wincing as my backpack seams let out a tearing sound. But instead of a masked robber or armed descendant or even Hyebin fetching me for another mission, it was only Kim Yejun.

"Oh, it's just you," I said, relaxing my shoulders.

"Yes, *just me*, who you ditched even though we had work to do," he said, glaring at me.

I thought of the girl I'd seen him with that morning, his hand around her waist, the way he'd looked down at her so kindly. I clenched my teeth and sharpened that feeling into anger, rather than risk crying.

"You do plenty of things outside of work, but I can't?" I said, crossing my arms.

Yejun raised an eyebrow. "What are you talking about?"

I shook my head. "Where's Jihoon?" I said, ignoring his question.

"I didn't kill him, if that's what you're implying," Yejun said, rolling his eyes. "He had to go to tutoring. Now, can we get back to saving the world, or did you want to play around with Jihoon some more?"

"I'm not playing with him!" I said. "And even if I was, I would rather do that than spend a single second with you!"

"Why are you suddenly mad at me?" Yejun said, throwing his arms up. "I mean, I know you're not my biggest fan, but you're acting like I spit in your coffee."

Because you can't just take me on what is basically a date and then put your hand on another girl's waist, I thought. *You can't bring me cheesecake and hold my hand and put your arm around me if it doesn't mean anything to you, because it means something to* me.

"I'm not mad at you," I said, looking away. "You're projecting."

"You're mad about *something*," he said. Then he pointed at me. "There, that facial expression! You're angry."

"Who *wouldn't* be angry around you?" I said. "You're smug, and annoying, and can't take a hint! You tried to mess up my infiltration mission. You think the world revolves around you and that I have nothing better to do than wait around for you. You think so highly of yourself, right down to your stupid blond hair!"

Yejun pouted. "You don't like my blond hair?"

"Why is that the part you're stuck on?" I said. "And no! I mean, if anything, you're way too aware of how good it looks. You're so full of yourself."

His face brightened. "You think it looks good?"

I let out a frustrated sound and turned away as a sharp pain bloomed across my palms. I looked down at my hands, which had four even cuts across each palm, bleeding slowly.

Yejun appeared over my shoulder. "I think you need to trim your nails," he said.

"No one asked you!" I said way too loudly. Everyone on the sidewalk turned to look in our direction.

Yejun let out an awkward laugh and grabbed my arm, tugging me down the sidewalk. "Can you keep it down?" he said under his breath. "I don't want to be the star of a K-drama."

I don't care what you want! was what I was about to shout back at him, onlookers be damned. But then he put his arm over my shoulders and tugged me close as a car raced down the narrow road, the side mirror nearly clipping my arm.

"And watch where you're going," he said. "I know you like sugar, but try your best not to actually become a pancake."

Any intelligent response melted away. I could feel Yejun's heartbeat through his side, which was still pressed against mine. I'd always thought I was too tall for Korea, but I fit so perfectly under his arm, two puzzle pieces slotted neatly together.

"Now," he said, finally releasing me, "how do you feel about sushi?"

"I thought you wanted to talk about saving the world," I said stiffly.

"I do, and we can do that over sushi," he said. "So do you like it or not?"

I frowned as he led us down a side street. This was a residential area, with no sushi restaurants that I was aware of.

"Are you assuming I like sushi because I'm Japanese?"

"I'm assuming you like sushi because everyone likes sushi, and you need to occasionally eat something besides cheesecake," he said. "There's a sushi place in 2010 near the next adjustment—which I was *trying* to tell you about today. Would that work?"

I crossed my arms, thinking it over. I didn't want him to get used to smoothing over his flaws with food.

But . . . my mom always said that there was very little that some good sushi couldn't fix. If I had to travel with Yejun anyway, I might as well get a meal out of it.

"It better be good," I said. "You're talking to someone who lived in Japan. I know good sushi."

"Oh, this is good, believe me," Yejun said as he grinned and walked faster down the street. He stopped suddenly, looked around, then yanked me down behind a parked car.

"No cameras here," he said, rubbing his hands together. "Okay, 2010, April 11, 14:45:11." Then he held his hand out, fingertips already sparkling blue.

I hesitated, remembering the last time we'd shared magic. For a brief moment, I felt like I'd seen Yejun's soul. Did that mean he had seen mine as well? I pictured his soft brown eyes unmaking me, tearing away every part of the human mask that I wore until there was nothing but time magic and dragon fire that no one else had ever seen.

Though I didn't reach out, ribbons of his magic unfurled from his fingertips, tracing gently across my cheeks. At their touch, I felt like sunlight bloomed inside me, my vision sparkling gold at the edges—that same feeling of weightlessness as before.

Slowly, I set my hand in his.

Our magic knit together instantly this time, the indigo light brightening, still tangled with both light blue and deep purple.

Like northern lights.

I jolted, because the thought wasn't mine. It echoed through me in Yejun's voice. I looked up at the blue light in his eyes.

Our magic together, he said. *It looks like the northern lights.*

I've never seen them, I thought. I didn't know if Yejun could hear me, but he smiled as if he could.

No need, he said. *This is better.*

· 🦋 ·

"You're right," I said—two words I never thought I would say to Kim Yejun, of all people. I put a piece of salmon egg sushi in my mouth and took my time before swallowing, ignoring Yejun's look of triumph. "This is the best sushi I've had outside of Japan."

"The sushi chef is from Ishikawa," Yejun said, stealing a piece off my plate. "You should know that I wouldn't joke about something as serious as sushi with a Japanese girl."

I groaned and leaned back in my seat. "I think I might explode if I keep eating, but there's no way I'm throwing any of this away."

"It would be a great sacrifice, but I think I could help you with that," Yejun said, reaching forward to snatch another piece.

I smacked his chopsticks away with my own. "Get your own sushi," I said.

"I'm paying," he said, pouting.

"I thought this was a gift?"

"*I* thought we lived in a civilized society where people shared."

"You thought incorrectly," I said.

Yejun laughed. "Fine, I should know better than to get between a girl and her sushi," he said, pushing his plate toward me. "Save a piece of salmon, though. We need to feed it to a pigeon."

"For the adjustment?"

"No, for my amusement," he said. "Yes, for the adjustment. You think I would waste salmon this good?"

"That's the only reason I would give up a piece of this to anyone," I said, taking a sip of water. "Are you going to tell me what you needed to talk about?"

Yejun shook his head. "You're trying to make me talk so I can't eat sushi."

I rolled my eyes and set my chopsticks on the table, holding my hands up in surrender. Yejun quickly popped a piece of my sushi in his mouth before setting his down too.

He fished out two folded pieces of paper from his pocket and slid them toward me. I raised an eyebrow, but he only gestured for me to take them. I unfolded them both and set them side by side.

Two copies of an article on dung beetles.

"This one is from before we made the change," Yejun said, tapping the article on the left, "and the one on the right is from this morning."

I used my dragon eyes to quickly scan for differences. Immediately, one line of text stood out to me. In the first article, it said:

The dung beetle was an insect native to the Korean Peninsula and Jeju Island, presumed extinct after a drop in population in the 1970s.

The article on the right said:

The dung beetle is an insect native to the Korean Peninsula and Jeju Island.

I looked up at Yejun, who grinned expectantly.

"We saved the dung beetles?" I said.

Yejun nodded quickly. "We're shifting in the right direction."

I'm getting closer to Hana, I thought. I could almost feel her next to me right now, leaning against my arm, snatching pieces of sushi off my place. I imagined her warmth, the scratchiness of her striped sweater against my arm, the way she might tie her hair back with a black elastic. Soon, she would be real.

I felt tears that I knew I couldn't stop, so I did the only logical thing: stuffed a bunch of wasabi in my mouth.

"*What are you doing?*" Yejun said, drawing back.

"I just love wasabi," I said as my eyes watered. I didn't have to pretend not to cry now—the wasabi was doing its job.

"I can tell," Yejun said, pulling out his phone and taking a picture before I could wipe my face.

"Delete that!" I said, grabbing a bunch of napkins and scrubbing my face before he could take any more pictures.

"Never," he said, clutching his phone protectively to his chest. "This is amazing blackmail material."

"*Do you want to die?*" I said, hurling a soiled napkin at his face. He laughed and looked as if he was about to respond, but then his gaze flickered to something behind me. I turned around just as another Yejun in a blue raincoat stormed across the restaurant.

The Yejun in front of me tried to stand up, but the Echo reached him first, snatched his water off the table, and poured it over his head.

"Idiot," the Echo said, then stormed away, casting the tin cup to the ground.

Yejun tossed his phone to a dry corner of the table, then wiped his face with the back of his sleeve. As his phone spun toward me, I caught a glimpse of his unread texts. My tears dried up as I read the name of the sender: *Mom*.

"Mom?" I echoed, looking up at Yejun, who had frozen with a handful of napkins. My gaze fell to his tattoo. "Your mom who you told me was erased?"

When Yejun didn't deny it, dread gnawed through my stomach. Yejun's phone screen went dark as he set down the napkins and looked away.

I should have been angry, but when the heat under my skin and the gold at the edges of my vision had faded away, I only felt cold.

"You lied to me?" I said. The words didn't feel real as they left my lips, like this was some strange dream. He was the only person I'd ever told about Hana, but now I wanted so badly to take that moment back. I'd traded my most precious secret for a lie.

I stood up to leave but froze at Yejun's next words.

"I thought it was true," he said, staring at the sushi scattered across the table. It was the quietest I'd ever heard him speak. "My dad told me she was erased and gave me a note on a napkin that he said she'd left for me. Last year, I got it tattooed on my arm."

I sat back down slowly. Not because his story made any sense yet, but because I had never seen him look so dejected, sapped of all his usual light and energy.

"I worked so hard before I went rogue," he said. "That's how I got so good at running scenarios. I thought if I got promoted, I could find out more about her, maybe even bring her back. Then, a few months ago, she called me." Yejun swallowed, tracing the lines of his tattoo with his left hand. "It turned out that my dad lied. She wasn't erased and she never wrote me a note. She just left because she didn't want me."

He looked up, his dull gaze meeting mine. "She wants to talk to me now, but it's too late. So I'm sorry that I lied to you, Mina, but it was because I liked that story better than the truth."

As he slumped back down against the booth, I tried to conjure anger but could only think of the sadness I'd tasted through his magic, the soft ache of grief. I thought of my own mother walking out on me, the gaping hole it would leave in my life and my heart. At least I could direct my grief over Hana toward the people who had taken her from me, but Yejun's mother had chosen to leave him.

My fingers felt warm, and I glanced down at purple ribbons of magic blooming to life in my palm, starting to reach toward Yejun. I clenched my fist and they disappeared.

Even if I wasn't angry, I wouldn't let him off the hook that easily. "No one gets to rewrite their life story," I said quietly.

There was no anger behind my words, but Yejun winced and looked away as if I'd scolded him. "You don't get it," he whispered. "Your parents want you."

Less than they want their jobs, I thought. But I knew what he meant, and didn't want to be pedantic about it. "But your mom wants to be part of your life again, right?"

Yejun shook his head. "She wants money. I gave her some, which I know I shouldn't have. But it wasn't enough, and now she's upset. I'm worthless to her if I'm not an ATM."

I didn't know how to respond. There were no words in any language that could fix this.

"Maybe she's right," Yejun said, stabbing a piece of sushi with a chopstick but making no move to eat it. "I worked so hard but have nothing to show for it but dung beetles."

"She's wrong," I said, frowning. "You're not worthless."

Yejun looked up, this time looking at me rather than through me, like he'd just remembered I was there.

"You're trying to save the world and are doing a good enough job at it to not destroy the timeline," I said. "That's worth something. It's worth a lot, actually."

Yejun set his chopsticks down, blinking at me like I'd just spoken a foreign language. I realized—too late—that I had actually sounded . . . *nice*.

Heat rushed to my face. I pressed back against the booth, crossing my arms and looking away. "I just mean that if you were totally incompetent, then that would make *me* incompetent for working with you. And I know I'm not great at calculus but I wouldn't hand my life over to someone who didn't seem halfway intelligent, and—"

"Thank you," Yejun said quietly, halting my deluge of words. I dared to glance back at him just in time to see him putting more sushi on my plate. "Here, eat more before you start sounding too nice and your soul climbs out of your body."

I picked up my chopsticks but hesitated before taking any more food.

"Kim Yejun," I said. "Don't ever lie to me again."

Yejun went still, as if pinned in place by my gaze. Then his shoulders slumped and he set down his chopsticks, bowing slightly. "Of course," he said. "I'm sorry, Mina. I only—"

"I understand why you did it," I said. "And you're right, I don't know what it's like to not have parents. So I'll forgive you, just this once. But this is the last time."

He nodded, bowing again. "Understood."

Satisfied, I finally grabbed another piece of sushi. Yejun looked up hesitantly, as if afraid I would jump across the table and bite him. When he saw me eating, his shoulders relaxed and he checked his watch.

"It's almost time," he said.

He wrapped a piece of sushi in his napkin, then slipped outside. I watched through the window as he held the fish up to a pigeon, who snatched it out of his hand, nearly biting his fingers off. I stifled a laugh as he jogged back into the restaurant.

"And that pigeon is going to single-handedly save the *Sewol* ferry?" I said.

"Not quite," Yejun said. "This is actually the biggest adjustment yet, and the causes are complex, so it will take a few more adjustments."

That wasn't surprising. The *Sewol* ferry sank in 2014 in the sea between Incheon and Jeju, killing hundreds of high school students. People had blamed a lot of different things—the crew, the coast guard, the president . . . it wasn't clear exactly what the main cause was, so it made sense that there were multiple factors that had to be changed.

"The pigeon will be too full after the sushi and will sleep in a tree, where a cat will kill it and bring it to its owner," Yejun went on. "The owner will scream in terror and pass out, smack his head on the table and get a concussion. That will knock a few points off his college entrance exam, and he won't get into his top school, so he'll decide to do his military service in the navy right away. He'll join the crew for a few different merchant ships, and eventually he'll get a job on the MV *Sewol* instead of one of the crew members who abandoned ship."

As he finished talking, Yejun gave a melodramatic bow, as if he'd just won an Olympic medal. "It's brilliant, I know."

"It's . . . elaborate," I said—the closest I wanted to get to actually complimenting him again. "And none of that will cause unwanted ripple effects?"

Yejun shook his head. "The vast majority of ripple effects are inconsequential. Most butterflies don't actually cause typhoons all on their own. A lot of factors have to line up for the typhoon to happen, and the butterfly is only one of them. It's actually not that hard to implement change without negative effects if you know what you're doing. The problem is, back when they first discovered time magic, no one knew what they were doing."

I blinked as his words sank in. It was so contrary to everything I'd learned in my descendant classes. "Then why do they teach us to be so neutral and obey the 'almighty timeline'?" I said.

Yejun rolled his eyes. "Because they don't want you making changes on your own. *They* want to be the ones who call the shots."

Then he straightened up and glanced at his watch. "But at any rate, the sushi in and of itself isn't going to save the ferry. The watermelons should help with that."

"Watermelons?" I echoed.

"Don't worry about that yet," he said, standing up. "I only calculated for a half-hour meal, so we should go back. Meet me in the bathroom in five."

He went up front to pay, and after four awkward minutes sitting alone, I followed him to the accessible restroom. I knocked twice, then Yejun cracked the door open and glanced around the hallway before letting me in and locking the door behind us.

"Duty calls," he said, smiling half-heartedly and holding out his hand. I reached for him, part of me alarmed at how natural the gesture felt, how familiar I now was with the color of his magic, the way it felt like silk caressing my skin and sunlight blooming in my bones.

The mirror shattered.

Yejun shielded his face as shards flew at both of us, white light spilling from behind the mirror like a dam unstopped. Whiteness crashed through the bathroom, peeling color from the walls, ripping up the tiles. *Another paradox*, I thought, scrambling back against the far wall.

Then the floor tiles disintegrated, and I dropped into the void.

Instantly, my whole body went numb. My mouth tasted like static, my vision blurry and monochrome. Below me, a vast canyon of nothingness yawned open like a stark white sea. Wind roared in my ears, tearing my hair in front of me, which I could see was slowly turning white.

A hand closed around my wrist, halting my fall.

Yejun was perched on the edge of the hole in the bathroom floor, holding me up. Blue light sparked between our skin, his warmth spreading through me. His eyes were wide, a screaming wind whipping his hair around his face.

"We have to go!" he shouted, sending a pulse of magic toward me.

I tried to move my hand toward the box of time magic in my pocket, but everything had gone numb.

"I can't move!" I said.

"*Try!*" Yejun said, looking around desperately.

The wind tore out my ponytail holder, more of my hair turning silver as it blew in front of my face. My feet were completely numb now, like they weren't there at all. What would happen if I was sucked into a paradox? Would it be just like being erased? Or would the timeline chew me up and spit me out in spaghetti strands?

Hana, I thought desperately. *You said you'd protect me.*

Warmth surged through my hand, brighter than before. My hair blew out of my line of vision, and there was Yejun, forcing more time magic into me.

"The descendants will be able to track you!" I said, shaking my head. Wasn't that the whole point of working together? Past a certain threshold, he would light up like a Christmas tree on the agency's radar.

The wind spiraled even louder around us. The only light I could see anymore was Yejun's eyes, searing blue from time magic. The only thing I could feel was his claws hooked into my wrist, tethering me to him, blood running down my forearm. He closed his eyes, whispering something to himself, and then a wave of time magic surged into my bloodstream.

It felt like Yejun had breathed me into his soul. His heart unfolded and lush green mountains filled the horizon, stark white skies blooming overhead. He was a thousand quiet summer mornings and warm citron tea, the scent of white silk drying on a line beneath the afternoon sun, soft grass and forbidden hope.

But the sun fell below the horizon, shadows suffocating the bright sky. There was that bone-deep ache of sadness that I'd glimpsed before, but this time it screamed within the tight cage of my bones.

Yejun's human face could pretend to be confident and careless, but the map of his soul whispered the truth to me.

The ground turned to glass between my feet, broken shards biting into my soles and plummeting into an abyss of hungry darkness. Gray clouds blurred my vision, choking me with freezing water, and I didn't realize until it was too late that I was tumbling into the empty sky.

And there, beyond the clouds, was . . . *me*.

There I was, asleep in a library on Yejun's shoulder as he read a book by warm lamplight. It was a moment that had never happened, but somehow I could feel the lamp's gentle glow, the scent of old paper, the softness of the blanket he draped over my shoulders.

And there I was again, sipping coffee across from Yejun at a café, walking beside him along the stream, pressed close to him in a packed subway car. They were moments I'd never lived, days that had never happened, yet each one felt glass-sharp in its vividness. Were these Yejun's dreams? The wishes he hid deep inside his heart? Somehow, I had a home within Yejun's soul.

I stepped into myself, no longer watching from above but beside him in a whispering field of silver grass beneath a white sky.

Mina, his soul said as he tucked my hair behind my ear, his touch as gentle as the silken grass swaying around us. I had the name of a spy and a liar, but from Yejun's lips, it sounded bright and true. I moved closer, letting him pull me in by my waist as he leaned over me and blocked the soft edge of the sun . . .

I crashed onto my side on concrete.

A car horn blared at me and I flinched at the sound, pushing myself up on my elbows.

I was back in Eungam—I recognized the intersection near the fruit stands, the café on the corner. The sudden brightness of the streetlights and solidness of the ground was so jarring that I wondered if I'd actually been hit by the car. But all my limbs were still there—tangled with Yejun's, in fact—and there was no pain, just a searing numbness like my whole body had fallen asleep.

Yejun scrambled to his feet and looked around.

"Yejun," I said, "did you actually—"

"I have to go!" he said, turning off and running.

I tried to follow him, but the driver of the car stepped out and stood in front of me. "I didn't hit you did I?" he said. A small crowd had gathered at the scene, so I hurried to my feet, brushing off my shirt.

"I'm fine," I said, and promptly stumbled against the side of the car because my legs were so numb. "Really, I'm fine," I said, hurrying away before anyone could call an ambulance. I melted into the crowd on the main road, slowly reminding myself of the feeling of shoes on my feet, sidewalk beneath me, one step at a time. After about a block, I was starting to feel normal again.

I looked back at the street where Yejun had run away, as if I could conjure him through sheer willpower. I thought of my own face carved into his sky, the scenes of us together that lived only in his heart.

I didn't know what to make of it. Yejun had never said anything out loud that suggested these were his dreams, and dreams that stayed locked in your heart didn't matter. Maybe our time magic tangling together had branded me into his soul whether he liked it or not.

I imagined the descendants catching him, throwing him to the ground and turning him to ash, all because he'd taken a risk to save me. The thought of Hong Gildong sinking his claws into Yejun made me want to burn headquarters to the ground.

But I knew that if I wanted Yejun to be safe, I had to keep my distance for now. Drawing more attention to him would be dangerous. Even though my bones screamed for me to turn around and follow him, I forced myself to keep walking home. Yejun was used to being a rogue, he was good at hiding and planning and surviving. I would have to trust that he would be okay.

Chapter Thirteen

My mom seemed blissfully unaware of the parade in my skull as she slammed the cabinets open and shut, rattled silverware in its drawer, and shuffled metal pots and pans around.

I should have been grateful someone else was home at all, because I couldn't have peeled myself from the couch if I'd wanted to—the overhead light was too painful. My mom plonked a cup of tea on the coffee table and sat down at my feet, rubbing a hand up and down my legs.

"Drink that when it's cool," she said. "It will help your headache."

I groaned. "Is it some Japanese drug again?" Once, my mom had sent me to some herbalist for insomnia who'd prescribed me a tea that knocked me out cold for fourteen hours.

"No," my mom said. "It has a shot of bourbon."

I cracked an eye open. "Seriously?"

"You're legally allowed to drink now, and it works on timesickness!" she said, putting her hands up defensively.

"I don't think this is timesickness," I said. "I don't have any open loops. Hyebin already checked for me."

In fact, she'd checked again today when I'd called out sick because of my headache.

My mom frowned and jabbed a finger behind my right ear. Pain flared where she'd touched, making me wince.

"It's classic timesickness," she said, leaning back and crossing her arms.

At first I thought it was a trick of light, but my gaze focused on her pinky finger, which was a different color from her other fingers. It looked oddly gray, blue veins visible beneath the surface, the skin wrinkled and nail yellowed.

"What happened to your finger?" I said.

My mom froze, recrossing her arms so I couldn't see. "What finger?" she said.

"You know what finger."

"It's nothing to worry about," she said, standing up and pretending to rearrange the cereal boxes, her back turned to me. "I got caught in a timeline fluctuation. It doesn't hurt, it's just a bit . . . aged. Like your new hairdo."

I sat up, wincing as the blood rushed from my head. "Can you fix it? What did your boss say?"

"My pinky is hardly a priority when the whole timeline is falling apart," my mom said.

Hyebin had told me that the timeline was not, in fact, falling apart, but she'd been known to lie. The good news was that she hadn't burst into my apartment to arrest me for timeline interference, which meant that Yejun was probably right about it not being our fault.

"Did you even ask?" I said.

"Mina, it's fine," my mom said. "I trust the descendants to figure it out, don't you?"

I took a sip of tea rather than answer, which seemed to satisfy my mom, who tucked my white hair behind my ear and headed back into the kitchen. I coughed as the bourbon burned down my throat, but I could already feel my headache releasing its claws from my skull.

As the fog cleared from my vision, it occurred to me that my mom hadn't even asked about my being caught in a timeline fluctuation.

She clearly assumed that a paradox was the cause of my white hair, but there was no *Oh my gosh, Mina, are you okay?* or *Did you see the medics?* or things that I knew moms were supposed to say when their only children were nearly devoured by the timeline. Last night, my dad had raised an eyebrow at me while I made myself a cup of coffee at midnight and said "cool hairdo" before kicking his boots off and heading to bed. Did they really trust the descendants that much?

I drained the rest of the teacup and set it down heavily on the coffee table.

They're just busy with work, I thought. *I don't need them fawning over me.*

Soon enough, they would understand. I was going to bring Hana back with me, and they would finally see exactly how much they'd lost.

The bourbon was already going to my head, so of course it seemed like the perfect time to try to dye my hair before I saw Hyebin again. The moment she saw three new stripes of silver in my hair, she'd know I'd gotten caught in another paradox and hadn't told her. I couldn't exactly explain that I'd been traveling on an unauthorized sushi date with Yejun.

I fumbled with the box of black hair dye I'd grabbed from Emart and realized belatedly that I'd forgotten latex gloves. I shrugged and started the process of dyeing both my hair and half my bathroom black as my phone lit up with a text.

I hurried to wash the dye off my hands and seized my phone from the edge of the bathtub. Yejun hadn't responded to my texts or shown up at school since running off yesterday. I hoped that meant he was hiding and being extra careful, not that he'd been caught because he used too much of his own magic to save me. The only thing keeping the panic at bay was the fact that I was still very much here and not being dragged off by a neutralization team, which meant no one had found out what Yejun and I had done.

When I tapped my phone screen and it lit up with a text from Jihoon, I sighed before I could help it, then immediately felt guilty for being disappointed.

From: Kim Jihoon
On my way! 😊

I frowned in confusion for a moment before gasping and dropping my phone to the floor.

I'm supposed to have dinner with Jihoon tonight!

I turned on the shower and frantically washed my hair even though I hadn't dyed all the silver strands yet, already mentally preparing my outfit and the half dozen excuses I could use that wouldn't make Jihoon hate me for being so late. I pictured him waiting at the restaurant with that same sad look on his face as when I'd run away at the river.

But then, like always, my thoughts shifted from Jihoon straight to Yejun. I imagined that Yejun was the one waiting for me at a restaurant, not just for work but because he liked me as much as Jihoon did. Yejun pulling out my chair for me, Yejun holding my hand as we left the restaurant, Yejun putting his hand on my waist and . . .

I turned the water all the way to cold to force myself out of the shower, or else I was going to be even later than I already was.

It occurred to me that I could always cancel on Jihoon. He would be sad, but probably a lot less sad than if I kissed him and then dumped him after. The idea of kissing anyone but Yejun felt wrong . . .

But why should it? It wasn't as if Yejun had staked his claim on my mouth, much less my heart. Why should I give up my mission—and any hope of finding my sister—for Yejun, who had no problem seeing other girls?

Jihoon deserved better than me, but if I had to choose between him and Hana, I would choose Hana every time.

I seared my mouth with mouthwash until I couldn't taste bourbon anymore, scorched my hair with a blow dryer, then hurried out to catch the train, still feeling as if the world was slightly off-kilter, thanks to the bourbon.

I put on some mascara and lip gloss on the train using my phone camera, then sprinted up the subway stairs at top speed. Somehow, against all odds, I made it to the date only twenty minutes late.

Jihoon stood waiting outside a ramen restaurant in Hongdae, backlit by white paper lanterns with tiny red cat faces painted on them. He was wearing a blue button-down shirt and holding a single pink rose in one hand. He brightened when he saw me, as if he wasn't actually sure that I would come.

"I'm so sorry I'm late," I said, jogging up to him. "I got caught up with work."

"It's no problem," he said. "I'm just glad you came."

"Of course I came!" I said, smiling. He flinched a bit, and I got the impression I was talking too loudly, that my smile was too tight across my face. My mom had truly picked the worst night to slip me a shot of bourbon. "I've been looking forward to this all week."

Jihoon smiled back, but it was thin, like he could smell the lie. "Really?" he said. "I feel like I get mixed signals from you sometimes."

Yes, because Yejun keeps trying to sabotage everything, I thought, hoping my smile hid my sudden urge to commit murder.

"That's strange," I said. I turned and gestured toward the rose. "Is that for me?"

Jihoon nodded quickly and held it out to me. "I picked out the prettiest one I could find, but it's still not as pretty as you," he said quietly, his voice shaking like he'd rehearsed the line before coming here. Something about his sincerity made me suddenly feel rotten inside. This meant something to him.

"Thank you," I said quietly, taking the rose. He'd even broken off the thorns. I slid my hand into his. "Come on, I'm hungry."

Like always, he grinned and followed me without question.

I truly, sincerely, did my best to listen to Jihoon tell me about his summer vacation to Japan. He knew a lot about Kyoto and asked me if I knew anything about the different palaces he'd visited, so sweetly careful not to act like an expert when he knew I was Japanese. But my mind kept wandering back to the wave of white devouring the bathroom, the way that Yejun had ripped me away from its teeth. I couldn't talk to Jihoon about the most important part of my life without putting him in danger. I had to smile in front of him and pretend to be a normal high school girl even when I felt like I was clinging to the back of a moving train. All his problems felt so minor compared to the world I was trying to hold together.

I pinched my leg under the table to ground myself in the present. I was here to finish my mission so I could stay in Seoul and save Hana. I could do it for her.

I was doing my best to nod emphatically as Jihoon talked but realized I must have missed something when he stopped and stared at me.

Quickly, I wiped my mouth on a napkin. "Sorry, did you ask me something?" I said. "I just . . . this ramen is so good, I kind of forgot what planet I was on for a second."

Jihoon laughed. "I'm happy you like it," he said. "I just asked if you wanted to go to the bunny café with me next week?"

Next week? Yep, I just need to go save the Sewol ferry from sinking a couple decades ago, then I can go pet some bunnies.

"I'd love to!" I said, because that was the right answer, the one that he wanted. "Have you ever seen videos of that architect who only builds bunny mansions?"

Jihoon's eyes went wide. "No, but I need to. Right this minute."

I grinned and started to dig through my purse for my phone. I'd thrown everything a bit haphazardly from my school bag into a somewhat nice-looking bag for the date, and my phone was currently swimming somewhere at the bottom.

A shadow fell over me. I looked up as someone wearing a hoodie drew to a stop in front of the table. I barely caught a glimpse of my own face before the Echo grabbed what remained of my ramen and dumped it into my purse.

"Are you serious?" I said, shooting to my feet as the hooded Echo ran off. Jihoon stood up too but luckily didn't try to chase down the Echo, saving me from having to make up a story about an evil twin.

I frantically dumped my purse out on the table as the Echo disappeared. I fished out my phone, which was already damp, the screen flickering dangerously. I bundled it in napkins, praying it somehow recovered. My wallet was slowly soaking up pork broth, which was rapidly spilling across the floor. I swore and tried to wipe it up with napkins as an employee appeared with a mop.

"Are you . . . okay . . ." Jihoon trailed off, clearly dumbfounded.

"It's fine," I said. "At least I ate most of it first."

To my surprise, Jihoon laughed. He grabbed a few more napkins and leaned over to help me clean off the table.

"What's so funny?" I said, still mummifying my phone in napkins.

Jihoon shrugged. "I don't know," he said, still giggling. "Everything is funny with you. You make things interesting."

I let out an incredulous laugh. *That's a generous way to put it*, I thought. Jihoon kept laughing—he truly had a ridiculous laugh, which sounded like squeaky windshield wipers—and soon I was laughing too. Why not? My bag was full of pork broth and noodles and I had to stop the apocalypse. My whole life was absurd.

Miraculously, my phone seemed to have survived the ordeal, though I couldn't say the same for my bag. Jihoon paid while I stuffed my bag with napkins and we headed outside. The sun had set and Hongdae glowed with neon street signs. A crowd was gathered around a group doing some K-pop dance, and I pressed closer to Jihoon so we could squeeze through. He put a hand on my waist to guide me, and at last we emerged on the other side.

It was slightly quieter here, the K-pop music a distant soundtrack to the night.

"Mina," Jihoon said airily. Something about his tone sounded so gentle, so earnest, that I turned around at once. He had such big brown eyes, which looked even bigger behind his glasses. He reached into his pocket and held something out to me. In the darkness, I couldn't figure out what it was at first. But then my breath caught in my throat when I realized.

The bracelet he'd picked for me.

"You fished this out of the stream?" I said.

"Of course," he said. "I got it for you. If you still want it, I mean."

He looked away, his cheeks pink. I took the bracelet from his hand and slipped it onto my wrist, the cool beads tight against my racing pulse.

"Thank you," I said. "Seriously, Jihoon, thank you. This was nice."

Jihoon's whole face was pink now. I took a step forward, but my foot slipped off the curb. Jihoon caught me by the waist and steadied me before I could fall on top of a storm drain. He didn't move his hand from my back as I straightened up. We were so close now, and all I could think was that he could definitely smell all the ramen on my breath.

"Jihoon," I whispered, not sure why I said his name. It was hard to think with him so close. *I'm so sorry*, I thought. *I wish I could be the person you want, the person you deserve.*

I stayed perfectly still—it didn't count if *I* kissed *him*—and dropped my gaze to his lips.

This time, he took the hint.

Jihoon leaned down and pressed his lips to mine.

It was such a soft, gentle kiss that lasted only a moment, like a flower petal brushing against my cheek as it fluttered into the sky.

I did it, I thought, my whole body alight as I tallied the points in my mind. I would get to stay in Seoul, where I would find my sister. Yejun and I would fix the timeline and get rid of Hong Gildong and all his corruption.

Then Jihoon pulled back with a smile, bumping his nose against mine, and let out a nervous laugh. He hugged me, tucking my face over his shoulder, and as I felt how fast his heart was beating, any trace of happiness melted out of me.

The fate of the world was supposed to matter so much more than one boy, but it was hard to feel like anything but a monster when Jihoon was so sincerely happy. He'd become yet another pawn in the great chess game of the descendants—his feelings, his life, his future were all expendable. Just like Hana.

My phone vibrated in my pocket, and I seized the excuse to pull away and start unbundling the napkins. Jihoon waited awkwardly as I wiped down my phone and a text from Hyebin appeared across the flickering screen, demanding that I report in.

It was a strange request. I never had shifts with her this late, and my quarterly report wasn't due for a few days, so I was pretty sure I hadn't missed any deadlines. I texted her back asking what she needed me for, but of course she left me on read.

"That's my boss," I said, pocketing my phone. "I have to go."

"Okay," Jihoon said, reaching for my hand. I let him hold it, even though I felt like a corpse he was now puppeting around as he maneuvered me to the subway. He walked me back to the train station and stood close to me in the packed train car, but I couldn't bring myself to look at him. We reached the mouth of the station, where he kissed me again before saying goodbye. I hoped he hadn't noticed how I hadn't kissed him back.

I turned and walked alone through the darkness, toward the heart of the dragons' lair.

Chapter Fourteen

Emart was closed this late at night, so I scanned my key fob at the side door and wound my way around the dark aisles. Only the refrigerator lights remained on after hours, the ghostly glow of milk and yogurt illuminating the polished concrete floor. I clutched my banana milk tribute to my chest as I walked up the frozen escalators, my every footstep echoing down into the basement. I kept glancing over my shoulder, unnerved by how quiet the whole store was, no sounds except for the humming of the refrigerators, which grew farther away as I climbed higher and higher toward the moon.

What could Hyebin possibly want? She worked all hours of the day and night, but the agency was generally good about leaving the agents-in-training alone after ten to do their schoolwork. The dread of not knowing what was in store made me feel like I was treading water in a black sea without a single star overhead.

I stepped into the elevator on the tenth floor and flinched when the doors slammed shut, thinking for a moment that my reflection was an Echo.

Calm down, Mina, I told myself, wiping away smeared mascara. *I know Hyebin is scary, but she would never actually kill you. She's probably just too busy to text you back.*

I repeated the thought again and again in my head until the elevator doors opened, then forced a smile onto my face as I held out the banana milk for Seulgi.

"You're the best," Seulgi said, setting down her paddleball and reaching out for the milk.

I headed for Hyebin's office, but Seulgi waved a hand to stop me. "Actually, you're going that way," she said, pointing to the left hall instead of the right.

I glanced down the hallway, which was dark except for the single door at the far end.

"But Hyebin called me in," I said. "Is she not in her office?"

"Hyebin called you in because Sajangnim wants to see you, and he doesn't like texting," Seulgi said, smiling sympathetically as she gestured once more to Hong Gildong's office at the opposite end of the hall. The long passage seemed endless, a ribbon of deep purple carpet that disappeared into the darkness. A gold dragon's head knocker gleamed in the center of the dark oak door.

I had never been called to Hong Gildong's office before. For a moment, I worried that this meant he'd found out about me and Yejun. But if that were the case, surely a team of neutralizers would have snatched me off the streets, not texted me to come in.

I walked hesitantly down the hallway, my footsteps muffled on the carpet. When I reached the door, I grabbed the ring in the dragon's mouth and knocked, the sound vibrating up the panels.

"Come in!" Hong Gildong called from inside.

Slowly, I shouldered open the heavy doors and stepped into the office.

Hong Gildong sat at a large executive desk, a marble scrying pool in the center. Floor-to-ceiling bookshelves lined the room like sentinels, some shelves packed with old leather tomes and others decorated with gold trinkets—tiny dragons, old coins in frames, embossed vases, even what looked like a gilded stapler. The whole room twinkled like its own galaxy from the sheer number of gold ornaments reflecting the streetlights.

"Mina," Hong Gildong said, rising to his feet. I had forgotten how tall he was, and it took everything in me not to step back as his head blocked the light, his shadow falling over me. "I think congratulations are in order."

I jolted as the door swung shut behind me. "Sajangnim, are you referring to—"

"You've crossed the point threshold," he said. "You're officially eligible for a full-time agent position. So, again, my congratulations."

My gaze darted to the golden clock on the wall. It was 10:15, which meant the timeline had refreshed while I was out with Jihoon. The points had been tallied, so of course Hong Gildong had been alerted.

I bowed quickly. "Thank you, Sajangnim," I said. "It's so kind of you to tell me personally. You really didn't have to."

"Oh, that's not the only reason I needed to speak to you," he said. "You are now *eligible* for a full-time position, but there's one additional layer of screening you need to complete before you can actually be hired."

"Screening?" I echoed, still pressed against the door. I had thought that the moment I kissed Jihoon, I'd get an automatic promotion.

Hong Gildong gestured for me to come closer. I walked stiffly across the carpet and sat in the chair across from his desk.

"All descendants must pass one final exam before they are cleared for independent travel," Hong Gildong said. "Something more challenging than your past assignments, in order to ascertain both your skill and your devotion to our cause."

I nodded, afraid to speak and say something wrong.

"Agent Jang Hyebin, for instance," Hong Gildong went on, "was tasked with destroying the Seongsu Bridge in 1994. A mission that she executed perfectly, leading to her senior agent position within the year."

Hyebin had never mentioned that, but few people probably wanted to chat about sending cars plummeting to the bottom of the river for the greater good. I had always known that the descendants were in the business of preserving truth, not saving lives, but that didn't mean I actually wanted to cause death. What kind of morally questionable assignment would Hong Gildong give to me?

"The timeline architects have selected an assignment for you that is equally challenging, and vital to the stability of the timeline," he said, gesturing for me to sign into the scrying pool on his desk. I wrote my signature across the cool water, trying to still my shaking hands. There was only one new mission waiting for me. I clicked on it, and the document expanded to fill the pool.

```
MISSION 874675
Agent 1475C, Yang Mina
Points: N/A—pass/fail
Date: October 16, 2025
Time: 19:10:00
Location: Front steps of National Assembly
Proceeding Hall
Principal Objective: Shoot presidential
candidate Min Sungho in left eye from distance
of 10.3 meters. Disperse with crowd before
apprehension.
End Objective: Initiate war with North Korea
```

My gaze lingered on the final line. I read it again and again, praying I'd just forgotten how to read Korean because there was *no way* that this was my assignment.

"There's going to be a war?" I whispered. "And I'm supposed to start it?"

Hong Gildong laughed, as if any of this was funny. "There's going to be a war whether you start it or not," he said. "A rogue tried to prevent it, but it was always going to happen. It *needs* to happen. That's the will of the timeline."

I clenched my fists, staring at the scrying pool rather than meeting Hong Gildong's gaze, afraid he would read the fire in my eyes.

The will of the timeline. What a joke. Even if this truly was the original timeline and not Timeline Beta, what made it so sacred and untouchable?

The descendants had no interest in saving lives, reducing suffering, or creating a world that was fairer even though they could have done so easily. They were so enamored with the idea that we were supposed to be neutral, that no one could make an impartial decision so no one should change the timeline at all.

But had the original timeline not already been determined by people in power? Didn't we all shape the timeline merely by standing on it?

It was one thing to bankrupt an amusement park or give a movie star some questionably cooked shrimp, but it was another to start a war. Korea still felt the scars of the last Korean War. Half of my class had grandparents who were war orphans. US military bases loomed over the Yellow Sea decades later. All Korean men still had to serve in the military for two years because of that war. How much damage would another war cause? Plus, North Korea had nuclear weapons now. What if the war caused them to wipe the entire Korean Peninsula off the map? Was "the will of the timeline" worth it?

I carefully smoothed out my facial expression, rehearsing my next words in my mind before I spoke them out loud. "Sajangnim," I said quietly. "Would a war with North Korea endanger our work here?" It wasn't the question I'd wanted to ask, but it was one that would express my reservations without making Hong Gildong mad.

"The descendants will not be in danger," Hong Gildong said easily. "Don't worry, Mina. What we do here is too valuable to risk losing descendants in a surprise attack. There are no surprises when you can see the whole timeline at once. You and your family will be safe."

"And the humans?" I said, daring to look up.

Hong Gildong blinked quickly, as if he hadn't expected the question. "Well, humans die every day," he said with a shrug. "It's inevitable."

"O-of course," I said quickly, dropping my gaze to my lap because his golden glare felt like it was unmaking me.

"Do you still feel compassion for humans, Mina?" Hong Gildong said, a hint of laughter in his voice, like he was asking if I still believed in the Tooth Fairy.

I swallowed, scrambling for a way I could object. "I just—"

"It's not your fault," Hong Gildong said, patting my shoulder. "Compassion is the inevitable result of dragon blood being so diluted with human blood over generations. You will feel it less over time."

"I see," I said, the only polite phrase I could manage. Hong Gildong's grip tightened on my shoulder, and I was sure he could feel the trembling deep in my bones. I felt like prey under his gaze—surely he was scanning my body language, cataloging my responses, making sure I was loyal even now. One careless facial expression could throw away everything I'd worked for.

"It's not supposed to be easy," Hong Gildong went on. Something sharp stung my collarbone, and I realized that his claws were just slightly tearing through my shirt. "That's why it's a final exam. But you've been entrusted with this because we believe you can help us hold the world together. The timeline architects ran through a thousand different scenarios and determined that you have the highest chance of a successful outcome. In part because you look like a rather... unlikely assassin. But also because your infiltration scores are impressive. This is your chance to show us that you'll wield those skills for good."

"That makes sense," I said, the words hollow. I imagined a war-torn Seoul in the window behind Hong Gildong, the ground maroon with blood and dirt, no end to the ruins until the churning black sea that lapped at the ashes on the shore. All because of me.

"Of course, we can't *make* you do anything," Hong Gildong said, releasing my shoulder. Hot blood trickled down my sleeve, but I forced myself not to look, not to show weakness. I sat perfectly still as Hong Gildong rounded his desk and sat in his chair once more. "Should you feel that our interests no longer align, we can discuss... alternate arrangements for you."

Like a brain scrub, I thought. I imagined Hong Gildong's claws extending and cracking my skull open like a chestnut, digging out brain matter and sloughing it on the floor.

One thing was certain: I could never start this war for him.

I had once thought I would do anything to get Hana back, but I'd meant sacrificing any part of *myself*, not other people. I couldn't end the lives of millions of humans in Hana's name.

But if I refused Hong Gildong now, I would lose any chance of restoring the original timeline and finding Hana. I would lose all my memories of learning about Timeline Alpha, and they would find some other descendant to start their war in my place. And this time, my family wouldn't be safe when the bombs fell.

I would have to find a way out of it that didn't leave me dead or with half a brain left, but for now, there was only one right answer, one way that I could leave this room alive.

"There's no need for that," I said, forcing my face into a tight smile. "Our interests have always aligned. I'm honored you would entrust me with a mission of such importance. I promise I'll execute it perfectly."

Hong Gildong watched me for a long moment, as if appraising me. I held my breath as his golden gaze flickered across my face, took in my breathing, probably even counted my heartbeats as if he could taste the lie.

At last, he smiled.

"This will mark the end of your missions with Hyebin," Hong Gildong said. "She'll assist with your firearms training, but after that, you're on your own. It's your chance to show us all you've got. I know you'll do well."

The words chilled my blood. Hong Gildong didn't toss out hollow platitudes—he could see the whole timeline laid out before him, and he must have seen me setting the world on fire.

Chapter Fifteen

Yejun didn't come to school on Monday, and I started seriously considering how to ask Hyebin about it. *Hey, Sunbae-nim, hypothetically speaking, do we have any time jails under Emart where we keep traitors before erasing them? Seen any new traitors lately? Asking for a friend.*

None of my texts were going through to his phone anymore, which I hoped meant he'd turned it off so he couldn't be tracked. All weekend, I'd stayed awake staring at the ceiling, paranoid that I'd miss one of Yejun's texts in the middle of the night, and now I was falling asleep a little bit in class every time I blinked.

At least Jihoon brought me coffee in the morning in addition to Yakult. Unfortunately, he also insisted on holding my hand and escorting me to all my classes even though it made him late for his own, and he had downloaded a date-counting app to track how many days we'd been dating, since apparently we were official now.

As sweet as Jihoon was, I felt like a liar whenever his face lit up at the sight of me. I needed to break it off somehow but couldn't figure out how to do it without feeling like a supervillain. Maybe I could tell him I'd had a religious awakening and had to become a nun, or gradually reduce how often I showered until he found me too gross to be around and lost interest?

But at this point, Jihoon seemed so hopelessly enamored with me that he would probably call my used tissues "art" and donate them to a museum.

And of course, there was the small matter of how to get out of starting a war.

The best solution I could think of at the moment was to "accidentally" miss when I tried to assassinate the politician and pray that Hong Gildong thought I was just nearsighted instead of a traitor, but surely he would either make me try again or give me something even worse to do instead.

I didn't expect Yejun to just hand me a solution, but it would have been nice to at least talk to someone about it. The mission was obviously classified, which meant my parents didn't want to hear about it, and Hyebin was . . . well, Hyebin.

"Have you ever wanted to try an escape room?" Jihoon said as we walked along the stream after school. He'd just bought me a dairy-free bubble tea, and I was gnawing on the straw distractedly.

"No, not really," I said. "I like my leisure time to be as low stakes as possible."

"Oh, uh, me too," Jihoon said quickly. "I hate them, actually."

"You can like escape rooms even if I don't," I said, suddenly tired.

"But I want to spend time doing things *you* like," Jihoon said.

I smiled, even though it felt more like a grimace. The problem was, I didn't know what I liked, because I hardly had time to like things. I liked not failing my classes. I liked not disappointing Hyebin. I liked getting closer to finding Hana. But Jihoon wouldn't understand any of that, and I could never tell him.

Something bounced off the side of my head. I winced and looked up at the tree branches. A falling eunhaeng, maybe?

"What's wrong?" Jihoon said quickly.

"Nothing," I said, taking another sip of bubble tea. "A squirrel dropping acorns or something."

Half a dozen eunhaeng rained down over my head.

I nearly dropped my tea as I stumbled back, glaring at the branches. But before I could curse out any squirrels, I caught a glimpse of blond hair and a sharp smile from up in the branches, shielded by yellow leaves.

I froze, unable to hold back my smile as I locked eyes with Yejun.

I suddenly felt wide awake, my whole body warm and light. Yejun was here, and he was okay.

Jihoon was frowning up at the tree, but I grabbed his arm and tugged him toward me before he could catch sight of Yejun.

"Just a squirrel," I said quickly. "Sorry, I forgot something at school, so I'm gonna run back. See you tomorrow?"

"I can walk back with you!" Jihoon said instantly.

I shook my head, already walking away before he could try to kiss me goodbye. "No, no, I don't want to make you late. Thanks for the bubble tea!"

I ran off around the corner and waited another minute until Jihoon was out of sight, then hurried back under the tree.

"Are you stuck up there like a cat?" I said. "Do I need to call the fire department?"

The leaves trembled as Yejun clambered down, landing easily on the path. "Cats always land on their feet," he said with a smirk.

I stepped forward and wrapped my arms around him, crushing him in a hug. He stumbled back in surprise, then his hands fell to my back and held me tighter. Here was the only person I could actually talk to about how the world was crumbling apart in my hands.

"Wow, you missed me, huh?" he laughed.

But when I said nothing and only gripped him tighter, feeling how fast my heart was racing compared to his, he pulled away.

"What's wrong?" he said, trying to get a better look at my face.

I clamped my hands to his jacket, not letting him. "You didn't get caught," I said into his shoulder.

He let out a sharp laugh. "Of course not," he said. "I'm too fast for them." Then he tried again to pull back, tugging some of my hair out of my face. "Did something happen?"

I glanced around the street, where people were still meandering on both sides of the road.

"I can't talk about it here," I said.

"Okay," Yejun said easily, taking my hand. We fit so easily together that I wondered why I'd spent so long resisting. "Where do you want to go?"

"I don't know," I said. "Somewhere else."

Yejun pressed his lips together in thought, then straightened up. "Did you like the cheesecake I brought you last week?"

"Yes, but—"

"Then that's where we're going!" he said, taking my hand and heading straight for the subway.

It was a quick two stops away, and he all but ran up the subway stairs the moment we reached our stop, as if I were dying from a lack of cheesecake and only he could save me. His pace slowed as we neared the bakery, and I realized why once he stopped in front of the dark storefront. A sign taped to the inside of the glass door said the owners were on vacation this week.

I pressed a hand to the glass and saw my own haunted reflection cast over the shadowed street. I hadn't realized how dark my eyes looked, how messy I'd let my hair get, how badly I'd gnawed my bottom lip until it bled. Ever since Yejun had disappeared and Hong Gildong had handed me my final assignment, I'd felt like I was trying to hold the threads of the world together all on my own.

My hand slid down the glass and I hung my head, letting my hair fall in front of my face to hide the tears that were splashing the sidewalk.

"I'm sorry!" Yejun said, an edge of panic to his voice. He tried to pet my hair, but it felt more like he was trying to soothe a dog, and he quickly dropped his hands when he realized it wasn't helping. "Okay, just . . . just stay here for a sec! I'll fix it, okay?"

"You don't have to—" I tried to say, but he was already charging down the sidewalk, ducking into the closest convenience store. I took a moment to wipe my face and tell myself to *get it together, you absolutely cannot cry over a piece of cheesecake*.

When Yejun popped out of the store, he was holding one of those big disposable bowls of ramen. He slammed the bowl down on a bench, peeled back the foil, tossed the dry noodles aside and emptied his water bottle into the bowl. I didn't realize what he was doing until the surface of the water started glowing blue.

"*Here?*" I said, bracing myself in front of him to make sure the couple passing by didn't see the magic-glowing ramen bowl.

"I'll be quick," he said as his fingers danced across the water. Watching him script scenarios was like watching a concert pianist perform. His fingers arced fluidly across the water, text appearing and disappearing faster than I could read it. After a few moments, he straightened up with a smile and the water went dark.

"October tenth," he said, holding out his hand. "The store wasn't closed then. We'll get you your cheesecake."

I let out sharp laugh. "Are you sure this one slice of cheesecake isn't going to destroy the world?"

"I ran the scenario, it's fine," he said. "All this will do is slightly alter a cloud formation in three days. It will look a little less like a hedgehog and a little more like a hippo."

It was a silly risk to take, and I should have told him no. That we could just as easily chat somewhere private in the present, rather than risk creating another paradox.

But in that moment, I wanted to be in a world that only existed with me and Yejun. I wanted to feel his magic wrap tight around mine, to fold myself up in the soft blanket of his soul and rest. I slipped my hand into his.

Yejun must have sensed how serious the situation was, because he bought me *two* pieces of cheesecake. He claimed it was for us to share but pointedly ignored his piece and pushed it toward me. A delivery truck had pulled up in front of the café window, blocking off our view of the street, so it truly felt like no one existed in this tiny world except for the two of us.

"That one is Basque burnt cheesecake," he said, pointing to the second piece, which I'd yet to try. "I firmly believe it can fix all problems."

"Let's throw some at Hong Gildong, then," I said.

"There might not be enough cheesecake in the world for that," Yejun said.

I took a bite, then my gaze snapped to Yejun in shock.

"It's good, isn't it?" he said, grinning.

I nodded, scooping up another bite. "If I eat enough of this, I might just forget all my problems entirely."

"Don't forget *all* of them," Yejun said with a smirk. "It was cute when you were worried about me getting caught."

"I was *not* worried!" I said.

Yejun only smiled and pulled out his phone. "You sent me . . . let's see . . . fifteen texts? I don't know, Mina, that seems pretty worried."

"You saw my texts and didn't bother responding?"

"I was a little busy," Yejun said, pouting. "I had to hide out for a while just to be safe. Aren't you glad I'm safe? Can we go back to that part?"

I rolled my eyes as the truck in front of the window pulled away.

The sun had started to set in the time we'd been here, and the lanterns in front of the restaurant across the street had lit up, illuminating little red cats in front of the ramen restaurant I'd gone to on my date with Jihoon.

Despite everything, the ramen had actually been amazing. Maybe I could convince Yejun to go there next. My gaze dropped to the couple in the booth by the window and their bowls of ramen with broth as thick and creamy as gravy. They looked a bit like . . .

I dropped my fork.

"Everything okay?" Yejun said, raising an eyebrow. Luckily, Yejun was facing away from the window, so I managed to smooth out my expression before he could turn around.

Across the street from us, Jihoon and I were on our date.

This was the night I'd finished my final assignment, when Hong Gildong had given me the small task of single-handedly destroying the Korean Peninsula. If I had never kissed Jihoon—or at least waited until after the political rally—would Hong Gildong have given me a different assignment? Something less terrible?

"I have to go to the bathroom!" I said too loudly, jumping up.

Yejun looked surprised but nodded warily. "Have fun," he said with a half smile.

I walked around him and headed for the bathroom before hurrying out the front door, across the street, into the ramen restaurant.

I could have told Yejun what I was doing—after all, he'd heard me and Jihoon set up the date, so it wasn't exactly a secret.

But for some reason, I didn't want Yejun to see.

Maybe it was that I didn't want him to make fun of me, or that I felt bad treating Jihoon like a spectacle, or because having a witness to my lies made me feel even crueler than I already felt.

But part of me knew the real reason.

I'd gone out with Jihoon mostly for my infiltration mission, but also to get back at Yejun for walking with the other girl, to show him he didn't own me, to hurt him.

I didn't want to hurt him—or anyone—anymore.

As I crossed the restaurant, I considered a dozen ways I could ruin the date. I could pretend to be the real Mina and insult Jihoon, but he was too damn nice and didn't deserve it. I could drag the other Mina out when Jihoon went to the bathroom so it looked like she'd ditched him. I could even set the whole place on fire, which would definitely ruin the mood.

I flipped up my hood so Jihoon wouldn't see my face, but slowed down to a stop as I realized what was happening.

An Echo in a sweatshirt had poured ramen into my purse on my date with Jihoon. Now, here I was, in the same sweatshirt, contemplating ways to ruin the date.

Pouring ramen into my own bag hadn't worked—I had no idea why I'd tried that in the first place and sacrificed my phone in the process—but maybe I could make one small adjustment that would change everything.

I reached the table, locking eyes with the other Mina, and picked up her bowl of ramen. In my mind, I could already see the scene playing out—ramen broth dumped over Mina's head, her hair ruined, makeup dripping down her face, her shirt see-through, noodles in her bra. If that didn't ruin the mood and make sure no kiss happened tonight, nothing would.

But then a sharp pain flared behind my eyes.

My timesickness headaches truly had spectacular timing. I lost my grip on the bowl, and instead of landing over Mina's head, it overturned into her purse.

"Are you serious?" the other Mina said, jumping to her feet.

I pushed past her and hurried out of the restaurant, wincing at the glare of streetlights.

I glanced back at the restaurant, but I knew my chance had been lost. I didn't want to go back and risk Jihoon seeing my face. The only thing worse than kissing him in the first place would be exposing him to magic and having to drag him into headquarters for a brain scrub.

I had already made the mistake of kissing him, and apparently I would have to live with it.

I slipped back into the café, where Yejun was waiting for me.

"Okay," Yejun said. "Now are you ready to tell me what's actually going on?"

· 🦋 ·

Yejun waited patiently while I stared at my empty plate and recounted my new assignment from Hong Gildong. With every word, Yejun's expression grew more and more grave.

By the time I finished talking, he looked like he wanted to murder someone. Hopefully not me.

"You can't do it," he said.

"I don't intend to," I said uneasily, his stern expression making me feel unbalanced—he was normally so bright and relaxed. "But I need to figure out what to do instead. Ideally something that won't result in me being wiped off the timeline."

"*That's not going to happen*," Yejun said, the sharp edge in his words catching me off guard.

"I mean, it might," I said. "I don't see a lot of options from here."

Yejun shook his head, jaw clenched, tendons taut in his neck. Abruptly, he stood up, grabbed his coat from the back of the chair, and headed for the door. "Come on," he said.

"Where are you going?" I said, untangling my bag from the chair legs before hurrying after him.

"I need a scrying pool," Yejun said over his shoulder. "I'll figure it out, Mina, I just need a little more time. Don't worry."

"*Don't worry?*" I said. "I feel like this is the exact right time to be worried!"

"I'll figure it out," Yejun said again. "I'll fix it."

"What, by yourself?" I said. "Slow down!"

But Yejun only took off faster and ducked into an alleyway, then squatted in front of a puddle and rolled up his sleeves.

"*Don't scry in mysterious liquids you found on the ground!*" I said. "Let's just go back. We can deal with this in the present, with a liquid that won't give you cholera."

"Mina, *there's no time!*" Yejun said, clenching his fists. "If Hong Gildong . . ." He shook his head, looking away as his shoulders drooped in defeat.

I knelt on the other side of the puddle. "Yejun?" I said, reaching for his face.

He caught my hand and held it close to his heart. "No one is going to hurt you," he whispered. His words felt warm, the undercurrent of fire beneath them, a latent tone that some dragon descendants could tap into.

"That's sweet," I said. "But I fear that you might lose to an ancient dragon like Hong Gildong in a cage fight."

I'd meant it as a joke, but Yejun looked up sharply, his eyes flaring gold. In a flash, Yejun had trapped me against the wall, his hands on either side of my head. This close, I could feel the heat radiating off him. I couldn't tear my gaze away from his golden irises, his pupils narrowed to thin black stripes, the sign of a dragon provoked. I had never had that kind of anger directed at me before, and I couldn't help the way my knees shook, the brick wall digging into my spine.

"Are you sure about that?" he said, the words low and dark, the vibration rattling through my bones. My heartbeat raced in my ears, and I knew what I was supposed to say next, what I could have said to stop this right here and now. I could have shoved him away and he would have yielded . . . but I didn't want to.

Instead, I turned my head slightly to the side, baring my throat.

"Prove it," I whispered.

Because I knew, even with the tiny amount of dragon blood in my veins, that dragons didn't back down from challenges.

Yejun blinked quickly, like he couldn't believe my words. Then his eyes flared brighter and he raised a hand to the side of my face, holding my cheek. I could feel the threat of his claws against my cheek, but he held me with exquisite care, not drawing even a single drop of blood.

For the briefest moment, like a comet flashing past overhead, I imagined a life with Yejun.

Days spent holding his hand, feeling our magic braided together, its warmth always with me. Nights spent on quiet journeys around Seoul, even something as simple as going to a sushi restaurant an adventure in and of itself because being with Yejun was exhilarating. For all I knew, it could be true—it was forbidden to look at your own file, so I had no idea what the future held for me.

"Mina," he whispered, and somehow I felt like he had said my name in every language all at once, like he had spoken to the whole of me, not the fragmented parts I offered to everyone else I met. His warm breath whispered across my face, one claw tracing a delicate line across my lip.

Then suddenly, Yejun drew back. He peered over my shoulder with a frown. I followed his gaze, and there we were—me and Jihoon—walking down the street.

Jihoon had his hand on my back, guiding me through the crowd. The other Mina looked at Jihoon and smiled before we disappeared around a corner.

I stayed perfectly still, wishing Yejun would say something, give me some clue as to what he was thinking. *I have nothing to be sorry for*, I told myself, even though it felt like a lie.

"The assassination," Yejun said at last, his voice low. "You said it was your final exam?"

I finally dared to turn around. Was Yejun actually going to pretend he hadn't just seen me and Jihoon on a date? Did he not care, or did he just understand that it was part of my job? He was still staring out the mouth of the alley, like he didn't see me at all.

"Yes," I said, trying to keep my voice even.

Yejun took a step back, his expression blank. The space between us suddenly felt like a thousand miles.

"That means you crossed the point threshold," he said, finally meeting my gaze. "What exactly was your mission with Jihoon?"

I tensed, feeling as if I'd fallen into a frozen lake. "I had to . . . get close to him," I said, gaze fixed on my shoes.

"You've *been* close to him," Yejun said. "What pushed you over the threshold? What did you do to him?"

Despite all my training that had molded me into an impeccable liar, improviser, and manipulator, I had no idea what to say next.

The key to getting what you wanted out of a social interaction was knowing what the other person wanted you to say, but that wouldn't help me here. I know Yejun would hate the truth, but he would hate a lie even more.

"I just let him kiss me," I said quietly. "That's all."

"*That's all?*" Yejun echoed, followed by a sharp laugh. He stuffed his hands in his pockets and turned away from me. "Unbelievable," he said under his breath.

My face burned, my hands clenching into fists. What right did Yejun have to be mad at me? Jihoon had never been a secret, unlike the girls Yejun went around with. "It was just an assignment," I said. "Why do you care?"

He looked back at me, and this time his eyes were no longer gold but so dark they were almost black. Even though we weren't touching, I could feel his magic like a frigid sea breeze from far away.

"I don't," he said.

The words fell like cold rain over me. We were no longer in a safe, warm world all by ourselves. I was alone.

He checked his watch and turned to the mouth of the alley. "Time's almost up," he said. "We should go back now."

"Right," I said quietly, offering him my hand. This time, as his magic flowed through me, I felt nothing at all.

Chapter Sixteen

After school on Tuesday, I was shooting bullets at a paper target, trying with all my might not to imagine Hong Gildong's face.

Hyebin had brought me to a shooting range in Myeongdong for firearms training. I'd been hesitant at first, not really wanting to start the day with a bullet in my foot, but Hyebin had only rolled her eyes and said *even a toddler couldn't get hurt at this range*. I hadn't understood what she meant at first. Then when I arrived, I was strapped into a Kevlar vest, safety goggles, and headphones, then pushed in front of a gun suspended on bike chains so that I couldn't turn it away from the target if I tried.

The recoil forced my wrist back, bullet casings popping out and falling to the floor around me. The air smelled bright with gunpowder, the echoes of the gunshot still stinging in my ears even through the headphones.

I tried to narrow my vision to nothing but the target, to forget about Jihoon and Yejun and everything except the mark in front of me. Still, Yejun's words from last night echoed in my mind. *I don't care.* I clenched my teeth against the thought and fired.

The staff member pulled my paper target back on a tether and made an impressed sound. My bullets had punched a tight ring of holes right through the center of the target.

"Remind me not to get on your bad side," he said, replacing the paper with a printout of a masked man holding a cartoon woman hostage.

"Don't get too excited," Hyebin said as soon as the staff member walked away. "Dragons have enhanced vision. If you weren't hitting your target, I'd be concerned."

"Thanks," I said flatly.

"Next time, we'll take you somewhere without childproofing. This is just to get you used to it."

I didn't think I would ever get used to handling a gun, or preparing to shoot someone made of actual flesh instead of paper. It had been a full day since I'd spoken to Yejun, and I still hadn't found a way out of my final exam. For now, I was only going through the motions of preparing for it so I wouldn't be executed on the spot, but I really hoped I could come up with an actual plan by the day of the rally.

Hyebin nodded toward the next target. "Now shoot that guy in the nose."

"He's wearing a ski mask," I said. "I can't see his nose."

"You know where noses are," Hyebin said. "Or is this too hard for you?"

"Yes, the idea of *preparing to kill someone* is pretty hard," I said, tightening my grip on the pistol.

Hyebin shushed me, glancing around in case anyone overheard. "Watch it," she whispered. "We all had to take a final exam. Stop whining about it."

My finger clenched reflexively on the gun and I fired without meaning to. The bullet flew somewhere into the corner, not even clipping the target paper.

"*Whining?*" I said. "About being forced to cause millions of deaths?"

"Mina, you're not the one causing their deaths," Hyebin said, crossing her arms. "You're doing your job. Or you would be, if you could hit the target without complaining so much. Try again, and try harder."

My skin suddenly burned, and I clenched my jaw so hard it ached. Nothing I did was ever good enough for Hyebin, or for any of the descendants. I'd given them everything, and still they'd pushed me between them and a nuclear war.

I tightened my grip around the gun, but this time the plastic creaked and snapped in my hands. It fell to the floor in jagged shards, the casing hitting the tile with a *thunk* at my feet.

"*Is that hard enough for you?*" I said. The words hardly sounded like my own. They had a strange edge to them, a weight that reverberated through the room, making the paper target shiver in the distance.

Hyebin narrowed her eyes, which were now searing gold. Fangs pierced her bottom lip and a bead of blood raced down her chin.

The heat melted out of me and I took a step back, instinctively lowering my gaze. Hyebin's presence eclipsed the sterile overhead light and darkened the small room, as if the sun had cowered back under the horizon.

"*What did you say to me?*" she said. Her words simmered, embers of a coal fire beneath each vowel, an ancient language bleeding through into her Korean.

I clenched my teeth against the dragon instinct to throw myself to the ground in apology. Hyebin wasn't going to help me out of my mission, so what did it matter? She'd left me all alone.

"Nothing is ever enough for you," I said, looking up at her

defiantly. Dragon manners weren't something any of us were taught, but I knew instinctively that I wasn't supposed to meet her gaze at a moment like this, not if I wanted to keep my head on my shoulders. "You think you're so much better than everyone else."

"I earned my position with my skill," Hyebin said, taking a challenging step forward.

I ground my heels into the tiles, forcing myself not to step back, but she didn't seem to notice.

"All *you've* done so far," she said, "is kiss a boy."

My jaw throbbed, and I felt dangerously close to shattering all my teeth from how hard I was clenching them. Of course my infiltration mission seemed silly to Hyebin, who'd blown up a bridge just because Hong Gildong told her to. Nothing mattered to Hyebin except her work—not anyone else's feelings, not the lives of humans, and definitely not me.

"You're good at your job because it's all you have," I said, taking a step forward. "You don't have any family or friends or anyone depending on you except Hong Gildong. You're a jerk to everyone else because you're jealous that we still have people who care about us!"

I braced myself for the attack, for Hyebin to grab me and shove me against the wall, or push me to the ground, or bare her teeth and go for my throat.

But instead, she went very still.

The gold in her eyes dimmed until her irises had faded to a dull brown, and her fangs disappeared behind her chapped lips. A single bead of blood traced down her chin, vivid in contrast to her sallow skin.

The staff member opened the door right at that moment, then let out a gasp at the sight of the broken gun. "What happened?" he said, hurrying to gather up the shattered remains of the weapon.

"These guns are pieces of crap," Hyebin said, turning away from me and grabbing her jacket off the hook. "Better look into that before someone gets hurt and sues. We're done here."

She turned to leave, tossing her jacket over her shoulder. I struggled out of my Kevlar vest and stowed it back on the shelf, then hurried after her. I hadn't actually hurt her feelings, had I? Hyebin had always seemed so impenetrable. Someone like me could never take her down.

"Sunbaenim," I said as I caught up with her halfway down the block. "I didn't mean—"

"Let's go back," she said stiffly, heading for the bus stop.

"Sunbaenim?" I tried again. "Are you—"

"Yang Mina," she said, "stop talking."

I clamped my mouth shut and drew to a stop beside her as we waited for the bus.

I had always seen Hyebin as the ideal descendant, the closest we could come to our dragon ancestors, fast and sharp and deadly. But without the light behind her eyes, she looked as if the sun had stripped all her colors away. She shivered as the wind blew her jacket back against the sharp line of her shoulders.

We boarded the bus together and rode in silence. When we got off in front of Emart, she turned toward headquarters.

"Go home," she said.

"Sunbaenim, I'm sorry," I said.

She looked over her shoulder, the sun lighting up her silhouette in gold, but wouldn't turn all the way around, wouldn't look me in the eye. "Go," she said again, stuffing her hands in her pockets and walking away.

I stood alone on the sidewalk, wishing I could send an Echo back to throttle my past self into unconsciousness before I could hurt Hyebin. I wanted so badly for her to yell at me, to tell me how worthless I was and how dare I speak to her like that, anything but calmly accept my insults and walk away.

I turned my face toward the white sun, which offered no warmth at all, then pressed my hand over my pocket, where Hana's note was tucked into my wallet.

Show me what to do, Hana, I thought. *I can't do it on my own.*

Yejun didn't bring me cheesecake that afternoon, which was how I knew he was still angry. The way he carefully avoided looking me in the eye and stood a calculated distance from me as we walked down the street were also good clues.

I glanced at him as we walked in silence, remembering his claws pressed against my cheek, his hands on either side of my face. As if he sensed me looking, he turned and locked eyes with me for a moment before I quickly looked away.

I wanted to scream. Nothing about Yejun made any sense to me. He acted like he liked me, but then he snuck around with other girls. He knew that my mission with Jihoon was part of my job, but acted like me finally completing it was a personal attack. It wasn't as if I'd married Jihoon. And even if I had, what right did Yejun have to be mad about it? We weren't together.

"This way," Yejun said, turning a corner so sharply that I nearly tripped off the curb when I tried to follow him. He pointed at a secondhand clothing store at the end of the block.

"We can travel in a changing stall here," he said stiffly. "We're not going back that far, so the stalls will still be here."

"What do you mean 'not that far'?" I said, frowning. "Didn't the *Sewol* ferry sink like ten years ago? How are we going to stop it from sinking after it's already sunk?"

Yejun sighed impatiently. "We're not the first people to try to stop it from sinking," he said after a moment. "Other rogues have tried, and other descendants have stopped them. We're going to stop a descendant from going back and interfering with a different rogue's plans. He'll show up late to work and miss his traveling window, then the rogue will report the ferry's owner for making illegal modifications that let him cram too many passengers on board."

"Wow," I said. "You take the butterfly principle seriously. That's so indirect."

"Why do work ourselves when we could let someone else do it for us?" Yejun said with a shrug. "It's less risky."

I said nothing out of fear that I'd accidentally compliment him again. Hong Gildong had truly messed up by losing Yejun as a timeline architect. I envied how easily he seemed to choreograph his plans across the whole timeline while my greatest skill seemed to be lying.

As we drew closer to the store, I walked faster so I could enter first and not wait to see whether he would hold the door for me or decide not to—I wasn't sure which was worse. I walked inside, then grabbed a random men's shirt off the rack and headed straight for the changing rooms. Luckily, this was a small store with only a tiny section of curtained stalls, which was easier than sneaking Yejun into the woman's changing rooms.

I pulled back the curtain to the closest stall, waving for Yejun to walk faster before someone caught us. He followed me inside and yanked the curtain shut around us as I hung up the shirt on a hook.

I had to stand uncomfortably close to Yejun in the tiny stall. He held his hand out, as far away from me as he could manage in the small space. I gritted my teeth and took his hand.

"Let's get this over with," Yejun said.

This time, his magic *burned*.

The blue and purple strands knotted together too tightly, my muscles tensing at the blaring surge of magic that forced its way through my bones. My mouth tasted like it was full of ashes, and each wisp of blue light stung my eyes as it lashed around my face.

The moment we landed in the past, I yanked my hand away from his.

"What's your problem?" I said.

"*Shh!* Mina, not here!" he said, trying to cover my mouth.

I shoved his hand away. "Why are you angry with me?"

"I'm not—"

"I can see it in your magic!" I said.

Yejun's expression darkened. "If you can tell what I'm feeling through my magic, then *stop pretending you have no idea why I'm mad!*"

I froze, remembering the thousand images of myself I'd seen in his soul. But I couldn't be the one to say it out loud, to be wrong.

"Um," said a timid woman's voice from the other side of the curtain. "Excuse me?"

Yejun sighed, then opened the changing stall curtain. An employee was standing just outside, gaping at us. Yejun brushed past her and stormed away, ignoring me when I called for him.

He shoved open the front door of the thrift store and hurried into the street. I chased after him but immediately choked at the taste of the air—somehow we'd landed in an awful air quality day, as if this couldn't get any worse.

"You said you wouldn't lie to me," I said, grabbing Yejun's sleeve and wincing as my timesickness headache flared up again. "Omission is still lying. So tell me what your problem is. Don't make me guess."

Yejun's expression pinched. He glared at the horizon, looking like he wanted to crawl out of his own skin. After a moment, he sighed and dropped his gaze to his shoes. "I just can't believe you actually went out with Jihoon," he said at last. His voice no longer sounded bright and annoyingly confident, but oddly fragile, barely above a whisper. "I thought we . . ." He trailed off, shaking his head.

My face suddenly felt far too warm, every muscle wound tight. Yejun was actually jealous of Jihoon. "How can you be mad about me going out with Jihoon when you did the same thing?" I said, a raw edge to my voice that I was sure gave away my sadness, but it was too late to take it back.

Yejun raised an eyebrow. "I didn't kiss Jihoon," he said.

I scoffed. "No, obviously not Jihoon!" I said. "You know what I'm talking about."

"I really don't," Yejun said, checking his watch. He jolted at whatever he saw, then took off down the sidewalk, waving for me to follow. "Sorry, but we're on a tight schedule here. I didn't script a lot of small talk when I ran this scenario."

I scowled but hurried after him anyway. We reached an intersection not far from our school. Yejun stopped just before the crosswalk and pulled a water balloon from his backpack.

"Cover me," he said.

"Cover you *how*?" I said.

But he didn't wait for me to figure it out. He only turned and reeled back, then hurled the balloon into the intersection, where it burst on the windshield of a passing car.

The car swerved as it sailed through the intersection, forcing a minitruck to turn sharply to avoid it. The truck was loaded with fruit and overbalanced at the sudden turn, spilling watermelons into the street.

Brakes screeched behind us as drivers dodged errant melons. One rolled over my foot and nearly toppled me like a bowling pin, but Yejun clamped his hand around my waist to steady me. I looked up at him, my left hand clutching the back of his uniform jacket for balance, my side pressed up against his.

I had been here before.

A day when the air quality was in the red zone, when an overturned cart of watermelons caused a traffic jam right outside my school, when Yejun had held another girl by the waist on the other side of the intersection. Except, it hadn't been another girl at all.

It was *me*.

"Oh no," I whispered, clinging to Yejun's sleeve, his bright brown eyes locked on mine. "Oh, this is all my fault, isn't it?"

"What?" Yejun said, frowning.

I used his arm to pull myself up but didn't let go of his sleeve. All this time, I'd thought Yejun was a player, sneaking around with other girls behind my back. But all he'd been doing was crossing the timeline with me.

Crap.

What was I supposed to do to fix this? If our roles were reversed, I probably would have bought the world's biggest apology cheesecake, but Yejun had never taken a single bite of any of my cheesecake slices, so I doubted that was his preferred dessert.

But maybe there was something else I could get him. He'd mentioned it once, on the day we went to Namsan Seoul Tower.

"Come on," I said, gripping his arm and tugging him around the corner. He seemed too startled at the gesture to protest, his arm limp as I dragged him down the street toward the nearest convenience store.

"Where are you going?" Yejun said. "The adjustment—"

"Just give me a minute," I said, running faster and stifling a cough. I really shouldn't have been running without a mask when there was so much fine dust in the air, but this was too important to wait.

I hurried into CU and rushed to the refrigerated section, then grabbed some banana milk, melon milk, and a bag of red ginseng candies. Yejun watched with wide eyes as I dumped the strange combination of foods onto the counter and passed the cashier a 10,000 won note.

"What are you doing?" Yejun said.

"Getting you your favorite snack," I snapped, accepting the bag from the cashier with a smile.

"But . . . why?" Yejun said, stepping aside as I pushed open the front door and dropped the snacks onto the metal table.

I sat down and kicked out the other metal chair, gesturing for him to sit. "Because you always get me my favorite food to make up for annoying me," I said. "So here is your banana-melon-ginseng monstrosity."

He stood awkwardly beside the table, eyeing the food like it was a trap. I sighed and dropped my gaze to my lap, fidgeting with the hem of my skirt. "About Jihoon," I said. "I did that mission so I could stay in Seoul. My family is moving to Hokkaido, and if I don't get a promotion, I have to go with them. I wanted to stay here. I wanted to stay with"—I dared to glance up, losing all my courage once my gaze locked with Yejun's—"with you," I finished quietly.

Yejun sat down slowly, blinking at the snacks like I'd presented him with radioactive rocks. Then, abruptly, he folded over laughing.

My face burned. "*What?*" I said. "Why are you—"

"Mina," he said, wiping back tears of laughter. "When I told you I loved mixing banana and melon milk with red ginseng candy, I was *joking*."

He flopped over on the table, laughing even harder while I felt my whole face heat up. "Who jokes about that?" I said. "I just thought you were a weirdo! Is that really so hard to believe?"

He couldn't answer, too busy laughing. It turned out his laughter was contagious, because despite everything, I felt a smile creep across my face. I started to laugh too once I realized the cashier probably thought we'd lost our minds, crying-laughing over a couple bottles of milk.

But my laughter didn't last long, because something tickled my throat, and I had to turn away to hide a grating cough in my sleeve.

Yejun quickly calmed down and opened the banana milk, offering me a sip. I waved it away, so he opened the melon milk for me, which I downed in a few gulps.

"Are you okay?" Yejun said.

I nodded, though my eyes had started watering from all the coughing. "It's the fine dust," I said, gesturing to the gray sky.

Yejun scowled and shook his fist up melodramatically at the hazy sky. "I'd fight the sky for you, if I could," he said. "Actually, maybe I can do you one better."

He pulled out his phone and quickly searched for something, then swept the snacks into the plastic bag and reached for my hand. "Let's go back a few days," he said.

I raised an eyebrow. "Aren't you going to run the scenario first?"

"Already did," he said with a wink.

"When could you possibly have done that?"

Yejun sighed. "I thought you'd realized by now that I am a huge loser and my only hobby is running imaginary scenarios. Most of them involve you. Adjusting them by a few hours is just some quick mental math."

"Is this why you're so good at calculus?" I said, breezing right over the "most of them involve you" comment.

"So I can take you on beautiful and seemingly spontaneous dates?" he said. "Of course."

My mind latched onto the word *dates*, and I couldn't help but smile. I reached for Yejun's hand and laced my fingers with his.

As his magic flowed through me, it felt like I was standing under a waterfall of light, its coolness smoothing away the sharp, unpleasant edges of the real world. I was tethered to Yejun's heart, and in our private universe there was no war, no points, no final exam. Nothing but the song of our heartbeats together.

When the indigo haze cleared, we were standing under a clear blue sky.

"*Now* this is perfect," Yejun said. He glanced down at the bag on his other hand, then set it on the table. "Well, almost perfect. How about I get you my *actual* favorite snack, for future reference, and we can share it?"

"Yes please," I said, glaring accusingly at the ginseng candies that were spilling out of the bag onto the table. He smiled as he stood up, ruffled my hair, then headed back inside CU.

For a moment, I allowed myself to think that everything would be fine. Yejun was happy with me again, so he would help me figure a way out of my mission. I would find Hana, I wouldn't start a war, and everyone would be safe. It was easy to be an optimist when the sun was out.

It was a beautiful thought for all of five seconds. Until I saw who was crossing the Bulgwang stream.

There I was, in my school uniform, clutching a bag of honey butter chips and walking across the stepping stones. Jihoon was following behind me, his backpack on his back and mine on his front.

This was the day Jihoon had given me the bracelet.

Jihoon looked over his shoulder, and I quickly turned away so he wouldn't see another Mina gawking at him. Through the fogged window, I could see Yejun's silhouette inside CU, making his way down the candy aisle.

If Yejun saw me with Jihoon, he would be upset all over again, and snacks probably wouldn't make up for it a second time.

I watched helplessly as Jihoon took out the bracelet. This was the part where I was supposed to fall into the stream and ruin the moment. If it happened fast, maybe Yejun would miss it.

But instead, the other Mina smiled as she took the bracelet, slipping it on her wrist.

That wasn't right.

Something must have changed. Yejun said he was good at adjustments, but maybe he'd made a mistake and I'd changed this day. Would I actually complete the mission this time around, just in time for Yejun to come out of CU and see me kissing Jihoon?

The wind blew my hair back as I glared at my past self. I remembered how, back then, using Jihoon had felt like a game.

One day, you'll regret this, Mina, I thought. *Don't do it.*

But the other Mina couldn't hear my thoughts, so she only smiled her same sharp lie of a smile and leaned closer to Jihoon.

Then suddenly, her gaze locked with mine.

She froze, the smile dropping off her face.

I tensed up, wondering if I should run into CU, but it was already too late—I'd been seen.

The other Mina was talking frantically to Jihoon now, gaze darting back and forth between me and him. Just as Jihoon started to turn around, Mina grabbed him and both of them toppled into the river.

I let out a sharp laugh, my shoulders relaxing.

There, I thought. *I fixed it*.

The other Mina made a quick exit, just as she was supposed to, and stormed over to me.

"*What?*" she said, crossing her arms.

Something about the way she spoke—the resigned tiredness of that single word—felt so familiar.

Here I was, standing in front of my past self, an open bottle of banana milk on the table beside me. All that was missing was . . .

The confetti, I thought. The confetti that Yejun had showered over me when I'd passed my calculus test. The confetti that was still in the pocket of the backpack I was currently wearing.

I was the organic Echo, just as Yejun had thought.

I dropped my gaze to past-Mina's shoes—at the time, I'd wondered what could have possessed me to pour banana milk all over them, but now I understood.

On the day I'd met Jihoon, he'd complimented my shoes—these shoes—and spilled orange juice on me. I'd found his apology so funny that we'd become friends and I'd decided that using him for my infiltration mission would be easy.

I wished it had never happened.

I picked up the banana milk, just as I was always destined to, and poured it over her—not my—shoes.

"Sorry," I said, even though I wasn't sorry at all.

"Is that all?" the other Mina said. "Any more infiltration missions you want to ruin for me while you're here?"

No, I thought, *though I do need to make a quick escape before Yejun sees you.*

I reached into the front pocket of my backpack, grabbed a handful of confetti, and tossed it into the other Mina's face.

She sputtered as one of the tiny pieces got in her eye. *"Are you serious?"* she said.

I didn't stick around to see what happened next.

Yejun was just coming out of the store with a plastic bag in each hand. I grabbed his arm and tugged him around the corner and down the street before past-Mina could see us.

"Where are we going?" Yejun said. "What happened to the milk?"

"Don't worry about it," I said, turning another sharp corner. I knew which direction *I'd* gone, but I had no idea where Jihoon had walked after parting ways and didn't want him to spot us.

It wasn't until I drew to a stop, certain we were out of sight, that I realized something strange.

My timesickness headache hadn't gone away.

The banana milk loop had been caused by an organic Echo, just as Yejun had suggested, but the constant ache behind my eyes hadn't lifted in the slightest. Did that mean I'd done something wrong and hadn't really closed the loop?

"It's honey butter chips, by the way," Yejun said.

I flinched, thinking about the other Mina holding the chips as she crossed the river. "Huh?"

Yejun pulled a bag of honey butter chips out of his plastic bag. "My favorite snack," he said. "The perfect umami blend of salty and sweet."

"That's not what *umami* means," I said distractedly as my phone buzzed. It was a reminder I'd set up in my calendar—my quarterly evaluation was due tonight.

"Crap," I said under my breath, slumping against the wall. "I have to go back and turn in my report. Or finish it and then turn it in, actually."

"Procrastinator," Yejun said, poking my side. "Okay, let's go back so Hyebin doesn't skin you alive. You can even take a bag of chips with you."

"My hero," I said, taking Yejun's hand. His fingers laced with mine, holding me tight as he carried us home.

Hardly anyone was working at headquarters this late at night. Lower-ranked office workers didn't stay for night shifts, senior agents like Hyebin were out in the field, and the timeline architects rarely left their private wing. I sat alone in the computer lab, which was dark because I was too tired to stand up every five minutes to dance for the motion-activated lights. I pulled up the half-finished draft of my quarterly report from Google Drive, plugged in some moderately flattering scores for my self-evaluation, and printed it.

I prayed I didn't have to actually see Hyebin and could just leave the report on her desk. I would have to give her extra Choco Pies tomorrow, or maybe the rest of the week, until she forgave me. As it was, I wasn't expecting a good score from her.

I clutched the report to my chest as I knocked on Hyebin's door, but the room was dark and the doorknob wouldn't budge. I debated just sliding the report under the door, but something told me that Hyebin wouldn't appreciate stepping on it as soon as she returned to her office. I sighed and went to the security desk to ask Seulgi.

"Hyebin was helping Sajangnim with something in his office," Seulgi said. She must have noticed my stricken expression because she laughed and shook her head. "Don't worry, Sajangnim is in a meeting. He left Hyebin in there by herself."

As if Hyebin is less scary than Hong Gildong, I thought grimly.

"Thanks, Seulgi-nim," I said, heading to the left wing, down the echoing hallway to Hong Gildong's office.

You're just handing her some paper, I told myself. *This is not the hardest thing you've ever done.*

I took a steadying breath and knocked twice on the heavy wooden door.

"Come in," Hyebin's voice called from the other side.

Cautiously, I opened the door.

Hyebin, still scrolling through something on Hong Gildong's scrying pool, didn't acknowledge me as I entered.

"Sunbaenim," I said, shifting from foot to foot, "I just wanted to say—"

"Do you have the report or not?" Hyebin said.

"I . . . yes," I said.

She gave me a cursory glance, then checked her watch and jolted to her feet. "Staple it, then leave it in the pile and go home."

I nodded and bowed as she strode past me, slamming the door behind her like she couldn't stand to be in my presence for a second longer. I sighed, trudging over to the desk.

Hong Gildong's scrying pool reflected the overhead light like a golden halo, a ring around my own reflection. If only I were Hyebin, and Hong Gildong trusted me to leave me alone with his own scrying pool and all his files . . .

All his files, which were currently right in front of me, unguarded.

I set my report to the side and glanced at the door, listening for the sound of Hyebin's footsteps returning. When no sound came, I hurried around the desk and tapped the surface of the scrying pool. Four glimmering words floated to the surface of the screen.

Please enter your signature

I sighed. Of course Hong Gildong's scrying pool was locked. Surely no one had access to files more important than him. I pulled open a couple drawers, hoping he might have jotted his signature down on a Post-it or something, but all I found were unorganized office supplies in various shades of gold—scissors, staples, paper clips, thumbtacks. Considering that most of our documents weren't actually paper, I figured this was just part of Hong Gildong's hoard rather than anything he actually used.

I sighed and shut the drawers, moving around the desk before Hyebin could catch me snooping and have yet another reason to hate me.

I grabbed a gold stapler off the desk and stapled the top corner of my report. As I started to set it on top of Hyebin's other papers, I noticed the file at the top of the stack, and my hand froze. There, in bold black letters, was the name of the last agent to turn in their report:

KIM YEJUN

Chapter Seventeen

I read the name over and over again until it no longer looked real.

Yejun didn't work for the descendants anymore, so it must have been someone else with the same name. Kim was a common name, after all.

I tensed at the sound of the elevator dinging at the end of the hallway. Hyebin could come back any moment, or worse—Hong Gildong. I dug my phone out of my pocket and snapped as many photos of the report as I could, then jammed the file into the middle of the stack and slapped my report on top.

The door swung open and Hyebin strode back in, hesitating at the sight of me by the desk.

"You're still here?" she said. "What the hell are you doing? Get out."

"Yes, Sunbaenim," I said, bowing and hurrying around the desk. I'd almost reached the doorway when Hyebin called for me.

"Wait," she said.

I froze, my hand an inch from the doorknob. There was no way

Hyebin could tell that I'd read someone else's report, right? Were there cameras in Hong Gildong's office? I swallowed hard, my mouth suddenly dry as Hyebin crossed the room and stood behind me.

"Here," she said.

I turned around slowly. She was holding her hand out to me, something shiny clenched in her fist. I held out both hands and let her drop it into my palms.

I half expected it to be some kind of grenade, but when I opened my palm to examine it, I saw a key chain with a tiny gold ladybug charm.

"I bought it last week," she said, stuffing her hands in her pockets and looking away. "Your graduation present. I can't return it, so . . . congrats, I guess."

It was cheap and silly looking and so very un-Hyebin-like that the thought of her buying it at the store actually made me smile. Then I felt ashamed all over again—she'd gotten me a present and I'd insulted her to her face. "Thank you, Sunbaenim," I said, bowing probably too deeply.

"Go home," she said, waving me off.

I wanted to say more, but I could tell I was no longer welcome. I trudged to the door and closed it behind me, clutching the ladybug in one hand. I held it close to my chest as I rode the elevator down.

Out on the street, I hurried against the flow of foot traffic. I came to a stop on the bridge across the Bulgwang stream and gripped the railing with one hand. The cold metal shocked life back into my palm, and I realized how badly I was shaking. I pocketed the ladybug key chain and took out my phone.

```
Quarter Three Report: Kim Yejun, Associate
Agent (1027C)
Supervisor: Hong Gildong [alias], Seoul Branch
President (003)
```

QUARTERLY ASSIGNMENT

Primary Objective: Ascertain the loyalty of Agent-in-Training Yang Mina (Agent 1475C).

Determine:

    a. The approximate level of Yang Mina's power with regard to her dragon energy and ability to control it effectively

        (Note: Yang Mina is flagged for extra review due to suspected genetic predisposition for enhanced powers—see file 1475B, "Yang Hana.")

    b. Yang Mina's susceptibility to outside influence with regard to unauthorized timeline interference

    c. Whether or not Yang Mina can be used as an asset to the descendants or poses too great a risk of disloyalty and must be eliminated (see Appendix A)

My findings:

Yang Mina strongly resisted my initial infiltration attempt, citing mistrust of my motivations and skepticism over the existence of an alternate timeline. As the operation was ineffective, I left the scene before she was able to contact another agent for backup.

    Yang Mina continuously resisted my attempts to persuade her to help me rebel against the descendants, even when presented with photographic evidence. She agreed to another conversation with me only when ambushed in the train station. There, I capitalized on her desire to remain in the descendants' good graces by passing her calculus class to support her current infiltration mission.

    a. Power levels: Yang Mina possesses strong but uncultivated dragon energy. She was able to call it forth on the first attempt with limited instruction.

    b. Loyalty: Yang Mina falls into category 4 of loyalty index (moderate susceptibility to outside forces).

    c. Future usefulness: Yang Mina would be a useful asset to the Seoul branch team if powers were harnessed.

Conclusion:
I believe that Yang Mina is not a candidate for erasure as she does not meet the established criteria. Her decision to assist me was motivated by her desire to complete her infiltration mission and continue to work as a faithful descendant.

    Out of the established protocols, I believe the best course of action is to proceed with Option C (see Appendix A).

Appendix A:

Option C: Determination of Loyalty
Proposal draft by: Hong Gildong [alias], Seoul Branch President (003)

Kim Yejun's final examination will be to supervise Yang Mina on her final examination mission (874675) [assassination of politician Min Sungho] to ensure completion.

If Yang Mina completes the assignment successfully, Kim Yejun will:
- Accompany Yang Mina to HQ for mission debrief, written warning for prior infractions, registration for corrective conduct classes.

If Yang Mina deviates from instructions in any way or otherwise fails to complete the assignment, Kim Yejun will:
- Immediately apprehend Yang Mina and escort her to HQ.
  If met with resistance:
  - Cleared for firearm usage
  - Cleared for termination

Cleared for termination.

I read the words again and again. At first, they meant nothing at all—like I was reading a novel about someone else's life.

Then I reached the last page.

There was Yejun's headshot, taken against the beige background of the costuming department. His hair was black in the photo, but I recognized those dark eyes. I had seen them sparkle with gold when he laughed and glow like amber when he was angry. But in this photo, he only stared impassively ahead in a way that felt so starkly un-Yejun, as if I'd never met this person at all.

Because I haven't, I realized, a strange coldness building in my feet and creeping up my body, like I was wading into a dark ocean. I'd met Kim Yejun the rogue agent who wanted to save the world, but that person didn't exist.

I locked my phone and dropped my hands to my sides. The sea was rising higher and higher, filling my mouth.

No one is going to hurt you, he'd said.

No one except for him.

I sank to my knees, my legs shaking too much to hold me anymore. The ocean roared in my ears, my mouth stinging with salt—maybe I'd bitten my tongue, or maybe I really was going to drown in the sea of my own mind. Dragons were water creatures, but until this moment, I had never felt like I came from the cold and lightless depths of the ocean. Now I only wanted dark waters to drag me home, to bury me in white sand.

Hana's absence yawned wider, as it always did in moments she should have been here. I imagined her fingers combing my hair, her warm hand on my back, her soothing words in my ear.

What does this mean for Hana? I thought, my throat closing up. If Yejun had made up Timeline Alpha to trick me, was there any hope of getting her back? I'd thought I could peel back Hong Gildong's offenses one by one until everything was undone and Hana came back to me, but how was I supposed to find her now? The only person who had more information about her was Hong Gildong, and I couldn't access his files.

Just this afternoon, I'd thought I was on the way to saving the world, and now I had nothing and no one at all, not even Hana. I had to start a war, or I would lose Hana forever, and Yejun would kill me if I ran.

I walked home, feeling like the cool autumn breeze was rushing straight through me, like I was made of silk.

My parents were already asleep since they were boarding a plane for Japan early tomorrow. I sat alone at the table, where the kitchen was mostly packed up in boxes that the movers would pick up tomorrow afternoon.

The door to my parents' room clicked open and my mom stuck her head out.

"Mina?" she called.

"Go to bed, you have an early flight," I said, not wanting her to see me upset.

"Do you want some cheese ramen?" she said, as if I hadn't spoken.

"No," I said, facing away as she entered the kitchen, pretending to be very interested in whatever was happening out the window. "I'm tired," I added.

I waited for the sound of her footsteps returning to her room and the door closing, but she lingered a few feet away. "Are you okay, sweetie?" she said.

I swallowed, tasting the easy lie on the tip of my tongue. *I'm fine, just stressed about school.* But I was so tired of lying to everyone.

My mom frowned at my silence and stepped into the room, then sat beside me at the table. "What's wrong, sweetheart?" she said, tucking a lock of my hair behind my ear.

I hugged my knees to my chest, wondering how much I could really tell her. *Maybe my mom can fix everything for me*, I thought, even though I was too old to believe it.

"My next mission," I said at last. "The descendants want—"

"Wait, wait," my mom said quickly, holding up a hand. "You know that's classified, sweetie. You can't tell me specifics. That's between you and your mentor."

My hands tightened around my shins. "I don't care about that," I said.

My mom sighed, patting down my hair. "I know it seems like there are a lot of rules, but they're all in place to keep us safe."

My hands tensed, fingernails biting into my legs. "They won't keep *me* safe!" I said, pushing her hand away. "You asked me what was wrong but you don't even want to hear about it?"

"Of course I *want* to, Mina," my mom said, frowning. "But it's not about what *I* want. What's best for the timeline is what's best for all of us. You have to trust."

Would you say that if you knew the truth? I thought, turning away and crossing my arms so she wouldn't see my tears. But I didn't need to ask, because I knew the answer. They had already lost one daughter to the timeline, and they didn't even miss her.

"I'm going to bed," I said, pushing out my chair and snatching my bag off the floor.

"Okay, honey," my mom said hesitantly. "I love you, Mina."

You don't know what love is, I wanted to say. *If the descendants can take it away from you so easily, then it isn't love.*

"I love you too," I said quietly, then shut my bedroom door.

My parents were leaving early in the morning, so that might be the last time I ever saw my mom. I would never be able to kill someone knowing it would start a war, which meant Yejun would take me to headquarters to be erased or kill me on the spot—either way, I'd be gone from their lives. Hong Gildong would probably do some selective mind wiping on my parents regardless, just to make sure they stayed obedient worker bees. The idea of my parents not even missing me was so much worse than them mourning me.

I tore a sheet of paper out of my notebook and set it on my desk. Yejun had said paper materials didn't reset as easily as phones during a timeline refresh, so maybe, somehow, this would survive.

I picked up a pen and wrote a letter to my parents.

My name is Mina. If you don't know who I am, then the descendants have already taken me from you. Once, I was your daughter. I love you always, even if you forget me. The descendants can never change that.

I crept back into the hallway and tucked the note into my mom's coin purse, where she probably wouldn't notice it for a few days, until she was safely in Japan. Maybe the timeline refresh would destroy it anyway and she would never read it. But I knew now that erasing someone wasn't a clean process, that there were always loose threads. I prayed that this was one of them.

I took out Hana's note and clutched it to my chest as I lay down in bed.

You have to trust, my mom had said.

But I couldn't trust the descendants, or Yejun, or even my parents. The only person I could trust was someone I couldn't even see. I was somehow both trapped under Hong Gildong's thumb yet still as isolated as a rogue agent. I might as well have gone rogue at that point, for all the good my friends and family had done me.

Slowly, I pulled Hana's note from my chest, letting the pale moonlight illuminate her words.

Hana had to have gone rogue in order to leave me this note. That meant she had survived the timeline refresh. And if she could, maybe I could too. It wasn't a hundred percent chance, but I liked the odds of surviving the timeline refresh better than my odds of surviving Yejun's gun to my head or Hong Gildong shoving my time magic down my throat. All I had to do was get Yejun out of my way before he could tell on me.

I crushed Hana's note close to my heart, feeling like she was here with me once more.

You're smarter than them, she would tell me. *Just like the ladybug, you can slip away when they least expect it.*

They'd tested me because I was foreign, average, no one special. But underestimating me would be their last mistake.

Chapter Eighteen

The next morning, I finished my red velvet cheesecake and wiped my mouth, reapplied my lip balm, then took out my phone and dropped Yejun a pin with my location, followed by a panicked text.

THERE'S A PARADOX HERE.

I pushed my plate away and leaned back in the booth. My phone lit up with texts, but I ignored them all and examined my new locks of white hair in my phone camera. It had taken a metric ton of bleach to make it look like the timeline had stripped part of my hair of color, and it still looked a bit too yellow, but I figured it looked convincing enough for Yejun. It wasn't like he was a hairdresser who would know the difference.

My parents had left for their flight before sunrise, leaving me full reign of the house to destroy the bathroom with bleach. I'd even bleached half an old shirt for good measure, which I was currently wearing. It was a pretty basic scenario setup—I wasn't Yejun, after all—but I was good at lying, and that was how I would sell it.

I silenced my phone, because it was still lighting up with texts from my dad, updating me on every nanosecond of their travel.

> Just arrived at the airport! Got through security—
> mom almost lost a shoe. Waiting at the gate eating a
> sandwich—not very good.

My phone started vibrating, but I ignored that as well, wondering if I had time to get another piece of cheesecake before Yejun showed up. It was tempting, but the last thing I wanted was for him to arrive and see me calmly eating cheesecake.

I'd come to a café in Hapjeong early that morning and tucked myself into a back booth, shielded from view by a huge model train—the café had some sort of steampunk theme, with giant gears and dissected clocks sparkling on every wall.

I'd chosen this location partially because all the chaos would make time travel easier, and partially because it was famous for its huge selection of cheesecakes. A long display case stretched across the room, filled with an array of cheesecake flavors—chocolate, red velvet, raspberry, coconut, peanut butter. I told myself that this was a strategic choice because most Koreans didn't want cheesecake for breakfast, which made the café less crowded this early in the morning, but mostly I'd just wanted to sample the different flavors.

I scrolled on my phone for another fifteen minutes, then scattered my silverware across the table, messed up my hair a bit, and tried to work myself up to near tears, which was hard to do when my dad kept bombarding me with ridiculous texts.

> Airplane food is OK. Was hoping no one would sit near
> us. Should I trust airplane sushi? Is it legal to paint nails on
> plane? Mom wants to know. Should we eat BBQ or ramen
> when we land?

I started to type up a response, when Yejun rushed through the door, his hair wet and sticking up, a bright blue raincoat flapping behind him, gaze darting around frantically. He locked eyes with me and hurried across the café.

I jumped up and rushed into his arms, letting him sweep me into a hug. It was almost physically painful the way his magic hummed through my bones, warming me as I pressed against him. Now that I knew all of this was a lie, each beautiful moment felt so sharp.

But I was good at infiltration missions, at pretending not to feel. It was the only reason I'd made it this far.

"Are you okay?" Yejun said, pulling back and examining my white locks of hair, my bleached shirt. He reached for my arm on the bleached side and held it up to the light as if checking for marks.

"I'm okay," I said, sniffling. "It only got a small part of the café and went away pretty fast. But I've never been alone when a paradox came before, and I almost fell into it, and I . . ." I turned away, letting my hair fall over my face as if to hide my tears.

Yejun cupped my cheek and angled my face toward him, his eyes so wide and concerned that the next tears that tracked down my cheek weren't a lie. *Stop pretending*, I thought. *I can't bear it.*

"Did you tell Hyebin?" he said, wiping my tears away gently with his thumb.

I shook my head, leaning into his hand. "I didn't want to talk to Hyebin," I said. "I wanted to talk to *you*."

The words felt so foolish now that I knew the truth, but it was what he wanted to hear. His touch scalded me as he wiped more tears away, a cruel reminder of what could never be real.

Yejun smiled sadly, then tucked my head against his shirt and petted my hair. "I'm here," he said, the warm words vibrating through his chest. "What can I do?"

I took a steadying breath, tugging at my sleeves while I pretended to contemplate the answer. "Can you take me somewhere else?" I said at last. "I don't want to be here right now."

He nodded quickly. "Anywhere," he said, holding my face so delicately in his hands. "Where do you want to go?"

I glanced forlornly out the window at the gray sky.

"How about that day when it was sunny last week?" Yejun said quickly, just as I'd planned.

I pretended to contemplate it for a moment, then nodded and grabbed a napkin to wipe my face.

"Okay, stay right here," Yejun said. "I'm gonna go clog a sink and scry for a sec. Don't go anywhere!"

He gave my hand a gentle squeeze, then dashed off toward the bathrooms.

The moment he was out of sight, my shoulders drooped. I could still feel the warmth of his chest against my face, the sound of his heartbeat against my cheek.

Remember why you're here, I thought, clenching my teeth and slumping over in the booth. *Focus, Mina. You're supposed to be scared. Think of scary things. Spiders. Clowns. Global warming.*

Yejun hurried back a few moments later. "Okay, got it," he said. "October eighth."

He glanced around to check for humans or cameras, then held out his hand.

I hesitated, memorizing the pattern of his veins, the shape of his nails, the sight of his slender fingers that I had seen dance across scrying pools, changing the world like it meant nothing at all. This would be the last time I held Kim Yejun's hand.

I took his hand and his magic sang through me. He would be able to taste my sadness, but he would think it was because I was scared after a paradox, not because I was about to say goodbye.

As we landed in the past, I squinted at the harsh morning sunlight through the windows, the unfairly beautiful sky.

"Better?" Yejun said, turning to me.

"Yes," I said, smiling stiffly. I leaned forward to hug him but this time didn't press my face to his chest. I locked my eyes with him, so close to his face, my hands clutching his jacket. "Thank you, Yejun," I whispered. "You're always here for me. You're the only one who is."

It was almost easy now. I had waded so deep into the lie that I felt like I was telling the story of someone else's life, a dream that would never be mine.

"I'll always be here for you," he lied, tucking my hair behind my ear.

I leaned closer, so close I could almost taste his next words on his lips, the sound of my name . . .

I slipped my hand into his pocket and closed my fingers around his yeouiju.

I turned away right as he leaned forward, pocketing his yeouiju before he could see the blue light between my fingers.

"I have a new plan," I said, sitting back down in the booth.

Yejun blinked quickly, startled by the sudden change in mood, but nodded and slid into the booth opposite me.

"I'm not going to do the mission," I said.

Yejun stared at me blankly. "Okay," he said. "So what are you going to do instead?"

"I'm going to go rogue," I said. "Like Hana. She has the gene, so I must have it too."

Yejun frowned. "Are you sure?"

"I don't have a choice," I said. "I've decided, so I need to do it now before the hour resets. This is the last time you'll see me, at least for a while. I'm sure Hong Gildong will be looking for me, so I should keep my distance to make sure you don't get caught. In fact, it's probably safer if I don't even tell you where I'm going."

Yejun had gone very still in the booth, as if afraid to move a muscle. "Mina," he said, "I think—"

"I've already decided," I said, because apparently I needed to make this clear. "Fuck Hong Gildong and his plans. I'm never going to do what he says. Unless they find me in the next"—I glanced at my watch—"fifty-one minutes, they'll never find me again."

Yejun dropped his gaze to the table, clenching his jaw.

Now he would have no choice but to apprehend me. Except, when he reached for his yeouiju, he would realize it was gone. I'd stranded him in the past with no powers. Neither of us would show up to my mission, Min Sungho would live, and there would be no war.

I waited for the moment he tried to take me, braced to jump and run. I couldn't wait to see the look on his face when he realized I'd tricked him.

But Yejun only sighed. "First of all," he said, "there are tests for the rogue gene. You should get tested before just throwing yourself into a timeline refresh."

I frowned. "Are you . . . trying to talk me out of it?"

He shook his head. "No, you should definitely go rogue," he said, "but in a way that doesn't leave you dead. Your plan has too many holes. For one thing, going rogue doesn't suddenly make you invisible. Hong Gildong will probably be keeping close tabs on you until the mission is over. You need to find a way to shake him before just running off, or else—assuming you actually survive the timeline refresh—a thousand alarms would go off in headquarters once they register that you're not on your origin timeline anymore."

I shook my head. This wasn't what was supposed to happen. I had deviated from my instructions, and this was his last chance to apprehend me. He should have been dragging me back to headquarters, but for some reason, he was helping me.

When I didn't answer, he started digging through his backpack. "I didn't grab a tray before I left," he said. "Maybe I should buy some bingsu, then we can eat it and use the bowl for scrying? We'll think of a better plan."

"*We?*" I echoed, clenching my fists. Tears burned my eyes, but this time I couldn't stop them. "Why are you still pretending?" I whispered.

Yejun raised an eyebrow. "Pretending?"

"I told you I'm not going to kill Min Sungho," I said. "Why aren't you dragging me to HQ like you're supposed to?"

He froze. "Why would I . . ." But he trailed off as he read my expression. Maybe it was the hate in my eyes, or maybe my words had finally sunk in, or maybe it was just because I'd been foolish enough to let him into my soul and he could see exactly what I was thinking. Understanding dawned on his face, and he dropped his gaze to the table as if ashamed. "Mina," he said unsteadily, "I—"

"*Don't*," I said, taking a shuddering breath to stop myself from crying more. "Please stop lying to me."

Yejun's shoulders drooped. He looked so pathetic and sad, but that only made the rage burn brighter inside me. "I know you were just doing your job," I said, talking louder to fight back the tears. "I know that's what all the descendants are doing. But that doesn't make it right, and that's not a good enough excuse for me anymore. I trusted you because I thought you knew that."

"Mina," Yejun said sadly, reaching out as if to take my hand.

I yanked it away before he could touch me. "And the worst part of all? You used my sister to sell me on your lie. I never would have used your mom against you, Yejun. And maybe that's why you're a good descendant and I'm not. I know I never would have been like you or Hyebin. But I don't think I deserved all this just for being so"—I unclenched my fists, looking at my pale palms scarred from nail marks—"human," I finished quietly.

"Mina, I'm so sorry," Yejun said. He sounded sincere enough, but his words meant nothing to me now. They wouldn't change what he'd done. "I didn't want to lie to you. But I wouldn't have hurt you or turned you in. Please believe me."

I scoffed. "Why would I believe you?" I said. "You lied to me about everything! Were we even going to save the *Sewol* ferry? You just used all those deaths to add some drama to your story? To make you seem like a good person?"

He shook his head quickly. "I petitioned Hong Gildong to really let me save the ferry," Yejun said. "I scripted a thousand scenarios telling him how we could pull it off without actually breaking the timeline, but he wouldn't even read my proposal. He kept talking about the 'integrity of the timeline.' I've been trying to find a way out of this, Mina, just like you. I swear."

"I don't believe you," I said.

Yejun sighed and raked his fingers through his wet hair, rustling his blue raincoat . . . which looked strangely familiar. It was the same bright blue as the raincoat that Yejun's Echo had worn when he stole Yejun's laptop and poured water on his head. Sure enough, there was Yejun's black school bag on the seat beside him.

"You got your bag back?" I said, frowning.

Yejun followed my gaze to his school bag. "Oh, yeah," he said. "Losing my laptop gave me an excuse to turn my mid-quarter report in late, so I had to make sure it happened. I was afraid Hong Gildong would make me test you even sooner."

"So you *mugged yourself*?" I said.

He shrugged. "I mean, gently, yeah."

I shook my head. My mind felt like it was full of sand flies. "And dumped water on yourself? How did that help anything?"

"It didn't," Yejun said with a grimace. "I was just mad at myself and thought I deserved it, like in those K-dramas when the woman does it to the man, but I knew you were too nice to do it to me. I swear I didn't want to turn you in, Mina. I wanted it to be different this time."

"I already told you, I don't . . ." I paused as the rest of his words sank in. "What do you mean, *this time*?"

Yejun leaned back against the booth, crossing his arms. "There is not a single timeline where I could hand you over to Hong Gildong," he said. "Do you have any idea how inconvenient that is for me?"

I tried to conjure a response, but no matter how many times I played back Yejun's last sentence, it didn't make any sense. This felt more like a fever dream than an actual conversation. "What are you talking about?" I said at last.

Yejun sighed, glaring down at the table. "The first time this happened, I really thought I could do it," he said. "I've always been the top of my class, and I was first in line for a promotion. All I had to do was get rid of you, and I would be the next Jang Hyebin. But do you know what I did instead?" He let out a sharp laugh, shaking his head. "I shot the supervising agent at the rally."

Yejun waited for my reaction, but I was still caught on the whole "first time this happened" bit that he glossed over. He already failed this mission once, and he got to try again?

"The descendants sanctioned a redo for you?" I asked.

Yejun scoffed. "Of course not. They threw me in a cell while they decided whether to erase me or just wipe my brain. I had to choke a guard through the bars to take his keys and get my yeouiju back. I barely made it before the refresh, but I managed to send an Echo back with a note for the shoe rack. I nearly put it in the wrong shoe, too. I'm honestly kind of shocked that I'm still alive."

He raked a hand through his hair, jaw clenched, all his muscles tense. "The second time, I spent as little time with you as possible. I tried to be just rude enough to you that you wouldn't open up to me, but nice enough that you would still work with me. But then we ran into my mom, and you defended me when she started insulting me in public, and of course I couldn't kill you after that. At least Hyebin spilled some coffee in my cell that time so I didn't have to nearly bite my own tongue off to make a scrying pool and figure out another plan."

He leaned across the table, his eyes swirling with gold, so bright that they reflected my own face back at me in shifting shades of sunlight. "I've tried so many times to make myself hate you," he said, "or at least not care about you so I could do this mission. But I don't think the timeline is as malleable as the descendants would like to believe. I think there are some things that even dragon gods can't change."

"What do you mean?" I whispered. He was so close to me, his words warm on my face.

"I don't know if there really is a Timeline Alpha or not," Yejun said, "and I don't know if it's too late to fix it this time around. All I know is that no matter how many times this plays out, I'll choose you every time."

I looked away as his perfect promise hovered in the air between us, the words he surely knew I wanted to hear. Every part of me wanted to forgive him, to let go of that bitter sting of betrayal and let our souls braid together.

But I couldn't just forget how I'd felt when I read his report. I'd come so close to feeling like a true descendant when I was with him, someone powerful and smart and capable. But I was only ever another casualty to the timeline. I was the Seongsu Bridge that Hyebin had destroyed, and the sinking ferry that we never could have saved, and the scorched, ruined world I'd imagined beyond Hong Gildong's office windows.

I'd managed to shove the sorrow down, smother it under my plans to go rogue and get revenge and find my sister. But only because I knew if I dared to stopped running, I would find out exactly how deep Yejun had cut.

And what if this was just another test? What if he turned around and wrote on his next report that I was stupid enough to fall for his lies not once but twice? He'd promised not to lie to me, and yet he'd lied to me every moment since I'd met him.

I leaned back, watching his eyes go dim. "It's too late, Yejun," I said.

His expression crumpled, but he nodded as if he expected this, then pulled a notebook out of his bag and set it on the table. "Luckily, it's never too late for a time traveler," he said, pulling a pen out of another pocket and starting to scrawl something on the blank page.

"What are you doing?" I said.

"Writing myself another letter for the shoe rack at the restaurant," he said, not looking up from the page. "So when I go back and try again, I'll remember."

"What do you mean, 'try again'?" I said, reeling. "I told you—"

"Hang on," he said, still writing. I caught a glimpse of my own name in the book and leaned closer, but he angled away from me.

"*You can't just try again!*" I said, reaching for the notebook. "You don't get to just go back and erase your mistakes!"

Yejun tried to tug the notebook out of my reach, but I grabbed the corner and snatched it from him. I started to tear out the note he'd just written, intending to crumple it up and throw it away, but hesitated when I read the first line.

Dear Yejun,

You've managed to mess this up once again, despite our best efforts, so here's all you need to know this time around: Soon, you're going to fall for a girl named Mina. When you touch her magic, you'll feel safe. And when you touch *her*, you'll feel like you're home.

Just do it again, and do it right this time. If she doesn't forgive you in this timeline, try again. Fall for her in a thousand lives if you have to. Don't ever give up until you get it right.

Sincerely,
A less-successful Yejun

P.S. She loves cheesecake.

Slowly, I looked up and met Yejun's gaze. His eyes were no longer gold with dragon fire or blue with time magic but a warm, human shade of brown.

I knew, in that moment, that he was sincere.

Not because I tasted it in his magic, or because I could see it written on the map of his heart, or because I could detect the speed of his pulse with my dragon senses.

I knew it because I knew Kim Yejun, and I always had.

It was funny the way the timeline worked—I didn't remember falling for him before, and the version of me who did was not the same as I was now. But being with Yejun was inevitable, and the timeline knew it, just as it knew that Hana's love for me survived against all logic. Just as some people believed in God, I believed in love that could not be seen, or touched, or explained.

"Kim Yejun," I said at last, "you're going to have to buy me a metric ton of cheesecake to make up for this."

He let out a sharp laugh, then reached for my hand once more. This time, I let him take it, lacing his fingers with mine.

"I fully intend to," he said, "but how about we figure out how to survive the rest of the week first?"

With my cheesecake replenished and an empty bingsu-bowl-turned-scrying-pool on the table in front of us, we got to work.

"Can your amazing architect skills find a way to save us and stop a war?" I said.

"I hope so," Yejun said, digging through his backpack. He pulled out a small, worn notebook and set it on the table. As he flipped through it, I caught a glimpse of tiny scrawl crammed into every page, so tightly that there was almost no white space.

"What is *that*?" I said, squinting to discern the writing.

"From the shoe rack," Yejun said, smoothing it out as he reached a blank page. "Plans I've tried before that haven't worked."

I gripped the edge of my seat. "You've tried all of that and none of it has worked before?"

Yejun shot me a withering smile. "It's a good thing—we won't repeat the same mistake twice."

I groaned and flopped back in my seat. "This is hopeless."

"It's not," Yejun said, pulling the bingsu bowl closer. "We just need to find a way to find your sister—"

"Wait," I said, dread lancing through my stomach. "If there's no Timeline Alpha to bring back, how can I save Hana?"

"If Hana is still communicating with you, then she can't be completely erased," Yejun said. "Maybe they didn't wipe her from a certain moment or place and she managed to move around the timeline. If we can read her file, maybe we can figure out how to help her."

I drummed my fingers on the table. "Okay, so we just need to break into Hong Gildong's office and scrying pool even though he can see the whole timeline and is definitely keeping a very close eye on both of us?"

"By tomorrow," Yejun added helpfully.

We stared blankly at each other for a moment before he sighed and stood up. "We're going to need more caffeine for this," he said.

While he went to order coffee, I scrolled through my phone and tried to think of anything I could possibly google that might help. I didn't want Yejun to do all the work, but there was a reason *he* was training to be a timeline architect while *I* was focusing on infiltration missions. I flipped back to the barrage of texts from my dad and typed out a quick response about BBQ restaurants, sending it before I remembered that I wasn't in the present and it probably wouldn't even go through.

Yejun returned to the table with two coffees in hand, then got to work at his scrying pool. His fingers danced across the surface as he typed with one hand and scrolled with the other, two different windows open at once.

"I'm searching your family file through the back end, but I can't find anything about Yang Hana," he said. "What do you know about her that I might be able to use?"

Hardly anything, I thought, too embarrassed to voice this out loud. "She had a pink sweater?" I said quietly.

Yejun lifted an eyebrow, his fingers hesitating over the water. "Anything else?"

"She left me a note? Does that help?"

Yejun looked up sharply. "When?"

"I found it on September second," I said.

Yejun nodded and turned back to the pool. "I can search the mission logs and narrow it by that date," he said.

"Aren't the mission logs classified?" I said.

"Yeah, if your hacking skills are worse than those of a twelve-year-old," Yejun said. "Most mission logs are only level two, which is easy to hack into. Level one is another story." Then his eyes lit up. "Found it," he said, waving for me to come to his side of the table. I shoved out my chair and hurried around. In the scrying pool, he'd pulled up what looked like an advanced search function, with only one item populated at the top.

```
SEPTEMBER 2, 2025, GREENVIEW OFFICETEL ROOM
325, UNAUTHORIZED AGENT, DURATION: 5 MINUTES
```

"That must be her!" I said, squeezing Yejun's arm. "That's when Hana went to my apartment!"

"I know, I know, I'm brilliant," Yejun said, grinning.

I hugged him from the side, feeling as though my whole body was made of sunlight. I had never felt so close to finding Hana before. It was like only a thin pane of glass stood between us, and all that was left was to shatter it.

Yejun's yeouiju glowed warmly against my side, and I remembered that I still had it on me. Before I pulled away, I slipped it back into his pocket.

"So we just have to intercept her there," I said as I leaned back.

"Well, yes," Yejun said uneasily, "but that still leaves the problem of how we could do that without getting caught. Hong Gildong knows you want to find Hana, and if *we* could figure out where she's been, *he* definitely has. He probably has supervising agents staking out your apartment on that day."

I sank back against the seat, glaring at the ceiling as if it would tell me the answer. Yejun let out a hiss, and I turned to see him examining a paper cut on his finger before jamming it in his mouth.

"I have Band-Aids, you monster," I said, reaching for my backpack. I slid my hand into the middle pocket for my first-aid pack, but my fingers closed around the ladybug key chain from Hyebin. It looked so smiley and silly—a complete contrast to Hyebin herself. I remembered us catching the ladybug together over the bridge, back when everything had seemed so simple. If only I were able to hide from the descendants the way the ladybug had.

I tensed, sitting up straight. The ladybug had managed to evade the descendants, so why couldn't I? What had Hyebin said again? Something about daylight savings. I closed my eyes and tried to remember the sound of her voice, imagining her on the bus beside me as we rolled through western Seoul.

Daylight savings was tested in 1988 for the Olympics. So there's no 2:00 A.M. through 2:59 A.M. in the spring, and there's duplicate times for 1:00 A.M. through 1:59 A.M. in the fall that year.

That meant there was an hour on the timeline that didn't exist.

Except . . . there were no holes in the timeline. Time flowed continuously and for all of eternity, but *measuring* time was a concept engineered by humans. The world had still existed from 2:00 A.M. to 2:59 A.M. in 1988, but for people who relied on the social construct of time . . .

It would be a blind spot in our records.

"Mina," Yejun said, "what about—"

"Shh!" I said, closing my eyes and trying to chase the thought, clinging to it like an umbrella seized in a storm.

The ladybug went from not being on the timeline at all to landing at 3:00 A.M. on May 8. It was kind of like being born on that day—1988 became its new origin timeline.

I pictured Hyebin squishing the ladybug inside the bag, just like Hong Gildong would squash me if given the chance. He'd mark my execution as MISSION COMPLETE in his scrying pool and I'd disappear into the abyss of archived files, forgotten . . .

Forgotten.

"What if," I said, sitting up straight, "I died at the rally?"

Yejun frowned. "You're not going to—"

"But *what if I did*?" I said, leaning closer. "What if I failed the mission and you killed me?"

"I wouldn't do that," Yejun said with a scowl. "I don't know what you're—"

"What if the descendants *thought* you killed me?" I said.

Yejun froze, slowly sinking back in his seat. "Then they wouldn't be watching you anymore," he said. "At least, for a few minutes. But as soon as the timeline refreshed, and your file stayed open, they would know you were alive."

"Unless I didn't exist," I said. "Unless I was somewhere they couldn't find me."

A small smile curled the corner of Yejun's mouth. "Mina, what are you planning?"

"Do you think one hour is enough time to save my sister and then the world?" I said, scooping up another bite of cheesecake.

"It might be cutting it close," Yejun said, "but I think you can make it work."

Chapter Nineteen

The first step in Operation: Fake Kill Yang Mina was to make sure that the agent supervising the mission would be standing far away at the rally so he wouldn't get a close look at our tricks.

Yejun's solution was to feed a squirrel a peanut butter and honey sandwich a few days in the past, which rendered it so full that it fell asleep instead of darting in front of someone's car and causing a fender bender. Without the accident, the rear car didn't realize that he needed his brakes checked. He wouldn't figure it out until the morning of the rally, when he'd skid through an intersection and slam into an ice cream truck. The whole intersection would have to be shut down, and the supervising agent would get caught in the traffic jam, making him show up late to the rally and unable to get a good vantage point.

Then, of course, there was the matter of making sure Yejun didn't have to actually kill me.

The most logical way to ensure my safety in that regard was, of course, by patching up a hole in an alley outside an Italian restaurant one day in the past. The mice that normally snuck scraps out of the kitchen had no choice but to hunt for food elsewhere, and a trail of breadcrumbs led them to a bakery, where they cleared out the cranberry bin in record time. As a result, the bakery made a batch of chocolate chip muffins rather than their usual cranberry muffins. The assistant at the firearms desk at headquarters bought one, assuming it was cranberry, and accidentally ate four chocolate chips, which triggered a migraine. When Yejun came by that morning to check out his live rounds and a Kevlar vest, the assistant was too dizzy and distracted to realize he'd given Yejun blank rounds instead.

"Are you sure these are blanks?" I said, rolling one of the tiny golden cylinders between my fingers as Yejun loaded his gun in the alley outside Caffebene. "This still looks like it could kill me."

"I'm positive," Yejun said. "There's no projectile on top. You see how it just looks like a tube instead of a little rocket?"

I passed it back to him, unconvinced.

"Hyebin never showed you blanks?" Yejun asked.

I shook my head. "Can't do target practice with blanks. I must have used them at some point, though. I've seen those somewhere."

Yejun handed me the Kevlar vest, which I stuffed into my backpack, then we parted ways so we could both get ready for the rally that night.

I managed to choke down some instant ramen for dinner, then strapped on the Kevlar vest, followed by a plastic bag of corn syrup, water, and red food dye, which I secured with packing tape to my abdomen. I pulled Hana's baggy pink-and-orange sweater over the top to hide it all, then practiced walking like I wasn't wearing a Kevlar corset.

In my front holster, I had the gun I'd signed out of headquarters that morning, since as far as anyone else knew, I fully intended to kill Min Sungho. I hated the weight of an actual loaded gun against my skin and was sure that despite all the firearm training, I was going to accidentally shoot my own toes off.

When I got to the rally, Yejun would shoot a blank at me, breaking the blood bag but hopefully not any ribs. I would play possum until the crowd dispersed, and then I'd commence my hour off grid.

I can do this, I told my reflection as I slipped on my shoes and grabbed my backpack off the floor. I was fairly certain I wasn't supposed to take something as big as a backpack to a political rally where security would be tight, but my purse still smelled like pork thanks to my failed attempt at ruining my date with Jihoon. I cast one last glance in the mirror at my skunk-streaked hair and headed into the night.

I kept double-checking that my wallet was in my bag as I walked, irrationally afraid that Hana's note was going to disintegrate the moment I couldn't see it. I'd hoped the note would give me courage, but Hana felt strangely far away today. Even though I was wrapped in her sweater, I didn't feel like she was hugging me like usual, as if the Kevlar was shielding me from both the bullets and her touch.

I took the subway, which was packed with people holding signs for the political rally. The train car rocked me back and forth, and I did my best to tug my sweater down, paranoid that someone would notice my gun.

When I finally arrived, I followed the crowd out of the subway station and up to the main street, which was lit with so many streetlights and neon signs that it might as well have been broad daylight, even though the sun had already set.

I locked eyes with Yejun, who was waiting for me on the stairs, just as we'd planned.

I walked up to him and angled myself so I was facing the street, where the supervising agent would get a clear view of all the blood but not much else. When Min Sungho headed down the walkway,

I would make a show of preparing to shoot and then changing my mind and trying to leave, at which point Yejun would grab me, I would resist, and he would fire his blank at me.

"Showtime?" I said with a small smile.

"Showtime," Yejun echoed, not meeting my gaze. His eyes darted around the rally, his fingers twitching and tugging at the sleeves of his jacket. He had always seemed so at ease, but now it seemed like his bones were trying to shake free from his body.

"What's wrong?" I said.

"Is that a serious question?" he said. "This is kind of an important mission."

"What, you think you'll miss?" I said, smirking and poking his stomach.

But he didn't return my smile. "A lot of things could go wrong," he said. "We could get caught. Or maybe the supervising agent will see through it, or the blood bags won't go off, or—"

"You have scripted hundreds of intricate scenarios," I said, "and *now*, of all times, you decide to drop your ego?"

He grimaced. "I'm nervous."

"You're not the one getting shot."

"Mina," he groaned. "Don't say that."

The noise of the crowd increased as a black car pulled up at the end of the walkway. Min Sungho must have arrived, judging by the swarming security guards. I scanned the crowd, being sure to look in the direction of the supervising agent, then tracked Min Sungho with my gaze as he began to ascend the walkway. I slipped a hand into my jacket, as if to grab my gun, then let my shoulders droop and turned to Yejun.

"In a dramatic turn of events, I have realized I am too kind and gentle a soul to do it," I said, keeping my expression forlorn even as my words were ridiculous. "I have no option but to betray the descendants. Whatever will you do, Yejun-ssi?"

Yejun only grimaced, unmoved by my melodramatics. I sighed and took a step closer. Soon, Min Sungho would be right in front of us.

"Go ahead," I whispered to Yejun. "I'm ready."

Yejun took a steadying breath, then withdrew his gun from the holster and pressed it to my stomach, shielding it with his coat. I braced for the impact of the blank, but he only let out an unsteady breath and rested his forehead against mine.

"Yejun?" I said. "Uh, you probably shouldn't let the supervising agent see this."

"Blanks are still dangerous, especially at this range," Yejun said.

"That's what the Kevlar is for," I said, frowning.

"It could still hurt you."

"I mean, maybe, but I wouldn't die," I said, shrugging.

It was the wrong thing to say. Yejun tensed up, then lowered his gun. "I've already hurt you so much," he said. "I don't want to hurt you anymore."

"Yejun—"

"Mina, I *can't*," he said, cupping my cheek with one hand. "Don't you see? Ever since the very first time around, that's always been the problem. I can't hurt you, no matter how much I need to."

His words didn't sink in until he zipped up his jacket, hiding his holster, and I realized that he was actually going to refuse to shoot me.

The voices in the crowd rose as Min Sungho approached, flanked by security. He would walk by us soon, and the moment Yejun was supposed to kill me would pass. The supervising agent would seize us both, and I would never find Hana.

"Let's go and get a head start, Mina," Yejun said. "If they're going to take us down, let's at least make it hard for them."

I shook my head, looking around frantically. "We can't leave yet," I said. "You have to do it, or else—"

My next words died in my throat.

A girl with a hood pulled over her face was pushing toward us.

The rest of the crowd faded into the background, all their voices blurring together into a drone, their faces melting away. The empty feeling of Hana's absence had lifted. The girl in the crowd had dark hair that turned coppery in the sunlight, a silver watch on her wrist.

"Mina, I won't do it," Yejun said, starting to sound frustrated instead of sad. "I can't."

The girl drew to a stop five feet away from us. Her hair blew around her face, her hood hanging over her eyes. I wanted to run toward her, but I couldn't move at all.

"Hana?" I whispered.

Then she squared her stance, raised a gun at me, and pulled the trigger.

The impact tossed me back into Yejun. Even through the Kevlar vest, it was like a solid punch to the ribs that forced all the air out of my lungs. For a moment, I couldn't think of anything except trying to draw in air. My side felt cold and wet, my whole body trembling with adrenaline. Had I actually been shot, or was it just the blood bag bursting? I was too numb to tell.

Yejun seemed to wonder the same thing, for as he caught me, one hand slid under my sweater and to my abdomen, worming beneath the Kevlar, his fingers cold against my skin. I knew, when I felt his fingers on smooth, unbroken skin, that it was only the fake blood.

I looked up at where Hana had been, but she was gone. I tried to recall her face, but with her hood down, I hadn't gotten a good look, and now all I could imagine was a black hole, an abyss instead of answers.

Why would Hana shoot me?

I hated knowing so little about my sister. She'd used blanks, so clearly she wasn't actually trying to kill me, but why would she shoot me at all?

The crowd had stilled at the sound of gunfire, and now everyone had spread out in a circle around me and Yejun.

"There's blood!" someone shouted, prompting a few people to scream and start pushing away.

"Are you okay?" Yejun whispered, one hand cupping my cheek.

"I'm fine," I whispered back, now that the ache had faded and I could breathe again. "We have to keep going."

The crowd was screaming now. Some people were pushing, everyone rushing for the exit. The police were trying to force their way toward us but couldn't make it far through the packed crowd. Yejun slipped one hand under my knees and lifted me up to avoid being crushed. I yelped in surprise, clinging to him so I wouldn't fall. My face was definitely bright red as I realized how easily he carried me, which was a far cry from the bloodless look I was going for.

"You're not doing a very good job at playing possum," he whispered.

I managed to loosen my grip, then flopped over. He stumbled, struggling to adjust his hold, and I swore I'd kill him if he dropped me. He headed in the direction of headquarters, because that was what the supervising agent would want to see. By now, the crowd was screaming and shoving in all directions. Yejun tucked me closer to his chest, shielding me from the crowd.

Though I couldn't see, I felt the change in temperature as he made it out of the crowd, ducking into the alley by the fruit market where there were no cameras, exactly as we'd planned.

He set me on my feet, his hands lingering over the fake blood, his expression pinched. I took his wrist and pressed it to my heart.

"It's okay," I said. "Just corn syrup. You can have a taste if you want."

He laughed sharply and drew his hand back, then took his yeouiju from his pocket and placed it in my palm. "Do it now," he said. "Before they catch up."

My right hand closed around the ball of light, my left hand holding my own box of time magic. Blue light wound its way up my right arm, purple light spiraling up my left arm, the whole alley glowing indigo around us.

Yejun and I had shared magic so many times, but now I was holding his soul in my hand, and he'd given it to me like he hadn't thought twice about it. I held it delicately, feeling the warm pulse of blue light in time with his heartbeat. *I'll take care of this*, I thought. *I promise*.

"Go," Yejun said with a smile, as if he'd heard my thoughts. "I'll see you and Hana when you're done."

Then he stepped back, waving with a soft smile as the ribbons of light around me grew brighter, devouring the street and Yejun along with it.

· 🦋 ·

I landed in an empty construction lot in the dark.

The bakery near the alley we'd been standing in hadn't been built in 1988, so it eliminated the risk of me appearing on top of a customer. Around me, there was nothing but loose scaffolding and cinder blocks abandoned at night, remnants of coffee cups and footprints in the pale dirt.

I checked my watch.

1:58 A.M.

Only two minutes until the timeline would reset, and I would find out for sure if the ladybug theory was right, or if the refresh would obliterate me.

If this doesn't work, I'm going to die anyway, I thought, hiking my bag higher on my shoulder and stepping carefully out of the construction zone.

Eunpyeong was quiet this late at night. All the shops were different in 1988, and some tall buildings were mysteriously absent, but I recognized it in the same way I was certain I knew Hana. Even now, no matter how much had changed, it felt like my home.

I squatted behind a dumpster and quickly shed the Kevlar vest and bloody shirt, dumping both on top of the trash, then pulled on a clean shirt from my bag and carefully tucked Hana's sweater back inside.

I walked to the Bulgwang stream and stood on the footbridge where I'd stopped so many times to look at the sky. It was a bit narrower now but had the same crop of purple flowers on either side, the same unhurried pull toward the sea. If I was going to be wiped from existence on the hour mark, I wanted it to be here, looking out at the stream that disappeared into the horizon, the white footbridges, the pale stepping stones, the clean pinpricks of stars in the dark sky. I wanted to be at home.

I checked my watch again.

Ten seconds.

I closed my eyes, my hands tense on the railing, and took a deep breath. I could smell rain, and gas, and echoes of fried food, and dew on the grass below, and wetness on stones, and so many other pieces of home that I would miss if this really was my last life.

I counted down the moments in my head.

Three . . . two . . . one . . .

My hands tightened on the railing, then released. I opened my eyes and checked my watch.

3:00 A.M.

I let out a breath. A breeze tore across the street, jingling the ladybug key chain hanging from the zipper of my backpack. I was now the second Mina Yang, the second ladybug, flying undetected. All that was left to do was intercept Hana on the day I moved to Seoul.

I clutched my two sources of time magic tight in my hands, let them warm my bones, and wiped my mind of everything but a girl bathed in sunlight, her hand reaching out for mine, and the time and date when we would finally meet.

I arrived two minutes before Hana.

It was enough time for me to hurry to my apartment and beat Hana to the scene, and not so much time as to blow through my fifty-nine-minute limit before the timeline refreshed once more. I walked in a daze down the street, unbothered by the crush of summer humidity or sunlight blaring around the skyscrapers because I was so close to finally seeing Hana.

Even though I'd since lived in this apartment and city for over a month, the day still felt exactly like the first day I'd arrived—my fingertips prickled with all the fear and excitement of a new beginning, a new life where anything at all could happen. I knew, from the first moment I saw the glimmer of Bulgwang stream under this same burning sun, that this place was different from all the others.

I reached the officetel where my parents and I would arrive in only a few minutes. I hurried up the cool marble stairs to the front door of our apartment, where the lock was set to 0000 before we picked up our keys. I punched in the code and slipped into the apartment, into my room that was still only a bed frame, mattress, and empty nightstand, everything covered in shadows and dust.

I'm here, Hana, I thought, every muscle tight as if bracing for impact. Any moment now, she was going to walk through the door and I would finally know my sister's face.

I was too nervous to sit on the bed, so I rocked back and forth on my heels, tugging at my backpack straps. What was I supposed say to Hana when I finally saw her? *I missed you?* But that was technically a lie—you can't miss someone you didn't know. *I love you?* That felt even crazier, because how can you love someone you've never actually met? But I felt the truth of it deep in my bones, in a way that time magic couldn't explain.

The front door unlatched.

"Take your shoes off first!" my mom's voice called from the hallway.

For a moment, I could only stand in the middle of the room and frown at the closed bedroom door. The panicked whirring in my mind fell silent.

This is all wrong.

I remembered this moment from the day we'd moved in. Next, my dad would say—

"Well, I can't squat down like I used to! You're gonna have to wait while I untie my shoes."

I heard my own impatient sigh in the hallway, the sound of me rolling a suitcase against the wall and sitting down on it.

This isn't how it's supposed to happen.

The day I'd moved in, the note from Hana had been waiting for me on my bed. Any moment, the past Mina was going to walk in, and there wasn't going to be anything here but me.

I messed around with the timeline too much, I thought, dread washing through me in a cold wave. I thought of all the silly, pointless missions I'd gone on with Yejun, the paradoxes that ripped holes in the timeline. I must have caused a butterfly effect that changed this moment, and now Hana wasn't going to show up. Or worse—what if Hana had finally gotten caught? If she didn't come now, everything would change.

That note was the first time that Hana had turned from a vague sense of loss into something tangible, someone I could believe in. What would my life in Korea look like if I didn't even know Hana existed? How many times had I taken out her note for strength?

Maybe I wouldn't have agreed with Yejun's plan if I didn't believe in Hana, but surely the descendants would have found another way to test me. If I never found the note, I might walk unknowingly into my own execution.

I set down my backpack and dug through it as quietly as possible until I found my English notebook, then ripped out a page. I winced at the sound, glancing at the door, but my dad was still taking his time untying his shoes.

I bit the cap off a pen and copied over Hana's note as quickly as I could. I had every word memorized, so I scrawled it all down without hesitation. Hana would just have to forgive me for interfering in the timeline and impersonating her. *It's for a good cause*, I thought, moving to set the note down on my bed. I couldn't make a perfect copy, but this would be good enough.

I hesitated just before I set it down on my pillow.

It took me a moment to realize what had changed. I'd grown so used to the constant ache behind my eyes that when it suddenly lifted, I felt strangely light. *My mom was wrong, it wasn't a timesickness headache*, I thought. It couldn't be, because that would mean I'd completed a time loop, when all I'd done was interfere.

I drew my hand back, staring at the note on my pillow, the torn edge of the paper that I'd ripped too far down the right side. But that was okay, Hana's note looked similar enough.

I should have left then, but I found myself taking out my wallet and pulling out the real note from Hana, then laying it side by side against my note.

I'm just making sure it looks similar enough so that I don't cause any more unintended ripple effects, I told myself, even though I sensed that something was very wrong as I drew my hand back.

The notes were exactly the same.

The one I'd kept in my wallet was more crinkled, but the messy handwriting was the same, aligned crookedly along the lined paper in exactly the same way. So was the jagged edge of the paper, the way my thumb had smudged the last line.

That's not possible, I thought, my feet rooted in place even as I heard suitcases rolling into the hall. *Hana wrote me this note.*

The doorknob to my room began to turn.

I snatched Hana's note off the bed and ducked into the closet, dragging my backpack in after me. I just managed to close the door before the other Mina entered.

I held my breath, peering through the thin seam of light where the closet door was slightly parted.

It will be different this time, I thought, clutching my backpack to my chest. *It has to be, because the note is different.*

But the other me sat down on the bed and picked up the note. I watched myself read it again and again, then jump to my feet and lock the bedroom door, just as I remembered. The other Mina sat cross-legged on my bed and took a picture of the note with her phone, terrified of losing it.

Don't do it, I thought, holding my breath. *Do something differently this time. Please.*

But, exactly the same as the first time, the other Mina tucked the note under her pillow. She stared at the pillow for all of two seconds before deciding better of it, then dug her wallet out of her bag and tucked it in behind her ID to keep it safe.

I closed my eyes, pressing my face against my knees as the other Mina unlocked the door and strode back out into the hall to grab her other bag.

Hana was never here, I realized, my stomach tight. Hana never came to my apartment to leave me a note, never promised to find me, to keep me safe.

I left the note for myself.

Chapter Twenty

Humans brushed past me as I walked down the stream, but I hardly felt them. I was barely even aware of my legs propelling me forward. Passing cars were shapeless blurs of headlights, the sky a dark veil overhead.

Hana's note—my note—was crumpled into a tight ball in my hand. I wanted to hurl it over the bridge into the stream but couldn't seem to unclench my fist. I dropped onto a bench, not sure if I would ever be able to stand up again.

I was supposed to meet Yejun back in the present, in the alley where he'd given me his yeouiju, but I'd returned an hour early because I didn't know what to say to him. I couldn't bear the idea of returning alone, of seeing the pity in Yejun's eyes. So now I was sitting here alone in the dark, wasting precious time. But what did all the time in the world matter anymore if I didn't know what to do with it?

Ever since I'd come to Seoul, I'd looked to Hana's promise like a North Star, the only thing I could turn to when the world was dark. I'd clung to the idea that there was someone out there whose love for me couldn't be erased, someone who would bend the rules of time and fate to protect me. The note was my proof of that love.

But now, I knew nothing about my sister at all. Not even if she loved me.

"*Hana*," I whispered to the stars, as if she could hear me somewhere out there. "What am I supposed to do without you?"

"Mina?"

A shadow was approaching me from under the footbridge. I half expected it to be Yejun, popping up unexpectedly like he always did. But a bike rolled out of the shadows, and there was Jihoon, unclipping his helmet.

"Are you crying?" he said, his eyes so wide and worried. He was probably coming home from his night classes right about now.

I shook my head and tried to wipe my eyes on my sleeve, but it was pointless to deny what he could so clearly see.

He sat down beside me, then dug through his bag for tissues. I blinked up at the moon, trying to stop my tears as Jihoon set a gentle hand on my back.

"I'm sorry," I said, wiping my nose. "I'm being gross. I didn't mean to—"

"Don't apologize," Jihoon said, shaking his head quickly. "Seriously, I cried over my breakfast this morning. It's fine, Mina."

I let out a sharp laugh. "Why did you cry over your breakfast?"

"Oh, uh . . ." Jihoon looked away, blushing. "My mom made me eggs and rice, but I dropped them. In hindsight, that's not a very good reason to cry, but in my defense, it was 6 A.M. and I was very tired."

"That is absolutely worth crying over," I said, wiping my eyes. "I once cried because I had a doughnut so good it changed my life."

Jihoon laughed. "I hope that's why you're crying now. And that you have more doughnuts to share."

"I wish," I said, slumping back against the bench.

Jihoon said nothing, but his unasked question lingered in the air. I'd lied enough to Jihoon, and I couldn't quite conjure up a good excuse when my brain felt like mashed potatoes.

"My sister is gone," I said. "I don't know where she is, or if I'll ever see her again. For so long, everything I did had meaning because it was all for her. But now I don't know what the point of anything is anymore because nothing will bring me closer to her. I gave so much to find her and now she's . . ."

I trailed off, looking away from Jihoon. I'd used him to find her, and now it was all for nothing. She was never even here.

"I'm so sorry, Mina," Jihoon said. He balled up a tissue and wiped my face, even though tears were still falling. I wanted him to give me a solution like Yejun had, to tell me I could bring her back if I was smart and strong enough, that there was still a way, that she wasn't gone.

But Jihoon didn't live in a world like that. The most he could do was wipe my tears and pat my hair, and something about giving in to that pathetic, human helplessness felt like a relief.

"Are you in a solutions mindset?" Jihoon said quietly. "Or would you rather just get some ice cream?"

I laughed, wiping my eyes. "Ice cream can be a solution," I said. "Maybe not now, but it can solve more problems than you'd think."

"I have never once underestimated ice cream," Jihoon said. "Or you, Mina."

I looked up.

"Your sister is lucky to have someone like you, who cares about her so much," Jihoon said. "Someone so smart and devoted. If anyone can find her, it's you."

I sighed. "I'm not smart," I said.

Jihoon frowned. "Of course you are."

I shook my head. "You have no idea."

"Oh?" Jihoon said. "Is that why you asked Yejun to tutor you in calculus instead of me?"

I grimaced. "Uh, I mean—"

"It's because you didn't want me to think you weren't smart, right?"

My shoulders drooped. "Yeah, basically."

"But I never would have thought that, Mina," he said, setting his hand on mine. "You work so hard at everything. Nothing ever stops you, no matter how difficult. You moved here in the middle of the school year and caught up so quickly. You were kind to me even when I spilled orange juice on you when we first met. Did you know that last year, before I grew six inches and got my braces off, no girls would even talk to me? I still feel like that person sometimes, but not around you. That's why I like you, Mina. Not because of your calculus scores." He swallowed, dropping his gaze to his shoes. "And, I mean, you're also really pretty, so that's part of it too."

I leaned forward and hugged Jihoon. As always, he was kinder than anyone deserved.

I never should have dragged him into this. It had been so easy to say it was my mission, that I had no choice because I was a descendant and this was what descendants did. But I'd known all along that descendants could be cruel and unfair. I'd tried to make myself one of them so I could find Hana.

But I would never be a true descendant, and I didn't have to play by their rules anymore.

"Jihoon, I'm so sorry," I said, pulling away. "I think we should just be friends."

Jihoon froze. "Oh," he said quietly, drawing his hand away from my back.

"You're going to have a good life without me," I said. "You're going to be an accountant, which is kind of boring, but you'll like it anyway. You're going to meet someone in grad school who you really love. You're going to get this cute little dog together and dress her up in sweaters in the winter. You'll have two kids, and you'll live to be ninety-four, and when you die, everyone will talk about how kind you were, even to people who didn't deserve it, like me."

Jihoon blinked at me with his big, adorable eyes, and I realized how strange this must have sounded to someone who wasn't a descendant and hadn't read the file of his life according to the current timeline.

"I mean, that's what I want for you," I said quickly. "That's the story I imagine for you."

He let out a laugh, shaking his head. "You're strange, Mina," he said, giving my hand a gentle squeeze before pulling away and sliding a few inches away from me. The distance that friends sat, not boyfriend and girlfriend.

"I've been called worse," I said, shrugging.

Jihoon nodded like he didn't really hear me, staring at a family of ducks bobbing down the stream. After a moment, he let out a sigh and his gaze dropped to his lap. "It's because of Yejun, isn't it?" he said.

I grimaced. "Yes," I said.

Jihoon nodded, like he'd expected it. "I hope he's good to you, Mina."

I turned my gaze to the sky that for once wasn't covered in smog, the stars so stark and perfect against the velvet night. There, mockingly bright, was Horologium, Hong Gildong's favorite constellation. Maybe I would always see it etched into the sky, as if he was watching over me, hunting me down no matter where I went. My mind traced the empty space between the stars, filling out the pendulum, the six prickly stars curved into an L. Almost like a scar . . .

Or a signature.

I sat up straight. "I have to go," I said. I had to find Yejun and get to headquarters. If I couldn't find Hana in the past, there was only one more place I could find her—in the descendants' records. The kind of records that only Hong Gildong could unlock. That was, unless someone else knew his signature.

"Okay," Jihoon said, standing up stiffly. "Do you want me to walk you home?"

I shook my head. Even now, he was too nice. Before I could forget, I took his bracelet out of my bag and held it out to him.

He shook his head. "It's for you, Mina."

"But I'm not . . ." I looked down, a thousand thoughts blurring in my mind. *I'm not the person you deserve. I'm not who you thought I was. I'm not even Mina Yang.*

"It's not like I could give it to anyone else," he said, smiling softly. "'Beautiful jade,' remember? It's yours."

I closed my hand around the cool beads. "Thank you," I said, for what felt like the thousandth time.

Jihoon moved to hug me, then hesitated, taking an awkward step back. He pressed his lips together as if contemplating something, then held out a stiff hand.

"A handshake?" I said, raising an eyebrow.

"Should we just bow instead?" he said with a laugh. "I don't know how to say goodbye to you."

"Then don't," I said. "Goodbyes are sad anyway."

"Right," Jihoon said. "Not goodbye, Yang Mina."

"Not goodbye, Kim Jihoon," I said.

He bowed stiffly, then pushed his bike the opposite way down the path. I slipped his bracelet back around my wrist, a relic of the life I once thought I'd have. I closed my eyes and felt nothing but the coldness of the beads, tight against my racing pulse.

Police had blocked off the main road to headquarters for the political rally, so I had to weave through side streets, cutting down on what little time I had left. I fought through the crowd but came up against a metal barricade. I would have to go through the rally to reach Yejun at the meeting spot.

I ducked into a clothing store and scanned the shelves for a sweatshirt I could steal. I needed something with a hood so the supervising agent wouldn't spot another Mina and realize something was amiss. As the employee at the counter headed to the back, I reached for a pink sweatshirt. It looked baggy enough to hide me and had an oversized hood that would cast shadows over my face.

As soon as my hand closed around the fabric, I froze.

I remembered Hana, a gun in her hands, wearing a baggy pink sweatshirt. Was this the same shade? It was hard to say, since Hana had been standing in the dark when she shot me.

But had it really been Hana at all? If I'd left myself the note in my apartment, maybe the shooter had also been one of my Echoes. My fist clenched tight around the sleeve, stretching the fabric. That moment was all I had left of Hana, and now it might not even be real.

I drew my hand back, then turned and pulled a blue sweatshirt off its hanger and hurried out the door.

I set down my bag outside and tugged the sweatshirt over my head, letting out a breath once I was safely swathed in blue—not pink—fabric. I might have tricked myself into writing Hana's note, but there was no way I could accidentally shoot myself. I didn't even have blank rounds on me.

The flow of the crowd carried me near the stairs where the other Mina and Yejun were standing. I didn't want to get any closer and alert the supervising agent, but it was the only way through. Maybe I would even get a better look at Hana this time before she ran off. I wanted to catch her and never let her go, but it was dangerous for her to show herself at all, much less in front of a supervising agent, and the last thing I wanted was for Hong Gildong to apprehend her because of me.

The crowd grew denser so close to the front, and I couldn't force my way through no matter how hard I tried. I would have to wait until everyone started running to make it to the other side.

I stood by a light pole as Min Sungho's car arrived at the far end of the walkway and security stepped out. As the other Mina and Yejun talked, I scanned the crowd for anyone in a pink sweatshirt, but counted over a dozen on this side of the barriers alone.

Then someone bumped into me from behind, jolting me away from the streetlight.

Hot liquid seared across my face and neck. I fell forward onto my hands, my eyes stinging. A boot stomped dangerously close to my fingers, but before the crowd could crush me, someone yanked me up by the arm.

Someone with a pink sweatshirt.

I rubbed the liquid from my eye as some of it trickled into my mouth. *Coffee*, I realized, as the scent wafted over me. *Someone spilled their hot coffee on me.*

"I'm so sorry!" a man was saying over and over again. "Are you okay?"

"I'm fine," I said, tugging off the soaked sweatshirt and using it to dry my neck and face. I squinted up at the man even though my eyelids felt gummed together with sugar and cream. He was young—probably a college student—wearing a pink sweatshirt and clutching a crumpled coffee cup.

His face suddenly turned red and he ripped his own sweatshirt off, handing it to me. "Here, you can have this," he said.

"I don't need your sweatshirt," I said, trying to look around him at Yejun, but he only pushed it closer to me.

"Your shirt," he said uneasily.

"What about my—" I looked down, and realized why he was so uncomfortable—the coffee had made my white tank top see-through.

I sighed and snatched the sweatshirt from him, tugging it over my head and moving as far away as possible. It didn't matter if I was wearing a pink sweatshirt anyway. I still wasn't going to shoot the other Mina.

Min Sungho was heading up the walkway now, and I could see the other Mina frowning as Yejun put his gun away. Hana needed to make her move soon, but I still couldn't see her in the crowd.

Counterprotesters started yelling as Min Sungho drew closer, trying to push their way to the front. The crowd carried me closer to the stairs, angry humans stomping on my feet and elbowing my ribs to get past me.

Something snagged on the ladybug key chain on my zipper, yanking me to the side. The left shoulder strap on my backpack finally tore, and my bag hit the ground. I reached for it right as something metal fell out of the front pocket and clattered to the ground.

Firearm cartridges.

The ones Hyebin's Echo had given me at school. I held one up to the streetlight, running my thumb over the flat paper surface where a projectile was supposed to be.

They were blank rounds.

I hadn't known it at the time, since I hadn't had firearms training yet, but now I was certain. I remembered how pale and unraveled Hyebin's Echo had looked under the yellow light of the bathroom stall. Had she come back to help me because I'd used live rounds and died, or because the descendants had caught me the first time?

I clutched the handful of cartridges tight in my palm, then rose to my feet and turned to the other Mina and Yejun, who were still in a tense discussion. There was no one else in a pink sweatshirt pushing through the crowd. No one but me.

I looked to the sky. *Really, Hana?* I thought. *You're gonna make me do this part too? Just how lazy are you?*

The sky crackled with thunder, and I let out a dry laugh. It was the most sisterlike interaction I'd ever had with Hana, if you could call it that. I could imagine her response, even if it was nothing more than a story I told myself and the real Hana was nothing like that at all. But, like Yejun said, sometimes stories were all you had.

You can't expect anyone else to save you, Mina, Hana would say. *This was your plan, so you can finish it.*

I sighed, my hand curling tighter around the cartridges.

Fine, I thought. *I'll have to save myself.*

I yanked my hood up, then pulled out my gun and emptied the live rounds onto the ground. It didn't matter who saw—the crowd was going to stampede in about thirty seconds anyway. I jammed the blank rounds in, hoisted my bag over my shoulder, and shoved through the crowd.

"I won't do it," I heard Yejun saying as I drew closer.

You can't, I thought, elbowing someone out of my way, *but I can.*

The other Mina had clearly noticed me approaching, her body angled toward me, one hand still on Yejun's sleeve.

I squared my stance and pulled the trigger.

In the moment after the gunshot, the world fell silent. Everyone turned toward the source of the sound, waiting for their brains to make sense of what they'd just heard. In that moment, I was in a world all by myself, pushing upstream through the paralyzed crowd. Then the first scream came, and the world exploded with noise.

Everyone started to run.

Someone elbowed me in the ribs, someone else shoved me forward, another person screamed in my ear. I stepped on something that felt suspiciously like fingers, but I couldn't stop now, not for anything or anyone.

I broke free from the crowd, falling into the glass doors of a convenience store that swung open and dumped me on the tiles. I was up before the cashier could ask if I was okay, disappearing behind the chip aisle and shrugging off my sweatshirt, which I stuffed into the gap on the shelf where fire ramen used to be. I put Hana's sweater back on, and only then, when I was neither crushed beneath a stampede or handcuffed in the back of a police car, did I let out a breath.

I bought a black mask at the counter and slipped it on as I headed outside, where cops were circling the block and the crowd had started to thin. I tried to even out my breathing and walk as casually as possible to the meet-up point, though I found myself running around the last corner and nearly crashing into Yejun.

He caught me before I could slip into a puddle, spinning me around and setting me on my feet in the alley.

"You're back," he said, smiling and brushing my hair out of my face. Then he looked around me, and the light left his eyes. "Your sister?"

I shook my head. Seeing the pity in his eyes stung just like I'd expected it to, but this time it was tempered by the fact that this wasn't over yet.

"There's one last thing I need to try," I said. "I need to get to Hong Gildong's scrying pool."

· 🦋 ·

Seulgi's eyes widened when she saw me and Yejun enter the building together. I grimaced, wondering if literally everyone in the office but me knew I was being played.

"Hi, Seulgi-nim," Yejun said, smiling and bowing casually as if we didn't just fake my death. "We have an appointment with the boss."

"You do?" she said. "He's not due back for another hour." I didn't miss the way her gaze fell to my empty hands. *I forgot the banana milk*, I thought. On the one day I could really use a bribe, I didn't have one.

"Can we just wait for him there?" I said, pointing toward his office and fighting the urge to check my watch. I knew seeing the time would only make me panic-sweat. It had taken us a good eleven minutes to rush over here from the rally.

It was the wrong thing to say. Seulgi's expression hardened and she crossed her arms. "You know that's not allowed, Mina."

"But Hyebin—"

"Hyebin is a senior agent and Sajangnim knew she was there," Seulgi said. "Why do you want to go there so badly?"

I looked to Yejun, but he was staring at his shoes with a grim expression, like he knew as well as I did that there was no logical reason for us to be in Hong Gildong's office, that no excuse was going to cut it.

Well, I thought, *if you can't outsmart a dragon, submit to them.*

I dropped to my knees and bowed to Seulgi, who flinched and backed away. "Please," I said. "It's an emergency. I can't explain right now, but I wouldn't ask you if it wasn't important."

Seulgi looked to Yejun as if he could explain, but he only shrugged pitifully. Some partner in crime he turned out to be.

After a moment, Seulgi sighed. "Did you at least bring me some banana milk?" she asked.

I hung my head, but Yejun was already heading for the elevator. "I'll grab you some!" he said.

"No need," Seulgi said, halting Yejun in his tracks. "I'll just have to go get some myself, I guess."

I looked up sharply. *She's going to leave her post?*

"It would be unfortunate if someone slipped by the desk while I was gone," she said. "But you two can keep a lookout, can't you?"

"Yes!" Yejun said quickly as I rose to my feet, bowing again. "Yes, of course!"

"Good," Seulgi said, winking as she stepped into the elevator and the doors closed behind her.

As soon as she was gone, we raced down the hall and threw the doors open to Hong Gildong's office. I froze in the doorway, as if Hong Gildong was going to pop out from a shadowed corner and kill us on the spot.

Yejun hit the light switch as the door clicked shut behind us. "It's all yours," he said, gesturing to the scrying pool.

I walked around the desk and sat in Hong Gildong's chair, my heartbeat loud in my ears. My reflection stared back at me in the still water, my eyes wide and petrified. *This is it*, I thought, raising a trembling hand.

I dipped a finger into the surface, and the water rippled as four words appeared.

Please enter your signature

I held my breath, then traced the shape of Horologium into the water.

Descendants cannot afford to overlook a single moment, Hong Gildong had said. *That is what this constellation reminds me.*

It was the only good advice he'd ever given me, since that particular moment would be his undoing.

The water glowed white, brightness washing away my reflection. I held my breath as the light cast dizzy shapes across my vision, the water churning in a slow circle.

Then the light faded away, and all of Hong Gildong's documents appeared in the water's surface.

Yejun peered over my shoulder, gaping at the files. "How did you do that?"

"I'll explain later," I said as my watch beeped again. My fingertips ghosted over the surface as I pulled up the search bar and typed:

Yang Hana

A single file popped up in the search results.

I tapped on it with a trembling hand, and the document filled the screen. There, at the top right corner, was a picture of my sister.

It felt like something out of a fever dream—my own features stretched and pinched into a new face so similar to my own. Hana had the same brown hair that turned copper in the light, the same wide medium-brown eyes, the same straight eyebrows. Her cheeks looked softer and rounder than mine, her gaze kinder. I touched the surface of the pool, forgetting for a moment that it wasn't paper. The water rippled, distorting her face.

I don't remember her, I realized, the thought pulling tight at my chest. I thought that the moment I saw her face, all the memories would come rushing back. But Hana was still a stranger to me, and she always would be. I scrolled down and read her file.

```
YANG HANA [1475B]
Aliases: Yamamoto Hana, Hannah Young
DOB: November 21, 2005
Status: Neutralized as of March 3, 2017
Lifetime Points: 345
Supervisor: Lee Siwoo [937]
Administrator Note:
Mission information has been encrypted
indefinitely due to agent termination. Agent
terminated on March 3, 2017, for following
reason:
-[Violation 488] Accessing classified files
without authorization (Operation 191H)
-[Violation 133] Verbally informing
unauthorized agents of classified information
(Operation 191H)
```

I tried to scroll down, but there was nothing left to read.

This can't be it, I thought, my hands shaking, my whole body cold with sweat. *There must be more.*

"What is Operation 191H?" I said, looking over my shoulder at Yejun.

"Let me see," Yejun said, reaching across the scrying pool and pulling up an advanced search alongside Hana's profile. After typing in a few strings of commands I didn't understand, he opened a file and stepped aside so I could read.

```
OPERATION 191H
Date of Execution: February 2, 2031
Sponsor: National Aerospace Industries Korea
Mission Objective: Korean government purchases
arms from National Aerospace Industries,
totaling no less than 100 billion won.
Adjustment Target: Declaration of war with
North Korea
Butterfly Origin: Spilled bottle of chocolate
milk at 37.50083, 127.02560, December 11, 2008
```

"National Aerospace Industries Korea?" Yejun said over my shoulder as he read. "That's an arms manufacturer. I thought Hong Gildong was just taking Samsung's money or something. He's taking money from people who make *bombs*?"

"That explains why he wanted me to start a war," I said, clenching my fists. "That would make a lot of money for people selling weapons."

I held back the urge to dump Hong Gildong's scrying pool out on the floor, or to take a hammer to it and shatter it into a thousand pieces. All this time, he'd said we couldn't save anyone because of the integrity of the timeline, but that had never been the truth. We couldn't save anyone because saving lives didn't make him money.

As I clenched my jaw so hard that my teeth ached and my burning blood screamed through my veins, I felt closer to Hana than I ever had before. She had found out this same information, and I imagined she'd felt exactly as I did now. Even across timelines, I shared this moment with her.

I gripped the edges of the scrying pool, staring at Hana's picture. I wouldn't let everything she had lost amount to nothing at all.

Hana hadn't been able to stop this war, but maybe I still could.

"Well, would you look at that," a voice said from the doorway. "Right on time."

Chapter Twenty-One

I jumped to my feet. Yejun moved in front of me as Hong Gildong entered the office, the door slamming shut behind him.

"Mina," Hong Gildong said, his fangs glinting as he smiled. "Welcome back from the dead."

I clutched Yejun's arm. "How did you know we were here?" I said.

Hong Gildong laughed, but it sounded less like a human laugh than something he'd studied and rehearsed, thorn-sharp as it echoed across the room. "Very little surprises me when I can see the entire timeline."

I shook my head. "I'm not on the timeline right now."

"But *he* is," Hong Gildong said, waving at Yejun, who flinched. "This wasn't just a test for Mina, but for you as well, Yejun. And in case it wasn't obvious, you both failed."

Yejun pressed me back against the desk as if to shield me, but Hong Gildong didn't move toward us. He only strolled toward the bookshelves and examined the spines, as if we were making casual conversation over tea.

"It's unfortunate," he went on. "You both would have been such valuable assets to our team, and we don't exactly have many descendants to spare these days. Yejun, your scenario planning is truly impressive. And Mina . . ."

He trailed off, appraising me with his golden eyes. "After Hana, I long suspected that you would possess similar abilities."

"Abilities?" I echoed. I thought back to Yejun's mission report.

```
Yang Mina is flagged for extra review due to
suspected genetic predisposition for enhanced
powers—see file 1475B, "Yang Hana."
```

Hong Gildong wiped some dust off the edge of the shelf with his finger, frowning at it as if that was truly the greatest inconvenience at the moment. "Yang Hana was an exceptionally powerful descendant. She retained many dragon abilities despite how diluted her bloodline was. You understand now why we couldn't simply wipe her mind—stripping her of her memories wouldn't remove her claws. We suspected there was a genetic component to it. But, despite all of Yejun's hand-waving in his report in an effort to convince me otherwise, it is painfully clear to me that you cannot compare to her."

I glared back at Hong Gildong, my skin burning. Not at the idea that I was less than Hana—that had never mattered to me—but the idea that he had known her better than I ever would.

Before I could respond, the ground began to tremble.

I fell to the right, catching myself on a bookcase. The whole room vibrated, potted plants overturning and books sliding off the shelves. At first, I thought Hong Gildong was using some sort of dragon power to rend the earth in half. But he stumbled against the desk and caught himself with one hand in his scrying pool, like he hadn't expected it either.

At the top edge of the bookcases by the window, color began to slough off the walls like dead skin, a wave of whiteness oozing across the room.

A paradox.

Yejun grabbed my wrist and pulled me away from the whiteness that was now dripping down the bookshelves, the rainbow of spines all fading to muted gray.

"We have to get out of here!" I said.

But Hong Gildong wasn't gawking at the paradox or running in fear. Instead, he let out an impatient sigh and checked his watch. He straightened up, then began chanting in a language I couldn't comprehend.

Each word sounded like a facet of a diamond glinting in the sun, sharp and bright. It must have been the ancient dragon tongue, which only the highest-ranked descendants were ever taught.

The paradox shivered and shrank back into the wall. Then the room settled, colors blossoming across the white stain.

Hong Gildong has dealt with paradoxes before, I realized as he straightened his tie with one hand.

At first, I had thought the paradoxes were caused by me and Yejun going against Hong Gildong's orders and messing up the timeline. But if Yejun was working for Hong Gildong the whole time, then Hong Gildong knew everything we were doing and would have made sure none of our actions damaged the timeline. No wonder Yejun was so certain it wasn't our fault, and was so perplexed that paradoxes were popping up anyway.

"Why is the timeline breaking down?" I asked Hong Gildong. "And why aren't you worried about it?"

Yejun scoffed, "Because all that matters is who gives him more gold for his hoard."

Hong Gildong growled, the sound like a low peal of thunder through the floor. "I don't expect children to understand," Hong

Gildong said. "Explaining the intricacies of dragon negotiations to you would be a waste of my breath. You'll both be gone soon anyway."

Then he turned, drew a gun from beneath his jacket, and pointed it at Yejun. I tried to step closer but froze as Hong Gildong clicked off the safety.

Instinctively, I reached for my box of time magic. Maybe I couldn't outrun a bullet, but I could go back and make sure we were never in this situation in the first place.

"Before you try to travel," Hong Gildong said, "there's something I think you should know."

Magic was already curling around my wrist, but I hesitated at his words.

"I've just flagged you both for neutralization," he said. "The moment you run to another time, the timeline architects will see it, and a team will already be there waiting for you. So, before you go anywhere, it's worth considering whether or not you like the taste of time magic crammed down your throat."

I remembered the hazy image of my last neutralization mission, the way the woman whose name I could no longer remember had turned to dust that the carpet inhaled. Even that broken shard of a memory made me shiver, and I reflexively pulled my hand from my pocket, the magic fizzling out.

"Good girl," Hong Gildong said, smiling darkly as he turned back to Yejun.

"Yejun—" I started to say, but froze as he smiled. He was no longer looking at Hong Gildong, but at me. He wore the same carefree, easy smile I once despised.

"It's okay," he said quietly. "This isn't the first time this has happened. I'll find you again."

I shook my head. *He's going to erase us this time*, I wanted to say. "Yejun, you can't—"

"*I'll find you*," Yejun said, his words tinged with desperation, like he wanted so badly to believe it. "I'll comb through every timeline, okay? Please don't cry."

I didn't even realize I was crying until he said it. I could only shake my head, for all words in every language seemed to have left me. I should have said something more to him. Something kind and comforting, an apology for how rude I'd been, gratitude for giving up everything for me, but I couldn't find the words.

I thought of Yejun bringing me strawberry cheesecake, holding my hand as magic flowed through both of us, telling me he would never hurt me. I thought that Hana was the only person to care for me exactly as I was, but it was always Yejun.

I couldn't let this happen.

"Wait!" I said, taking another step forward.

But before I could do anything else, the door to Hong Gildong's office slammed open. All three of us turned toward . . .

"*Dad?*" I said.

My dad was standing in the doorway, waving awkwardly as my mom peered over his shoulder. At this, Hong Gildong actually did lower the gun as confusion crinkled his face.

"Allen-nim?" Hong Gildong said.

"Um, hello, Sajangnim," my dad said, giving half a bow and staring unsubtly at the gun in his hand.

My mom pushed him into the room so she could see, bowing slightly before she noticed the gun as well.

"It seems I've interrupted a . . . training exercise?" my dad said. Then he noticed Yejun and his eyes brightened. "Oh, Yejun! Good to see you!"

"Uh, you too, Mr. Yang," Yejun said. "Despite the circumstances."

Hong Gildong narrowed his eyes and turned fully toward my parents. His towering silhouette blocked the city lights from the window behind him, casting darkness across the doorway.

"*Leave,*" Hong Gildong said. "This is none of your business."

I expected my parents to bow and then scurry away at the direct order from their boss, but neither one moved.

"Mina," my mom said hesitantly, "I found your note in my bag."

Oh no.

They weren't supposed to come back. Now they knew too much, and Hong Gildong might decide to erase them too.

"Your note had us worried, and you wouldn't answer your phone," my dad said. "Why are you talking about us remembering you?"

"*Both of you need to leave,*" Hong Gildong said, his words thundering across the floorboards. "We will discuss this tomorrow."

Still, neither of my parents moved.

"Sajangnim," my dad said, bowing his head, "I'd like to leave with Mina and Yejun."

"That's not possible," Hong Gildong said. My dad flinched at the sharpness of his words. "Everything will be in order by tomorrow, Allen-nim. You can trust me. This is all part of the timeline."

My dad opened his mouth to respond, but then his gaze settled somewhere beyond Hong Gildong, and his face drained of color.

"What exactly is this training?" my mom said.

"Eri," my dad said, tugging at my mom's sleeve.

"Please just leave," I said to my mom. The longer they stayed here, the more likely it was that Hong Gildong would decide to just erase my whole family and be done with it. It's not like they could ever stop him, even if they wanted to.

"Are you even old enough to use firearms?" my mom said.

"*Eri!*" my dad said.

He was no longer looking at me, or my mom, or even Hong Gildong, but at the scrying pool.

The pool where Hana's file was still open.

My mom followed his gaze, and after reading for a few moments, clapped her hands over her mouth.

"Hana," my dad whispered, as if testing out the word. He looked to Hong Gildong, his face deathly pale. "I had another daughter, and I forgot her?"

My mom shook her head quickly. "I wouldn't forget my own daughter," she said. "I . . . there's no way I . . ."

Hong Gildong stepped forward and tapped the scrying pool, wiping away Hana's file. "*Go home*," he said. "This doesn't concern either of you. Trust in the timeline that this is how everything is supposed to be."

"Trust," my father echoed, nodding slowly, his eyes distant. My mom was still staring at the scrying pool as if trying to remember the image, the only photo of Hana any of us would ever have.

At last, my father let out a breath and looked away from the pool. As always, he trusted in the agency above all else. It was easier that way. He couldn't feel the pain of Hana's loss, and he wouldn't feel the pain of losing me either. I wasn't even surprised at this point.

But instead of leaving, he crossed the room and stood in front of me.

"Allen-nim," Hong Gildong said, teeth clenched as his fangs descended, "you don't want to get involved in this. You are a dependable employee."

My mom stood beside my dad.

"Eri-nim," Hong Gildong said. "This doesn't concern you."

"*Of course it concerns us!*" my dad said. I flinched, realizing I'd never heard him yell before. He always spoke in the same low, infinitely patient voice. Even Hong Gildong flinched at the sound before frowning and steadying his grip on the pistol.

"For twenty-eight years, I did everything you asked," my dad said. "I never once asked why. I never asked for more of anything. Not money, not stability, not even answers. I believed in you, in this cause. And now, after all these years, I find out that *you killed my daughter?*"

The room seemed to quake from the force of his rage. He wasn't a true descendant, so he shouldn't have had that kind of power. But somehow, the bookshelves trembled, the water in the scrying pool rippled, and the curtains shuddered at his words. His face was red, fists clenched and shaking. Beside him, my mom, dangerously quiet, had narrowed her eyes at Hong Gildong.

I felt halfway out of my own body, sure that I was dreaming. I had never seen my parents get angry, and certainly not at their boss.

"Both of your daughters have put the entire timeline at risk with their carelessness and defiance," Hong Gildong said, his eyes flaring gold, his claws biting into the gun.

"Fuck your timeline!" my mom said.

It was the first time I'd ever heard her swear at someone. I would have laughed if Hong Gildong didn't still have a loaded gun, now pointed at my parents.

"You care about her more than all of humanity?" Hong Gildong said, jerking a clawed finger at me. "She could have ended the world!"

At this, the redness faded from my dad's face, his shoulders drooping. He shook his head slowly. "There is no world without her. Not for me," he said. "She's *my* world."

Then he looked back at me and smiled softly, like he knew this might be the last time he could.

I had always known that my parents cared about me. But I also knew that love was not just cooking someone dinner or driving them to school or braiding their hair. It was rage and grief and anger, like what I felt for Hana. It was foolishness and audacity, like when I nearly attacked Hong Gildong for Yejun. I never thought my parents were brave enough to actually love me, to understand what that meant.

But now, as they held hands and refused to move even when Hong Gildong sighed with his pistol pointed at them, I realized far too late that I was wrong.

"Suit yourself," Hong Gildong said. "I have enough bullets for all of you."

Then he leveled the gun at my dad.

I stepped forward, but Hong Gildong didn't even bother holding his hand up to stop me. He squared his shoulders and pulled the trigger.

The sound tore through the room. Crisp and bright, like the world had cracked in half. Someone slammed into me, elbowing my ribs, forcing the air from my lungs. My head slammed against a bookshelf and books rained down around me as the echo of the gunshot faded, the air alight with the scent of gunpowder.

My dad clung to the bookshelf beside me, his face pale and hands shaking. I grabbed his arm, searching for the wound, but couldn't find even a drop of blood.

With a thump, Yejun fell to the carpet.

He pressed a trembling hand to his stomach, his face drained of color as he gasped down an unsteady breath. I let go of my dad and turned to Yejun, but before I could reach him, blood gushed through his fingers.

A wave of coldness washed through me. Scalding hot blood soaked through my tights as I knelt beside Yejun and reached for his hand, which was already shockingly cold. I pressed him back against Hong Gildong's desk to get a better look, but all I saw was red red red, the color devouring his white shirt, the pool of it yawning wider across the floor.

"*Why would you do that?*" I said, my hands trembling. I didn't care anymore that I had my back to a man with a gun who would probably aim for me next. I couldn't imagine doing anything else but holding Yejun as his cold, blood-slicked hands gripped my arms. My dad had already shrugged off his jacket and was trying to wedge it against Yejun's stomach to stop the bleeding. My mom had tackled Hong Gildong against a bookshelf and sunken her claws into his arm, trying to wrestle the gun away from him.

Yejun coughed, sparks of blood flying from his lips. "You have parents who love you," he said, the words so soft that I must have been the only one who heard them. "I won't let Hong Gildong take that from you."

I shook my head, tears blurring my vision. My dad was telling me what to do, but I couldn't focus on anything but Yejun. His pulse hammered beneath his white skin, his blood scalding hot against my palms.

Hong Gildong shoved my mom back with a frustrated cry. She tripped backward over a potted plant, which shattered beneath her. Then he brushed off his jacket and turned back toward the three of us. "It's a wasted effort," he said. "All of you are going to die anyway. The order hardly matters."

At his words, fire rushed through my veins, all my blood ignited. Every part of me felt so searingly alive, like I could raze the world to ashes.

I rose to my feet, my hands throbbing. Something sharp stung my lower lip and I tasted blood.

"Mina?" my dad said. But I ignored him, taking another step toward Hong Gildong, no longer afraid of the gun leveled at my chest. The room had a strange tint, like it was drenched in sunlight, every surface blazing gold. Sounds echoed as if I'd fallen to the bottom of an abyss.

Hong Gildong narrowed his eyes. "Careful with those," he said.

But I didn't know what he was talking about and I didn't care. "I won't let you take them from me," I said. "*I won't let you take anyone else from me.*"

At my words, the room trembled. Just like when the paradox had rattled through the room, wood creaked and books jumped off the shelves, the curtains shivering at my words.

Hong Gildong opened his mouth, but I couldn't hear his response because the ocean was roaring in my ears, a chorus of screams. My vision glinted and sparkled, my gaze focusing on Hong Gildong's pale throat—exposed, soft, vulnerable.

I vaulted over the desk and struck my claws across Hong Gildong's face.

I have claws, I thought, barely processing the discovery as we both crashed into the carpet and the gun flew out of his hand. I hardly felt the impact, like my body was no longer made of flesh and bones but of searing light.

I lunged for his throat with claws that I could now see were sharp and silvery as starlight. Hong Gildong seized my wrist before I could strike him again, yanking me to the side.

I crashed against his desk, sending water from his scrying pool sloshing over me. Hong Gildong stormed toward me, but I was faster. I tackled him around the legs, and we both fell against a bookcase. He barely moved out of the way of my next strike, and my claws ripped across the shoulder of his shirt instead of his face, raking blood to the surface.

I had never felt like anything but a human girl until that moment. But suddenly, despite the cage of human bones, I felt as endless as a river reaching for the sea, my every movement fluid as water, my teeth shards of sea glass, my vision burning with brine. Hong Gildong's blood splashed across my face, and the taste of it only made the gold in the room glow brighter. My claws tore open the side of his jacket, and something bright blue rolled across the carpet.

His yeouiju.

I climbed off Hong Gildong and seized the ball of light. By the time he got to his feet, I had his yeouiju clenched in my fist.

"*Careful with that!*" he said, holding his hands up in surrender.

I pinched it between my claws and he winced, letting out a wounded sound. "What happens if I pop it like a grape?" I said. My words came out strangely with my fangs scraping across my bottom lip, but Hong Gildong clearly understood me well enough, because his frown deepened.

"Don't," he said, lowering his head in a half bow. "Please," he added through clenched teeth.

Every part of me wanted to end him once and for all, but there was one last thing I needed from him.

"Bring my sister back," I said.

I expected him to throw himself at the scrying pool to comply, or tell me he needed more of his time magic to do it, or anything except what he actually did, which was stare at me blankly.

"Bring her back?" he said, raising an eyebrow. "It doesn't work like that."

"The timeline is a toy to you," I said, pinching his yeouiju harder, pulling a strangled sound from him. "You can do anything you want with it, so *bring her back*!"

"*I can't!*" Hong Gildong said. "Neutralization is permanent. Once your source of time magic is destroyed, you can't come back."

I shook my head quickly. This was just another one of his lies. "There must be enough of her left," I said. "She's been communicating with me—"

"You've been communicating with yourself," Hong Gildong said. "You might have noticed her absence—it's difficult to completely eliminate someone—but she has never once interacted with you since she was erased. She can't."

I took a faltering step back. "I don't believe you," I said, even though I could smell his fear with my dragon senses, even though I knew he wouldn't lie to me now, with my fist around his yeouiju.

When Hong Gildong didn't answer, I shook my head again, hugging myself because my arms had broken out in goose bumps and I couldn't stop shaking. My claws and fangs were gone and everything ached, my head throbbing and my skin sticky with blood. There must have been another paradox coming, because I felt like the room was collapsing in on itself, the sound of my breathing deafeningly loud.

"She helped me," I said, tears burning down my face. "She saved me."

Hong Gildong shook his head. "You did that yourself."

"I didn't," I said, though the protest sounded so small and childish. I wasn't supposed to save myself. That's what sisters were for—to do what I wasn't strong enough to do. To make sure I was never alone. Hong Gildong was wrong, because even now I could feel Hana here, gently taking my hand, uncurling my tightly clenched fist, running her fingers over my bloodstained palm and silver-tinged nails where my claws had once been.

My claws.

I turned my hand over, staring at my throbbing nails that still looked slightly metallic, like the shifting shades of a dragon's scales.

I wasn't supposed to have claws. It was rare for any modern descendant, since we were so far removed from our dragon ancestors. It was even rarer for someone with one human parent like me. Claws were a mark of a powerful descendant, like Hyebin, Hong Gildong, and Seulgi . . .

And, apparently, me.

The descendant who couldn't even pass calculus on her own, who was so weak that the other descendants decided to sacrifice her to the timeline for the greater good. Too stupid, too clumsy, too human to be anyone of importance.

But all along, Hana had known—*I* had known—that that wasn't the full story.

My fingernails lengthened into sharp points, glinting in the light.

I had always thought of myself as more human than dragon, but now I felt as if I was seeing my own hands for the first time in my life. Of course I'd always looked out of place in every photograph—I'd been wearing the skin of a lost, lonely human, not a descendant. Hong Gildong had *feared* me.

Slowly, I leveled my gaze with Hong Gildong.

Without the power of his yeouiju, he no longer seemed like a tsunami of darkness, an all-powerful dragon too strong and wise to challenge. He was just a lanky young man in an expensive suit who thought the world was his inheritance.

"Mina," he said—the same smug voice that had once ordered my sister's death.

I lunged forward and closed my claws around his throat.

With his yeouiju clenched tightly in one hand, I crushed him into the carpet, holding him down with my knees on his chest. He struggled against me, but he felt like a butterfly beating its wings against a glass window.

I wrenched his jaws open with a clawed hand and brought the yeouiju to his teeth. He thrashed in my grip but didn't dare bite down with the yeouiju so perilously close. I raised the heel of my palm to jam it into his mouth, but before I struck down, a gentle hand squeezed my shoulder.

At first I thought it must have been my parents, but when I turned around, they were still a few feet back, helping Yejun. No one was stopping me. Everyone knew Hong Gildong deserved it, and yet...

There it was, that same gentle touch on my shoulder that I'd felt so many times before. Hong Gildong said Hana couldn't interact with me anymore, but maybe there were things that he—as a cold-blooded dragon—couldn't understand. The warmth on my shoulder that bloomed like sunlight on a spring day, the invisible hand that tucked hair behind my ear and gently pulled my wrist back... maybe it wasn't a rogue Hana in another timeline reaching out to stop me. Maybe it was the lingering traces of love, the memories that Hong Gildong could never erase. Whatever it was, I trusted it. That was what sisters were for—loving you through the darkest times.

I pulled my hand back, releasing Hong Gildong. He stayed perfectly still, as if afraid I would change my mind. I put his yeouiju in my pocket, then picked up the discarded gun and sank my claws into it, snapping it in half. I didn't know what to do with Hong Gildong, but I knew I would never let him hurt anyone again.

Footsteps pounded down the hallway. I braced myself in front of Yejun, claws bared as the footsteps drew closer and closer. Then the office doors swung open and the doorway filled with gold.

At first, it looked like all of Hong Gildong's hoard had burst out from behind the bookshelves and filled the room with glittering piles of sunlight. But as my eyes adjusted to the light, I realized that a gold dragon had curled around the perimeter of the office, its massive head resting on Hong Gildong's desk. It blinked its gilded eyes at me, and I found myself staring at my own petrified reflection within them.

Logically, I'd always known that I was descended from dragons, but I never imagined I'd actually see one. I felt impossibly small, yet something about the dragon felt natural and safe, as if I instinctively knew that despite our different bodies, we were the same.

Hyebin appeared in the doorway, Seulgi close behind her.

"Sunbaenim," I said. "What are you—"

"This one overheard what was going on and called for me," Hyebin said, nodding toward Seulgi. "I figured this was a matter for someone above Hong Gildong. Now bow, you idiot. This is the Dragon King."

I jerked my head back to the dragon, then threw myself to the carpet in a bow. "I'm sorry, uh, Dragon-nim," I said, not missing Hyebin's groan of disappointment at what I was sure was the wrong title.

The dragon let out a huff of warm air over me.

"It's all right, Mina," said a voice in Japanese.

I turned to a woman in a kimono standing beside the dragon, one hand resting gently on its head. I was so shocked at the dragon that I hadn't noticed her at first, but now it was impossible to look away from her beauty. Her turquoise eyes appraised me coolly, her pale blue kimono fluttering as if rustled by an ocean breeze. Her skin had a pearlescent sheen, like the inside of a seashell.

"It's Otohime," my mom whispered in awe.

I all but slammed my face back into the carpet in another bow. This was my ancestor, the daughter of the dragon god who bestowed time magic on Japan . . . and she was standing six feet in front of me.

Otohime laughed. "Relax, Mina," she said. "You've done well."

I peeled my face from the carpet, wincing at the sting. "I have?"

Otohime nodded. "Hyebin called your sajangnim's supervisor," she said, gesturing to the dragon. "We happened to be out for lunch together, so I came along as well."

The dragon huffed, its eyes glinting across the five of us.

"He says that he wants to thank you and Kim Yejun personally for uncovering Hong Gildong's corruption," Otohime said. "And he assures you that accepting bribes to alter the timeline is not in alignment with the principles of dragon culture, in Korea or Japan." She glanced warily at Hong Gildong's ruined desk, the golden office supplies spilled across the floor. "It is unfortunate that some with higher concentrations of dragon blood are too drawn to riches. Of course, we also agree that Hong Gildong cannot erase our children as he pleases. That decision should have been brought to us first."

Yejun coughed wetly and I turned back to him, kneeling by his side.

"Otohime-san," I said quickly. "Please, can you help Yejun?"

Otohime turned to Yejun, her vivid eyes taking him in unhurriedly. "He is not one of my descendants," she said. "It's not my place—"

"Urashima Tarō wasn't your descendant either, but you took

him in!" I said. "You cared for him and gave him time magic! How is this any different?"

Otohime stilled at my words, her gaze drifting back to Yejun.

The whole reason that Japan had access to time magic at all was because Otohime had loved a human and gifted him a box of time to protect him. That man—Urashima Tarō—had opened the box and unleashed her magic on the world.

"Please," I said, dropping my head and bowing. "None of this was his fault. He was injured protecting your descendants."

Otohime turned to the gold dragon, exchanging a long glance. After a moment, the dragon nodded.

Otohime knelt in front of Yejun. His tired eyes fluttered open as she pressed a hand to his cheek, then closed again as she pulled back.

"I cannot save him," she said.

I gripped Yejun tighter. "But you're—"

"My domain is time, not healing," she said. "He cannot be saved."

I felt my fangs descending once more, claws digging into Yejun's shirt. I hadn't planned on fighting a god today, but for Yejun, I would try.

"However, perhaps there is something else we can do," Otohime said.

I straightened up, quickly retracting my claws.

"We can reset the last hour, so that this tragedy never occurs in the first place," she said. "It's probably for the best, as I see there has been a lot of . . . meddling with the timeline."

Reset the last hour? I thought, my stomach sinking. I should have expected this—all my unauthorized time traveling probably poked a few too many holes in the timeline, and I was lucky I wasn't actually getting punished for it.

But I didn't want to forget the way my parents stood up for

me, the way Yejun was willing to die for me, the way I learned that Mina Yang wasn't a failed descendant and disappointment after all.

I looked down at Yejun, who was breathing shallowly, his face sickly gray.

"Okay," I said. "Yes, please do whatever you have to do to save him."

"What about him?" Hyebin said, gesturing at Hong Gildong, who was still curled up in the corner.

The dragon huffed out a breath, and Otohime laughed. "Oh, don't worry, Hyebin-nim," she said. "We have plans for him as well."

A hand gripped my sleeve, and I looked down at Yejun, whose eyes were now barely open.

"Hey," I said, taking his hand. "It's okay. Otohime is going to help you."

He made a wordless sound of acknowledgment. I squeezed his hand a bit too hard until his eyes opened wider.

"If you can hold on for another minute, you might want to do this first," Hyebin said, kneeling in front of us. She passed me a notebook and two pens.

"What's this for?" I said.

"I figured there are some things you might want to remember," Hyebin said with a shrug. "If you want to write yourselves notes, I can drop them off at the restaurant for you to pick up later."

I glanced over Hyebin's shoulder at Otohime. "Is that okay?"

"It wouldn't be the first time it's happened," she said with a soft smile.

I turned back to Hyebin. "Thank you," I said. "Not just for this but . . . everything. And I'm sorry."

Hyebin crinkled her nose and waved her hands as if wiping my words out of the air. "It's in the past," she said. "And for what it's worth, you weren't wrong about me, even if you were pretty rude about it."

I shook my head quickly. "I was wrong," I said. "When I said no one cared about you, that wasn't true. I've always cared about you, Sunbae."

Hyebin's face scrunched up like she'd eaten something sour. "Don't get sappy on me," she said. "And don't expect me to say that back. I literally went behind my boss's back for you, so read between the lines."

"Got it," I said with a smile.

Not wanting to waste any more time, I tore off a piece of paper for Yejun and helped him hold a pen, then hurried to jot down my own note.

Yejun only scrawled a quick note before folding it in half and setting the pen down with a shaking hand.

"That's all you're going to write?" I said.

Yejun nodded. "I'm not worried," he said, smiling palely.

"How can you not be worried?" I said. "So much has happened."

He coughed, clearing his throat. "I don't need a note to remember how I feel about you," he said. "It's inevitable."

My face was suddenly on fire, even before my mom let out a happy squeal behind me. "Are you two officially dating now?" she said, tugging my dad's arm in excitement. "Mina, he's so handsome!"

"*Mom!*" I groaned.

"Actually, this is perfect," my dad said. "They're both descendants, so their children won't have diluted powers, but their ancestors are different, so they can skip all the genetic testing."

"*Dad!*" I said. Even Yejun flushed red at this comment. This was one part of the day I wouldn't mind forgetting.

"Are we all ready?" Otohime said, smiling.

I hurried to finish my note, then handed it to Hyebin. I laced my fingers with Yejun's, turned to Otohime, and nodded.

The scales along the dragon's body began to glow. I winced at the sudden light that swallowed the room, so much like the paradox, but this time full of warmth instead of emptiness. Otohime set her hand on the dragon's head, and the whole world was swallowed by brilliant, blazing gold.

I spotted Yejun in the crowd at the political rally right away.

It was hard not to—he was wearing a raincoat in a glaring shade of blue and waving at me so enthusiastically that he nearly elbowed someone else in the eye. No one had the right to look that carefree with a loaded gun under their jacket, but then of course, this was Kim Yejun.

I made my way toward him through the dense crowd, but it took long enough that his arm started getting tired and his waving looked more like a tree swaying in the breeze.

"Stop before you dislocate your shoulder," I said when I finally reached him, poking him in the side.

"Just wanted to make sure you saw me," he said with a smile.

I rolled my eyes. "Try to look a little less joyful," I said. "You're supposed to be on a mission."

"Right, right," he said, smoothing out his expression. "How's this?" He scowled at me, and I choked back a laugh.

The last time I'd seen Yejun, we'd gone back in time to feed peanut butter to pigeons in order to set the stage for this final mission. We were supposed to meet again in the morning before the rally so I could take his Kevlar vest, but I'd had an unexpected visitor at my apartment before I could step out the door.

"Did you know that the restaurant between dimensions serves brunch?" I said.

Yejun raised an eyebrow. "What, like American brunch?"

"Yeah, pancakes and everything, but only before one o'clock. I'd never been there that early before, but Hyebin dragged me there this morning."

Yejun looked up sharply. "Did she?" he said, his voice oddly light. "That's funny, she made me grab a coffee with her there right before I got here. She's not even my mentor, so she basically just kidnapped me."

"That sounds like her," I said.

Yejun jammed his hands in his pockets, suddenly fascinated with his shoelaces. "How . . . how were the pancakes?" he said after a moment.

"They were awful," I said, "but is that really what you want to ask me?"

Yejun swallowed, then met my gaze for a brief moment before looking back down. For the first time since I'd met him, he looked like he wanted to hide his head in the sand. What had happened to the cool, confident Yejun I knew?

"Did you happen to find anything unusual there?" he said at last.

I reached out and took his hand.

His gaze snapped toward me, his hand tensing around mine. "Mina—"

"As a matter of fact, I did," I said, leaning against him. "I found a letter. A pretty long one, actually. But the gist of it is that we don't have to worry about this mission anymore. Oh, and that there definitely isn't going to be a war, so I shouldn't shoot anyone."

That hadn't been all of it, of course. There was a lot about how I should trust Yejun and not doubt my parents' love and how Hana was always with me even though I was never going to find her.

But none of it mattered, because I hadn't needed the letter at all.

As the dragon's golden light had devoured Hong Gildong's office and carried all of us into a gilded sea, a hand had shielded my eyes from the apex of brightness.

Thank you, Mina, a woman's voice had whispered in my ear, though it might have been nothing more than the song of wind across a vast blue sea.

When I'd opened my eyes, I remembered.

I remembered the endless eyes of a dragon, and a princess of the sea, and stars in the shape of a clock and pendulum.

I remembered the heat of Yejun's blood on my hands, the sting of my fangs in my lip, the sound of Hong Gildong's cry as I seized his yeouiju.

I remembered Hyebin, and Seulgi, and my parents, and Yejun, and the warmth of a hand on my shoulder that no one else could see.

Yejun laughed, the sound bright as starlight. "Yeah, definitely don't shoot anyone today," he said.

"Don't worry," I said. "I didn't even bring a gun."

"Me neither," Yejun said, pulling back his jacket to show that he wasn't wearing a holster.

"Did *you* get a note?" I asked, when it seemed like he wasn't going to volunteer the information himself.

"Oh, uh, yeah," he said, looking over his shoulder as if something incredibly interesting was happening to the trash can five feet away.

"And what did it say?"

He let out a sharp laugh. "Not much, actually," he said. "Just that I should stop being an idiot and do it already."

I frowned. "Do what?"

He took a deep breath, then met my gaze.

"This," he said.

Then he put a hand on my waist, pulled me close, and kissed me.

Cheers rose up around us as Min Sungho stepped out of the car and onto the walkway, but my whole world was Yejun, his hands on my face, his heartbeat so loud against mine, and the glimmer of our magic tangled together.

Epilogue

On the eightieth day of my life as Mina Yang, I walked along the Bulgwang stream hand in hand with Yejun, who was carrying my absurdly heavy school bag. It was November and the trees were stripped bare, the sky an empty white. As much as I missed the blue days of fall, I didn't mind the empty sky all that much. It felt clean and new, like anything could happen.

Yejun hadn't left my side all day, going so far as to peer in the window of my history class. He had a whole slate of activities planned for us today—everything from an escape room in Gangnam to pancakes in Itaewon to renting bikes along the Han River. I told him it was too much to do in one afternoon, but he insisted. He hadn't explicitly said why he was so determined to keep me busy today, but I had a pretty good guess.

We'd only just finished our first stop of the afternoon—the restaurant between dimensions—and I already felt too full to go anywhere else.

It turned out that Hong Gildong was now a dishwasher at the restaurant for all of eternity.

Otohime and the Korean Dragon King had determined that Hong Gildong had been too impactful to the timeline to fully erase without causing a thousand unintended ripple effects, so they'd dropped him in the restaurant and destroyed his yeouiju, leaving him stranded in the only place that existed outside of any timeline. He was powerless, now at the mercy of the dozen elderly Korean women who worked in the kitchen.

Hyebin hated the idea. She said she could sense him glaring through the kitchen window whenever she sat down to eat. But the gods had consoled her by promoting her to Hong Gildong's position, so she stopped complaining pretty quickly once she got to take his office.

Hyebin had adapted surprisingly well to her new position. It helped that the timeline ran a lot smoother without Hong Gildong intentionally poking holes in it. Leadership—or rather, authority—seemed to come naturally to Hyebin. No one ever dared to question her.

In the first week of her position as head of the Korean branch of descendants, the first thing she did was take down all the creepy dragon statues and paintings in the main hall.

In their place, there were now photographs of everyone who had been erased.

The photos were stark and serious—they came from their ID photos after all, the only remnants of those people we had. Now, since everyone had to walk through the hallway, we were forced to look at their faces every day. They were so familiar at this point that they felt almost like coworkers. I memorized all their names and greeted them every time I went to headquarters.

Sometimes, I lingered by Hana's photograph before I headed into the scrying room, wanting to reach out and touch but not wanting my fingertips to leave a mark on the glass. It was all I had left of her, and it wasn't enough, but it was *something*, and I'd have to be content with that.

I still felt her here at times, even though Hyebin said it was impossible. Sometimes I rolled over in bed in the morning and I could almost see Hana in the sunlight streaming through my window. I felt her presence, the same way I could feel rain or snow or sunlight on my skin. Her love for me was not something that even the most powerful dragon in the world could completely destroy. It lingered like the scent of smoke in the air long after a fire is extinguished.

"Is it illegal to bring pine cones to Japan?" Yejun said, scrolling on his phone with his hand that wasn't currently holding mine.

I glanced at his phone screen, where he was zooming in on a photo of a red squirrel with pointy ears.

"Don't feed Korean pine cones to Japanese squirrels," I said, for what felt like the hundredth time.

My dad had invited Yejun on our family trip to Hokkaido over winter break, and ever since I showed him a picture of an adorable Ezo red squirrel—a species with catlike ears indigenous to Japan—squirrels had occupied his every waking thought.

I was surprised my dad invited him, but then again, everyone—from my parents, to Hyebin, to Otohime herself—was conspiring to make our relationship as convenient as possible. Most dragon descendants married humans these days because marrying among descendants always carried a risk that you'd fall in love with your cousin. But because Yejun and I had different dragon ancestors, that wasn't an issue. It probably also helped that Yejun had already laid the groundwork for making my parents fall in love with him by bringing them cheesecake at every opportunity.

"Hey, there's your friend!" Yejun said, pointing to the other side of the stream.

"My friend?" I said, squinting through the glare of the sun to see who he was looking at.

There, across the stream, Jihoon stood frozen as if Yejun had pointed a gun at him.

"Stop tormenting him," I said, elbowing Yejun. I felt bad enough for leading Jihoon on without Yejun making it worse.

"I'm not!" Yejun said. "He's with a girl."

Sure enough, a girl—Im Daeun, from our calculus class—peered around Jihoon and waved, smiling at us.

I smiled and waved back. *So that's why there were still Yakult bottles in the trash, even though Jihoon stopped giving them to me*, I thought.

"He's not going to marry her," Yejun whispered, even as he smiled at them.

"*You read his file?*" I said, tugging his arm to make him keep walking.

"So did you!"

"Yes, because it was relevant to me once," I said. "You're just nosy."

"And you're just"—he paused, letting go of me and stuffing both hands in his pocket—"shit."

"I'm just *what*?"

"No, not you," Yejun said, spinning around and looking back at the path we came from. "My wallet fell off my phone."

I groaned. "I told you the MagSafe wallet was a bad idea."

"It's okay, it has a tracker," Yejun said, tapping his phone screen. After a moment, his shoulders drooped. "Which doesn't work."

"You probably dropped it in another decade, that's why," I said.

We'd been going on a lot of missions together lately, our twenty-year leash extended to fifty years. I was excited to go back to ancient Korea one day, though less so ever since Hyebin had given me the rundown on how many ancient diseases I could catch.

"Oh, I know where it is!" Yejun said, grabbing my hand and pulling me toward the Eungam station elevator. "September thirtieth," he said. I sighed and let him drag me along. Who knew having a boyfriend came with so many errands?

As the elevator descended, Yejun stood behind me and wrapped his arms around my stomach, resting his chin on top of my head. "Are you doing okay?" he asked.

"Yes," I said, setting my hand on top of his so that he held me tighter. It was true—I was fine for now. It was easy to stay grounded in the present when Yejun was there. Time magic began to tangle between our fingers, violet light illuminating our reflections in the glass as we slipped back in time.

"I thought about getting a cake," Yejun said, "but I didn't know if you wanted today to be more of a celebration or . . ."

"Or a funeral?" I said, turning my head to face him.

He winced. "We can also just go home if you want."

I sighed, shaking my head and leaning back against him as time magic fully tangled around us both.

Today was Hana's birthday.

She would have been twenty years old today, if she still existed. I couldn't stop wondering how we celebrated her last birthday before she was erased. What kind of cake did she like? What did I buy for her? What did she wish for when she blew out her candles? Sometimes, late at night, those kinds of questions drowned me.

Yejun squeezed me a little harder, then let go as the elevator doors opened two months in the past. A crowd of grandpas were waiting to board the elevator, so we let them in and decided to take the stairs back to the top, rather than risk their wrath.

We emerged from the station on a dark, smoggy night. Yejun hurried over the bridge, past the fruit market, and into the alley near my apartment.

"Slow down!" I called as he jogged ahead.

"I can't!" Yejun said. "What if someone steals it?"

"Then you go on ahead," I said, stopping in the parking lot and waving him forward—I didn't really want to vault a fence in my school skirt after inhaling a gallon of kimchi jjigae for lunch. Yejun climbed over it easily and ran down the side street.

"I see it!" he said. He bent down to pick it up, pulling out his yeouiju, which had already started glowing blue.

Careless, I thought, smiling and shaking my head. He didn't even bother to check the scene.

Suddenly, Yejun froze. He looked toward the end of the street, at something I couldn't see on the other side of the building.

"Mina?" he said.

I'm over here, I thought. *What are you* . . .

Then I realized, all at once, who he was looking at.

Yejun was wearing half a school uniform and a black mask, just like the first day I saw him. When I actually met him in the café the day after, he denied ever seeing me there. He hadn't been lying after all—he just hadn't met me yet.

The Mina on the other side of the building had no idea that this was just another beginning.

I was very good at beginnings, because I'd had so many of them. I was an expert at lying and sneaking and burning my old life behind me.

But this time, for this beginning, I was no longer worried about the ending.

Yejun glanced at me, then back at the other Mina. He shrugged apologetically to her, then ran back toward me and clambered over the fence.

I took his hand once he reached me, and we traveled back to the present. I knew that when the other Mina chased him around the corner, both of us would be long gone.

We landed in the shade of the parking lot outside my apartment complex, this time in daylight.

"You really should look before you start shooting blue light out of your hands, you know," I said, poking him in the ribs.

He smiled. "What fun would that be?"

Then he put his arm over my shoulder as we walked down the stream, under the hazy blue sky of the place I was lucky enough to call my home.

Acknowledgments

I would not have been able to write this book without the help of so many amazing people. Not just in terms of my skill as a writer or my access to the publishing industry, but also in terms of the content; this is by far my most lighthearted book to date, and for a long time, I never thought I would write anything like it. I thought I was too cynical to write something this happy and was deeply afraid that I didn't know how to do it. Luckily, so many people in my life have taught me how to make space for light in these dark times, and have helped me grow as a writer so that I can tell all kinds of stories, not just ones that involve decapitations.

As always, endless thanks to my agent, Mary C. Moore, for making this dream possible. I sent this book to Mary after a series of proposals that I decided were trash about ten minutes after emailing her. I felt stuck after the release of *The Scarlet Alchemist*, so Mary encouraged me to write what I wanted regardless of how commercial I thought it might be, and the result is the book you're holding now.

Immense thanks to my editor, Holly, whose incredible ideas made this book infinitely better and reignited my excitement for this project. Thanks as well to the whole Feiwel and Friends team for all your hard work behind the scenes. I'm truly impressed with and grateful to all of you.

Thank you to my friends for your endless support both of me and my strange stories, especially KP for her help with Korean! Hopefully this book is less traumatizing than my previous ones, which you valiantly read for me.

Special thanks to the Flying Ducks and the Monstrous Misses for becoming my author family and weathering the highs and lows of this industry together.

Thanks to Rebecca Kim Wells for guiding me through this industry and supporting me on every step of my journey.

Thank you to all the booksellers who have championed my work. I appreciate you and all you do for the book community! Thank you as well to all the librarians, teachers, bookstagrammers, and booktokkers for keeping our community alive.

Thank you to my parents for bragging about my books to everyone who will listen, and for always supporting my dreams.

And of course, thank you to all my readers, both new and old. Thank you for joining me on these journeys to different worlds and timelines. Thank you for opening your hearts to my stories. Thank you for the honor of lending me your time. It's a privilege to embark on these adventures and know that I'm not alone.

About the Author

Kylie Lee Baker is the *Sunday Times*–bestselling author of *The Keeper of Night* duology and *The Scarlet Alchemist* duology. She grew up in Boston and has since lived in Atlanta, Salamanca, and Seoul. Her writing is informed by her heritage (Japanese, Chinese, and Irish) and her experiences living abroad as both a student and teacher. She has a BA in creative writing and Spanish from Emory University and an MS in library and information science from Simmons University. For more, go to **kylieleebaker.com**.